Pound Of Flesh

A Horror Novel
James Atkinson

Paperback ISBN: 979-8-9887039-2-1

Cover Design: James Atkinson

Edited By: David-Jack Fletcher @ Chainsaw Editing

Printed in the United States of America.

Other Works:

The Cold Black: A Collection Of Terrors

Lake Life

Please visit the author at:

www.authorjamesatkinson.com

You can also find James Atkinson on most social media outlets:

Facebook, Instagram, TikTok, X (formerly Twitter), Slasher, LinkedIn, Goodreads

For Amy, Hailee, Aaron, and Maddie
You are the magic

Contents

PROLOGUE

Samuel was so engrossed in *Silver Bullet* he didn't notice his mother, Gloria, was home until her keys hit the porcelain bowl on the entry table in the foyer.

"Shit," Samuel hissed. He'd been instructed to have Benji ready by 7 p.m. Here it was, five after seven, and he hadn't even begun to dress his little brother. The babysitter, Anna Claire, had already reminded him once.

Sam told his mom Anna Claire was no longer needed. Not that she was a problem. She was really cool—and super pretty—but he was old enough to watch Benji. His mom gave a weak excuse about how she felt better having someone there, but Sam overheard her arguing with his dad, Rodrigo, a few months ago. Gloria had warned Rodrigo to stay away from her family, before slamming the phone down.

One muggy summer night two years ago, Rodrigo went out to have drinks with his buddies at the Sand Dollar in Shallotte, and never returned. Word quickly got around that he'd split back to Mexico. Gloria called around and found the rumors were true. He was shacked up with his ex-wife in Santa Caterina and had no plans of returning to America anytime soon.

Gloria struggled the first few months, depressed and crying all the time. Sam tried to help with chores, and with Benji, stepping into his new role of man of the house. Anything to ease the burden. The Latino community pulled together and helped the family weather the storm; food was delivered daily by one family or another. Money was left in envelopes on the counter, twenty dollars here, a hundred dollars there.

A few connections led Gloria to a hospitality management position at a luxury hotel in Holden Beach, a job with a considerable pay bump above her meager salary as a part-time housekeeper for the Browning family. Things improved with a surprising quickness. Gloria cheered up, her new job a source of pride.

The last few months, Sam had noticed she smiled less. Seemed agitated. Gloria was mum on the subject—not that she'd worry her kids with it anyway—but Sam was sure his father was the reason.

Which explained Anna Claire.

Sam hurried to Benji's room, leaving *Silver Bullet* to play without an audience. His little brother was on the floor playing with his plastic train set. Sam pulled Benji to his feet so he could lower the top half of his costume on. "Take it easy Sam," Benji complained. "You're hurting me."

"Sorry," Sam whispered. "We gotta hurry." Sam dropped to one knee to tie Benji's shoes while he strained to hear the conversation between Anna Claire and his mother.

"Look at you," Gloria said. "That's a sexy get-up, but you're going to freeze your tail off."

"I'll be inside the sorority house all night. I'll only freeze from the car to the door."

"What did Chuck say about that dress?"

"I didn't show him." Anna Claire sounded annoyed at the name. Chuck. "He would flip."

"No social media for you," Gloria said, laughing.

"I'll be sure to wear my trench coat."

Anna Claire's footsteps clopped toward the front of the house. The front door squeaked open.

"They're almost finished." Sam tossed Benji the conductor's hat off the dresser and ran to his room to slip on his boots.

"You're awesome," Gloria said. "Thank you for doing this on such short notice."

"No problem," Anna Claire said. "Have a good night."

"Have fun." Gloria added as the door closed: "And no drinking." Then it came, the yell. "Let's go, boys. It's now or never. The taxi leaves in five or not at all."

Sam hustled Benji down the hall with a hand in the small of his back.

"You guys look so cute," Gloria said, bouncing on her toes.

Sam was going as Jason Voorhees, one of his favorite horror characters. The hockey mask was a little big for his face, and his breath was hot under the plastic, but the costume was badass. The plastic machete in one hand totally rocked.

At seven years old, Benji was still into *Thomas the Tank Engine*, hence the train costume. A blue train conductor hat engulfed his little head, his big ears stopping it from landing on his shoulders. He wore the obligatory blue conductor shirt, black pants, and black shoes. Thomas himself was draped over his shoulders and sat around his waist, a blocky thing made of fabric and plastic framing, designed to look like a train, the eyes of Thomas wide with eternal surprise.

"Okay," Gloria said, squeezing Sam close to his brother. "Picture time." She turned her cell phone to the side for a landscape view. Sam aimed the machete at the camera while Benji pulled back on Thomas as though he was about to charge down the track. Gloria giggled and started tapping the screen. One photo turned to ten. Sam and Benji patiently endured the photo session, trying to remain excited even when their mother suggested another round of terrible poses. It was the first time either of them had seen her smile in ages. A *real* smile, too. Neither kid could take that away from her.

Gloria finally slipped the phone in her jeans pocket when she was satisfied with her social media haul.

"Load up. We gotta meet the Bell's in twenty. Grab your jackets."

"But, Mom, then you can't see my costume," Sam whined. He wanted to show off the fake chain wrapped around his chest, imitating the iconic design from *Friday the 13th VI: Jason Lives*.

"Too bad. It's thirty degrees outside and it is only getting colder. The other option is you can stay home. I'm not totally okay with you guys going to a haunted carnival as it is."

"It's a haunted *house* and hayride, Mom." Sam rolled his eyes.

"Whatever. Get your jacket and get to the car." Her smile was gone now, and Sam felt a pang of guilt.

Having grabbed their jackets, the two boys climbed inside the back seat of the silver Kia Sorento while Gloria started the engine. Benji's costume proved tricky to maneuver inside the SUV, but after a few adjustments he was buckled in.

"Mom," Benji called as Gloria turned out the driveway. "Lee told me the boogeyman is really real. He said I better watch out tonight because the boogeyman loves to eat kids." He paused, picking his nose. "Is...the boogeyman...real?"

Sam shook his head. Lee Galp was a hairy ball sack. A bully pretending to be Benji's friend. Sam wasn't a fan and had told Benji to stay away from the guy.

"Lee is a pendejo, Benji," Gloria said, staring at him through the rear-view mirror. "I don't know why you associate with that kid." She sneered the last word. "He does these kinds of things to you all the time. No, the boogeyman is not real. Stories about the boogeyman are make-believe tales meant to scare children. It's all for fun. Lee is wrong. He is *always* wrong. He will always be wrong. Okay? The boogeyman is not real."

Benji nodded and looked out the window as the city of Supply, North Carolina zoomed past. Benji had already mentioned the conversation with Lee earlier today. Sam had told him pretty much the same as Mom, but Lee was like a splinter; once he was under the skin, it took a lot of pain—and a little blood—to get him out.

Sam peered out his own window as the glow of Supply dissipated and the blackened landscape of Green Swamp blurred past. The people running Creepy Swamp Haunted House and Hayride picked the perfect location for this attraction. Green Swamp was lush and beautiful during the day, but at night it was downright scary. His thoughts crept to the haunted house, the excitement building. It was his first one, not counting the church carnivals, where the thrills were innocent and lame. His first *real* haunted house and hayride. A few of his friends had already been, and said it was spooky but not scary. The TV commercials were cheap advertisements, but Sam was excited regardless. He loved all things horror. His mom wasn't aware he watched scary movies all the time. On his phone after bedtime, under the blankets with headphones on. The scarier the better.

A distant glimmer above the dark silhouettes of pine trees indicated they were close. Sam leaned forward and pointed. "There it is."

"I see it," Gloria said, slowing, leaning forward herself to search for the entrance.

Benji kicked his legs in anticipation. Gloria turned beside the flashing sign that announced: CREEPY SWAMP HAUNTED HOUSE AND HAYRIDE. A statue of the grim reaper stood next to the sign. Except the statue moved and swung a sickle at her SUV. Gloria screamed and yanked the steering wheel away from the danger, unloading a string of expletives. Sam almost cracked a rib laughing.

Gloria parked beside the Bells' black Mercedes C-Class sedan. Sam and Benji were out before the Kia stopped.

"This is going to be awesome," Hunter said. His costume was a camouflaged sniper grille suit. He loved to hunt: deer, wild pigs, turkey, duck, gator.

Colt, on the other hand, was a ghostbuster. He was obsessed with *Stranger Things* and loved the costumes the characters wore in the second season. The Bells were identical twins, the only visible physical difference the one-inch height advantage Hunter had over Colt. That, and the fact they had different styles, made them easy to tell apart. "Liam said there are some pretty good frights in the woods during the hayride. He said they grab at your ankles."

Sam smiled as he imagined how scary *that* would be.

"Guys," Gloria said to them.

"Yes, ma'am?" the boys responded in unison.

"Stay together. Do not speak to strangers. And you three older boys are to always keep Benji at your side. Sam, I am especially talking to you. Watch. Your. Brother. You fail to do any of these things, and you won't go out again until you're thirty. Got it?"

"Yes, ma'am," they answered and gulped. Gloria Ramirez was only 5'4", but she was an intimidating figure.

"Same goes from me," Bella Bell called out her window.

Sam pulled Benji along as he hurried to the ticket booth, paid for admission, and followed the crowd of people filing into line.

"Did you see the fight yesterday between Zeke and Brad?" Hunter asked as the crowd moved a few feet forward.

"No, but I heard it was crazy." Sam shook his head. The mask made it hard to talk and he could smell his own breath, so he sat it on top of his head like a hat. "Library shelves knocked over, books everywhere."

"I was there," Hunter said, eyes wide as though he'd seen something special and rare. "Zeke actually suplexed Brad onto Mrs. Kennedy's desk."

"What did she do?" Sam tried to imagine the mean librarian, red-faced and yelling at Zeke and Brad to sit down and shut up.

"She went in like a referee, broke it up, and pulled them to Principal Gershawn's office by the ears. Funniest thing you ever saw."

Sam could picture it like he was there. "That had to—"

Someone tapped Sam on the shoulder. Emma Lou Danning, the prettiest girl in school, smiled while Sam tried to think of something to say. She rarely spoke to him.

Emma Lou was recently dating mule-mouthed Scott Swearinger, but she broke up with him because she caught him talking to her mortal enemy, the one and only Karie Young. Emma liked jocks and Sam was not a jock. His cheeks flared hot when he noticed she was not in costume.

"Hey, Emma Lou," he said. The words sounded stupid as they left his mouth.

"Hi, Sam. Nice costume." Her face was blank, he couldn't tell if she thought he looked cool or stupid as hell.

Sam debated running away. *I am an idiot.* "Thanks. I dressed up for my little brother. Gotta play along, you know how it is."

Emma Lou smiled at Benji. "You're a cutie." To Sam, she said, "That's cool of you, being a good big brother and all. I would never do that for my little sister."

The line moved forward.

"See ya," she said, twiddling her fingers at him, and disappearing somewhere in the crowd. Surging forward again, the thrill seekers hurried to board the flatbed trailer.

The driver blew a whistle, and smoke poured from the exhaust pipe like steam from the bowels of Hell. The girls on the trailer screeched and the boys laughed. The tractor lurched forward, vanishing into the darkness of the woods. The line shifted forward again.

Hunter punched Sam in the arm. "You ass monkey. Emma Lou likes you."

A nearby mother shot Hunter a stern look of disapproval.

"No, she does not," Sam said, rolling his eyes. The thought made his stomach feel funny. "She's just being nice."

The Bell twins gawked at each other, sharing one of their silent, mind-reading twin moments. So creepy. So cool. Hunter said, "She ever been nice to you, Colt?" Colt shook his head. "Me, either." Grinned at Sam. "She likes you."

Sam shook his head, feigned exasperation, but secretly his knees were weak.

A piercing whistle blow announced the return of the hayride. The driver ground through some gears, and the roar of the engine brought the tractor and empty trailer out of the woods, where it stopped before them. The line wasted no time getting onboard. The best seats were on the edge, where legs dangled in the darkness for some creature to wrap its cold, dead hands around unsuspecting ankles. Sam hurried to take one of the last remaining spots on the edge next to the twins. Benji was at the end, the last pair of feet among dozens of others.

"You okay?" Sam asked his brother, his arm draped over the small shoulders.

Benji nodded, but Sam knew he was lying.

Sam had been afraid of everything when he was younger. The closet had been like a doorway from another dimension, hiding monsters capable of incomprehensible savagery behind a thin piece of wood.

Those monsters loved to snatch little boys while on their knees to pray. Eyes closed, minds innocent, godly words on their young lips. The monsters, hungry for that tender flesh, would drag the little kids through the dark, to another plane, before he or she could scream for help. Never to be seen again. In an effort to thwart such attacks, Sam had shone a flashlight into the closet every night, then shut the door with an emphatic slam. With age, his fears ceased.

It was like his mom said earlier, there was no such thing as the boogeyman.

Sam patted Benji on the back. The spotlight on the back of the tractor shut off, and the night dropped like a coffin lid. The tractor engine whined with effort as the trailer lurched forward, drawing squeals from all the girls onboard—some of the boys, too. The trailer bounced side to side as it rolled over ruts and roots.

A smoking chainsaw roared to life. A masked man lunged from the shadows and jumped aboard the trailer, swinging the chainsaw above his head. Oily smoke billowed from the two-stroke engine. Everyone screamed and shrunk away, despite laughter and the failed pretense by some boys that they weren't even marginally frightened. One guy, bearded and wearing a Carolina Panther's hat, took a shot from a flask while his wife—or girlfriend—buried her head in his chest.

As the chainsaw swung again, the trailer was suddenly assaulted by a clown, and a werewolf. The hairy beast ran down the trailer growling and grunting like a rabid animal. The clown skipped around, bonking people on the head with a plastic, oversized dead blow hammer.

A vampire dropped from a tree limb, eliciting a cacophony of screeches. Sam caught the actor detaching the cable from his body harness before grabbing at squealing girls to suck their blood.

One by one the actors disappeared into the night. The trailer ground to a halt next to a rundown dwelling. The haunted house.

Sam was sad the ride was over, but excited about the horrors that lay within.

"Okay, Ben—" he began, but stopped and looked around.

Benji was gone.

Sam hopped down and searched the trailer and its departing occupants. "Hey, have you seen a little boy wearing a *Thomas the Tank Engine* costume?" Sam asked, over and over, to everyone getting off the ride. Hunter and Colt asked as well, concerned about the possible wrath of Gloria. An adult working the hayride heard the commotion and came over.

"Who's missing, son?" the lady asked, pulling the three boys to the side. Her voice was gritty, like a smoker. A three-pack-a-dayer as his father would say.

"My little brother," Sam said, panic setting in. "We were on the hayride. He was beside me, all the stuff happened with the chainsaws, and I just noticed he was not on the trailer when we pulled up here. You gotta help me."

"What was he wearing?" the lady asked, grabbing a walkie-talkie clipped to her side.

"*Thomas the Tank Engine* costume. He's seven. Black hair, brown eyes."

She held up a hand for him to quiet down and spoke into the walkie talkie. "Allen, come in."

"Yeah, Sherri?"

"We have a kid who appears to have fallen off the trailer during the hayride. I need you to delay the next run. Send Jack, Weasel, and Phil out on four-wheelers to find the boy. He's wearing a *Thomas the Tank Engine* outfit. Seven years old."

"Oh man, yeah, I remember seeing that kid. Okay, gotcha." The voice disappeared into static.

Sam's stomach twisted and dinner rose up his throat. He swallowed to hold it back and tried to breathe. His mom was going to kill him.

"Hey," Sherri said, placing a hand on his shoulder. "He's fine. We'll find him and this will all be a scary ordeal we can laugh about later."

Wishful thinking. His mom would never allow them to visit another haunted house attraction again. The stress she was under with her estranged husband. She would never find this funny. He was grounded from now until he died of old age. At least.

A bullhorn blasted across the landscape. A flare popped, illuminating the night sky, screams of help rattling the trees. The radio in Sherri's hand crackled with shouting and chaos. There were so many people talking over one another it was impossible to make sense of the jargon.

But Sam caught four terrible words that cut him to the bone. Words that would haunt him until his final breath.

"He's in pieces."

CHAPTER 1

There was nothing northern about Northern Eason. A southern girl born and bred, she was raised on a farm since birth, accustomed to early mornings, hard work, and dirty hands. Her father, Ray Eason, was a third-generation farmer. Her great-grandfather, Hilliard Eason, won fifty acres of wooded land in a lawsuit settlement. Hilliard's father, Hobbie Eason, was tragically killed when a fifty-foot pine tree fell in the wrong direction. Hilliard's mother had died the year before from the flu, so the settlement went to him as next of kin.

Hilliard chose land over money. Even at the age of twenty-four, he saw the opportunity. It was back-breaking work, but Hilliard was a man of keen vision and stubborn determination. He planted more corn and tomatoes and potatoes and green beans and snap peas. The one-acre garden grew to three. Eventually spreading to ten—the beginning of an organic empire.

Hilliard built a one room hut by the road in front of his house and started selling his goods to coastal travelers and locals. Word spread Eason Farm sold fat, juicy, red tomatoes, hog-head sized potatoes, corn sweet enough to eat out of the shuck, and finger-thick green beans. Within two seasons he was seeing regulars from Myrtle Beach, Wilmington, Whiteville, and Tabor City. Ten acres turned to forty. When he ran out of land, he bought more.

Northern's granddaddy, Earl Eason, was born in 1940, with a hoe in his hand and took over farm duties for the aging Hilliard in 1975. Earl and his wife, Norma, welcomed Ray Eason into the world on March 6th, 1972. Ray was raised learning the life of a farmer. He fell in love with Maggie Henderson and the two married in 1997. Northern Rose Eason was born three years later. Eason Farm, LLC, started on a fifty-acre plot, but had grown to 200 by the time Ray took the reins in 2002.

Now the Eason Farm approached 300 acres. No longer were the fields tilled by mule; now it was motorized and mechanical. Fifteen barns and warehouses held the likes of tractors, combines, plows, bush-hogging equipment, four-wheelers, and trailers by the dozens. Several bunkhouses for the seasonal workers were clustered at the back of the property along the treeline.

Northern was a proud Eason, hands as calloused as her father's. No one in her family had gone to college. Now a student at UNC-Wilmington chasing a business degree, she was the first in the bloodline to seek an education higher than the soil beneath her boot. The gratification was intoxicating.

Northern was a farm girl who wore old jeans, flannel shirts, and cowgirl boots most of the time. But she liked to dress up, put on make-up, and wear designer jeans, even sporting the occasional dress.

On this crisp November Friday night, a week removed from Thanksgiving, Northern dressed for a special occasion. Special, because it was her first date with Garrett Inslow. Just thinking of him made her stomach flutter. A smile spread across her face as she eased a mascara brush through her eyelashes. The brush tip tapped her eyeball, and she blinked to clear the burning smudge in her vision.

What was it about him that made her so nervous? He was handsome, sure. Aqua blue eyes, wavy dark brown hair, solid jawline, 6'3", athletic. But it was more than that. His confidence. The way he carried himself. Not cocky or condescending, but someone at ease with himself. Well-mannered, respectful. Last week, before UNC let out for Thanksgiving break, Garrett helped a handicapped student not be late by running him across campus to class. Those small acts of kindness showed her all she needed to know about who he was as a person.

He was her kind of guy, even if Daddy wasn't so sure.

"Why isn't he picking you up? A respectful man picks up the girl." Ray Eason said to her from his recliner as she was leaving. He lounged in his fleece pajama bottoms and long-sleeved t-shirt by the fireplace, watching the flames chew on a log. In one hand, a clear tumbler was half-filled with Maker's Mark and ginger ale. In the other, the sweet aroma of a San Cristobal floated about the room, mingling with the smoke drifting from the fireplace.

"Daddy," Northern said, kissing him on the forehead, "things are different now than they used to be. Women are not the meek little puppets from yesteryear."

"Puppets or no, the man should be picking you up. All's I'm saying."

Northern smiled. Daddy was old-fashioned. He didn't even own a cell phone. The new ways of the world were leaving him in the dust, and as much as it bothered him to chew on the grit, he refused to catch up.

"I hear you. I love you." Northern patted him gently on the arm.

"Love you, too."

Northern stopped in the kitchen and kissed her mother on the cheek. "That's one ornery old man."

Maggie laughed. "Always has been. Always will be. He's just set in his ways."

"I know," she sighed. "Bye, Mom. Love you."

"Love you, too. Be careful, please. And don't be out late. That storm is rolling in sometime in the morning."

"Yes, ma'am."

The route to Shallotte took Northern down Highway 211. It was thirty miles from the Eason homestead to the one red light community of Supply, but it felt like a hundred. It was a stretch of road that always felt empty, even during the summer months when vacationers used the beach connector to flock to the coast. At night, during this time of year, the desolate stretch of asphalt felt isolated from the world. The weighty darkness pressing against the windows like a tenebrous ocean only intensified the solitude.

The entrance to Creepy Swamp Haunted House and Hayride swept past. The advertisement sign canted to one side, missing letters, pocked with bullet holes and graffiti. The gate was closed and locked, a triangular **NO TRESPASSING** placard dangled from the rusted steel tubing.

Icy fingers climbed her spine like rungs on a ladder. Slow and creeping. It never felt right, being here, and she had the same reaction every time she passed the place in the dark. The fact that a child died right there, and the details of how the child died, freaked her out.

Northern pressed the power button to her radio to ward off scary thoughts. Morgan Wallen kept her company for the remaining twenty miles to the small coastal town of Shallotte, North Carolina. She pulled into the parking lot of Blanchard's Restaurant and parked next to Garrett's big Ford F-250. He climbed out of the thing like a monkey from a tree.

"It's not high enough you know." Northern teased as they hurried inside from the brisk air. The outer edges of the storm were already approaching.

"I know. I ordered a lift kit for it. Gonna raise it six more inches."

Blanchard's was one of the oldest restaurants in Shallotte. Opened in 1977 by Blanchard and Rich Kappen, the restaurant became a destination for upper-tier food and spirits at a time when one needed to drive forty miles to Wilmington or fifty miles to Myrtle Beach for such dining options. The one-story structure was a sprawling 5,000 square feet of subdued opulence. Blanchard and Rich, concerned about losing ground to evolution, remodeled the building every ten years to remain ahead of the times. Northern had witnessed one of these transitions, but the walls were decorated with images from the restaurant's past, like a running obituary of what it used to be.

Blanchard's was busy tonight, but the floor-to-ceiling partition around each booth gave the impression of being alone. Hushed lighting and the faint sizzle of jazz created an elegant ambience perfect for a date night.

"My dad was not happy you didn't pick me up," Northern said as she slid into a booth.

Garrett smiled. "I offered. You declined. Did you inform him of that decision?"

"I did. He's beyond old-fashioned. He should have been born in the forties."

The waitress, a bubbly eighteen-year-old named Tiffany, stopped at the table to take their drink order: water for Northern, sweet tea for Garrett.

After she left, Garrett leaned forward in his booth. "When do I get to meet the family? Or is that an old-fashioned sentiment?"

"It is an old-fashioned sentiment that fits my family perfectly. I just—"

"Want to see if this is real?"

Northern bit her bottom lip, pulled an unruly strand of hair from her face, thinking how to word the answer, when Tiffany materialized with drinks in hand. She set the glasses on coasters, and said, "What can I get you tonight?"

Northern had yet to open the menu. She flipped to the salad selection and chose the Lemon Herb Mediterranean. Garrett went with the Shrimp Fettuccine Pasta en Blanco.

"Sounds good," Tiffany said with a smiling nod, and left to turn the order in.

Northern fidgeted with her glass, giddy and nervous about the ramifications of what he was asking. "I guess. My dad is very protective. I'm his only child, his baby girl. He still sees me as the eight year old who rode on his knee, steering the tractor through the fields. He'll always see me that way, I guess. I don't want him to scare you or run you off."

"You're in luck," Garrett said, sipping sweet tea. "I don't scare easy, and I despise running."

Northern laughed. The nervousness was gone like that, but the giddy remained. "My dad will have you quaking in your boots, sonny boy. He, for real, told a former boyfriend—on the night of my prom—that if he touched me in any way other than the 'natural contact that comes with dancing'"—she deepened her voice to imitate her father—"no one will find the body. Said Green Swamp is the perfect burial site. No one around to hear the screaming."

Garrett's mouth dropped open. "You're kidding me."

"I wish. Paul refused to hold my hand or dance. He sat at the table all night and pouted while I danced with my girlfriends. He broke up with me the next day."

"Damn. What did your dad say about this Paul fellow breaking up with you?"

"He said Paul obviously wasn't man enough to handle an Eason." She leaned toward Garrett and lowered her voice. "Then he asked if I wanted him to *disappear* Paul."

"And?"

"He's still alive and well…as far as I know." Northern paused for effect. "But it was a coin toss."

The waitress returned with platters precariously balanced on one extended arm like a circus performer. With smooth and well-practiced movements, Tiffany placed the food in front of them. "Do you need anything else?" she asked, a smile tattooed to her cheeks.

"We're good, thank you," Northern said. More of a "go away" answer.

The conversation turned to food. Garrett held a fork of pasta up for Northern. She sucked the spicy noodles into her mouth with a "Mmmmm." She saw Garrett gulp and smiled to herself.

Northern watched Garrett eat, listened to his voice, observed his mannerisms, his facial expressions. She was looking for a habit that annoyed her—biting a nail, chewing with his mouth open. She only found perfection. Or, rather, her perception of perfection. She had been raised on a farm in the constant presence of coarse men. She had witnessed the disgusting traits of field workers: farting and laughing about it, blowing sticky wads of snot out of each nostril, hocking gobs of dusty spit into the dry dirt, the creative strings of cuss words thrown about in meaningless conversation. She had watched the farm hands piss on trees and squat in the woods when they were too far from the outhouse—even done it herself. She was desensitized by her upbringing, but knew she was grounded in reality and could award an honest judgment.

Garrett was wholesome, honest, trustworthy, respectful, handsome, funny, smart. She trusted her assessment. She wanted to get to know him better. The idea of spending more time with him gave her butterflies.

He seemed to feel the same. He touched her hand often, just a graze, but charged with electricity. She loved how he looked at her. His eyes probing, studying, learning her. As if she were the only person in this crowded restaurant. A pretty brunette walked by in a figure-fitting dress that emphasized her cleavage, and his eyes never wavered—not even a peek. His focused attention made her self-conscious, and she fixed stray hairs and brushed her tongue over her teeth. Nervous *he* might find an imperfection.

Walking out of the restaurant, Northern decided to kiss him. The timing had to be right. She fumbled the car keys out of her purse and clicked the unlock button. The moment arrived when he opened her car door. She kissed him; deep, warm, open. It was their first kiss, and one she hoped would be as memorable for him as it was for her.

"Wow," Garrett breathed hard, his arms wrapped around her.

She could feel the heat of his body. She liked it. A little too much. "Thank you for dinner. This was the nicest evening I've ever had."

"Even better than the prom?" Garrett asked, his eyes twinkling under the parking lot lights.

"By a smidge," Northern said. She kissed him again, the nerves replaced with something else—a rising warmth in her midsection. "Good night." Northern reluctantly pulled away and climbed inside her car. Her body was thrumming like a guitar string, and she knew if she lacked the willpower to walk away at that moment, she would give in to the desire.

Garrett pulled away as she waited for the heater in her own car to kick in. She hardly needed the heater; the blood in her veins was molten. The yellow "Low Gas" light lit up her dashboard, and that tempered the fire. She hated getting gas.

Half a mile from Blanchard's, on the corner of Main Street and Holden Beach Road, was a Quicky Gas 'n Gone. While the gas pumped, she went inside for gum and water. A trucker, whose work shirt badged him as Tank, held the door open for her. "Thank you," she said. *He's built like a tank.*

The trucker tipped his Bonneau cap at her. "Yes, ma'am."

The kid behind the register looked up from a torn paperback to ring up her purchases. "What are you reading?" Northern asked, leaning forward to see the book cover. She was an avid reader herself and loved finding new novels.

"Umm," the kid stuttered. He seemed flustered, wouldn't look her in the eye. "*The Relic,*" he finally managed, raising the book for her to view the cover.

"Preston Child," she read aloud. "Any good?"

The kid nodded. "Pretty scary. If you like monster books."

"I like all kinds of books," Northern said. "I'll give it a try. Have a good night."

"You, too."

Northern returned the nozzle to its rightful place and headed out of Shallotte. She merged onto Highway 17 and pointed the headlights northeast toward Supply. She was settling into the drive when her phone rang. The infotainment screen read: Garrett.

"Miss me already?" She joked.

"I missed you before I left you," he said.

Good answer. "Are you home?"

"Yes, about to take a cold shower."

Northern giggled. "Cold showers are good for the pores."

"Yeah, they're good for other things, too." He took a deep breath. "Just want you to know that I had a really good time tonight. I loved every minute of it. Be careful driving home and I'll call you tomorrow."

"Ditto to all," she said. Her cheeks hurt from smiling. "I'll talk to you tomorrow."

The call was heavy with unspoken words, and Northern could tell he wanted to say something. As much as she *didn't* want him to say it, she also craved to hear those three timeless words. He clicked off, drowning the car in silence once more.

She reached the intersection of 17 and 211 in Supply and made a left—back down the winding, solemn, empty Highway 211. The meager lighting in Supply faded fast and the black hole of Green Swamp swallowed the glow of the moon and stars. Ten miles down 211, her mind firmly set on Garrett, Northern was yanked from her reverie by movement on her right side. She squinted to make out what could possibly be moving with her at fifty-five miles per hour. She had an "Uh oh" moment when she thought it was a deer. She'd hit one a few years back and totaled her first car. She had heard horror stories of antlers piercing the thin car door metal and stabbing the driver in the thigh, or deer being thrown through the windshield by the impact.

Darkness and cold weather were the perfect combination for deer to run. But this shadowed creature was loping almost like a horse. Not bouncing like a deer.

Is it a horse? She wondered. *A bear?* A bear couldn't run that fast, surely. Whatever it was, it looked much larger, heftier, than a horse. Or a deer.

Northern eased her car to the center of the two-lane road to put some distance between herself and the strange creature, hoping the peripheral glow from the high beams would illuminate its identity.

Thankfully, there was no oncoming traffic at this hour. When she looked for the creature again, it was gone. Nothing in the door mirrors, nothing in the rearview, except the crimson flare of the taillights piercing the darkness in her wake.

"Must be seeing things," she said, though the hammering in her heart, the trembling of her fingers, told her she was wrong.

The Honda Accord was rocked from the side, as though hit by another car. Northern gripped the steering wheel, fighting the swerve as she searched for the assailant. Most likely, a car had pulled out of one of the dozens of logging roads that snaked throughout Green Swamp and hit her.

Another metal-crushing blow changed her mind.

The car dove into a sideways skid. The brakes locked, tires screeched.

Northern had been behind the wheel her whole life, driving tractors, four-wheelers, four-wheel drive trucks, and running dogs at seventy miles an hour on one-lane backroads. She understood the mechanics of feel and throttle and brake and horsepower. How the subtle tap of a brake or gas pedal worked wonders in situations such as this. Northern was not one to panic on her worst day, so she felt none now.

She tapped the gas pedal, like a drummer playing triplets with his right foot, and eased on and off the brake pedal with her left, a double-pedal beat in a syncopated rhythm. The car responded and began to right itself, the tail coming around by her gentle coaxing, the nose correcting course.

Smashing the gas pedal to the floor, the car straightened and the small but powerful six-cylinder engine roared. The odometer was pushing seventy when she saw it in the driver's side rearview mirror. She was not sure what *it* was exactly—it was shrouded in shadow—but got the gist of the thing: a large dog.

A very large dog.

She was unable to contemplate the strangeness of such an occurrence because the dog careened into her car again. Gravity and bad timing had its way.

The Honda Accord spun sideways again. Black smoke poured from the tires, fighting to grip the asphalt. Northern pinched her eyes closed as a bridge guardrail flew at her like a spear, and for the first time in memory, she felt something she'd never felt behind the wheel.

Fear.

CHAPTER 2

Scott "Tank" Friar was entering the Quicky Gas 'n Gone at the same time as a pretty blonde. His momma raised a gentleman, so he opened the door, and the young lady displayed a rare trait in this day and age. Respect. She thanked him, smiled, and nodded. Her actions gave him hope for the future, restored a touch of faith in humanity.

He was pouring a large shot of caffeine in a cup and couldn't help but overhear the exchange between the kid behind the register and the beautiful young lady. *Poor kid. Hasn't learned how to talk to the ladies yet.*

Tank shook his head and stepped up to the counter as the blonde was walking out.

The kid watched her a little too long and ignored Tank.

"Mmhm." Tank cleared his throat. "Cup of joe."

The kid was slow to report to duty, his mind the victim of sensory overload. "Wow," he muttered as he slipped the dollar bills in the register.

"Wow, for sure, kid. But she's out of your league." Tank picked up his coffee and headed for the door, enjoying the dissipating fragrance of the departed young lady's perfume.

"That's okay, mister," the kid said dreamily, pushing his glasses up his oversized, pimply nose. "She's out of *everybody's* league."

Tank laughed all the way to his rig.

The Peterbilt 389 was Tank's prized possession. His only point of pride, besides the double-wide sitting on two acres in Tabor City. Thousands of miles of travel and frugal investments allowed him to afford his own truck. Now he was self-employed and fortunate to have a few loyal customers who used him exclusively. Life was fine.

If not for the divorce, life would approach perfection. Damn woman. What he saw in Lorraine was a puzzle. From the beginning he questioned whether she was "The One". Highly strung, overreacted to everything, especially the bad. Her mother was a sour lady who'd gifted her daughter the same grim personality. He worked hard to give her everything possible, hopeful the materials would mellow her into something lovable.

Never happened. She remained dour until the day he walked out the door, a glass plate following him across the yard, missing his head by inches. He filed for divorce while on a week-long trip to Seattle. He returned home expecting her to still be in the house. But no, she was gone. She wasn't one to do anything quietly so he certainly hadn't expected her to leave without drama. Her parting shot was to throw everything he owned in the yard, even his beloved eighty-five-inch 4K TV. A two-day rain ruined it all.

"Damn woman," Tank grumbled, still bitter about it.

He returned the diesel nozzle to its hanger and walked the perimeter of the trailer to double check all his lights and connections. He climbed into the rig, careful not to spill the hot coffee. Main merged with 17 and took him northeast. He turned the volume up on the satellite radio just in time to catch Merle Haggard.

The Quicky Gas 'n Gone coffee tasted like motor oil. He was tempted to throw it out the window but was afraid it would permanently kill the grass and contaminate the local water supply. Motor oil or not, he needed the caffeine to get him home.

Tank turned left onto 211 in Supply and moseyed toward Bolton. He'd driven across the country, across the longest state in the union—Texas—and every other state, but this fifty-mile jog of 211 between Supply and Bolton was the longest, most boring stretch of blacktop in the country. Especially at night. The glowing possum and raccoon eyes lined the ditches on either side of the road almost the entire length from dusk to dawn. It was not unusual to spot a few dozen head of deer as well. They stared at his headlights, drawn to his rig like moths to a flame.

He checked the sky for the moon. Bright as all get out, but the light failed to reach the road. Like Green Swamp was haunted by some invisible barrier that reflected its glow. He eased back in his hydraulic chair, shifted gears, and let the voice of Kris Kristofferson guide him home.

CHAPTER 3

Below the bridge, the engine ticked. One tire spun as if searching for the road. A lone headlight lit up the woods thirty feet ahead. Lainey Wilson sang on the radio at a cracked whisper, only one busted speaker now in operation.

Northern opened her eyes, half-blinded by a thudding pressure so immense she thought her brain would leak from her ears. Her mouth was gummed with copper-rich blood and her tongue ached with shooting pain. She moved it around her cheeks and teeth to check she had not bitten it in half.

The interior lights of the dashboard gave her enough distinction to know she was upside down. And partially submerged in a shallow creek. Blood dripped from her head and plopped in the water. She blinked a few times and looked around to assess the situation. She was alive, she knew that much.

She placed one hand on the roof to hold herself up and pressed the red seatbelt release button with the other. The buckle was jammed, and she fumbled with it, yanking impatiently and pressing the button again and again.

A splash in the water stopped her cold. She held her breath as the splashing got closer, scanned the dark swamp through blurry vision. A deep growl from...something...sent her mind scattering for a defense.

Thoughts were thick and slow. An idea flirted just beyond recognition, dodged her frantic mental fingers. She squeezed her eyes shut, shook her head to knock the spiderwebs loose.

Mace.

That's it. Northern searched her surroundings. Her purse was lying on the roof in the water. She stretched until her elbows popped, fingers twiddling back and forth, the tips brushing the strap, but falling short.

She whimpered and felt shame for a show of weakness. She was a fucking Eason, and Eason's were not weak. She shoved her body against the restraints of the seatbelt and felt a flood of relief when her middle finger looped the strap. She uncapped the pepper spray as the animal's snout appeared in the smashed driver-side window.

Yellow teeth bared, its black lips peeled back, a throaty growl rumbled from its flaring nostrils as it inched closer. As the eyes glared through the window—fiery, red, evil—Northern sprayed the thing in the face. The animal howled in agony, flipped on its back, flopping around in the creek, rubbing its enormous taloned paws across its snout. It jumped to all fours, whining in pain, and disappeared into the forest.

Northern let out a tight breath. *What the fuck?*

Despite the throb in her skull and the spiked pain in her ribs, Northern pushed against the roof with all her strength. Perhaps the weight of her hanging against the buckle kept it from releasing.

She pressed the button again, a silent prayer going out to the man upstairs, and enjoyed a stress-alleviating laugh when it released. She dropped into the water, the freezing temperature biting at her flesh. She grabbed her purse and scampered out of the wreck to the bank. She collapsed in the darkness, her legs unsteady, and stared back at the mangled car. The front half—visible by a still-working headlight, dashboard lights, and a few side lights—was crumpled like crepe paper, and smoking from under the hood. The passenger side door was wedged in from the fall, and all the windows were smashed to pieces. The back half had been thrown into thick brush on the opposite bank, dead as a dismembered body part.

How am I alive? she wondered. She rubbed her forehead. Her palm came back bloody. She opened her purse and hunted for her cell phone. It had been in the console. She waded through the water on her hands and knees and searched but found nothing.

If the phone is within range of my Bluetooth, I can make a call with my car. Stumbling back to the car, she punched the Infotainment screen and scrolled to contacts. The list was empty. The Bluetooth disconnected.

"Damn it."

She opened the glove compartment and removed her handgun, a Glock 43. Locked and loaded. A second clip was slipped into the back pocket of her jeans. If that thing came back, she was damn sure going to be ready.

The shock of the accident was beginning to wear off. Dull aches began to sharpen into acute pain. Abrasions burned. Her right side felt like a knife was buried to the hilt, and her head pulsed like a heart. On a positive note, her legs were regaining a modicum of strength, and adrenaline provided much-needed energy.

Northern climbed the embankment to the highway. It took ten minutes and a few cuts to her hands to make it to the top. From the bridge she looked down to the creek. The water crashed against the rocks and stumps and—now—her car, but the wreckage wasn't visible, even with a lone headlight shining. If she had died down there, it would've taken days to find her body. Months, maybe. A scary thought, but one she refused to dwell upon.

She started walking toward home, as brisk as she could. Her clothes were soaked, and the thin cold air was sinking into her bones. She had to move. Had to hope a car would come along and give her a ride. Whether or not she would accept a ride was another story. In today's world, that was a risky proposition. Green Swamp was less than an hour from Myrtle Beach and the much-publicized disappearance of multiple young women on the coast had shed light on a booming sex trafficking market. She was okay to make a hitchhiking decision when and if it became necessary, especially with the Glock tucked away in her belt.

Northern began to jog. The bouncing caused her brain to jostle inside her skull, and poked bruised muscles—especially in her chest and ribs—but she refused to slow. Her boots slapped the asphalt and her breathing settled into a rhythm. An owl questioned the night from a tree somewhere nearby, speaking to her—like a warning. Glowing eyes stared her down from the roadside ditches, and skittered away as she got close, their passage marked by the rustle of underbrush and a panicked squeak.

A tree limb cracked. Something big was out there, stalking her. Too loud, too sudden to be a small animal. She quickened her pace, adrenaline pulsing through her.

The creature was back.

Northern pulled the gun from her purse and slowed to a fast-paced walk. She wasn't going to outrun it; it had loped beside her car at fifty-five miles per hour. She scanned the woods surrounding her in all directions. Limbs popped and leaves crackled, but the creature's position remained unknown. The gun in her hand provided little security, but she flicked the safety off anyway, and held it firm. Even so, she felt weak.

Helpless.

Higher ground was necessary. She had an idea. Northern darted across the road and ran as fast as she could through the woods.

Being raised in Green Swamp, hunting the land from one end to the other allowed her to know things. Like the locations of the fire observation towers; scaffolded structures, five stories high, designed for viewing wildfires.

One stood nearby.

She broke through an opening in the forest and, sitting in the middle of the clearing, was the tower. There, the moonlight was doing a better job of penetrating the stubborn darkness. Northern hurried across the clearing, the waist-high weeds grabbing at her thighs and ankles. The cold air burned her lungs, but she dared not stop. She reached the tower and climbed up the ladder rungs to the mini shed at the top. She crawled inside the covered structure, pressed her back to the corner, and tried to calm her ragged breathing. The Glock still shook in her hand, though the need for it was now unknown.

Up there, in the tower, the cold air blew more briskly. Northern's wet clothes began to harden to ice. In the opposite corner sat a plastic container with a dust-caked lid labeled "Emergency Kit".

Thank Christ.

Inside was a hard hat, a blanket, a whistle, binoculars, a flare gun, and a walkie talkie. All the tools necessary to watch for a fire. The walkie talkie crackled to life with white noise, but her jubilation dampened when the batteries died almost immediately. She wrapped the blanket around her shoulders. Pressed the binoculars to her eyes to search for any sign of movement.

In the pale moonlight, nothing moved across the clearing. She scanned the entire field but found nothing. Then more of nothing. Maybe the cracking tree limbs were nothing more malicious than a deer. Deer in rut make a lot of noise. The consideration to climb down was fleeting. *I'll wait until daybreak, then walk out.*

The plan was made and settled. Northern leaned back in the corner and pulled the blanket around her shoulders.

The creature was odd. The features—the eyes, the teeth—were feral. A beast of unknown origin. She'd never seen anything like it outside of horror movies. To be so strong and fast that it crashed into her like a demolition derby. What kind of animal was capable of that? Nothing in Green Swamp.

The tower shook. The steel stilts vibrated. The guide wires designed for added strength during hurricanes twanged from tension. Northern leaped to her feet and peeked out the window, down to the ground. The beast was slamming its body into the corner poles. It growled and grunted with each assault. It paused after several tries, sniffing at the steel tubing and tearing into the earth with sharp claws.

Northern held her breath and waited. *Will it give up and go away?*

It began to dig around the footer of one corner post. Within minutes, the ground beneath the footer was hollow and the concrete slab canted and dropped away. The beast went to the next post and a dawning horror injected ice into her veins.

It's going to make the tower collapse.

Northern put the beast's thick hairy body in her gunsight and fired a shot. The fur jumped so she knew she'd hit the target. The beast roared and spun in circles. Dropping to its haunches, its blazing eyes stared up at her, hot with pain and anger. It howled, and gooseflesh rippled down Northern's back.

It went back to work with ferocity, the pain of its injury driving its rage. Northern tucked the gun into her belt milliseconds before another footer dropped, pitching the tower to one side. Northern was thrown across the shed floor. She slid out the door, about to plummet five stories, but her fingertips latched onto each side of the door frame. As cold and numb as her hands were, she gripped onto the frame harder than anything in her life.

The tower miraculously stopped falling. The guide wires committed to the job intended. Northern refused to look down at the distance she would fall or the snarling beast awaiting whatever was left.

She concentrated on refreshing her grip. She walked the fingers on her right hand across the metal frame until the hold firmed. She repeated with her left hand. Her feet hunted for a cross bar to step on, kicking forward and side to side. Her right toe tapped a bar. She slid her body to the right as much as possible. Her hands were white, and the feeling was leaving her arms.

I've got minutes at best. Then I'm dead.

The stark realization of mortality boosted her desire to live. She got one toe, all the toes, the whole right foot, on a bar. She let her weight settle on that leg to give her arms a break. One hand stayed clamped on the door frame while she let the other arm dangle. She shook it to get the blood circulating. The numbing tingle left her fingertips. She traded hands and repeated the process. Northern took a deep breath and jumped as hard as she could. She pulled her body up and into the doorway and rolled sideways to lay against the wall of the shed, the gun prodding her lower back.

Northern was at a loss. The beast was determined not to allow her to wait it out. Bullets were unsuccessful in killing or hurting it. Options were limited and shrinking by the second. The tower shook again, one guide wire popped.

Northern scooted on her butt to the ladder. She wasn't thrilled about climbing down but this platform was going to fall, and a five-story plunge was a death sentence. She was tired, concussed, and her bruised body hurt all over. Fighting for life was taking its toll. She took a deep breath, clambered down the ladder. The monster stopped attacking the tower and waited with greedy, snarling lips.

How are you this smart? she wondered.

She stopped one-story up. The beast jumped and swiped, its razor-sharp claws slicing at her legs. It missed but the claws struck the steel rungs a few feet down, and sparks flew. Northern removed the gun from her belt and emptied the magazine. The beast danced in circles to avoid the bullets, before disappearing through the weeds. Northern dropped the final story, rolled, and ran in the opposite direction, slapping in a fresh magazine mid-stride. She was almost at the tree line when she heard the furious roar of the monster behind her. She spun and fell to her back, trigger finger spasming, gun cracking.

CHAPTER 4

Tank always wanted to be in a band. Drumming would be cool. He pounded his left fist against the steering wheel to simulate the thud of the bass drum and tapped with his right fingers for the snare. He felt the beat, the timing, the rhythm.

Yeah, I could do this.

Maybe he'd go online tomorrow and hunt for a nice cheap set of drums and give it a try. How hard could it be?

As Tank slowed to take a bend in the road, he noticed skid marks from one side of the pavement to the other. They looked fresh—he'd seen enough traffic accidents to know the difference.

The skid marks swerved to the left, fishtailed back to the right, then formed a squiggly pigtail as the driver corrected and got control. He slowed further when he saw another set of skid marks that slid straight into a guardrail protecting the bridge. A plastic bumper lay on the bridge, just off the road. He stopped in the middle of 211 and rolled down his window. Flashed back to the station. The gorgeous blonde had climbed out of her little import—a bright-red Honda Accord. Sporty thing. Flared fenders with scoops and indentations for the dual purpose of aerodynamics and cosmetics. This discarded bumper was identical.

Tank pulled the truck past the bridge and eased off the side of the road into the grass. The brakes hissed as he let the air out. He shrugged into his Carhartt jacket, grabbed a flashlight out of the door pocket, and went to see what he could see.

He wasn't positive it belonged to the blonde, but if he were a gambling man, he would lay a thousand down that this was from her car. Water gurgled as it rushed toward its destination. The canopy of trees and overgrowth blanketed the creek, however, obscuring sight.

The swamp was peaceful. An owl hooted, its night song haunting. The only evidence anything had happened here was the bumper and skid marks. And that could have happened weeks ago, even if the marks looked fresh; dark black, not faded with time and vehicle passage. Was there a hint of burned rubber in the air? Or was that his imagination?

Tank removed the phone from his pocket and saw he had no service. There was cell coverage in Green Swamp, but it was spotty at best. All the folks who lived out here had to keep a home phone activated for just such a reason.

Tank contemplated his next move and saw only one option: drive to Bolton where he knew he would get a strong signal and call the police. Have them come check this out. He would even meet them here to make sure. Last thing he wanted was to find out that young lady was down there in the creek, and he dropped the ball helping her. He rushed to his truck and got the big rig moving.

Getting up to speed, the needle nudging fifty-five, a gigantic black shadow darted across 211 in front of him. "Jesus!" He jerked the wheel. The truck and trailer swerved. As Tank fought to correct and straighten his little freight train, a concussive blow to the trailer knocked it into a tilting skid, the brake-locked tires bouncing along the asphalt. The trailer seemed suspended in the air as it debated whether to completely flip on its side or drop back to the designed position. Tank snatched the wheel in the opposite direction in the hope that ergonomics would push the trailer in his favor. Another crushing blow sent the trailer sprawling on its side in the middle of 211. In a blink, the rig was twisted to its side.

Tank's arm snapped at impact. He heard it more than felt it. His head slammed against the door frame and glass ground into his skin. His mind raced, begging for the truck to stop sliding, begging for the pain to ease.

Tank moaned from the hurt. Everything pulsed in anguish, parts of his body he didn't even know could feel pain. A volcanic heat wrapped his fractured arm, and he tried to move it, to see if it still worked. He bellowed when the bones jutting from his skin bumped the steering wheel.

His head was split in two, a bass drum beater thumping against his eyeballs. Even his bunions hurt. Felt sick to the stomach. He snapped out of his harness and crawled one-armed through what used to be the front windshield. Pieces of glass cut his knees and arms, a jagged shard sticking from his thigh. Some of the sharper chunks had slipped through the tender flesh, burying into thick muscle.

Tank made it to the grass on the side of the road, gripping the greenery with blood-stained fingers, and vomited on some trash caught in the weeds. Why he was concerned about hurling in his demolished rig, he was unable to say. People weren't supposed to puke in the car. It was a law or something.

Tank lay half in the road and half in the grass for several minutes, clutching at his fractured arm. He was unconcerned about traffic, almost prayed for someone to hit him. At least the pain would end.

He was a country boy, though. Giving up was not in his vocabulary. He climbed to his feet, stood swaying in the darkness, his knees weak.

The trees whipped around him like he was spinning, playing the childhood game of making yourself dizzy on purpose then trying to walk without busting your teeth. He spewed the rest of the oily gas station coffee and dinner and junk food into the grass, wiped his mouth and slowly straightened. The forest stood still. He limped back to the truck and climbed into the cab via the windshield. He was searching for his flashlight when he heard the crunch of glass behind him.

A deep, rumbling growl.

Almost like a souped-up Camaro with a high-performance exhaust. He eased his head around to confirm what he already knew. The owner of the rumbling growl was the thing that had rammed him. Red eyes consumed him. He stumbled back and threw up his arms defensively.

He screamed when both arms dropped to the floor of the cab, the stumps below the elbow spurting blood like a fountain. He couldn't believe this was the end. He closed his eyes and waited.

Waited for the end.

Nothing.

The obnoxious blow of a horn startled him. He opened his eyes in time to catch headlights and a chrome, Fleetwood grill.

CHAPTER 5

Tin Shed was the most famous location in Green Swamp. Or, in this case, *infamous*. The story had gone through generations of telling and, as such, tended to be grossly exaggerated. How far the story strayed from what actually happened that day had everything to do with the teller.

Levi Stuart, Tommy Stuart's grandaddy erected a lean-to—four posts and a tin roof—for loggers to shelter if Mother Nature got quarrelsome in the middle of a long shift. Nothing special about the area or the modest refuge.

After Levi and his wife, Joan, settled in Green Swamp, he took to hunting—his favorite spot was three hundred yards east of the tin shed. He built a blind at the base of a tree, wrapped it with sod, draped twigs and moss over it, and used it until the day this whole tale came to pass.

Levi walked in early that day. It was a warmer-than-usual October morning, foggy. 3:30 a.m. Rain from the previous night had been heavy enough to wash away some of the muddy sod from the roof of the blind. It was too dark for Levi to notice, and he climbed inside and settled. He opened a coffee thermos and quietly tugged out half a wedge of PB&J. Without the sod on the roof, some of his camouflage was missing—more smell than sight.

A black bear rambling around that morning caught a whiff of a strange, nutty odor. The sweet scent of jelly calling to it. Hungry and curious, the bear went to investigate.

Levi was not aware of the bear until it stuck its snout in the gun slot of the blind. He pressed back against the tree and threw the sandwich to the side. Choking on the last bite, he dug through his knapsack in a frenzy. Levi's hand came out with an ammonia-filled spray bottle—every hunter had one, bears hated that smell. He squirted in the bear's direction, thankful to hit the muzzle dead on.

With a low roar, the bear barreled from the blind and plowed its nose through the wet wire grass. Wiped, swiped, rubbed its muzzle against the ground to remove the ammonia. The bear gave up, focusing instead on the person responsible for its condition: Levi.

It was such a shocking turn of events, Levi hadn't the time to pick the gun off the floor. The angry bear attacked the blind with rabid ferocity, clawing and tearing and growling. The shelter of the blind felt thin and weak, and Levi scrambled for his weapon while pressing into a corner.

The boards—rotted from weather exposure—splintered around rusty nails. The first board fell away, a giant paw with razor-sharp claws, swiped at Levi as he cowered. The bear, realizing the human was out of range, doubled its efforts on the boards. Another slat fractured down the middle and tore away. The bear's teeth gnashed, hungry for what it had smelled. Hungry for Levi.

Desperate and scared, Levi knew doing nothing was signing his death warrant. Pulling the rifle to him, risking a paw to the face, he raised the rifle, jacked a round into the chamber, aimed at the head.

Squeezed the trigger.

In the split second before the striker detonated the primer, the bear's paw tapped the barrel of the rifle and knocked it off course. The bullet missed, but the sharp crack of the weapon succeeded in scaring the bear off. It disappeared in the rolling fog, still scratching at its own face.

Levi climbed out of the blind, rifle at the ready, and ran as fast as he could toward Tin Shed. A country boy, sure. Hard, and tough as gristle, absolutely. A marathon sprinter, no way. Within a minute, all the oxygen seemed to vanish. His lungs gasped and begged, but nothing came in, as though some invisible demon was hacking at his lungs with a scythe.

His pace slowed to a fast walk as his elbow pushed against his ribcage, where the knifing pain pierced through to his intestines. A bass-toned growl echoed through the fog and the bear burst from its misty shroud.

Less than fifty yards behind him and gaining.

Levi gasped, forgetting about the demon. His legs pumped under him on autopilot, finding ground again and again to push him forward. Trees and limbs flashed by, puddled water splashed underfoot, glassy-eyed night creatures scampered away, a flock of nesting birds skittered for the safety of the sky.

Tin Shed came into view, and a flood of relief overcame him. *Almost there.*

He didn't chance a look back—the bear was close. The snapping of twigs, the thud of paws, growling, panting. Levi imagined the beast performing a leg sweep with its enormous claws, pouncing on him as he scrambled to stand. Massive jaws spreading to engulf his head, clamping shut so hard his skull imploded.

The imagery spurred him on, one last gush of energy pushing him the last ten yards to Tin Shed. In a remarkable, once-in-a-lifetime feat, Levi tossed the gun on top the tin roof, and scrambled up one of the posts like a squirrel. He was standing on the roof by the time the bear arrived, his lungs burning, his legs wobbling under him.

Roaring at him, angry that Levi had thwarted it again, the bear stood on its hind legs like a man. It ambled to the shed and attempted to climb the post.

Levi tugged a round out of the ammo holster slung around his torso, jacked another .38-40 cartridge into the barrel, aimed at the roaring monster, and took the shot. The pelt disappeared from the crown of its skull as the bullet crushed its cranium. The black bear fell backward. Dead. He'd faced the beast and lived to tell the tale.

Levi removed one of the bear's teeth, drilled a hole in it, and made a necklace. The story was recounted to anyone who'd listen—and some who wouldn't.

When his son, Dale, was older, he passed it on to him, the infamous bear tooth family heirloom. In turn, when Dale's son, Tommy, turned sixteen, it was passed to him as a gift. A rite of passage. A reminder of the perseverance of the Stuarts.

****

Tommy Stuart dreamed he heard gunshots. Which was weird because he was sitting in a deer stand with his dead grandfather, Levi. Granddaddy was a skeleton. Only one cloudy eye remained, and it was beginning to ooze clear fluid like an egg when the shell was cracked. Long, wispy, white hair bloomed from a grayish, desiccated patch of flesh atop the skull. A filthy, white t-shirt with I LOVE MYRTLE BEACH on the front hung like shredded curtains from his shoulders, the ribcage exposed and empty. A pair of jeans, discolored by time and grime, covered his legs.

Levi pointed a bony finger through the opening in the blind and whispered, "That's a nice one." His voice was dry as a corn husk. He choked on something, coughed, and a water bug flew out of his mouth. Landed on his lap. He picked it up, skeletal fingers like chopsticks, and dropped it in his mouth. Chewing the bug with the few teeth he had left, the slick innards squirting down his chin, Levi ignored the juice dripping in his lap.

Tommy winced in disgust, then checked on the deer Levi suggested to him. Through the scope was something resembling a deer, but with critical differences. It had two heads; one was normal, a six-point rack perched atop its head like a proud crown. The other head looked dead. The flesh on one side was ripped to shreds, hanging like ribbons. One eye was missing. But this head darted side to side, suspicious. The damage wasn't confined only to the head.

The body was the artwork of a savage, like a disfigured version of *Monarch of the Glen*. Entrails suspended from the stomach, dragging pine needles and cones as the deer stepped slowly forward in search of fresh blades of grass. Cuts of surgical precision and cleanliness exposed the ribs and spine of the animal. Exposed the steady beat of a black, shriveled heart.

"Perfect," Granddaddy croaked in his ear.

Nothing perfect about it. Only rot and death. He was not going to shoot that thing. He opened his mouth to tell Granddaddy his decision—

BANG!

BANG!

Granddaddy grabbed his feet and shook them. He looked down but Levi was nowhere to be found.

"Tommy!"

Tommy sat up. He was wrapped in a sleeping bag inside his tent, not in a deer stand. He checked his tent. Empty.

"Tommy!"

The fog of the dream dissipated, and he made eye contact with Steven, whose head was stuck inside the zippered flaps of the tent. "Yeah?"

"Something's going on. Get dressed and grab your gun. We heard a wreck, screaming, and gunshots."

Tommy slipped into his thermal camouflage coveralls and tugged on his boots, hurrying after his friends. After six days of not seeing any deer, the group had decided to stay one more night, hit the stands early in the morning, then return home in daylight. In hindsight, maybe not such a good idea.

He grabbed his shotgun and ran to catch up with the other three: Cliff and Steven Gainey, and Jerry Landon. Every year, the four of them went on a hunting trip in the Swamp. A ritual. Only the men. No children, no women, and no cell phones. A time of solitude, bonding, and connecting with nature.

Not roughing it—with a few creature comforts from home—but damn near. Tin Shed was miles from the nearest residential dwelling. Until four years earlier, Tommy's father, Dale, always accompanied them. A heart attack put a stop to that. Dale made it through the surgery alive, but his days of long hikes through the woods, sleeping in tents, and climbing tree stands were over.

Another burst of gunfire clipped the night before the swamp went silent. A handgun, by the sound of it. The four jogged, the underbrush whipping their legs, tree limbs popping them in the face. Tommy was sure the sounds came from the direction of Pop's Place, an abandoned, dilapidated house which once belonged to Pop Munerlyn.

Pop had committed suicide years ago. Shot himself on the front porch. Cliff found the poor bastard. Pop sat there for days, hunched over and rotting, before Cliff went to visit. In that time, animals had eaten the meat from his legs to the stomach, the bones licked to a glistening shine, his ribcage a hollow shell. Cliff said even Pop's dick and balls were gone.

Without family members to claim the property, the house was abandoned and now rotted away in Green Swamp.

They hurried into a clearing where one of the dozens of Green Swamp watchtowers stood. It canted to one side, looking half destroyed.

"What happened to it?" Tommy yelled between ragged breaths.

"Don't know." Cliff huffed over his shoulder.

The pale moonlight cast an eerie reflection off the floating mist. The cold, damp night sank into their skin, forecasting the coming winter storm. A cramp was forming in Tommy's side, but he was damned if he was going to stop. Cliff was twenty-five years his senior and still trotting along at an age-defying clip.

Mid-step, Cliff stopped. "What in heaven's—"

In front of them.

A body.

The glow of the moon dulled the ravaged flesh, but even in the dim light, the torn mass was lacquered in a dark liquid. It glinted like freshly polished furniture. The stench wafting over the grass was anything but, and Tommy covered his nose.

The four of them tiptoed forward as if they might awaken the corpse. Tommy thought of Granddaddy Levi and shuddered. The tangy odor of copper was redolent and arresting. The ripped flesh and chunks of meat made it hard to distinguish the sex of the victim.

"Looks female," Cliff said with disgust. He used the barrel of his rifle to loop something in the weeds. He raised it toward the moon and Tommy's eyes went wide when he saw the severed hand, blades of grass sticking to the moist nub. The white skin was paired with manicured nails of bright red on slender fingers.

Tommy was vomiting before his stomach made him aware of a problem. It surged from his lips in a steaming, chunky spray. He hurried away from the group and finished the business in the highest weeds. "Sorry," he said, returning to the scene, wiping his mouth.

"We need to call the police," Jerry said. "I think one of us should return to camp, grab a few belongings, and head home. Get the law out here. The other three should stay and watch over the body. This is a crime scene." He paused, then added: "We don't want animals eating any more of her."

Cliff nodded toward the girl's body. "She's already been chewed on. But I get the point."

"Anybody recognize her?" Steven asked. He'd been standing back a bit, sucking air that didn't stink of death. He stepped forward to join the others. "I see blonde hair, I think. Hard to tell but those strands look blonde."

Cliff raised his face to the moon and closed his eyes. "Lord, I sure do hope that isn't who it might be."

"And who might it be?" Steven asked his dad.

"Ray Eason's daughter. Don't know why she'd be out here. But she's the only person in the Swamp that has blonde hair. That I know of."

Steven shook his head, muttered a cuss word.

"What about that black smoke over there?" Tommy asked, pointing toward 211, miles away. "Must be one helluva wreck."

"Let's take it one problem at a time," Cliff answered. "The police can look into the wreck when they get here."

"I'll go," Tommy said. He wanted to get away from the nauseating smell. The sight of her body made his head light. And to think it was Northern Eason was too much. "I'll go call nine-one-one."

Cliff nodded. "Okay. Hurry. We don't want to be out here anymore than you do," he said, as if reading Tommy's thoughts.

Tommy took off at a dead blast. The burst of energy compelling him to leave was short lived. A needle stitched barbed wire through the muscle in his side, and he slowed to massage the area. Gunfire erupted from behind him, from the direction of the tower. Screams echoed through the forest. He spun around, scanning the night and seeing only random bursts of gunpowder.

More screams—begging for help. More gunfire.

What the hell?

One bellow was cut off instantaneously.

Tommy held his breath. Listened.

A limb cracked. Dry leaves rustled. The trees around him shuddered. The moon deserted him, leaving him in almost pitch black. Two candle flames floated toward him in the dark like fireflies. The candles promised a reprieve from the cold, from the dark. Warm as a country hearth. The smell of decomposed meat pummeled his nose, and Tommy realized the promise was for fools. The flames held nothing but the cold black, and they beckoned Tommy with a searing grin.

He thought of Mary and his kids. Of all the good times, the laughter. He closed his eyes to brighten their faces.

And those images accompanied him into the darkness.

CHAPTER 6

Worry was the worst. Like a termite infestation. Slow and methodical burrowing, hollowing out the insides until the body was weak and frail. And Mary Stuart was consumed with it.

She stared at the percolating coffee pot and contemplated, while the black liquid filtered into the glass bowl. Tommy wasn't home yet, that was the problem. It was Saturday morning, November 30th. Tommy, Jerry Landon, and Steven and Cliff Gainey were supposed to be back last night. They never returned late. Ever. Especially Tommy. He enjoyed the trip but was always ready for a hot shower, a good meal, and a warm bed.

Mary hadn't heard from the other wives. She wondered if they were concerned. She wanted to call but was not one to cause undue alarm.

This yearly ritual was coming to an end. Tommy's father, Dale, was the first to drop out after a heart attack. Cliff's days were numbered as he approached his mid-seventies. Jerry had already been through one knee replacement surgery and was limping toward another. Steven was showing signs of disinterest. Only a matter of time. Maybe the boys were thinking the same thing and were taking a bit longer to soak up the last vestiges of their ritual.

Maybe I should just check up on them. Invasive, she knew, but necessary for her peace of mind. She dialed Tommy's best friend, Buck Williams. He knew where the camp site was located.

"Unhh.... Hello?" Buck yawned.

"Hey, Buck, it's Mary."

Buck rustled awake and Mary knew why. She never called, and certainly never at 7 a.m. "What's wrong?"

"Well—" A barrage of sirens cut her short. "Hold on." She went to the window looking out at Highway 211. A convoy of emergency vehicles screamed by her house, splitting the peaceful morning like an ax.

"There are fire trucks, police, and ambulances flying past my house, headed toward Supply. Something's wrong... I've got a bad feeling it's something to do with Tommy."

"Tommy? He came home last night, right?"

"That's why I'm calling. He didn't."

Without hesitation: "I'll check it out."

"Thank you."

Buck lived in Bolivia, about a thirty-minute drive to Mary's house.

"I should wait for Buck," she said to the windowpane as another patrol car sped past. She shook her head. "Damn that."

Slipping on a pair of jeans, a pullover, and a pair of tennis shoes, she jumped in Tommy's Ford F-150 and followed the noise.

In all the time she and Tommy had been living in Green Swamp, there had never been a wreck on 211. Surprising, but true. With all the logging trucks and equipment, the multitude of dirt roads that spit those trucks onto the highway like conveyor belts, one would expect a wreck every other week.

"Oh my god." She breathed when she rounded the bend and saw the wreckage, her heart pulling tight. Two patrol cars blocked her from getting closer.

An officer stepped to her window. "Sorry ma'am, but you'll have to turn around," the young man said.

"What in the world happened?" Mary asked, shocked by the incredible mess.

"Not sure, yet. But it was bad." He looked back across the scene, his eyes conveying it was worse than bad, and he was still trying to process what he'd seen.

"Officer, I don't want to tell you how to do your job, but this is a busy highway. You'll have traffic backed up for miles with nowhere to go if you don't block off the road at each end."

"Already blocked off in Supply and Bolton. Have a good day, ma'am." With that, the officer stepped back and waited for her to follow orders.

Mary three-point-turned and slowly pulled away, trying to make sense of it all. A trailer lying on its side, blocking the road. Two rigs crushed together and burned to the steel frame. Truck parts and pieces scattered about like a bomb had exploded. The acrid tang of burned rubber. A white sheet covering the inside of the truck lying on its side, the contours of a body underneath.

Despite the scene, Mary was filled with relief. Her Tommy wasn't involved. He was okay, taking the long way home with the boys. A pang of guilt stopped her from smiling; even though Tommy was okay, people had still lost their lives.

As she pulled into her driveway, Arlene Gainey walked across the street. They were neighbors and Arlene was like family. She helped Mary adjust to country life when she and Tommy first got married. Mary grew up in Wilmington, knew nothing about living away from civilization. Arlene taught her all about the way of life in these parts. Hundreds of tiny things that were anything but inconsequential.

Arlene's son and husband were with Tommy on the hunting and camping trip. Mary wondered about her take on their lateness.

"Good morning," Arlene called, pulling her housecoat tight against the frigid temperature. Her hands were wrapped around a coffee cup. "What was all that commotion about? I was about to call when I saw you leaving to nose around."

"You caught me," Mary laughed nervously. "Arlene, it's crazy. There are two eighteen-wheelers piled up seven or eight miles down toward Supply. Got the road blocked off. They crashed basically head-on, best I can figure. And caught fire. Biggest mess you ever saw."

"Oh my," Arlene said, thoughts lost as she conjured up such an image. "That is crazy. But I'm not surprised. These truckers blow by here moving so fast they about knock the house off its foundation. Maybe this will teach them to slow down."

"Officer said they got 211 blocked on both ends."

Arlene nodded and took a sip of coffee. "That's a good idea."

"Hey, uh, have you heard from the boys?" Mary tried to sound casual.

"No, I haven't, but Cliff and Steven don't take their phones. Wouldn't matter; no signal out there."

"Tommy doesn't either. Honestly, I'm concerned they're not home yet. We have this storm moving in and Tommy swore he'd be home last night. It's not like him to not keep his word."

"Cliff said the same, but I'm not worried. Not yet. They may have tapped into the bottle a little too hard last night, and just decided to walk out this morning on steadier legs."

Mary fake smiled. "I'm sure you're right. I'm being silly."

"Mom, my stomach hurts," Conner called from the front door.

"Coming," Mary said. She hugged Arlene. "Thank you for calming me down."

"No problem. You go take care of those babies. Try ginger ale. I'll call you later."

Mary found Conner curled up on the couch. "Do you feel sick?"

"Yes. I already threw up a few minutes ago. I couldn't find you."

"I ran down the street for a sec. I'm back. Let me get you some medicine. Try to drink some ginger ale."

Mary was tending to Conner when Buck stormed in the front door. He was family, so knocking was unnecessary.

"Hear anything?" he asked, pouring coffee into his thermal cup.

"Nothing," Mary called down the hall from Conner's bedroom. She spoon-fed Conner some StomaRight, and cracked the tab on a can of ginger ale, helped him sip. He laid back as she tucked him in.

"They're not at Tin Shed. The wreck is two eighteen-wheelers piled up in the middle of the road. Has nothing to do with them."

Mary returned to the kitchen but decided not to tell him she already knew about the wreck. "What do you mean they're not at Tin Shed? You didn't see them there or on the way back here?"

"Nope. They *were* at Tin Shed. The campfire was smoldering. Their tents are set up but empty. No sign of them."

"That's odd." Mary frowned. "Do you think they're out hunting?"

"That crossed my mind but the one stand that I know about is empty. I'm sure they have more but I don't know where those are."

Mary's shoulders slumped from the weight of the news. They were capable men. Each great shooters and hunters. They were hunting, that's all. The craving to bag an eight-pointer before calling it quits like an addiction. No need to worry.

So why is my stomach in knots? "Buck, I hate to ask this. Could you take the Polaris and go ride around and find them? This storm is rolling in before noon and I don't want them getting caught in that."

"Yes, ma'am."

Buck grabbed the four-wheeler keys from the key hooks by the back door and left. A few minutes later she heard the engine fire up, rev, and Buck was gone.

"Where's Daddy?" Maribeth asked wiping the sleep from her eyes. Her *Dora the Explorer* onesie scratched against the floor as she shuffled into the kitchen. She just turned six on November 7th. She and Tommy privately referred to Maribeth as "the surprise". They were not trying to get pregnant. After such a long-term battle to get pregnant with Conner, they were in no rush to try again. When the doctor delivered the stunning news, she thought it a prank. Mary asked him to repeat it three times before she accepted the truth. She had rushed to Tommy's office to give him the good news in person. They received a standing ovation from all his co-workers.

"He'll be home shortly," Mary said. Trying to manifest the hope into reality. "You want some breakfast?"

CHAPTER 7

Sarah Grace Elliot had her eyes on the scrambling eggs and her ears on the weatherman. Grits bubbled in a pot on the back burner. Bacon and link sausage sizzled in a pan next to the eggs. The coffee pot was full. Fresh orange juice purchased from Eason's Market chilled in a bowl of ice on the island counter.

The guy from *The Weather Channel* was broadcasting from Wilmington. If he was in town, a doozie of a storm was on the way. Snow was unusual in the south and even more so in coastal communities. The last snow event was eleven years earlier, nothing more than a dusting. The last major snow event in Brunswick County was back in 1989. Two feet of snow had fallen over a two-day span. That storm stood today as one of the worst winter storms on record. If the predictions were accurate, this incoming system would shatter those existing accounts.

Sarah Grace had lived through numerous hurricanes but had never witnessed a forecast like this. She was glad her husband, Ron, had insisted on a household generator a few years earlier after Hurricane Matthew left them powerless for a week and a half. If the guy on TV was right, power could be down for longer this time.

Jason and Addie entered the kitchen. Jason still half-asleep, Addie wide awake, tail bouncing. Addie was technically Ron's golden retriever, but she followed Jason everywhere. He spent a lot of time with her, throwing balls in the yard, running through the woods, petting her, allowing her to sleep in his bed. She no longer belonged to Ron.

Jason's porcupine hair shot to all compass points, his eyes puffy with sleep, pajama top and bottoms wrinkled. He yawned, and sat quietly, picking at his fingers.

Sarah Grace was still learning the mannerisms of this little human. He was new to the family. The Elliot's adopted him sixteen weeks earlier, after his mother was killed by his father in a drug-fueled rage. The father had returned home to their melancholy trailer after a night of snorting cocaine and drinking with friends and found her having sex with a neighbor on the living room couch. Jason was watching TV in the living room, his back turned—but ears open—to the shenanigans. The father had grabbed shotgun—loaded and leaning in its usual spot by the front door—and shot them both as they pleaded for mercy. The father, struck with grief, dropped to his knees, put the gun under his chin, and pulled the trigger. Jason watched the whole thing in the reflection of the TV. The counselor responsible for Jason's case had told Sarah Grace and Ron that Jason confided in her his father's final cryptic words.

"You'll die there, boy."

Jason had no idea what those words meant, the counselor had told them. He was too traumatized from the murder-suicide to care.

Sarah Grace and Ron were reminded daily of Jason's extraordinary character. His fortitude and attitude in the wake of such a tragedy was jarring. He was a normal twelve-year-old boy even when life attempted to beat all the normal out of him. He loved superhero movies, riding the four-wheeler through the Swamp, playing basketball, and video games. He spoiled Addie rotten and seemed to be adjusting to school.

New friend Jesse Griffin just invited him to his birthday party in January. He was excited to go, and that was everything to Sarah Grace.

"Looks like school is canceled next week," Sarah Grace said, watching him from the corner of her eye. "You'll get a winter break, then a Christmas break. Nice vacation, huh?"

Jason nodded and continued to pick at his fingers; Addie wagged her tail at his feet.

"Would you like some orange juice?"

He nodded again. She poured the sweet, pulpy liquid in a glass and slid it in front of him. He took a sip, then stared at the juice.

"You know," she said, her voice lighter, more playful, "they're calling for three to four feet of snow. I'll bet Ron will pull you around behind the four-wheeler on the sled. That'll be fun, right?"

Jason frowned and shrugged.

Sarah Grace propped her face in her hands on the counter in front of him as the eggs continued to sizzle in the pan. "Something's wrong," she said quietly. "I can tell. And you can talk to me about anything. I want you to know that. You can always talk to me about whatever. Even if you think I'll be mad."

"I don't think you'll be mad," he whispered, his voice husky with sleep.

"What do you think I'll be?"

Jason's eyes rose from the juice to meet her stare. "Scared."

A shiver tickled her spine. "Why would I be scared?"

"Because...my daddy came to see me last night."

A nightmare. "He did, huh?"

Jason nodded. "His face was gone. His tongue flopped side to side like a dancing snake. When he spoke, it was hard to understand, 'cause he had no lips or jaw. But it was like I was being told the words in my head. He said that something bad is happening. He said something bad is *going* to happen. He said"—his lower lip trembled and his eyes watered—"something bad is going to happen to you and Ron."

The counselor warned them of this. Jason lost his parents in the most tragic way possible. She said he may act clingy and express fear of losing his new parents. Part of the process of healing.

"Baby, listen to me closely," Sarah Grace said, cupping his cheeks, her tone soothing, "neither Ron nor I are going anywhere. Nothing is going to happen to us. We are here with you, and we will be here for a long, long time. You have nothing to be afraid of."

"He showed me," Jason said.

"Showed you what?"

"I don't know what it was, but—"

"But?"

Jason licked his lips and gulped. "It has killed people."

Sarah Grace was momentarily stuck. He had a nightmare, and in his current state of recovery, believed the negative connotations. She wanted to assure him that everything was fine while not pandering to his fears. "Jason, I love you. Nothing bad is going to happen to you or this family. Okay?"

Jason nodded slowly.

"As far as whatever you saw, dreams can be real. Several years ago, I dreamed my dad was alive and picking tomatoes with me out of the garden. He was talking to me like I'm talking to you. It was so vivid I went out to the garden that morning to make sure I didn't see an extra set of footprints in the dirt. I've woken from a nightmare screaming because it was so real. Dreams are like that. They're like movies in your head. Some of them are like the old, made in the fifties, grainy and fuzzy and not very clear. But some of them are in high-definition 3D and every monster in the dark is larger than life. But it was just a dream. You have nothing to be afraid of."

"Swear?"

"I swear," Sarah Grace promised, relaxing as the stony weight of concern rose from her shoulders. "Now, would you like for me to fix you some breakfast or would it be okay to let those eggs burn until they catch fire?"

"Breakfast," he said, smiling.

Ron walked in, yawning and stretching. He lifted Jason from the barstool and tossed him over his shoulder. The two played make-believe wrestling, laughing and giggling. Addie danced around their legs, barking excitedly until Sarah Grace called for breakfast.

The conversation with Jason dwindled from her thoughts, but the residue of unease remained. And uneasiness was like a ghost. It may fade, but it was always there, roaming the corridors of the soul.

CHAPTER 8

The rear tires of the four-wheeler sprayed red clay in a rooster tail. The cold air bit Buck's cheeks like hornets, and his uncovered hands quickly tinged blue. He rode the side of 211 until he reached Two Mile Road. At its end, he took a left on Peak's Pass and drove deeper into the heart of Green Swamp. The sky was the color of a day-old corpse. The shuttling clouds angry and threatening. The sun hid in fear like a scared child.

Green ash, long leaf pines, oak, and river birches swept by Buck's vision in a teary blur. His nose dripped like an old faucet.

Green Swamp was normally a hive of activity as logging companies hauled cut timber from the land. In anticipation of the coming storm, everyone was sent home. Unmanned logging equipment was parked randomly around the Swamp. He shot by a beat-up logging truck. A few minutes later, a utility truck with a stump grinder attached to it flew past.

Buck slowed to take the sharp dog leg left at Deadman's Turn. Many a hunter had missed that turn and wound up in the bottom of the ditch. Clear of danger, he cranked his wrist back to accelerate again, and the engine was happy to accept the challenge. A mile further and he took a right onto Possum Trail Road.

Buck had always thought the backroad's nicknames were funny. He'd learned over the years that each name given to the road came from a story. And hunters loved stories.

He remembered Tommy mentioning a deer stand somewhere on Possum Trail. Tommy had said he always forgot where the stand was located so he used a landmark to help him remember: a tree mangled by a lightning strike.

Sliding to a stop beside an American beech, split down the middle like a giant had chopped it with a flaming ax, Buck considered the tree. The wood inside was charred black, the sides flaky white with rot and pockmarked with bug holes.

Under normal circumstances, Buck would practice hunting safety. Wave his arms and yell loud and clear before approaching. Anything not to be mistaken for the wrong kind of buck. These were not normal circumstances, and time was wasting. The four-wheeler roared as he cut through the flora and fauna that carpeted the forest floor. He found the stand hovering in the fog like a shroud.

"Tommy," he called from below the wooden structure. It was hand made by Cliff and Pop Munerlyn years and years earlier. The wood was almost black with age, thousands of cracks in the fibers, the wrinkles of time. The bracing boards were new. They carried the weight of the stand and, therefore, the old boards were replaced with new two-by-twelves every few years. "You up there?"

No one answered.

Buck emerged from the woods on the back of the mechanical thoroughbred and continued on Possum Trail. He took another left half a mile down at Black Bear Crossing onto Rabbit Hole Road. Rabbit Hole merged onto Tin Shed Road, and ten minutes later Buck was back at the campsite.

The site was basic in nature, sensible in necessity. Four tents surrounded the campfire. White smoke drifted from ashes in the fire pit, curling and dissipating in the chilly morning breeze. A black, cast-iron pot hung above the fire pit. Beans and franks—last night's dinner—caked the bottom of the pot. Around the perimeter of the camp was a short wall of stones, placed and left to protect against curious snakes and critters. Further away from the camp, nailed to the trees around the site, hung fishing line with bells attached. It was a redneck alarm system. If, say, a bear were to wander into the campsite, attracted by the mouth-watering scent of beans and franks, or frying fish, or beef stew, the four hunters would be made aware and could bring the necessary entertainment favors to the party.

The tin shed was wrapped with a blue tarp and housed the cooler and various camping bric-a-brac. The camp was tidy, neat, and displayed no outward signs that anything was amiss. The tents were whole. No tears or bullet holes. All signs said they were out hunting.

Yet, Buck was troubled. His gut was rumbling, and it had nothing to do with those beanie-weenies. A troublesome pang gnawed at him.

He checked each tent again, mimicking his earlier scrutiny. The sleeping bags and contents showed no evidence of distress or trouble. He found a Smith and Wesson under Cliff's pillow, locked and loaded. Buck checked the magazine and the one in the pipe; all were accounted for and no bullets missing. Under Tommy's pillow was a paperback, *My Heart Is A Chainsaw* by Stephen Graham Jones. Whoever that was.

Jerry Landon's tent also had a pistol under the pillow, a six-shooter, all chambers full. Steven's tent produced a 15-round Glock under the pillow and a shotgun wrapped in the folds of a blanket beside the sleeping bag. Beyond that, not a lot. A bottle of ibuprofen, a tube of ChapStick, roll of toilet paper, a spray bottle of deer piss.

They had to be out there.

"Wherever the hell out there is," Buck said to himself, dropping the zippered flap to Steven's empty tent.

Buck was not a tracker but felt that was his best option. He duck-waddled around the site, looking for clues. The ground was hard, but he was able to make out boot prints. He followed them over the wall, across Tin Shed Road, and into the woods heading west. He lost the tracks in the foliage. He decided to move west.

He would find them soon. Surely.

CHAPTER 9

Jason finished breakfast and asked if he could play video games for a while.

"Absolutely," his new mom, Sarah Grace, answered while she filled the sink with water and suds.

His new dad, Ron, was reading a *Writer's Digest* at the breakfast table. Ron wanted to publish a novel he'd been working on since childhood. Ron's father had published some stories twenty years earlier through a local boutique press. One story caught on and became a movie for TV. Jason watched it one night with Ron and Sarah Grace. A decent movie if you liked romance and mushy kissing scenes.

Jason closed the door to his new bedroom. He turned on the TV for background noise. Not really interested in video games, he stared outside at the pressing cold. The wind whistled around the old window. A chilly draft wormed through invisible cracks in the sill and found its way to the back of Jason's neck. He shivered.

Jason lacked the ability to accurately explain his feelings to Sarah Grace. He wanted to convey the fear he felt inside, to beg her to understand they were in danger. Wanted to take her and Ron by the hand and lead them somewhere safe, to tell them what he'd seen in his dream. What his now dead father had shown him.

But he didn't have the words.

Sarah Grace was an adult. She was the most wonderful adult he had ever met, but she was still an adult. And adults lost certain senses as they aged. Most notably, the subtle one, the most important: *awareness.* Not physical awareness. Awareness to vibrations, like a tingle. Children were sensitive to vibrations in the atmosphere. It was the pureness, the innocence of the soul. The world had yet to pollute the brain. Yet to pound a jaded perception on life, dismissing the idea of the fantastic.

Adults dismissed these vibrations as immature or childish, losing knowledge of their existence. Refused to acknowledge the evidence. Labeled the phenomena folklore, tall-tales, fiction, supernatural hogwash.

Jason knew better.

He had seen ghosts before. A little girl haunted the trailer he lived in before his parents died. She was nine. Her eyes were bloodshot and bloody tears crept down her cheeks like plump red ticks. She told him her name was Megan. She died when her mother shot her full of heroin to shut her up. Jason was well-versed in drugs by then and understood that unforgivable truth. It also explained why Megan smelled like dirty diapers.

His parents never saw Megan. She was invisible to them. Being adults, they ignored the signs of her existence: the open door that had been closed the night before, the bathroom sink faucet running water when no one had been home, toilet seat down when it had been up. Megan enjoyed the games. She said ghosts had nothing better to do than play pranks. Jason had never considered what life as a ghost was like until Megan. She explained it all with a fascinating indifference.

Jason once asked her how it felt to be dead. She said it was always cold, like living in Antarctica, only colder. She said there was a sadness in her, like black water tickling her throat, choking the tears from her brimming eyeballs. She said she fought hard not to cry every second of every day. He understood that all too well; he fought the same battle.

Megan was sitting beside him the night his father killed his mother and the perverted neighbor Charlie Reilly. And then himself.

Jason and Megan were watching TV when Charlie came over. He'd sat on the couch, made a few pervie comments to Pauline. She asked if he had any pills on him. He'd inquired how bad she wanted them. Jason heard the familiar unzipping. Glanced back and grimaced at the sight of his mother's head on the guys lap.

"Don't look," Megan had warned.

Jason was rising to his feet to go to his room when his dad blew through the door like a tornado. Megan held his hand when Daddy killed the naked and pleading pair of cheaters. The blasts had been sharp and brutal in the small trailer. Bloody chunks of tissue sprayed all over the cheap brown wood paneling walls and dirty shag carpet. The bodies had flown back on the flower-print couch and twitched. The air smelled like an entire Master Blaster Mega Pack of fireworks went off at once.

Megan whispered to Jason with great compassion and care as his father dropped to his knees, weeping uncontrollably, his body seizing with guilt. His father propped his chin on the barrel of the shotgun and looked at Jason.

Jason got a shock when his dad looked at Megan, staring intently. Then his bloodshot eyes settled on his son one last time. Jason had lied about his father's last words. He had lied because he'd been too afraid to repeat them out loud. The ramifications were immense and scary and barbed with possibilities and mysteries.

She can't help you. No one can. You'll die if you go there, son.

Jason shivered. His new house was warm, his room cozy and comfortable, and the nicest bedroom he'd ever imagined. Yet, he was cold. Deep in his bones.

He tugged a pajama sleeve up to check the bruises on his bicep again. Still there. He'd hoped they would fade, as the nightmare faded, but neither were going quietly.

Last night, his father grabbed him by the arm, his fingers clammy and hard, and pulled him across the sky, the two soaring like eagles on the wind. He pulled Jason into the dense forest to allow him a glimpse at the harbinger of death.

"When the moon rises, so does the beast." No explanation for the enigmatic statement.

Then they sailed through the clouds, his father guiding him with a deliberation he had lacked when he was alive. Homes with smoking chimneys passed beneath their feet. His dad paused above a structure that was more shack than house, and together they descended. The roof was shingled with rusty tin. The walls sheathed with weather-rotted boards, light from within shining through the cracks. Jason was barely able to see through the sooty glass panes, but a figure lay on a cot, a book in his hand. He was not aware of the identity, but his father squeezed his arm like a vise, and pointed at the figure.

"The dumpster diver. Your only chance."

Jason had gasped awake in the safety and warmth of his bed. His arm had been throbbing. He hadn't been surprised when he discovered the bruises.

Absent-minded, he rubbed the sensitive, discolored flesh, and stared blankly at the TV with a commercial about a new video game. He wished for a commercial explaining the enigma of the dumpster diver.

The complexity of the problem boiled down to a simple equation: Mysterious Figure − Identification ÷ Lack of Location^2 = Totally Clueless Kid.

Jason picked at the issue, worked it from every angle. The clock on his nightstand read 10:48 a.m. With every passing minute, the pressure to figure this out mounted exponentially.

Evil was on the way, and time was running out.

CHAPTER 10

Maggie knew something was wrong. Northern was not home. She was not answering her phone and the location app installed on Northern's phone was showing location unavailable. Northern was the most responsible girl she had ever known, mature beyond her years. She was not the type to go off-trail. It scared Maggie damn near speechless to think bad thoughts about her daughter.

But something wasn't right.

Maggie found the number for Beth Gunther, Northern's best friend from UNC-Wilmington. Her cell claimed "No Signal"—*Of course!*—which required her to use the landline.

"Hello?" Came a sleepy voice.

"Beth," Maggie said, "this is Maggie Eason, Northern's mother. You and I met a few months ago."

"Yes ma'am, I remember." Beth's tone shifted. The strangeness of the call. "Mrs. Eason, is everything okay?"

Maggie sighed, deep and long, not sure where to start. "Honestly...no. Northern didn't come home last night after her date with this new guy. I can't even recall his name. Northern *never* goes off grid. You haven't heard from her, have you?"

"No ma'am, I haven't. Not since yesterday afternoon. She went out with Garrett Inslow last night. And you say she never came home? That's not the Northern I know."

"No, it's not. You wouldn't happen to know Garrett's number, would you?"

Maggie heard Beth fumbling around on the other end. Flinging covers off her, getting out of bed. Then: "Actually, I do. I'm the one that hooked them up. Northern is the toughest chick I know, but she was scared silly to ask him out."

Hearing this insight into her daughter's personal life, the side of her reserved for her girlfriends, those of the same age and plight, was endearing and heartbreaking.

Lord, please let my baby be okay. She prayed as she waited for Beth to scroll through her phone for the number.

Beth read the number and Maggie thanked her.

"Please call me as soon as you talk to her," Beth said before hanging up. "I'll kick her butt for you."

Maggie dialed Garrett's number twice. Her hands were shaking so badly she missed a number on the first try.

"Hello?" Garrett answered. He sounded wide awake.

"Is this Garrett Inslow?"

"Yes, it is. Can I help you?" He seemed amused.

"Garrett, my name is Maggie Eason, Northern's mother."

"Ah...yes, ma'am. It's nice to speak to you." He was caught off guard and, like Beth, his tone shifted. The weight of something strange streamed through the phone. "Is everything okay?"

"Garrett, Northern didn't come home last night. I'm worried." She started to cry. She tried to keep her composure, but failed. Maggie despised herself for a show of weakness. But she was so scared her knees were weak.

"Mrs. Eason, Northern and I left Blanchard's around ten last night. I came home and she said she was going home. She said she promised you not to be out late with this storm rolling in. She should've been home no later than eleven."

Maggie nodded, unable to speak. There was a lump the size of a softball in her throat, choking her.

Garrett seemed to understand this, and said, "I'm on the way." He hung up before she could protest.

Maggie wiped her face and called 911.

"What's your emergency?" the dispatcher asked.

"I'd like to report a missing person," Maggie said. She took a deep breath to stop the sobs begging to be set free.

"How long has this person been missing?"

"Since about ten-thirty or so last night. She was supposed to come home and didn't. Her phone isn't working to call her."

"Ma'am, we require a person to be missing twenty-four hours before we can officially start a search. With this storm moving in, that wait period might—"

The front door slammed shut and Ray appeared. He was fighting mad. Maggie hung up.

"There is a pile-up about fifteen miles down toward Supply," he said, leaning against the cased-opening frame leading into the kitchen. "Two eighteen-wheelers. Biggest damned mess you ever saw. Pete Dawson's working traffic. He said no car was involved. Northern's, or any other. Just the two trucks. The road is closed on both ends of 211, except for residents. They're detouring everyone else. He said the roads would probably stay closed because the storm is about to make investigating the crash and vehicle recovery impossible. At the moment they're just trying to remove the two bodies and document everything else. He did say that the death of one of the truckers is looking highly suspect."

"Suspect how?"

"He wouldn't say." Ray shrugged, stiff, hands stuffed in his pockets.

"So, where the hell is our daughter?"

Shaking his head, Ray said, "I asked Pete if there had been any reports of wrecks or incidents involving a blonde in a red Honda. He said no. He said he would pass it on to dispatch to put it in the system for officers to be on the lookout." His voice quivered, which was rare for the hardened farmer.

Maggie was slightly relieved but not much. Northern was still missing. And Ray was worried. He *never* worried.

"I called 911. They won't do anything for twenty-four hours. I also spoke to Garrett, the guy she went out with last night."

"I told her he should pick her up," Ray said, salty.

"She left Blanchard's to come home around ten. He hasn't spoken to her today. He's on the way. I need to call and tell him about the roads."

Maggie relayed the information to Garrett. He was undeterred. He was coming if it meant driving through the fiery pits of Hell.

"I like this kid," Ray said. He took the phone from Maggie and gave directions. There were dozens of dirt roads from Supply and Bolton that lead through the swamp and came out at various points on 211. Ray instructed Garrett on which roads to take, which turns to make, which doglegs were hazardous. He gave him landmarks to help with the journey.

"And it's a trek, son," Ray said. "Be damn careful. You'll drive thirty miles of dirt road to go ten miles as the crow flies. Just be cautious on some of those tight turns and you'll be fine. The phone companies have been slow to get towers erected in the Swamp. You don't get a signal out here, so don't get lost." Ray hung up.

Maggie paced back and forth, the worry and dread coalescing into a tightness in her chest. She decided to call a few neighbors.

Leslie and Jackson Mangold, and their three teenage children, lived a few miles from Bolton. Leslie was a weekly regular in the market. Neighbors watched out for neighbors.

"Good morning, Maggie," Leslie said. There was the clinking of pots in the background.

"I catch you at a bad time?" Maggie asked.

"Not at all. Just washing breakfast dishes. Got the boys doing some chores outside to get ready for the storm. I sent Jackson to Bolton to fill up the gas and kerosene cans. What's up?"

Maggie filled her in on Northern and the wreckage.

"Oh my, Maggie, can I do anything?"

"Not at the moment. If you see or hear anything, would you give me a call?"

"*Of course*. And call if *you* need anything."

Maggie scrolled through the contacts on her phone. Arlene Gainey.

"Hello?" Arlene answered.

Maggie repeated the story. Asked if Arlene was aware of anything amiss beyond the rig pile-up.

Arlene was quiet. Maggie thought she'd hung up. After a full minute, "Cliff and Steven didn't come home last night. They're on a hunting trip with Jerry Landon and Tommy Stuart. Neither Tommy nor Jerry have shown up either."

It was Maggie's turn to let silence fill the void. She was unable to make a connection, but she *could* add, and the math said five people were now missing. "Were they coming back from Wilmington or Whiteville?"

"No. They were on their yearly hunting slash camping trip back at Tin Shed. Mary Stuart is worried sick. Jerry lives alone."

This can't be coincidence, Maggie thought. She said, "I can ask Ray to go check Tin Shed."

"Mary has Tommy's friend Buck checking right now. He should be back with them in a bit." She added: "I hope."

"Call me if you hear anything," Maggie said. The two exchanged goodbyes and Maggie hung up.

She repeated it all to Ray who was watching the news.

The updates on the storm were getting worse by the minute. A storm front was going to collide with below-average temperatures, and the result was going to shut down South Carolina, North Carolina, Virginia, and all points northeast for days. Perhaps even weeks, if the warmer trough couldn't break through the push of frigid air to melt the snow and ice. The weather forecasters were visibly giddy with the news of such a crippling storm blanketing the Eastern Seaboard. This was a ratings bonanza, as millions of Americans tuned in to stay updated on the latest developments. Advertising dollars practically fell from the rafters of the broadcast studio. Bad weather, like any disaster, was good for business.

Maggie shook her head in disgust. This weatherman was smiling about how bad it was going to get. "Get your coats, folks, because it's about to get bbbbbreeeeeezzzy!!" He laughed too hard at his own joke, wrapped up in a stupid faux-winter outfit.

Ray said, "I can't sit around. I'm going to ride over to Tin Shed and have a look. If you hear from Northern, tell her to stay where she is, and I will come get her. This goddamn storm is rolling in fast and furious, and I don't want her out in it."

Ray visited his office and came out holding a rifle, a handgun strapped to his waist.

"Why the guns?" Maggie asked.

"We're missing too many people for this to be chance. Something ain't right. I'm not going to be caught with my pants down." He rushed down the stairs, hopped in his truck, and was gone again.

A disturbance in the air drew Maggie to the porch. She held her hand out and snowflakes tickled her palm.

The storm was here.

CHAPTER 11

People threw out the best stuff. Utter nonsense. Grills, bicycles, jewelry, books, clothes, coins. The discarded waste was mind-boggling. The dumpsters were full of good trash.

"Another man's trash is one man's treasure," Skeeter DuPray said to himself. It was a popular motto, repeated several times a day. He sifted through the metal recycling bin at the waste yard, taking in all the shiny bits and bobs. Feeling the trinkets with his fingertips.

"Hey, Skeet," Herb Gardner yelled as he threw trash bags into the compactor, "if you find a chicken leg in there, would you save me a bite?" Herb laughed heartily and another gentleman within earshot laughed as well, all enjoying the joke at Skeeter's expense.

"Su...su...sure thing, Herb," Skeeter stuttered. He hated when someone like Herb got the better of him. It made him nervous. Caused his tongue to tangle.

"O...O...O...tay." Herb mocked, and guffawed. He drove away, the sound of his abrasive cackling following him from the property.

Skeeter put his head down to hide the shame. Ridicule was life, having been a victim of verbal abuse since he was a child. He embarrassed easily when other people were witness.

Several cars were in line to toss their garbage. The occupants heard the exchange, and snickered. His face reddened. He hid and waited for them to leave.

Skeeter was a life-long resident of Green Swamp. He was raised in the little shack he still called home in the middle of Green Swamp. His mother ran off when he was six, leaving his father to raise his younger brother, Joseph, and himself. His father had a good heart and meant well, but he had been a drunk with little education and no expectations of himself. The burden of raising two boys had been dumped on him when Mom bolted in the night. He handled the responsibility the best way he knew—by drowning in bourbon, soaking in it until the world blurred to stupidity.

The night Joseph disappeared, his dad had been passed out on the couch, unaware the boy was gone until Skeeter shook him awake. The two of them had gone looking; Joe was prone to sleepwalking, and his dad was sure they'd find him in the woods, right as rain. He *had* been in the woods, but he'd not been right as rain. His body lay beside a bear trap, his right foot amputated at the ankle. Joe had stepped in the trap and bled out.

Skeeter's father had never recovered from that loss. The gallons of bourbon he'd consumed couldn't obliterate the sight of Joe from his every waking—and sleeping—thought. The bleached skin. The milky eyes. The gaping mouth. The bite marks around the bloody stub.

Six months after Joe passed, while on a walk through the woods, they passed the spot of Joe's death. His dad had stood still for a moment, like he was communing with some unseen force. He choked back a sob, then screamed and ran.

Skeeter chased him, lost sight, but eventually caught him standing at the edge of a swampy bog. The depth of anguish in his father's eyes caused Skeeter to take a step back.

"I'm sorry, son," he wailed. "You're better off without me."

Skeeter stood helpless as his father—and only living relative—waded into the muddy water, sinking like a stone. He never tried to escape the sticky grasp of death. Only accepted it, wanted it, needed it. His head disappeared. The only sign were bubbles. Those stopped after a few minutes.

Skeeter dropped out of school after that. What was the point? No one cared about a seventeen-year-old loser like him. His life was rife with suffering, heartbreak, poverty. He was meant to be a nobody; it was his destiny. Who was he to change the course of fate?

So, he learned, adapted. His father was useless at most things, but he taught Skeeter the tricks of living with nothing.

Skeeter pillaged dumpsters for goods to be sold on the street corner, or aluminum cans on the side of the road to be scrapped at the recycling bins. He cleaned the vacuum canisters at all the Shallotte car washes for free in exchange for keeping whatever change he found in the canister, and the occasional bag of food from the owners. He stood on street corners and tolerated the stares and laughter, the cruel remarks, the name-calling. He dug food scraps out of the dumpster at Boone's Market and Deli/Bakery. Sometimes the Sub Factory or Chuck Roger's left food out, too. Even Blanchard's set out a plate for him occasionally. Several times a year, he raked and bagged leaves for old lady Mosley in return for a bag of sandwiches, a few cold soda pops, and a five spot.

There was no refrigerator at his house. No television set. He had no job to buy such pleasures. But he rarely went hungry or in need. Some people in Shallotte were mean and nasty, but not all. Most were good people, happy to help when possible. The rest of the time, he helped himself.

An ornate metal container at the bottom of the dumpster caught his eye. He pushed his arm as hard as he could through the maze of metal scraps. His fingers danced on the lid, the raised decorum like Braille. He pushed harder, the leg of a broken chair biting into his collarbone. He pushed anyway. His hand wrapped around the container, and he knew by its weight he had something valuable before he opened the lid.

Inside was an old pair of glasses, a broken watch, a twenty-dollar bill, and change equaling three dollars and forty-nine cents.

An unbelievable haul. His face scrunched up and his eyes went to the turbulent sky as he tried to remember a better score in a single pop. He couldn't recall. He pocketed the money, slipped the glasses and watch in his book bag.

He shook his head, marveling at his bright luck on this dismal day. "Another man's trash is one man's treasure."

CHAPTER 12

Jason laid in his bed, staring at the ceiling, and worked the problem. He walked back through the dream, listening to every word his father spoke. When they arrived at the shack, he paid extra close attention. His father had pointed at the man, and said, *"Dumpster Diver. Your only chance."*

"Dumpster diver," Jason said aloud.

He recalled his father jumping inside a dumpster once to retrieve a bike he said was fixable. But he never *attempted* to repair the broken thing. The last time he'd seen that bike was the same night he was escorted into a government vehicle, lots of blue lights and gawking neighbors in attendance, never to return to Beaver Creek Trailer Park again.

He went to his computer and typed it into a search engine. Dumpster diving was salvaging discarded items from trash dumpsters.

"Ewww," Jason said to the computer. "That's gross."

Now another problem: where was the dumpster and how would he get there?

He tackled the first part of the problem. He knew there was a waste site here in Green Swamp. He'd been there with Ron a few times. But that site consisted of a trash compactor and one big dumpster for yard waste. He and Ron had used the yard waste container several weeks earlier after a tree limb broke off and landed in the driveway. Ron let him use the chainsaw to cut it up. Lots of fun, the tingling vibration running through his hands for hours afterward.

They stacked the cut pieces with the rest of the wood for the fireplace, and the twigs and limbs were loaded and dumped into the yard waste container. There was nothing at that site worth salvaging.

He searched the internet for other waste sites. There was one heading toward Wilmington, one in the direction of Southport, and a nice one in Shallotte. He researched the Shallotte site and found that to be the most likely candidate. It was large, paved, held over a dozen containers, and served a large portion of Brunswick County. A dumpster diver's wet dream.

That has to be it. But how do I get there?

An idea formed almost immediately.

He went to the kitchen and found Sarah Grace and Ron at the table. Ron was still reading *Writer's Digest* and Sarah Grace was checking her Etsy sales on a laptop. Addie was at her bowl slopping up wet food.

"Guys, I need a favor," he said. He put on the saddest sad face he could muster.

"Sure, honey, what is it?" Sarah Grace said, pulling him over to sit on her lap.

"I need to throw some things away. Some personal things that belonged to my"—Jason hung his head. Despite himself, he started to cry. That wasn't part of the plan, but the body responds to unpleasant memories like it does pain. He wiped his eyes and finished—"dad."

She hugged him tight, the clean scent of her shampoo comforting. "Of course. You pack those things up and Ron will run them down to the dump."

"I want to go. And I want to take it to the dump in Shallotte. I need a few things from the store anyway. Before this storm gets here." Gauging their expressions, he added: "I'm sorry but I need this stuff gone so I can move on. It's like...a ghost that keeps haunting me. After my nightmare last night...I need closure." He frowned, hoping he wasn't laying it on too thick.

Sarah Grace looked at Ron, who shrugged. "You know," she said, "why don't I take you? I actually could use some creamer for my coffee and another dozen eggs. Just in case. But we need to hurry—I see snowflakes already."

"Yes, ma'am," Jason said, wiping his wet eyes.

He almost jumped to his feet in excitement when he remembered he was supposed to be sad. He hung his head until his bedroom door closed. He celebrated with a fist pump. The contents of his book bag were dumped on the bed. He threw in a few items that had belonged to his dad: a Yankee's baseball cap, his wedding ring, a silver pocket watch on a broken chain, and a postcard with stony mountains surrounding a plush green valley with AFGHANISTAN in yellow lettering on the front. The back held a message to Jason's mom, written in his trippy script—Miss you much and see you soon!

It was all the memento's he possessed. He wasn't keen on tossing them, but this was life or death. And he'd seen enough death to last him a lifetime.

Sarah Grace tapped on his door with a knuckle. "You ready?"

"Yes, ma'am." He was still getting used to having parents that were polite. They never barged in on him. Allowed him space and privacy.

"We'll take Ron's truck. It's four wheel drive. Just in case the weather gets crazy before we get back."

They turned right out of the driveway, toward Supply. In Supply, a highway patrolman stood guard in front of two ROAD CLOSED signs.

"What in the world?" Sarah Grace said aloud. She stopped by the officer. "Excuse me, why is this road blocked off?"

The officer stepped over to her car. His shoulders were hunched against the freezing wind. His trooper hat was wrapped in plastic and dusted from the falling snow. "A tractor trailer accident down about seventeen miles. Got the road blocked completely. No one can get through so we're only allowing residents to enter. Where you headed?"

"To Shallotte. We won't be there long. Just got to pick up a few things from the store."

"My advice..." He looked up to the sky, and then around at the snow. "Hurry. I'm getting updates on my radio and this thing is coming in hot. The wreckers aren't even willing to remove the wreckage from the road. 211'll be closed for non-residents until after the storm passes."

"We'll be quick. Thank you."

The trooper waved them on and returned to his post. Sarah Grace merged into traffic and ten minutes later pulled into Boone's Market. The two quickly got the needed items.

Jason was spooked for some unknown reason when he passed a tall, gangly fellow in a white apron with blood stains on the front. His name tag read JEFF. Jason stared at Jeff after he passed and got a return glare. Jeff disappeared into a swinging door in the meat market, but he lingered with Jason like cheap cologne.

"You okay, baby?" Sarah Grace asked Jason.

He realized he was stopped in the middle of the aisle, staring at the polished floor. "Yeah, I'm okay. Sorry."

"No sorry. It's all good."

By the time they were back in the car, Jeff was a fading silhouette. By the time they arrived at the dump, he was forgotten.

Jason searched the dumpsters as Sarah Grace eased forward in line. City workers hid inside block sheds, no doubt a space heater running to keep them from freezing. The windshield wipers squeaked across the glass and removed the light snow accumulation. A horn blared as a car tried to cut in line.

"These people are lunatics." Sarah Grace marveled, as the man who blew the horn jumped out of his car and berated the line cutter. The line cutter jumped out of his car and a case of road rage ensued. The horn blower punched the line cutter square in the jaw, grumbling a cuss word. The line cutter went down fast, one hand at his bloody mouth, the other breaking his fall. Slipping back to his car, the horn blower hurried away, narrowly escaping a fender bender.

Jason hardly noticed. He was busy scanning the site for the mystery figure. He wasn't sure what he looked like, how tall, what color hair, what style of clothing, but somehow, deep inside, he knew he would recognize the man when he saw him.

It was the other sense that was going to help identify the stranger. The sense that once saw Megan. An extra eye, an extra set of ears, at the back of his brain, like the subconscious but not. A sixth sense.

"Okay," Sarah Grace said. They were at the trash compactor. The snow was swirling around a surly city employee wearing a dirty waste management puffer as he motioned for people to move along. "You want me to do it?"

Jason swallowed his disappointment. He bowed his head. "No, I need to do this."

He dashed to the compactor, the smell of decomposing food flaring in his nostrils, and threw the bag of belongings in with the other black and white trash bags. It only took a second but he was already dusted with snow.

"Let's get home before this gets worse," Sarah Grace said.

She stopped at the Quicky Gas 'n Gone to top off the tank. Jason was deflated and wondering what to do next when, through the white haze of snow, he saw the stranger. The man was pulling a wagon, loaded with junk. He was heading out of the parking lot and down the street. Not even fazed by the snow.

Sarah Grace climbed back into the truck. "Shew, it is cold."

"Sarah Grace," Jason tugged on her coat sleeve. "We have to pick that man up." Jason pointed at the stranger.

"Who, Skeeter?" Sarah Grace looked at him, curious.

"That's his name?" Jason didn't take his eyes from the man.

"Yeah, he's been around forever. Lives out in the Swamp some-where, I think."

"We *have* to give him a ride."

"Jason, honey, I love that you have a heart and are such a caring boy, but—" Sarah Grace stopped talking. She looked at Jason, back to Skeeter, then nodded. "You're right. We have to give him a ride."

Sarah Grace eased down a busy Main Street and pulled up alongside the snowman walking on the edge of the asphalt pulling a wagon. Jason rolled down his window.

"Skeeter," Sarah Grace said over the howling wind, "let's put your wagon in the bed of the truck and I'll give you a ride home. You don't need to be out in this mess."

Skeeter moved to object, but his eyes settled on Jason. A dawning recognition lit his face into a smile. "Yes, ma'am," he said, excited. "That's mighty fine. Mighty fine, indeed."

Sarah Grace was already climbing out of the truck, missing the acknowledgment. A car horn bleated, and Sarah Grace waved them around. She helped Skeeter unload the scraps from the wagon and set the wagon in the bed. She slammed the tailgate shut and returned to the driver's seat. Skeeter stood outside with the door open, and shook the snow from his jacket, hair, and pants before he climbed in.

"It's okay, Skeeter. It's just water."

The smell flooded the truck cabin as soon as Skeeter closed the door. It was the stench of homelessness. No bath, no shampoo, no soap, no running water, no washing machine—what Jason's future would have been like, if it weren't for Sarah Grace and Ron.

Sarah Grace raised her eyebrows at Jason.

He smiled back. "I saw you in my dream," Skeeter said from the back seat.

He was looking at Jason.

CHAPTER 13

The truck slid to a halt at Tin Shed. Ray Eason stepped out, grabbed his rifle.

Snow-blanketed tents were set up. A fire pit occupied the center of camp, as was custom. Ray used his boot to open the zippered flaps. Each tent was empty. The thickening accumulation of snow on the ground showed no signs of recent passage. A blue tarp hung from the sagging, rusted roof of the old tin shed. He used the rifle barrel to push the tarp aside. A seafoam blue B-loZero cooler sat in the dirt, four mud-caked wheels and a handle on one end for easy mobility. A few cast-iron pots and pans sat haphazardly on top of the lid of the cooler, a scattering of utensils, a dented metal plate. Ray let the tarp fall back in place and propped the gun on his shoulder. He slowly turned in a circle, searching the surroundings, listening to the music of the Swamp.

As a man grown from the very soil on which he stood, Ray was as familiar with the songs of this land as he was his wife's body. The cracks and drips and whorls, like a vinyl record spinning beneath the needle of the old Victrola in the living room. The slender arms of loblolly pines, the bowed branches cracking beneath the burden of ice and snow. The dense viridescent undergrowth of titi, evergreen shrub bog, wire grass, and gall berry clicking and popping as the frozen rain and snowflakes crash landed on each frond. The slap of frozen moisture on butterworts and sundews. The wind manipulating the precipitation to move in this or that direction as it whistled and moaned like an epicedium. The vibration and thud of hoof-fall as a buck returned home to bed down and stay warm. The air perfumed with damp soil, bloated atmosphere, a potpourri of fauna and flora.

And then, a disruption. The record skipped; the music stuttered. Ray heard the faintest of rumbles, a frequency unlike anything produced by the Swamp. Several details spoiled the symphony.

First, on Tin Shed Road, the messy accumulation associated with a four-wheeler spinning its tires. The snowfall was trying to hide this detail like a murderer hiding a body. But Ray was a life-long participant of running these roads and knew the dirt, the grains, the potholes, the mud pits, the deep ditches. A four-wheeler was here not long ago, just before the snow fell. Arlene said a guy on a four-wheeler was out here performing a wellness check.

The second spoiler was a glint, a hint, a difference in state and stature a long way off. The Swamp was not just music; it was art. The browns, the greens, the yellows, the oranges, the whites, the flow of pigments, the coloration of landscape. All familiar and beautiful.

Which made the hard line in the distance strange. A metallic glint, non-indigenous to the Swamp. A trespasser. As was he, as was his truck, as were the loggers raping the land. Ray hurried to his vehicle and went to find the driver.

Tin Shed Road delivered him to the four-wheeler, six hundred yards later. It idled in place. Ray was not a professional tracker, but he knew enough that he was able to follow the passage of the four-wheeler driver with ease. The evergreen shrub bog was thick. Each step like walking in the ocean.

Ray smelled it before he saw it. A stench as distinguishable as coffee. The aroma of blood. The rifle stock shot to his shoulder as his arms brought the barrel up and up, sight set ahead, the motion practiced and performed thousands of times. He went down to a squatting walk, slowly stepping with toes leading to the ground, quiet as a mouse. A quick scan of the environs told him he was alone.

Then why do I feel like I'm being watched?

It was the Swamp, speaking to him, through him. It was atmosphere, the subtle shift of air, oxygen, the particulates drifting with the snow and ice, the interruption of the music. He wasn't sure of anything, but he trusted tingle. The tingle was real.

I am being watched.

Ray eased around a longleaf pine and saw it. A heap of bloody meat. The crimson liquid coagulating, freezing stiff, but not before tinting the snow red as it filtered through to the dark soil beneath.

"What the—"

"Don't move," someone said, and the ice-cold barrel of a gun pressed against his neck.

CHAPTER 14

Sarah Grace almost pulled the truck over. Skeeter was harmless, so far as she knew. But the Mr. Creeps vibe was wafting from him like the stench of his filthy clothes. She raised her foot from the gas, about to stomp the brake—not smart in an ice and snowstorm—when she saw Jason's face light up like a light bulb. He smiled and turned to Skeeter.

"I saw you in my dream, too," she heard Jason say.

Unbelievable. Impossible.

But the way Jason stared at Skeeter, and Skeeter stared back, it was hard to argue. She realized Jason had duped her.

Jason had asked to come to the dump in Shallotte. The crap in the wagon told her Skeeter had been at the dump.

How did Jason know? Sarah Grace asked herself. *We'll get to that later.*

Jason spotted Skeeter walking, knew who he was, and pleaded to her softer side to give him a ride. The whole thing was a ruse.

But how did Jason know Skeeter? Through a dream? That was impossible. There had to be another connection she was missing.

Jason was not from this area. He moved from Ohio sixteen weeks ago when the adoption was finalized. Skeeter had been a resident of Brunswick County his entire life, hocked scraps to eat, was damn near homeless. Jason had been to Shallotte only half a dozen times. They generally went to Wilmington to shop or to eat out. Shallotte was growing by the second, but it was no match for Wilmington.

Why had Jason been so determined to get to Skeeter?

"Okay," Sarah Grace said, holding her hand up. Jason and Skeeter, mid-conversation, stopped. "I'm not sure what's going on here, but you two are going to explain it to me."

Jason looked at Skeeter, who stared back Jason. Skeeter's bottom lip poked out, and Sarah Grace could see he was nervous.

"I will," Jason said. "But you're not going to believe me." He looked down at his hands where his fingers absentmindedly picked at broken nails. She'd seen the same fidgeting earlier in the kitchen, before he told her about the nightmare.

"Jason," Sarah Grace said, twisting her grip on the leather-wrapped steering wheel. The windshield wipers beat away the onslaught of swirling snowflakes and icy rain. "I'm on your side. I *will* believe you. Because you have yet to give me a reason *not* to believe you. You did lie to me about the trip to the dump. For reasons unknown to me, you did that for Skeeter. I see that, even if I don't know why. Maybe you can explain." She looked at him, then Skeeter in the mirror.

Jason stopped fiddling. "I told you I had a nightmare last night about my dad, but I didn't tell you everything. I thought you'd think I'm crazy and not want me anymore."

Tears bubbled in the corner of Sarah Grace's eyes. The statement hurt her in places she never knew existed. She wanted Jason to feel loved and safe and secure and free to express himself. She wanted him to know he could talk to her about anything. The confession made her question whether she was doing a good job of being his mother. And *that* was like an ice pick to the heart. She blinked away the tears. "I will never think you're crazy. And I could never not want you. You are the greatest thing to ever happen to me. We are family now. No matter what."

"No matter what?" Jason asked, still not sure.

"No matter what," she said, pushing her fingers through his thick, brown, silky hair. His bright blue eyes searched her face for signs of reassurance. She smiled to reinforce the statement.

Jason hesitated, then began. "I see things sometimes. Things that you would consider not there or not real."

Sarah Grace wiped her eyes. "What kind of things?"

"At the trailer, a little girl lived with us. My mom and dad couldn't see her. Or I *thought* my dad couldn't, but I think I was wrong about that. Her name was Megan, she was seven, and she died in that trailer four months before we moved in." Jason stopped, watching her.

There was a lot to unpack in those first few sentences. There were questions, but Sarah Grace decided to wait, hear him out. "Okay."

Jason continued. "She died from a drug overdose. Her mom was an addict and was tired of her crying because her stomach hurt. Megan hadn't eaten in two days. She was having hunger pains. Her mom shot her up with heroine to put her to sleep. Megan never woke up."

"Jesus," she whispered, her hand rising to her mouth. Trying to imagine such a thing was beyond her capabilities. Her own mother? Drugging a child?

"She became my friend. My first friend from the other side. She was with me the night my parents died.

"Megan helped me understand what was happening and what I was seeing. She didn't know why it was happening, but she gave me a new perspective. She helped me learn how to deal with the things I saw, felt, heard. She even helped me understand previous encounters."

"Like what?" Sarah wondered.

"Like the Hodge twins."

****

Jason is the new kid. He walks into his class after getting signed in by his mother. Feels hostile stares prick his skin like darts. The teacher is Olivia Nesbitt. She's pretty and understanding, compassionate. Jason likes her.

Ms. Nesbitt introduces Jason to the class and gets the expected response: laughter, under the breath "jackass" calls, a few curls of the lips from the Prissy Girl Club. She quiets the class and pats Jason on the back.

"Have a seat, Jason," she says quietly, her cinnamon breath tickling his ear. He sighs, lifts his chin, and walks to his desk. His seat is at the back of the class, and, from the safety of Ms. Nesbitt's side, looks miles a way.

He hears the "uh gross" and "looosseerrrr" and "nice dirty pants, is that a new fashion?" He tries to ignore it.

He sits, only to find everyone staring at him like he's from outer space. Jason busies himself. He places his books into the bin underneath his seat, opens his composition notebook, and looks to Ms. Nesbitt for guidance.

At P.E., Jason and two other boys are sent downstairs to the basement to the sports storage room to retrieve another bag of basketballs and orange cones for drills. The two boys make fun of Jason's filthy and ill-fitting clothes and his choppy home-cut hair. His thrift store shoes apparently bother them, so they make rude comments.

Down in the basement, Jason grabs the bag of basketballs, and his two classmates divide the tall, cumbersome orange cones. He follows them. As he plants one foot on the first riser, the boys kick him in the chest, and he sprawls onto the floor. The dozen basketballs spring out of the bags, bouncing helter skelter across the basement floor.

The boys laugh hysterically and leave him behind. Jason shakes his head and picks himself off the cold, cracked concrete floor. With the empty sack in his hand, he begins retrieving each ball. Dropping the eleventh ball in the bag, he searches the large room for the final ball. A portion of the basement is unlit, pitch black. He takes a step toward the shadowed area but stops when the basketball bounces back to him out of the darkness. He stops the ball with his foot.

"Hello?" Jason calls in the dark. "Is anyone there?"

A pair of silver-dollar eyes appear. They float like fish in a syrupy lake. Another pair open next to the first. Together, they drift forward. The faintest outline of two faces emerges but stops short of a full reveal. Their bloodshot eyes bulge from the sockets, almost to the point of plopping onto their cheeks. The images are dim, but Jason can see they're twins. They look alike, move alike, same height. Blonde hair clotted with chunks of muddy soil, matching mud-caked t-shirts with We Love Myrtle Beach *barely visible through the filth, wet and grimy jeans browned from age and dirt, identical mottled sneakers. As if they just dug their way out of the grave. One smiles like broken glass and his brother mimics.*

"Would you like to play with us?" The two questions in perfect harmony. The voices are sing-song sweet and melodic. Fingers massage his scalp, caress his face.

A four-alarm siren is blasting in his head. Stranger Danger! Stranger Danger! *But he feels helpless. His head is light, his eyes heavy. Jason thinks about lying down for a second. A quick nap is just what the doctor ordered. The twins beckon him toward them with the simultaneous motion of their fingers, hand, and wrist.*

"Take a nap with us, Jason." They chant.

He steps forward. He is powerless to stop. His body is fatigued, and the dark corner looks like a hammock on the beach. Myrtle Beach, perhaps.

His foot lifts, moves forward, drops down, and the other foot follows the lead. His eyes drift closed as he arrives within touching distance.

A tattered rope dangles around their necks. The skin is raw and whelped, riddled with seeping pustules. The fragrance of the grave has followed them here. The sweet, sick malodor of decay. The earthy tinge of mold and mildew. The siren in his head has grown faint. As he steps into the shadows, the twins touch him. It's like a bolt of lightning electrifies his body. He feels every inch of his existence—skin, bones, toenails, fingernails, the hairs on his head and the tiny hairs across his body. He feels the subwoofer thump of his heart, the quivering air rasping from his lungs.

Still images flash through his mind like a shaky movie reel. Memories, grungy with time and torment.

The twins.

They're cute eight-year-old boys—brown eyes, wavy blond hair—laughing as they build sandcastles. They're at the beach. The crash of ocean waves and the squawk of sea gulls is the soundtrack. A prop plane flies along the shoreline pulling a banner advertising Myrtle Beach T-Shirts for.99 at Blue Skies Beachwear.

Behind the two boys are a man and a woman. The hereditary traits of DNA are easy to see. There's another couple with them. The man is big-bellied, hairy bodied, with greasy thinning gray-brown hair, and designer sunglasses. The woman with the greasy man is pretty, brown hair, nice smile, pale skin, younger than potbelly by ten years. One can wonder the attraction.

"You sure you're good with watching your nephews tonight?" the mother asks. Her blonde hair is mostly hidden beneath a floppy beige sun hat. Her eyes shaded by sunglasses.

"Of course, we don't mind," the greasy man says heartily. "You two enjoy your anniversary. The boys will be just fine."

The images fast forward like a tape in a VCR, white noise lines at the top and bottom of the video, fuzzy bent images scrolling past.

Uncle Grease Ball is tucking the boys into separate twin beds. "I'll check on you guys in a bit."

The twins fall asleep, but one twin is awakened. There's something under his covers. He raises the sheet and is shocked to see his uncle. The uncle places one finger against his grinning lips. SSSHHH.

The twin drops the sheet and lies trembling, scared beyond measure. The uncle slides up and up until he is face to face with the twin, his breath reeking of alcohol and cigars. "You tell anyone, Trevor, and I'll gut you like a fish."

Trevor begins to cry silently. He nods.

The uncle moves to the other twin. Trevor watches, his body trembling. His brother cries but is helpless. After an eternity, the uncle leaves.

Jason cries out and tries to break the hold. The grip of electricity loosens but does not relinquish. The movie reel thankfully fast forwards.

The boys are at school. In the basement. The two are poster children for sadness. They are gathering supplies for P.E. One of the items is a thick-braided rope for tug-of-war. They hold the rope and stare.

And stare.

And stare.

They share a look of desperation, and without saying a word, decide.

Trevor carries the rope and Ryan grabs two plastic chairs. They take the items to the far corner of the basement. Trevor is unable to find a beam to throw the rope over, so he settles on a fluorescent light bar hanging from the concrete ceiling. The two boys grab an end of the rope and tie a loop and a knot.

They are Boy Scouts. They know how to tie knots.

It takes minutes to get the rope the right length on each end. Trevor climbs up on the chair and drops the loop around his neck while Ryan does the same. Neither child is crying. Neither child appears upset. This is an escape. An escape from shame and fear. An escape from more abuse. They embrace it.

Without speaking, the two kick the chairs out from under their feet at the exact same moment, twins sharing a telepathic connection. They choke, spit flies from their mouths, they grope for each other's hand. The eyes bulge and the whites fill with blood from ruptured veins. Their feet kick involuntarily. Piss runs down their legs. One last kick of the leg is the final movement.

The P.E. teacher comes downstairs and finds them. He screams and runs to them. Yanks them down. The fluorescent light bar breaks in half, sparks shower the floor, and the lights go out in the basement corner.

Jason is released. He falls backward, and once again finds himself on the cold, concrete floor. He hears footsteps and the P.E. teacher trots up to him. The teacher is older now but the same man. He's looking into the dark corner, like he sees ghosts, too. He looks down at Jason, and the fear pulses off him like a fever.

"You okay, Jason?" he asks holding out a hand.

"You found them," Jason says. "The twins."

The teacher stumbles as if struck, eyes all wide, brimming with tears, recalling the bodies, though he sought counseling to stop seeing them. "How'd you know that?"

"I saw them," Jason answers. He sees something else as well. No matter what, he is different now. In the mind of his physical education teacher, Jason is a freak. Harmless, perhaps, but a freak nonetheless. And word would spread through the school like wildfire.

Jason is labeled now. Just like his last school. His chest hurts from the pity he feels for himself, but is powerless to stop from saying, "They hung themselves down here."

Mr. Manheim slaps his palms over his eyes to ward off the reality of what he'd discovered.

"I know who did it," Jason says, though it has never occurred to him to offer this kind of information. Maybe that's why these lost souls reach out to him. For help.

Mr. Manheim responds by dropping his hand, opening his eyes, and crouching by Jason. His eyes are fire now, brow furrowed. "What do you mean? They committed suicide. Nobody knew why, but there was no one else involved."

Jason holds the teacher's stare. "They were molested by their uncle Joey. Really bad, nasty stuff. That's the who that explains the why."

Mr. Manheim falls back on his butt, the color drained from his face. "He was at the funeral. Upset, crying. Comforting the parents." His cheeks flushed and his face went red. "That sick son-of-a-bitch." He looks at Jason, like he is really seeing him for the first time. "I've got some calls to make."

The lights in the dark corner begin to strobe off and on. The strobing stops and the lights flash on in a brilliant surge. After a few seconds, the surge fades, the light ballasts hum, and a steady wash of illumination blankets the corner. The teacher looks at Jason and back to the empty corner. He helps Jason to his feet. Jason grabs the last basketball, drops it in the bag, and follows the teacher upstairs.

****

"My God," Sarah Grace said. She was on Highway 211, the snow a driving force now. She was in shock that Jason had witnessed such a tragedy. Another trauma to add to his already traumatic life.

As absurd and unbelievable as it sounded, she believed him. Totally. He was so genuine in his telling. His sad eyes went away, back to the moment. His body language became jittery. His fingers clawed at the cuticles. Sarah Grace was convinced he was telling the truth.

"You believe me?" As if she had spoken aloud.

"I do." But she had a question: "What happened to the uncle?"

"His house was searched and the police found boys underwear in a locked chest. Belonging to Trevor and Ryan, but others too. He was arrested. He was killed by another inmate before he could go to trial."

"Wow." It was all Sarah Grace could think of saying. So many questions demanded a voice.

Jason cut through the noise. "Okay, now let me tell you why Skeeter is in the back seat. And why he needs to come home with us."

CHAPTER 15

"We have to go," shouted the firefighter. "It's getting bad. You should go, too."

Detective Sean Bates waved him off. "I'll leave shortly. I'm just checking a few more things."

The firefighter nodded and loped to his truck. It took more than three points to get the thirty-five-foot monstrosity turned in the right direction.

Detective Bates was glad they were gone. The scene was quiet now. Most emergency personnel and fellow boys in blue were headed home before the storm locked North Carolina down. Only essential personnel were on standby.

Bates understood he was taking a chance of getting stranded by staying. The Department of Transportation wasn't advertising the information, but the state had run out of the salt brine used on roadways. The country was a shit show right now with inflation and supply chain disruptions on most items due to politics and greed. Which left the NCDOT with just enough brine to salt major interstates, highways, bridges, and overpasses. 211 was a highway, but being a two-lane connector relegated its importance to the back of the pile. Not an ounce of brine was sprayed except for a quick squirt on its bridges. Good thing the road was closed on both ends. More accidents than this were being avoided.

Speaking of this one—what a mess. At first glance, the wreck appeared straightforward. An eighteen-wheeler lost control and overturned. Another truck hauling logs bound around the turn and, unable to stop, plowed into the wreckage. The fire had engulfed both vehicles, killing the drivers. Open and shut.

But.

Always a but.

The driver of the overturned Peterbilt, one Scott Friar of Tabor City, North Carolina, was found burned to death. Expected. Both of his hands were severed at the forearm, cut clean through the bone. Not expected. The scorched bones of his hands were found lying near his feet. The cuts surgically precise. The coroner, Leo Willis, mentioned the cuts were so clean that the bones weren't chipped on the edges. Leo refused to speculate on the meaning until an autopsy was performed. Scott *could* have lost his hands during the wreck. A freak amputation.

Maybe. Maybe not.

Detective Bates paced slowly around the wreckage, trying not to shiver. Snow and ice pelted his rain jacket.

As a detective investigating a post-accident scene, it was his job to recreate the events of said accident. Sometimes the puzzle pieces were simple, large, easy to adjust, the picture clear from the start. Sometimes the pieces were tiny, thousands of them, clarity a distant goal. Bates was beginning to think this was going to be the latter variety. The incoming blizzard was only going to complicate matters. Time was the enemy in cases like this, and he was going to lose a lot. Contamination was the other problem. Precipitation played hell on a crime scene. Which explained the oversized blue tarps now covering Scott Friar's cab.

He crunched across ice and broken glass behind the trailer lying on its side. The trailer was devoid of logos or markings. A simple dirty white. An earlier check found it to be empty. Scott was on the way home when this occurred.

Snow now covered the top side of the trailer, the burnt husks of the trucks, the road, the ditches, tree limbs. Leave now or not at all.

Screw it.

He was about to head to his running unmarked when something odd caught his eye. It was on the back of the trailer, the bottom hinge of one giant trailer door. Fibers fluttered in the wind. Nothing abnormal. Scott snagged his jacket on the hinge.

Bates squinted, got close. Using his numb thumb and forefinger, he tugged the fiber strands out of the crease between the pin. It looked like hair. Animal hair. He removed a plastic Ziplock baggie from his back pocket and placed the strands inside. Why strands of hair would be in the hinge was a head scratcher, but he doubted it was anything significant. Probably had hit a deer a while back or something. Still, it paid to give each clue its due diligence, even if it led him down a dead-end street.

He climbed behind the wheel of his sedan and rubbed his hands together in front of the warm air blowing from the vents. He debated whether to head home—a place now cold and empty—or head to the station.

Station. He threw the shifter into drive.

The end of a shift was always tough. It meant he was off work, the job unable to distract him any longer from his personal issues. She was no longer home to welcome him with a kiss when he entered the front door. The memories were all over the house. On the mantle. On the nightstand by the bed they'd once shared. In the bathroom drawers. A painful reminder of what he lost. Even her fucking half-used toothpaste choked him up. He threw himself into the job and let time eat away at the hurt.

The sedan's tires handled the slippery conditions well along 211. As long as he wasn't venturing above fifteen miles an hour. A four-wheel-drive GMC Sierra passed him, heading in the direction of the wreck. A woman behind the wheel, leaning forward, concentrating. Doing fifty with no trouble.

"I sure hope you live down here lady, or you're going to have a helluva trip back," he said to the snow cloud she left in her wake. He thought about flagging her down, just to check, but her quickly vanishing taillights told him to let it slide.

On Highway 17, the ride was smoother, and he was able to get to fifty. Highway 17 had received the salt brine treatment—albeit thin—making travel possible. A smattering of cars navigated the treacherous weather.

Ahead of him, a minivan hit an icy patch and the tail twerked. The driver overreacted and the van was sideways in a blink.

"Ah, hell." He slapped his fingers against the steering wheel and gave a disgruntled sigh. "Just what I need."

The tires bit, and inertia had its way. The black Honda Odyssey flipped on its side, rolled to the roof and slid down the center of 17 like a hockey puck.

Bates snatched the receiver from its clip, and said, "Dispatch, this is Bates. We got a 10-50 out on Highway 17 just past Queen Toyota. 10-33. 10-58 needed."

"Gotcha, Bates," Linda said back. She switched to the live channel and said, "All emergency personnel, this is dispatch. 10-50 on eastbound 17 near Queen Toyota. 10-51 and 10-52. Please respond."

A rapid-fire succession of responses crackled through the airwaves from the limited but gung-ho emergency personnel still on duty. Bates stopped short of the wreck, threw on his emergency lights, and ran to the overturned vehicle.

He heard crying in the back. Yanked on the sliding door. It refused to open. He retrieved a center punch from his sedan and busted the rear window. Four children hung upside down, all unconscious, arms dangling. The crying was coming from a car seat. Thankfully, it was properly strapped down, and the child inside was secure in the harness. Bates belly-crawled across the strewn luggage and golf clubs to the baby. He held the infant girl in place while he unbuckled the harness. Boots crunched over broken glass as help arrived. A highway patrol officer stuck his head in the back window.

"Take the baby." Bates handed the infant to patrolman. "Keep her wrapped up." Bates helped the other four children out of their seatbelts.

The wail of sirens from a distance informed him the calvary was on the way. As he unbuckled each child, they began to stir, disoriented and scared. He calmed them and helped them out of the van.

In minutes, the sight was a beehive of activity as the victims were rescued and treated. Word came that all of them were going to be okay. It was a family of six, heading to the beach for the weekend. They were somehow unaware a blizzard was on the way.

Bates arrived at the station two hours later than intended. He was informed that all the lab techs had gone home. It would be tomorrow at the earliest before the hair specimens could be analyzed, and even then, with a backlog of requests, he'd have to throw his weight around to get it moved to the front of the pile.

"Nothing is going to happen tonight, anyway," the lab director, Taylor Grinoch, said as she left the building.

Bates sat at his desk. Again, debated going home. The building was almost empty. The usual bustle of activity was now the hush of a library, save the occasional ringing of a telephone. There was a picture of her beside his computer screen. He placed it face down and began perusing his notes. Filling out the preliminary accident report was preferable to the loneliness waiting at home.

CHAPTER 16

The weather forecast continued its downward spiral. Not only was a blizzard about to suffocate the South, but graupel was expected to be significant.

Mary sipped on a fourth hot cup of coffee when the doorbell dinged. She slapped the mug on the counter, the contents sloshing over the sides of the cup, and ran to the door. The person on her porch was neither Tommy nor Buck. It was a woman, and she looked familiar. She wore a stylish toboggan, a huge parka with furry edges on the hoodie, leggings, and expensive snow boots. A subtle whiff of perfume pushed through the doorway. Too fancy for Green Swamp. More suited to Aspen.

"May I help you?" Mary asked after a moment.

"I am so very sorry to bother you," the woman said. Her teeth were perfect, straight, pearly white. Her bright green eyes practically sparkled. "I'm your new neighbor. I bought what was called the Houghton House by the locals. Across the way." The woman tossed a thumb over her shoulder in the direction of her new home, a Green Swamp landmark.

"Oh, yes!" Mary said. *Now I remember.* "You're the real estate agent I see on all the billboards around town." She snapped her fingers as the name jumped off her tongue. "Victoria Naughton."

"That's me." A confident smile.

"Please, come in," Mary said, moving out of the doorway. "Some storm, huh? The weatherman said we haven't had a storm like this in over thirty years. Pretty rare."

Victoria stamped the snow off her boots and stepped inside the foyer. "Beautiful home you have." She gazed around, her realtor eyes taking in the furniture, colors, and features. "I love how you refurbished the old and added new flooring and doors and furnishings. It looks fantastic."

"Thank you. My husband Tommy did most of it himself." When Victoria's eyebrows raised in suspicion, Mary explained. "He's an architect, so he has the know-how. Whatever he didn't know how to do he subbed out to contractors. Took three years but I think it turned out nice."

Nodding with enthusiasm, Victoria said, "He did a great job. I need to get his card. I've started buying properties to flip. I'm always looking for good architects. Finding reputable and trustworthy professionals is getting harder and harder by the day. Everyone is out to scam you. I had a tough time getting Houghton remodeled. I fired three contractors before I found one who wanted to do it right."

"Tommy agrees with you."

"Is he around? I'd love to ask him a few questions." She poked her head around the corner to search the kitchen.

Mary looked down at her feet, unsure how much she wanted to unburden. "He...uh...he isn't home *just* yet. He was supposed to be home last night and never made it. I have a friend out looking now."

Victoria's face blanched. "Oh my. I am so sorry. Was he out of town?"

Mary explained about the annual trip, keeping it short and sweet so as not to feed the horror writhing in her veins.

Victoria shook her head and moved to the front door. "I'm sorry to be bothering you then. You have more pressing things to worry about."

"It's fine. Nice to talk to someone." Mary realized the woman had shown up at her door, but the purpose of the visit remained unknown. "Is there something I can help you with?"

Victoria waved her off. "Absolutely not. My SUV won't start, and I came to see if you had jumper cables, but it is fine. I shouldn't be out in this weather anyway. I'm from up north and I'm used to driving in this mess, but 211 is getting bad. Do they not salt the roads here?"

"Usually, yes. For some reason not this year." The lack of county trucks salting 211 had slipped her observation until now. "Not sure if you know, but the 211's closed. A wreck."

"I thought I heard sirens earlier. I was cleaning and had music on, but I thought I heard that. What happened?"

Mary gave the details of what she knew.

"Wow. All kinds of drama in the Swamp today," Victoria said.

"Sure is." Mary decided to help the woman. She'd do nothing but pace the floor until Tommy returned, anyway. Might as well be useful. "Let me help you get your car started. That way if you need to go somewhere, it will crank. Tommy has a battery charger in the shop he keeps for the four-wheeler and the tractor. You keep it plugged in and it'll charge the battery. As long as we have power anyway."

"I had a generator installed. Living in hurricane country and all."

"Smart girl. Give me a sec."

Mary told Conner and Maribeth she would be back soon. She grabbed her jacket, gloves, and slipped into her own duck boots. Victoria followed her out to the building to grab the battery charger. The horse barn next to Tommy's shop was all quiet. Willow must be sleeping.

"I'll be with you in a bit, girl," Mary called. To Victoria, she said, "Maribeth's filly. She started asking for it as soon as she learned to talk. Girl loves horses."

Victoria smiled. "I've never ridden a horse. Looks fun though."

Mary retrieved the charger, drove a quarter of a mile down the street, and turned into the winding driveway that cut through the woods leading back to the house.

****

The Houghton House was built in 1921 by Robert Houghton. Robert died of pneumonia in '59, leaving his wife, Celeste, a widow. She sold the house to the first couple who knocked on the door and ran back home to Boston.

George and Esther Kittle were the lucky couple who knocked. George was the heir to Kittle's Furniture in Whiteville. He knew little of the world, but he knew he despised sales. Fluorescent lights, dress shoes, smooth talking. No, thank you.

His mother, Georgene, died in '54 in a freak hit-and-run, so when his father, Clyde, died in '61, he became the sole owner and operator. For some, a dream come true. For George, a nightmarish reality he worried would suck the soul from his body.

George dreamed of owning land, plowing a garden, owning some goats. When he and Esther discovered the Houghton House by accident, George said it was fate.

He'd been driving his wife to Southport in their convertible Ford Thunderbird for a sunny day at the beach when the front tire blew. George pulled over and came to a halt in the driveway of the Houghton House. A "For Sale" sign stood two feet from where they'd stopped. He forgot about the tire and the couple never made it to Southport.

George marched down the driveway, a man on a mission, Esther chasing after him. He knocked on the front door of the charming house and waited while bumble bees buzzed around the pink and white azalea bushes, and a wind chime tinkled in the soupy summer breeze. A red robin chirped from a nearby Weeping Willow.

Celeste answered the door and was gracious with her time. She showed them the house, the property, and a rusting whiskey still left behind by Robert Houghton. George was not discouraged by Robert's former trade craft. He loved the property, saw the potential, and wanted it immediately. He bought the place, sold the business, and used the money to start a farm. The Eason Farm twenty miles down was growing by the day, but George was undeterred by the competition. He *was* a salesman, after all.

Turned out George was great at selling furniture, not so great at farming. He shut the endeavor down after two years of failure and disappointment. Thankfully, he was frugal during those years and a good portion of his money remained. He opened a furniture shop in Southport, followed by a second location in Shallotte four years later. He offset the melancholy dread of sales by cultivating a nice-sized garden. He grew vegetables and fruit for his family's consumption. Built a pen and bought chickens for eggs. Bought a cow for milk. A goat, just because. Esther got pregnant in '63 and they were blessed with a healthy baby girl, Becky. Six years later, another baby girl, Winnie. When Becky was seven, George bought her a dog.

George owned a successful business that provided financial growth and stability. He owned fifty acres of real estate where he gardened and raised farm animals. He was married to the most beautiful woman in twenty counties, and the pair had two beautiful daughters. He even had a damn dog. Life was grand.

When he hung himself from the exposed living room beams, everyone was shocked. The suicide made no sense. He had everything.

A traumatized Esther no longer wanted to live in the house. She saw George's naked body every time she walked in the living room. Saw the claw marks around his neck from tearing at the rope—he'd changed his mind, the coroner had said, like they always do. His limp husk of a body, pale and empty, began to haunt the family. She and the girls moved to Southport to be near one of the stores.

But she couldn't bring herself to sell the property. It had been George's dream. It had once been her dream. Even if the dream had killed him.

The Houghton House sat dormant and empty, the ghosts of Robert and George left to roam the empty halls together. The untended fields went to the weeds, the manicured yard followed suit. Time, weather, gravity, and insects chewed away at the forlorn house like a starving dog on a meaty bone.

Esther and Becky died a few years later in some mysterious way, leaving Winnie to control the family business. The house remained a sad monument to the past, slowly rotting back to the soil from which it sprang. But the daughter and executor of the Kittle Estate refused to sell the Houghton House, even after she sold both furniture stores and moved to California.

****

Somehow, Victoria had convinced Winnie to sell. A feat attempted—and failed—by dozens of suitors before her, including the paper company.

Mary wondered if Victoria knew the sad history of the place. She was tempted to ask, but resisted. If the beautiful realtor was not aware of its past, Mary wasn't going to be the one to dampen her spirit.

As the trees cleared, the house came into view through the downfall of snow. Mary was stunned by its renewed beauty.

"Wow," she said, truly awestruck.

"It is wow, isn't it," Victoria said, smiling at Mary's reaction.

"I haven't been back here in over ten years."

It was remarkable. A two-story modern farmhouse. The window frames were black as well as the gutters and downspouts, the glass panes were mirrored, the HardiPlank siding a blinding white. The porch was massive and furnished with pillowed wicker chairs, a daybed swing, multiple ceiling fans, fake plants. It was beautiful, elegant, inviting, and homely. Straight off a magazine cover.

"It's amazing." Mary marveled.

"Nothing that money and elbow grease couldn't handle. A lot of the original structure was used. The bones were still in good shape. The skin, however, was beyond repair. We stripped it, replaced floor joists, roof trusses, studs, seal plates, anything else that was rotted from weather or termites. Added some rooms, sheeted it back, and went from there. New electrical, plumbing, data wiring, all that jazz. New roof, new sheetrock, new flooring, new millwork, new doors, new furniture. Cost more than I should have spent but..." Her voice trailed off. She completed the sentence by holding her arms out toward the house.

Victoria climbed out of Mary's truck and punched in the code for the garage. The door slid up and out of the way. Mary parked nose to nose in front of the SUV. She retrieved the jumper cables. With both hoods raised and the jumper cables hooked up, she instructed Victoria to start the Ford Explorer. It turned over on the first try.

Victoria climbed out, smiling. "Thank you so much."

"Happy to help. Let it run a bit to charge the battery. Let me show you how to hook up the battery charger, just in case you need it." Mary explained which clip went to which post and what the gauge on the front meant, then climbed into the truck, mindfully knocking the snow off her boots before putting her feet in.

"I hope everything's okay with Tommy and the others," Victoria said, standing beside Mary's truck.

"I'm sure everything's fine." Mary was sure of nothing, but she just met Victoria and wasn't comfortable unloading her fears on a stranger.

"I'll have you guys over for dinner one night once all this crappy weather is out of here. Repay the kindness."

"You don't owe me anything. The right thing to do is always the right thing to do. But it would be great to get to know our neighbor better. Plus, I want a tour of that beautiful home of yours."

"Sounds like a date. Be safe and thanks again."

Mary waved and u-turned. She looked in the mirror as she eased down the driveway. Victoria waved goodbye until the snow blotted her out.

She wasn't out of the truck when Maribeth yelled from the front porch. "Conner's throwing up again!"

Mary hurried inside with a sigh, wishing this day would give her a break.

CHAPTER 17

Sarah Grace passed a slow-moving unmarked police car but barely noticed. She focused on where the road was located, now that it was dusted in snow. She also digested Jason's incredible story. His dead father. The thing in the woods. Skeeter.

What it meant, she wasn't sure. Jason's father showed him something, but he wasn't able to fully describe it. It was dark outside. He only knew it was savage and deadly.

Skeeter backed him up. He saw the monster, too. Thought it was nightmare. Added the detail about the fiery eyes of a demon. Jason clapped and agreed. He had forgotten to mention that feature.

"Where did you see this creature?" Sarah Grace asked. They were almost home.

"In the woods of Green Swamp," Jason answered, looking out the window at the hurricane of snow. "I'm not from here, so I don't know where in the woods. But it *was* in the Swamp."

"Near Tin Shed," Skeeter said flatly from the back seat. The cab of the truck smelled like him now, but Sarah Grace no longer noticed.

"What was it doing when you saw it?"

Jason picked at his fingers again. "Eating something."

She shivered.

She was thankful when she pulled into the driveway. Her nerves were shot. From the story and the drive.

Ron was beside himself. "Where in the hell have you two been? What took so long?" A long pause. "Why is Skeeter in my foyer?"

Sarah Grace waved him down. "Chill, okay. We're fine. I'll explain." She turned to Jason and pointed at Skeeter. "Take him to your bathroom. Give him a towel, a rag, soap, and shampoo. Let him take a shower. Get his clothes in the washing machine. Come get a pair of Ron's pajamas and one of his housecoats for him to wear while his clothes wash and dry. Go."

Skeeter was not offended or mad. He seemed thrilled to finally get a warm bath.

Sarah Grace pointed at a confounded Ron. "You, come with me."

"This ought to be good," he said, following her down the hall.

In the bedroom, door closed, Ron sat on the bed while Sarah Grace paced back and forth. "Okay, so, I have something to tell you. A story, really. You're not going to believe it. I didn't. At first. But I want you to know that I believe it now. As incredible as it sounds—and honey, this is *batshit*—I believe it's true. I don't know how it's possible, but it is. With me?"

"You're going to tell me a batshit crazy story that I'm not going to believe." He nodded. "Got it."

"Good."

Sarah Grace told him the full story. All of it. He sat silently, listening. His expressions shifted from amused to doubtful, to oh shit, to wow, to contemplative. She concluded with her belief in their son.

"You weren't kidding," he said when she was finished. "Complete batshit." He paced the room frowning, gnawing on his fingernails. It was his thinking tick. Sarah Grace always knew when he was lost in thought. Mostly when he was stuck while writing. He'd stare at the blank page in his old ribbon typewriter, as if waiting for the words to type themselves, while chewing his nails to the quick.

She waited patiently. He needed to accept or deny the premise on his own.

"That is an incredible story." Pause. "I'll be honest, I don't know what to think. It's a lot to swallow." He paced more.

Sarah Grace grew agitated. Not that she expected him to automatically go with it. Doubt was understandable. The story came off like a horror script for an M. Night Shyamalan movie. Kid communicates with ghosts, sees monsters, shares some sort of telepathic connection with a stranger. She got it. Batshit.

But still. "What's the problem?" she asked, knowing the problem.

Ron stopped pacing. "Really?"

"I'm just wondering why you're struggling so much with this."

"The fact that you're not struggling with it gives me pause," Ron stated, an edge on his voice.

The fuck does that mean? she wanted to ask. She bit her tongue. She knew an argument when she saw one. A quarrel was not what they needed today. "I never said I didn't struggle with this. But, Ron, Jason has not lied to us—"

"Yet," Ron interrupted. "He hasn't been here long enough for us to learn all his quirks."

All manner of flagrant responses struggled from Sarah Grace's lips, but she swallowed them back. She took a deep breath to silence the cacophony. "Jason has *not* lied to us. He has never given us a reason to doubt him."

"I reiterate my previous statement." Ron crossed his arms, held her gaze with steadfast resolve.

"You think he's lying?"

"Didn't say lying. Maybe this is his way of getting attention. He's had a tough life, Sarah Grace. No argument there. But we can't jump every time some past trauma springs up. He has to learn how to let that stuff go, live in the here and now. Trust that we aren't going anywhere."

Sarah Grace refused to believe this was a call to be noticed. Jason was loved, treated with the utmost care and respect. She made every attempt to include him in everything. Trips to Wilmington, Charlotte, Charleston, Myrtle Beach were taken just so he could experience different adventures, have fun. One of his Christmas gifts was going to be a trip to Disney World.

Ron's excuse made no sense.

"What about the connection with Jason and Skeeter?" *Explain that away!*

"It's weird, yes," Ron acknowledged, "but Skeeter raids the school dumpsters, as well. I saw him there while waiting in line to pick up Jason a few weeks ago, when you had your dentist appointment. He could've met Skeeter while outside for recess. One traumatized human recognizing another. Who knows?"

Sarah Grace couldn't believe what she was hearing. An excuse for everything. *Makes sense though,* the ever-practical voice of her mother rang in her ear.

Through a cloud of stubborn irritation, Sarah Grace saw this was true. It was sensible. Holes could be found all through the story. "He wouldn't make something this elaborate up for attention, Ron," she pleaded. More to herself than her husband, she realized.

Ron shrugged. "I'm just saying there's a common sense explanation for all this. Ghosts and goblins aren't common sense."

Sarah Grace started when she noticed Jason standing in the doorway. For how long, she wasn't sure. She wanted to speak but her tongue was stuck to the roof of her mouth. His eyes verified the betrayal, and she felt a sick sadness twist her insides.

"Mr. Vernon was your grandfather, right?" Jason asked Ron.

Ron fidgeted on his feet, then answered, "Yes. You know he was."

"He hates the renovations you made on the house," Jason said, his tone like a razor. "He said your grandmother put that wallpaper up in the bathroom in 1985 and you ruined it when you covered it with tile."

With that, Jason grabbed the pajamas and housecoat from the dresser and slammed the door on his way out.

Ron stared at the closed door, his mouth agape, face white as a sheet.

CHAPTER 18

Ray stood still. Waited calmly.

"Who are you?" the gun-holder asked. Very southern.

"Who the hell are you?" Ray asked.

"I'm Buck. I'm looking for my friends. They were camping at Tin Shed."

"Why the fuck are holding a gun to my head, boy?"

"I don't know who you are. My friends are missing. You're out here looking around, funny like. There's some sort of torn up animal over there. Seemed like the right thing to do until we sort this out."

"I'm Ray Eason."

"Shit." The gun disappeared. "I'm terribly sorry, Mr. Eason. I got carried away."

Ray grunted as he turned to face the gun holder, no doubt the guy Mary mentioned. At six-foot-four, barrel belly wrapped inside a thick brown winter coat, an open, friendly face with a bushy beard, Buck looked more bear than man. He wanted to be mad about having a gun held to his head, but the circumstances tempered his anger. "You see anything?" Ray asked after a beat.

"Nothing but that maimed animal behind you."

Ray hunkered down, examined the mutilation. The animal was once a deer, but all traces of that graceful creature were gone. A bloody heap of broken bones and flesh was all that remained.

"What could do such damage?" Buck asked from over Ray's shoulder.

"A bear." *And a big one.*

"They say they got the one that killed that Ramirez kid. You think they were wrong?"

"Hard to say," Ray answered as he pushed his old bones to erect. "Plenty of bear in these woods. Does concern me that your friends ran up one. They were in the vicinity."

"So where are they? It's as if they just disappeared. Like those people in Roanoke in the 1500s."

Ray knew nothing about Roanoke, so he moved past the subject. "My daughter is missing, too."

"Northern?"

"Yeah, you know her?"

"In passing. I changed her tire one time a few years back."

"She told me about some genteel country boy coming to the rescue. Said he was two of the average man. I appreciate your kindness."

"What anyone would do, I guess."

"But anyone didn't. You did. So, thanks."

"When did she go missing?" Buck changed the subject, shifting from one foot to the other.

"Last night. My guess, somewhere on 211."

"Why 211?"

"She would've been spotted by now on 17. It's busy with traffic, highway patrol, police officers, and such. 211's a bit like the Bermuda Triangle. The right circumstances, you disappear. She's somewhere out here. Just like your friends."

Pete Dawson said the accident happened around midnight. Northern *should* have been home by then. She should not have gotten caught up in it. But if Pete was off by an hour, then maybe she was stopped by the wreck. That would mean Northern had to find an alternate route, which would put her driving through the backroads of Green Swamp. Which would potentially put her driving by Tin Shed.

Except Northern was not about to drive home if she came upon an inferno such as the one those two eighteen-wheelers with all that diesel would have created. She would have turned around and driven back toward Supply until she had a phone signal to call 911.

Pete said a local phoned it in that morning, when the local headed to Supply for milk and discovered the road impassable.

Northern was not rerouted. She was somewhere on 211.

"How do we find them in this storm?" Buck asked. "It's getting worse." The wind blew the frozen crystals in circles, right, left, sideways. Tornadic and intensifying.

"I don't know. That's the damnable truth of the matter. I was raised in this Swamp. I could find them if not for all the snow cover." Ray shielded his face from a hard gust blasting icy buckshot in his face.

"Maybe we should regroup," Buck yelled over a sudden gust of howling wind. "Get a plan. Layer up in extra jackets and pants. If we can find a few to help, we'll start a search party. Whatcha think?"

Ray nodded. "I don't think we have any other choice. Follow me."

CHAPTER 19

Arlene Gainey folded laundry while Kurt Lewis—the weatherman out of Wilmington—prattled on about the incoming blizzard. He initially predicted the storm was going to miss Brunswick County by a country mile, downplaying the severity and longevity. Told viewers nothing was going to happen, maybe a few snowflakes would fall. Stay calm.

Arlene huffed in irritation. *Boy was he wrong about this one.*

Unfortunately, the digital antennae provided limited channel options way out here in Bum Fuck Egypt. She was stuck listening to Kurt. She had been asking Cliff to buy a media stick so she would have better options, but he was content with the antennae. The current selection of channels included a 24/7 western station. Cliff was just fine watching Matt Dillon and John Wayne until his eyes bled.

Cliff.

Arlene folded a wash rag with an unsteady hand. She was not exactly truthful with Mary earlier. She and Cliff had been married for over fifty years. They'd been through the ups and downs of life and marriage. Their daughter Elizabeth had been killed in a car accident two weeks after sixteenth birthday. Arlene had survived ovarian cancer. Cliff had been severely injured when his tractor dipped in a sink hole and threw him over the side. The tractor rolled over on top of him, pinning him in the mud. He survived suffocation and a broken back that day. Asked how, he had saltily replied, "Cause I'm one tough bastard."

That was Cliff. Rugged as the land.

Now she was scared. He had never stayed anywhere longer than the intended time. He had always come home. Arlene knew Cliff from top to bottom. Something was wrong.

Arlene was hesitant to share her concerns with Mary. "I don't want that young lady worrying herself sick," Arlene said to her sleeping shih tzu-Maltese, Misty. Misty's hind legs kicked as she dreamed of chasing a car or a rabbit, but her eyes never opened.

Mary and Tommy bought the Tucker residence across the street over fifteen years earlier as a newlywed couple. Tommy and Arlene's son, Steven, had been friends since grade school. Steven quickly suggested Tommy buy the Tucker property the minute a "For Sale" sign was hammered in the front lawn. Old man Tucker had died in his sleep after a one-way call from the Widow Maker. His children had no interest in living in the country. The house had gone up for sale before the ink was dry on the probate paperwork.

Arlene took to Mary immediately. Maybe she saw Mary as a second chance. Elizabeth died so young. She never even attended a high school dance. Without her daughter, Arlene had felt incomplete, some biological branch ripped from the family tree. It had been the mother in her. Instinct and genetics. The desire to pass on her maternal knowledge.

When Mary came along, Arlene gravitated toward her youth and inexperience. Mary was raised in the city, but she had country in her bones. Arlene taught her how to work a garden. She learned to cook from Arlene. Cliff and Tommy taught her how to chop wood. She acclimated to well water, bugs, wharf rats, snakes, and poison ivy. A meek, sweet young girl who liked dresses and make-up transformed into a jean and flannel-wearing, callous-handed woman, right before Arlene's eyes.

The real breakthrough in their friendship came one early Saturday morning while the two picked snap peas in Mary's garden, a few hours before the summer sun reached its full blistering potential.

"Tommy and I have been trying to have children," Mary said, while on her hands and knees in the dry, dusty garden soil. Arlene sat on a bucket beside her, too old to crawl around in the mud. "The doctors can't figure out why. We are both healthy and fertile. Do you think it could be me? Maybe punishment for some past sin? I was raised in church, yeah, but lost sight of the point and stopped going. Could this be the way He gets back at me?"

Arlene was profoundly moved that Mary would share something so intimate. She took her time answering. "I don't believe God would ever punish someone for not going to church. God knows what's in your heart and your soul, whether you're in church or not. Mary, you are of pure heart and soul. Maybe you've made mistakes. You are human after all. But that's not the reason."

"What is it then?"

"Nature, sweetheart. Nature." Arlene palmed a handful of dirt and let it sail into the humid breeze. "There is a time for everything. During the winter, these snap peas won't grow. But during the summer, they flourish. Asparagus grows year-round.

"Nature has its way about things, a period of renewal. If the doctors say nothing is wrong, then nature will have its way with you when the time is right. My advice: stay patient, enjoy the 'trying to make a baby' part, and let the process flow."

And flow it did. Mary and Tommy were parents to a handsome young boy and a beautiful little girl. Arlene had babysat those two countless times, and she considered them grandchildren.

Arlene *was* worried. But she wasn't going to pass that worry to Mary until she had a reason to do so.

"...accumulation of at least thirty to forty inches is expected for parts of northern South Carolina and North Carolina," Kurt said, while standing in front of a giant map of South and North Carolina. Snowfall totals in giant fonts spread across the region.

Arlene was folding the last towel in the pile when something banged against the back door. Misty cracked awake like she'd been prodded with a sharp stick. She yelped and spun in circles, a sign of excitement.

"Quiet down, Misty." Arlene hushed the dog as she walked through the dining room, back through the kitchen, and into the laundry room to the back door. She parted the curtain with her finger and peered through the crack. Snow was falling in furious drifts, swirling on the hastening breath of the wind, but there was—

BANG!

Arlene jumped back from the door with a startled cry. Misty howled from the living room. Arlene watched the door rattle in its frame for only a second, then stop. She tiptoed to the curtain and peaked out again.

Nothing.

Her backyard was fenced in for Misty; the crazy dog would chase tractor trailer tires if let free. In one corner, an old shed housed several tractors and her now deceased father-in-law's ancient Cadillac. A new big and bulky shop with two roll-up doors, and all the fixings, occupied the other corner. Two swaying pine trees stood in the center of the yard. A perfect, white blanket covered the yard like carpet. Unblemished and—

What is that? Arlene wondered, squinting. To her right, the snow was disturbed. Not by prints made from stepping, but from the mess of dragging. The crisp whiteness was streaked with red. Stark and defining.

BANG! The door rattled in the frame, the glass trembled.

Arlene opened the curtains further and pressed her forehead to the freezing glass. Her ragged breath fogged the windowpane. From this vantage point, she could see the porch stoop. Hanging off the porch were a pair of snow-coated boots.

Cliff's boots.

A bloody hand smacked the glass, then fell away.

CHAPTER 20

The fibers were bagged and tagged, but not placed in evidence. Detective Bates flipped the clear baggie between his fingers. Thinking.

The black/brown fibers were hair. He was sure of it. Dog hair, bear hair. A few possibilities.

How would dog or bear hair get caught on a hinge four feet off the ground?

Bates reached the forensics lab. The door was locked but he had a key that allowed him entry. One door inside the lab led to the evidence room of any open cases. Only forensics staff possessed the proper credentials to access those rooms. Bates only needed a microscope.

Back in the beginning, when Bates was entering law enforcement, he had considered forensics. CSI was a TV show that had him thinking it was the way to go. He quickly learned they were overblown bullshit. CSI techs and law enforcement in general hated those dramatized serials because they were so preposterous, and included technology that doesn't even exist.

Bates had been a natural-born problem solver his whole life. He had the keen ability to retrace steps, apply common sense to actions and movements, see past the smoke and mirrors. CSI was all science. What you saw was what you got. Not the right field for someone who loved to explore the why as much as the how and what.

Used to love, he thought bitterly, slipping behind a desk with a microscope on its top. The past month and a half had gone by in a fog. He was still coming to terms with her being gone. Attention to detail had waned, patience had disintegrated. His passion for the work had deteriorated. It left him with a hole inside, deep and wide and empty.

He shook his head to rattle those thoughts away. He still wanted to be a great detective. That would get him through until the heartbreak subsided.

He powered on the light microscope, applied a thin coat of solvent on a slide to hold the hair flat, and used tweezers to place the specimen on the solution. Another slide was carefully placed on top to sandwich the hair, and the sample slid onto the microscope tray. Looking through the lenses, Bates dialed the magnification to 10X, 20X, 50X. He tweaked the focus knob to clear the image.

The hair cuticle was scaly, almost fish-like. The scales overlapped in slim rows, the tips pointed and barbed. Varied pigmentation. Defined medulla. Jagged root. Short in length.

Not human.

He magnified the hair follicles but could discern no helpful hints. A nuclear or mitochondrial DNA test would provide a more detailed analysis.

He searched animal hair images in the national database. The sample was comparable to a wide variety of species. Canine was a possibility. Mammal was feasible.

Not much help, but he chased hunches and leads until they provided another lead or went nowhere. Though this lead provided little clarity, Bates was convinced the hair sample meant something. If he had found the hair strands around the bottom of the truck, he may not have given them any thought. Discovering them four feet high—in a place they had no business—proved puzzling. Perhaps the answer was simple, and he was overthinking.

He twisted his knuckles against his eyeballs. *What a day.* And it was only two-thirty.

Bates shut the computer down, flipped the power switch on the microscope, and locked the door on the way out. The roads were worsening. Unless he was planning to sleep at the station, he better get on the road.

Shallotte was Antarctica, from Bates' perspective, anyways. This was the South. Hurricanes were the rage here, not blizzards.

Right after Halloween, a cold snap and rain brought the area an eighth inch of ice and people lost their grits. The stores sold out of bread and water. Gas stations sold out of gas. Highway Patrol reported over three dozen wrecks with four fatalities in a twelve-hour span in this area alone.

"Halloween," Bates said as he climbed inside his car. A strobe of recognition. "Halloween."

Then he had it. A seven-year-old boy was killed in Green Swamp. At the Creepy Swamp Haunted House and Hayride. Bates hadn't investigated that case. He'd been in a room under hospice care, watching his soulmate scratch out her final breath.

But word got around.

Benji Ramirez had been killed by a bear. Or so the official statement had read. Bates heard CSI unofficially had questions about the murder; the claw marks for one. While the patterns were consistent with a bear, a fifth claw was detected in one spot on the Ramirez kid's body. Bears possessed a dew claw that *could* make that mark but was highly unlikely. The coroner also noted that the cuts were surgical, clean. Bear cuts were more ragged. A cutting *and* tearing.

Parts of Benji were missing. Bears were omnivores but were not known to actively eat humans. Benji was missing his heart, spleen, intestines, and kidneys. His skull had been chewed on. CSI admitted that under the right circumstances this type of behavior could occur but was not typical to the species.

There was also the location of the attack. A haunted hayride. A loud, large tractor pulling a flatbed trailer loaded with screeching people. Pitch black woods teeming with actors dressed in costumes and wielding chainsaws. Not an environment conducive to bear activity. Bears were solitary creatures. Finding a bear amidst that much activity was considered an improbability.

And how was the bear not seen entering or exiting the area? Bears were not stealthy animals. They were big and scary and would have attracted the attention of someone.

The final abnormality—most relevant to Bates today—was CSI were unable to positively identify hair strands found on the boys mutilated body. The hair follicles were similar to a bear's but not identical. Bates recalled hearing the CSI tech responsible for working that angle of the case say the hair was unusual and did not match any samples in the database. Even the nuclear DNA tests were inconclusive.

Despite the uncertainty, the public outcry was loud enough to bury the doubts. The department was forced to release an official finding. The boy's death was blamed on a bear. Green Swamp was populated with mammals and, though there were concerns and questions, no one could categorically deny that it was a bear attack. The official cause of death was ruled as such, and the case was closed.

"I need to see those hair samples." Bates hurried back inside.

CHAPTER 21

Past the store lay the driveway to the Eason home, a beautiful country structure with a wraparound porch. Several trucks and a four-wheeler were in the driveway, and four people stood on the porch. He spotted Mr. and Mrs. Eason quickly and easily enough. He saw Northern in them both. One visitor was a tall, burly country boy, and the other guy appeared to be about Garrett's age. They watched him park and climb down from his truck.

"Garrett?" Ray asked from the porch.

"Yes, sir," Garrett answered, climbing the steps quickly with his head hunkered from the frigid wind and icy precipitation.

"Nice to meet you," Ray said, shaking his hand. "This is Buck. He's also missing a few people. This is Brent, a friend of Northern's."

"Ex-boyfriend," Brent said with a scowl. "You were the last one to see her alive, I hear."

"Apparently," Garrett said. He knew where this line of questioning was going.

"You mind enlightening us as to where she is then?"

"If I knew, I wouldn't be here right now. We left Blanchard's at about ten, just as they were closing. She said she would call me today, and we left separately. I called her about fifteen minutes after our date to see how she was doing. She was good, driving. My phone didn't ring again until this morning when Mrs. Eason called me. That's what I know."

"Not sure why she would be on a date with someone like you," Brent hissed, stepping closer to Garrett.

"Guess she was tired of assholes," Garrett said evenly. This prick was not about to scare him off. "I can relate." Brent took another step, so Garrett added: "Ex-boyfriend."

Brent lunged forward but Ray jumped between them. "Hey!" Ray said, nose to nose with Brent. "I will not tolerate that on my property, or in my presence. We are here to find my daughter and the missing hunters. If you can't handle that, hit the road."

Brent, red-faced, bowed his head. "Sorry, Ray."

Northern was right. Ray was a presence. When he raised his voice, it rumbled in your gut.

"Did she say where she was when you talked to her that last time?" Mrs. Eason asked, her voice shaky and desperate.

"No, ma'am," Garrett answered. "We talked for only a few minutes." Garrett pulled his phone from his pocket and went to his call log. He showed them the call was made at ten-thirteen and ended at ten-seventeen. The next call was this morning. Mrs. Eason, just as he'd said.

"If you guys left Blanchard's at ten, she should have been home by ten-thirty," Ray said, his eyes searching the snow for answers. "Ten-twenty would definitely put her on 211."

"Did you say Northern's not the only person missing?" Garrett asked, trying to catch up.

"My friend, Tommy," Buck said. "He and a few friends went on their annual week-long camping trip back at Tin Shed. They were supposed to be back last night. They never showed up. The campsite is empty."

Garrett nodded, remembering the tents. "I passed that camp a while ago. No cell phones allowed on these trips, I guess."

"Not that it would do much good out here. The cell service is shit."

"I think we should get four-wheelers and ride 211 toward Supply," Ray suggested. "She has to be somewhere along the road. A wreck maybe. Only thing that makes sense."

"What about the two trucks?" inquired Buck. "The police won't let us pass."

"They're gone now," Ray answered. "Maggie saw the emergency trucks leave. I don't care if they are still there. I'm finding my daughter, no matter what." Ray bound down the stairs and headed toward a rear building.

Garrett hurried to catch up. Garrett could feel Brent staring a hole through the back of his head. *Let him stare.*

Ray disappeared inside a metal building. A roll-up door rose automatically. Inside was a fleet of four-wheelers and utility vehicles. "Grab one and let's go," Ray called, as he climbed aboard the biggest one, a yellow Honda.

Garrett hopped aboard a camouflaged Honda with a gun-case mounted on the side. The engine fired on the first try. He followed Ray out the bay door. He waited beside Ray as the other two joined the parade. "We want to look in ditches, woods, check down any logging road, anywhere that looks suspect. Got it?"

"Yes, sir," they all said together.

"Let's go."

Ray led the convoy to the road where he stopped with more instructions.

Ray pointed at Buck and Brent, and said, "You two ride the left side of 211. Garrett and I will ride on the right side. Eyes peeled."

They slowly moved forward, searching deep and shallow ditches, and the woods beyond. After three miles they came to a driveway, woods lining either side. A quick inspection showed nothing of importance. They resumed moving down the desolate highway. The usually busy connector to the coast was completely devoid of traffic. Even the locals were hunkered down.

On the opposite side of the highway, Buck and Brent were passing a residence when a woman called to Buck from the front porch. "Why are you out here?"

"We have multiple people missing now," Buck answered. "Northern Eason is also missing."

"What?" The woman gaped in astonishment. "This can't be coincidental, can it?"

"I don't know. I found nothing at the campsite so I'm checking into this. I'll update you when I get back."

Garrett pulled up next to Ray. "Who was that woman Buck was talking to?"

"Mary Stuart," Ray replied. "Tommy is her husband."

Each logging road or driveway or fire lane was checked. A suspicious mound in a ditch was investigated—one such mound a dead deer. Miles of roadway brought them to the eighteen-wheeler wreckage. The sight was cordoned off with police barricade tape. A blue tarp covering the rig on its side popped like sails from the buffeting wind.

Garrett was glad to see Ray veer clear of the charred accident scene and move on. A mile and a half further, Ray stopped suddenly, and Garrett had to react quickly to not backend him. "What's wrong?"

Ray pointed ahead. They were at one end of a bridge and on the other end lay a red bumper, now almost hidden beneath snow. Red paint marks scratched the concrete railing like bloody prints.

"Is that—" Garrett whispered.

Ray popped the clutch and bolted forward.

Garrett whistled at Buck and Brent, who were further back.

Ray was off the four-wheeler before it stopped rolling. He lifted the bumper out of the snow. "It's her bumper," Ray said, choking back emotion. "When we bought her the car, she liked the sporty bumper. Said it made the car look fast."

Garrett peered over the concrete railing. No sign of a car, due to the dense canopy of overgrowth, but he noticed some broken tree limbs. The creek gurgled and swallowed like a dog lapping water from a bowl.

"She's down there," Ray announced, before sprinting down the steep embankment without hesitation or care for personal safety.

Garrett followed, terrified of what they were about to find.

CHAPTER 22

Saucers, empty save muffin crumbs, sat before each occupant at the kitchen table. Jason and Skeeter sat side by side. Skeeter wore Ron's pajamas and a robe, his massive hands wrapped around a cup of coffee. The TV in the kitchen was still broadcasting *The Weather Channel* but the sound was down to a hushed whisper. Addie lay curled at Jason's feet.

Ron and Sarah Grace sat on the opposite side of the table, elbows on the surface, staring at the two of them.

"How do you know about the wallpaper in the bathroom?" Ron asked, heat on each word.

"I told you." Jason was still miffed Ron claimed he was making this up for attention. Defiance seemed the best course of action. Ron was scared and shocked by all this, trying to grip its impossibility. Jason knew this but still refused to baby Ron through it.

"And I don't believe you."

Sarah Grace placed her hand on Ron's arm, squeezed until he looked at her. No words were spoken but the intentions were clear.

"I can't help what you do or do not believe," Jason said calmly. "The truth is the truth."

Ron laughed, but it lacked humor. Jason knew the tone. Ron was angry and getting angrier. Ron nodded with his whole upper body.

"I've seen Skeeter at your school, nosing through the dumpsters. Is that where you two met?"

Now it was Jason's turn to get angry. Ron was not just suggesting Jason was looking for attention. He was blatantly calling him a liar. "Your granddaddy nicknamed you Alfalfa as a kid because your hair always stuck up in the back. You were born with a major cowlick. It's still there, but Janice is really good at cutting your hair so it's not noticeable."

Ron plopped back in his chair. He looked at Sarah Grace, who stared at him with an amused curl at the edge of her lips. An "I told you so" look if ever one existed. "I hated being called that," Ron said, thinking back. "Mom took me to a barber who got rid of it. It worked too, because grandaddy stopped calling me Alfalfa. In about the sixth grade." Ron looked at Jason, his lower lip trembled. "It's impossible for you to know that. I've never even told my wife."

Jason's cheeks flushed. He didn't want to embarrass Ron and felt bad about it. But he needed him to listen. If it meant revealing a few not-so-pleasant tidbits about his past, then so be it.

"I'm not seeking attention," Jason said quietly. "You guys are wonderful. I appreciate everything you do for me. I've never been treated so well. But this isn't about me." Jason looked at Ron, Sarah Grace, and Skeeter. "Something is out there. And if we want to live, we better get on the same page."

"What is it?" Ron asked after a few moments of silence. "Do you know?"

Jason shook his head. "Only that its eyes burn like fire. It's large. Bigger than any bear I've heard of. The claws are not like bear claws or dog claws; they're like knives."

"Do you know why it's here?" Sarah Grace asked.

"No."

"Green Swamp has a pretty substantial population of bear," Ron offered. "Big ones."

"I don't think it's a bear," Jason said. He wasn't an animal expert, knew only what he'd learned in school. He saw the thing in the dark, more shadow than figure. His feelings were more instinct than anything concrete.

"If not a bear," Ron said, his brow furrowed in thought, "then what?"

"I don't know," Jason said.

"I'm still processing this, so be patient," Ron said. "What does Skeeter have to do with all this?"

Jason and Skeeter exchanged glances. "I'm not exactly sure. My dad showed me Skeeter's cabin and pointed in the window. Said 'Dumpster Diver. Your only chance.'"

Skeeter pointed at himself, nodded, and said, "Dumpster diver."

"What does he mean by Skeeter being the only chance?" Sarah Grace asked.

"I don't know. I can only assume he meant what he said." Jason placed his hand on Skeeter's arm. "He's our only chance."

"Skeeter, when I picked you up, you recognized Jason and said you saw him in your dreams. What did you mean by that?"

"I saw him," Skeeter said, looking at Jason. "When I was sleeping. He was in my window. A scary man was with him." Skeeter swallowed. "His face was missing."

"That was my dad," Jason explained. "He's dead. He shot himself. That's why his face is messed up."

Skeeter's mouth went "Oh" as he digested this bit of morbid information.

"Skeeter, do you know what this thing is?" Ron asked.

Skeeter shook his head uncertainly, as if he was afraid to get in trouble for not having an answer.

"Jason, do you know where we can find it? Like...a cave?"

Jason shook his head. "I only saw a glimpse of it. Just enough to know that it's an awful killing machine. Sorry."

Sarah Grace posed one more question: "You said you're not convinced it's a bear. What do you think, feel, or guess it is?"

"You'll think I'm crazy."

Ron laughed. This time with actual humor behind it. "Too late," he said, with a tense giggle. Sarah Grace shot a scowl his way and he hushed.

Jason smiled at the joke while his brain worked to formulate the words to explain his theory. After a moment, he said, "I think it's a werewolf."

CHAPTER 23

Arlene Gainey snatched the door open. The bloody body of her husband lay face down on the back porch stoop. Misty spun in circles, yapping in panicked excitement. Arlene dropped to her knees and placed two fingers on his neck to check for a pulse.

Weak. So weak.

"Cliff?" she whispered in his ear. "Cliff?"

Cliff moaned but his eyes remained closed.

In the distance, Arlene heard the drone of four-wheelers, but it was background noise, like a radio with the volume low. She needed to get Cliff inside, out of the numbing chill of the storm. Snow was fluttering through the doorway and melting on the washroom linoleum.

Arlene hurried to the hall linen closet and retrieved a blanket. She spread the blanket beside Cliff's unconscious body, rolled him on it. She grabbed the corners of the blanket and pulled him across the threshold, through the washroom, into the kitchen, her worn out back screaming from the stress.

She used a warm, wet dish cloth to wash his face. On his right cheek, the flesh was sliced open deep enough to expose his denture-less gums. The cut was surgical, perfect. As soon as the wound was cleaned, it bubbled and oozed blood over the creases of his cheek. Soaked into the collar of his flannel shirt.

Arlene unfolded his tattered puffer jacket, unbuttoned the flannel shirt beneath. His chest was ripped to shreds. The marks claw like.

A bear. The boys were attacked. Where were the rest of them?

Cliff needed a hospital, but the wreck blocked the road to the nearest medical facility in Shallotte. No Urgent Care in Bolton. The next closest was in Wilmington and she knew he couldn't make it that far. Navigating the back roads of Green Swamp was possible, but she'd never used the back roads to travel to Supply or Bolton.

Arlene grabbed the cordless phone from the kitchen counter and dialed Mary.

"Hello?"

"Mary," Arlene sobbed, "I need help."

No questions were asked. "On the way." Mary was gone from the other end of the line.

Arlene hurried to the front door and opened it just as Mary bounded up the slippery, snow-caked steps. Mary gasped when she saw the blood on Arlene's clothing. "What happened?"

"It's Cliff," Arlene cried and pointed to the kitchen.

Mary rushed inside. "Oh my god!" She dropped to her knees beside Cliff. "What happened to him?"

"I don't know. I found him at the back door. He dragged himself here."

"Bear attack?"

"My best guess."

"Did he speak? Tell you where the others are?" She inspected the wounds.

"Not a word."

Wiping slick blood on her jeans, she looked at Arlene. "We need to get him to a hospital. Fast. We'll have to take the back roads."

"That's what I thought, but I don't know the way. I've never driven it." She placed a hand over her face. "Mary, I don't think he can make it."

"Arlene, he will make it." Mary pulled the trembling woman's hands down and looked her in the eyes. "He's the most stubborn man on this planet. He'll make it."

Arlene nodded, her lips twitching.

"I'm going to get Ray Eason. He knows the swamp like the back of his hand. He just rode by on a four-wheeler."

"Why is Ray out on a four-wheeler?"

"He's looking for Northern."

"Maggie called me earlier," Arlene said, unable to take her eyes off her husband. "What's happening?"

"I don't know, but I am going to get him. Stay here and try to wake Cliff. Warm him up a bit. Talk to him. See if he responds. We need to know where the others are. Okay?"

Arlene nodded. "Okay."

Arlene eased to her knees beside Cliff as the front door slammed in Mary's wake. His breathing was ragged, his body ravaged. Despite what Mary said, she knew her husband wasn't going to make it to a hospital. This realization broke something inside her. It shattered into a million jagged pieces. When you've been a part of someone as long as she had been with Cliff, the pieces were the sum. The two of them were no longer a separate entity. Cliff was her heart. If the heart died, the brain followed, as did the body.

Life wasn't worth living without him. She knew what needed to be done.

She placed her lips to his bloody ear and whispered, "Cliff? Cliff? Can you hear me? I need you to come up for air one more time." She ran her fingers through his thinning gray hair, still wet from the snow, and kissed his forehead. "I know you want to remain in the dark and rest. You're tired. You must be. You've worked hard your whole life and got the calloused hands to show it. You made a home for us. Made a wonderful life for your family. You've been through so much and you deserve to rest, but I need you to come up one more time. I need you. Steven needs you. Tommy and Mary need you. Do this one thing for me and I'll go with you. We can rest our tired old bones together. Okay?"

Arlene raised her head, combing her fingers gently through his hair. Waited patiently for him to surface.

Cliff gasped awake. His eyes fluttered open just a crack. They were filmed with pain, but they stared at her just the same.

Arlene hugged him, the blood sticky on her arms. She pulled away, wiped a single tear from a wrinkle in the corner of his eye and asked, "Where are the others?"

CHAPTER 24

Mary rounded a bend and stopped near the yellow police tape. CAUTION was stamped on the side repeatedly, as if the persistent warning would stop someone from entering the area. An oversized, blue tarp covered an area inside the overturned truck. With the roadway blocked, if Mary wanted to continue without walking, she was going to have to drive around the wreck. Four-wheeler tracks showed her where to drive, so she decided to chance it.

Once clear of the wreck, Mary drove slowly, hoping Ray and Buck weren't almost to Supply by now.

A bridge lay ahead and on the opposite end sat four ATVs, empty of drivers. Mary pulled up beside the machines and hopped out. Snow was piling up on the four-wheelers. In an hour they would be nothing but white mounds.

No one was around. The only sound was the moaning wind and soft patter of snow.

No, there was another. A gurgling. Mary peered over the concrete bridge railing, the gurgling volume increased.

So did the sound of voices.

The dense tree canopy prevented Mary from seeing anyone, but she heard them. It was then she noticed the broken tree limbs and the haphazard way the brush was crushed and damaged. As though someone had made a path by simply driving through whatever lay in their way.

Northern.

Mary slid down the embankment on her butt. Negotiating the underbrush and broken limbs was taxing but she made it through and arrived creekside without fracturing an ankle. The front half of a red Honda Accord was upside down in the middle of the water, roof crushed, glass shattered, rear half missing.

Four men were moving down the creek, searching for clues.

"Hey," Mary called. They all whirled, surprised by her sudden appearance.

"Mary?" Buck called back. "What are you doing down here?"

"It's Cliff Gainey. He came back but he's almost dead."

The four men jogged to her.

"What happened?" Ray Eason asked.

Mary had met Ray on several occasions and was always slightly taken aback. He was an intimidating figure. Not by size or stature, but in demeanor. He was super nice, cordial, said "Thank you, ma'am" and "Yes, ma'am" and "Yes, sir" to everyone, held the door open, showed the utmost respect to all humans. But he carried an air of authority with him, a confidence of his place in the world. He was handsome in a rugged way, though his looks only accentuated his strength. The chiseled jaw line, the broad shoulders, the deep hazel eyes that never wavered from yours, the vice-grip handshake, the deeply tanned, leathery skin. The total package said, "I am man. I know who and what I am. I know my purpose. I am fulfilled and happy to be that man."

Mary swallowed. "He's mortally wounded. Looks like a bear attack. Deep claw marks, lots of damage. He needs to get to a hospital, but I don't think he would make it if it was right down the street."

"Did he say anything?" Buck asked.

"No, he's unconscious." *Probably dead by now.* But she couldn't vocalize it. *What does that mean for Tommy?*

Splashing through the freezing creek water, seemingly impervious to the temperature, Ray hunkered down at the creek bed. "Over here," he called.

Mary hissed when the water filled her boots as she high-stepped through the creek. She knelt next to Ray. A faint but visible paw imprint with claw marks at the end of each toe. "The bear was here, too?"

Buck, Brent, and Garrett searched the sides of the creek where the water was shallowest and discovered more tracks.

"Ray, there are tracks all along the creek bed," Buck said, following the pattern of the animal's movements. "But they seem erratic. Almost like the bear was searching for something. Then the tracks move toward the car, and then away. The snow is too thick to follow where they go."

Joining Buck beside Northern's car, Ray dropped to his knees, leaned over so close his nose almost touched the water. A shoe indentation in the mud with a bear print inches away. The tracks told the story. "She survived the crash, climbed the embankment to the road." Ray pointed to the top of the hill. "It followed."

"Where would she go?" Mary asked.

"Home."

"Does she have a gun?"

"Yes. It's missing from the glove compartment."

"Have you tried locating her phone?"

"We've tried Connect247, Locate My Phone, all of those, but we got nothing."

Mary's eyes climbed the embankment to the top. She imagined the car t-boning the guardrail, the cabin careening down the hill, smashing through the trees, bush, undergrowth, and flipping like a gymnast to land on its roof in the creek. She imagined Northern hanging from the seatbelt, unconscious or, at least, dazed. Maybe the bear was down near the creek, hunting for food. Northern was bleeding and the smell drew the bear to the car like a shark in water. Northern shot the bear and it retreated. She got loose from the seat belt and climbed the hill to the road. She would have headed in the direction of Eason Farms, no doubt about it. The eighteen-wheeler pile-up was also in that direction, just down the street.

"Could the eighteen-wheeler wreck have anything to do with this?" Mary asked.

Ray looked at her. "I'm not sure how."

"Just hear me out," Mary sighed. She needed to get back to Arlene. But she knew Cliff was dead. Cliff's lungs had rattled with every strained breath. Her father died from pancreatic cancer six years earlier. He, too, had succumbed quickly once the rattling began. While time was of the essence, there was a potential link in these occurrences. Mary felt a need to chase this line of thinking. "She climbs the hill, as you said. What does she do when she gets up there?"

"She would head home. Maybe try to flag down a passer-by. Unlikely at midnight. Traffic is few and far between out here."

"She goes left toward home. Just down the street in that direction are two burned husks of trucks that collided head on. But one truck is lying on its side. How could two trucks hit head-on if one is lying on its side?"

"One truck had already wrecked. The other truck rounded the bend and didn't see the wreck until it was too late to stop," Ray said, catching on. "Okay, but I still don't see a connection. They only found the two truck drivers."

"What if Northern was walking down the street and the truck that flipped came barreling along 211, didn't see her until it was too late? Overreacted, overcorrected, and lost control of the rig? Maybe Northern was disoriented from her wreck and was walking in the middle of the road. She would be injured, right? Whiplash, concussion, at the very least. Maybe more."

"So, the trucker hit her?"

"Not saying that. My point is, the police wouldn't have checked the ditches too closely if they thought the accident was a simple head-on collision."

Ray began clawing his way up the embankment.

"We already checked the ditches," Buck said, winded from the climb.

"We'll check again," Ray demanded. He shoveled snow off his machine.

Mary's feet were ice cubes, her body numb from the cold. When Arlene called, she'd run out the door without a jacket, leaving her kids home alone in the storm. The long-sleeved shirt she was wearing was damn near frozen to her skin. The heated cab of Tommy's truck was like heaven.

She followed Ray and Garrett, and prayed they were not about to find Northern's body in a ditch or hanging from a tree limb.

CHAPTER 25

Detective Bates powered on his computer. A few passwords later and he was inside the secure database which housed the police department's crime files. Five years ago, the small, underfunded department decided to join the twenty-first century and upload all case files to a secure server for convenience. It had been a game-changing decision. Detectives spent a lot of time looking at old cases when investigating new ones. No longer having to request files and wait for them to be pulled and delivered saved an immense amount of unforgiving time.

A few more clicks and a photo of Benji Ramirez appeared on the screen. A school picture, taken the previous year. He was a handsome kid. Big brown eyes, black hair buzzed short, nice smile with one lost tooth filling in. Benji was open to all the fascinations of the world, the promises of dreams coming true. But not for Benji. A hayride had doomed him. A stupid fucking hayride.

Bates shook his head in dismay and scrolled down. More photos of Benji rolled across the screen, but these were not the smiling, happy Benji. Crime scene photos. Washed in floodlights, the blood glistening. The torn and mangled flesh robbed of life. The innocence now morbidly unrecognizable. Chalk-white bones poked through the skin where the slices were deep. A close-up showed the severed head lying away from the body tucked in the hollow of a tree—a detail never made public. Benji was missing an eye but the one remaining was turned up as if watching his assailant to the final breath. The nose, ears, and lips were missing.

Bates shoved away from his desk and went to the restroom, splashed cold water into his burning eyes. Took a sip to dilute the sour acid in his stomach. After all he'd seen, this was the worst. What kind of world was this to allow such a tragedy?

Bates dried his face and returned to his seat. It took a moment to work up the courage, but finally he scrolled to the next page.

The autopsy report was nothing but a verbal summation of the photos. Lots of damage and blood loss. Over one hundred lacerations. Teeth bites. Missing organs. Decapitation. A body diagram accompanied the autopsy report. The page was scrawled with incoherent notes, arrows pointing to hundreds of injuries.

The next page was a description of the crime scene. Detectives Monroe and Finn typed out their accounts, observations, details, crime scene placement in relation to the property, notes covering the timeline of events. From Benji and his brother, Samuel, leaving home with their mother, Gloria, to the beginning of the hayride. From climbing aboard the trailer until the end of the ride, when the victim was discovered missing. Where he was found along the route. This helped narrow down the estimated time of attack to 8:54 p.m. The temperature was a crisp thirty-eight degrees with clear skies and a full moon. The official head count on the property was 269. That number included thirty-one staff members.

The next document began the hundreds of pages of witness interviews, with matching photos. Upon law enforcement arrival, the exits were sealed, and no one was allowed to leave. A nearby storage shed was used as a makeshift crime scene headquarters. Several event tents were promptly erected outside the shed where the 269 attendees were held. Space heaters were placed in each tent to keep everyone from freezing. One by one, the subdued witnesses were led inside the storage shed and questioned at length, photographed, driver's license—when applicable—scanned, then sent on their way. Minors were questioned with a guardian present.

Bates paused at the last witness testimony page and looked into the eyes of Benji's brother, Samuel. He was older than Benji but the resemblance was so close they could have been twins. The same eyes, the same dark hair, the same open face.

Bates clicked play on the witness testimony video accompanying Samuel's profile. A frightened boy appeared on the computer screen. His head hung, weighed down by the unfair burden of guilt. Beside him, Gloria Ramirez sat in stunned silence.

****

Detective Finn: "Can you tell us what happened?"

Samuel sniffled and raised his head. He wiped his nose and greasy strands of snot spread across his cheeks. His bloodshot eyes held so much hurt Bates had to look away for a moment.

"My mom brought us here for the hayride and haunted house. I've been wanting to come for years but she said we weren't old enough. I was excited when she agreed this year. So was"—Sam lowered his head again to hide a moan—"Benji."

Samuel slipped into an emotionless, monotoned recounting of the incident. It was the only way he could cope, the only way to keep the savage murder of his brother from driving him crazy.

"Did you check on Benji after the werewolf went away? Before you arrived at the haunted house?" Detective Monroe asked quietly.

This broke Sam. He doubled over into gut-racking sobs. For him, the catalyst of the whole damn thing. Samuel Ramirez would go to the grave convinced he was at fault for his brother's death.

After a long few minutes. "No, sir. I did not. The Bell twins and I were laughing and cracking jokes. I was distracted."

"Did you notice anything unusual while on the ride?" Detective Finn asked again, softly, empathetic. "Anything in the woods? Maybe something you dismissed in the moment as a costumed actor working the carnival. Did you perhaps see something in the darkness that you thought was nothing but another actor? Anything. Anything at all."

Samuel's pained expression showed dogged concentration as he recalled the hayride. "I didn't see anything. I looked at the woods. Hard. I knew they were coming at some point, but I didn't know when. I watched for them. I didn't see those three until they were almost on the trailer. It was so dark out there."

"Is there anything else you can think to add?" Detective Monroe asked.

"I wanna go home," Samuel answered. His head dropped on his mother's bosom and the video cut just as he began to wail.

****

Bates wiped his eyes. He was relieved to know his heart was not calloused to the suffering of man. Susan had told him of her concern for him. It had been the reason she wanted him to retire as soon as possible.

"I don't want you becoming desensitized to the things you see," she'd said one night in bed. He'd come home late after working a long shift investigating the murder of a nine-year-old at the hands of her neighbor. The investigation uncovered some startling facts in the victim's diary. The pedophile neighbor was trying to seduce the little girl. Offered her drugs and money. She decided enough was enough and—Bates alleged—told him she was telling her parents. Motive and means. A deadly combination.

What Susan saw in him that night he had not seen in himself. He had arrived home tired but not especially upset. Bothered, sure. The crime was disturbing. A child robbed of all those years of life. But a clinical detachment was necessary. It was necessary in all homicides. Otherwise, he'd eat a bullet.

"I'm not," he told her. "But I can't allow emotion to enter what I do because then I'll see what I want to see, and it will be clouded by judgment and anger."

"I understand," she whispered into the darkness as he crept into the bed. "You must remain objective. But that is a self-taught mentality. After a while it becomes a habit. In time, it becomes who you are, whether you mean for it to happen or not. Then one day, you walk onto a crime scene where you feel nothing. You will have trained yourself to be blind to humanity and see nothing but a victim. That will be the day you are lost. And I fear that day. I fear what you'll be here at home. Behind closed doors when there is no one but the two of us and the real you is on full display. When we're lying side by side as we are now, and I'm opening up to you, and I get nothing but you rolling over. I fear for that day."

Bates had kissed her forehead. "That'll never happen. I won't let it."

Deep down in the darkest portion of his heart, where thoughts and ideas and feelings not shared with anyone hid and flourished like poisonous mushrooms, he had known he was already heading in that direction. He was becoming trained to see the lifeless body as a police report, a coroner's report, the reason for his job, duty, mission, nothing more.

That night, long after Susan's breathing had settled into the easy rhythm of sleep, he made a pact not to lose empathy. Work hard to solve the crime and get a killer off the streets, but do it with compassion, always mindful the victim was once a living, breathing soul.

Times like today, when reading through a report such as this, with all the horrid details of a child killing and mutilation, he wished the clinical detachment would return. The photos, the coroner's report, the witness testimony, were almost too much for a single mind to handle.

A bustle of activity pulled Bates' attention from the computer screen. A handful of uniforms hustled down the hall toward the rear parking lot where patrol cars were parked. Over the police scanner came Linda's voice. "Got a ten-sixty-five with a ten-sixty-one at Duffer Brother's Bank. Be advised, ten-sixty-four."

Translation: Report of armed robbery and homicide, crime in progress.

Bates signed for one of the spare cruisers and hurried into the violent weather while slipping into his still-wet parka. The department had covered the parking lot in salt, so the cruisers were not snowed in. Fortunately, the house mechanics had wrapped a few cruisers and a few patrol cars with covers in case of an emergency. He snatched the cover off and threw it in the trunk. The tires were bare of chains, but Bates wasn't surprised. Snow was such a rarity on the North Carolina coast the department had never purchased any. The budget was tight enough already.

It was slow going on the side roads but once he was on Main the salt brine kept the road clear of accumulation. He turned into the unsalted parking lot of the Duffer Brother's Bank and the tires spun across the ice.

Six patrol cars, lights flashing and sirens blaring, surrounded the entrance of the building. The officers leaned across the snow-blanketed hoods with pistols pointing at the bank.

Standing behind the storefront doors was a ski-masked assailant with a gun pressed to a woman's head.

CHAPTER 26

John Munson awakened from a chest-rattling cough. A knocking throb behind his temples was the first thing he noticed. Every heartbeat was like the racking of a pump-action shotgun. He winced as the light sliced his vision in half. He untied himself from a blanket and noticed the second discomfort; the bedroom was like a deep freezer.

"What the hell?" He groaned and winced again. Even his voice ground against his brains like a cheese grater. An uneasy tide of nausea sloshed against his throat, but he swallowed it back. He grabbed a two-day-old, half-empty can of beer from the nightstand and downed the remaining contents. It tasted like sweaty pig ass, but it helped clear the gritty film of bile from his tongue. At least it was room temperature, which was to say, cold.

A hazy flashback from last night hit him and he wrangled the covers to be sure she wasn't in bed with him. Whoever *she* was.

John vaguely remembered being at a bar in Holden Beach, shooting pool and knocking back shots. She was hanging around, flirting with him. He flirted back. He had some blow and asked if she wanted a taste. She agreed and followed him to his truck. Turned out she'd never partaken of the substance. Shit had her crazy with paranoia. He took her for a midnight stroll on the beach, hoping the chilly night air would clear her head. She pulled him down against a dune and unbuttoned his pants, let her freezing fingers roam inside. A few dark figures came walking toward them. John tugged her out of the sand and helped her to his truck.

The memories got splotchy after that, the alcohol and blow settling in. The mystery girl fumbled around in his pants while he was driving, and he thought he was going to get lucky but she passed out. He had to slam on brakes at a light and inertia dumped her in the floorboard. He laughed about that for twenty minutes. And then...

And then what? Where did I take her?

Everything was blurred from that point on. Hopefully, she went home.

John rose from the filthy bed sheets and shivered as he wobbled around the room, picking through the dirty clothes on the dresser and the dirtier clothes on the floor to piece together an outfit. He tugged a sweat-stained John Deere cap over his greasy brown hair and dropped an old thrift store jacket over his shoulders as he stepped outside.

The flimsy storm door scraped across a growing mound of snow on his porch and shoveled several inches out of the way. The wind whipped at his legs and back like a leather strap. John ducked his head down into the collar of the jacket and dug his already freezing hands into the pockets.

He shuffled over to his beat-up, faded-blue '89 Ford Ranger. It burned more oil than gas, had a bad power steering pump, and the clutch was acting up, but it took him from point A to point B, so that was a much-needed positive. He swiped a dusting of snow off the driver-side window and peered inside. The cab was full of trash but devoid of a female. A flood of relief washed over him, and his headache eased a bit. Recollecting where he dropped her off was a distant hope, but at least she wasn't here.

John limped around the trailer to the tired HVAC unit. The trailer was thirty years old, and the unit was original. Multiple repairmen had warned he was living on borrowed time. The parts were worn and rusted, the wiring frayed, the coils leaking, the heating element was shot, the condenser whined when it powered on, and the fan squeaked.

John was down in funds. His bank account was empty. So empty, in fact, the bank closed the account. His job at the fencing company was on life support due to his drinking and lack of dependability. The only reason he still had a job was because he was damn good at it. When he went to work anyway.

His boss, Kevin Teller, warned him every time he was a no-show the end was near, his patience was onion-paper thin. John continued to push the issue and Kevin continued to threaten. Eventually, Kevin would stop giving ultimatums.

And what will I do then? John wondered as he stared at the dead, rusting, metal box. *I've been fencing since I was a teenager.*

Fencing was his first job and for some odd reason, he liked it. Maybe it was the solitude, the outdoors, the monotony, the application of muscle and determination to the post-hole digger against the earth. Whatever arcane psychological bullshit someone wanted to use to describe his enjoyment of physical labor. John went to work, calloused hands on the handles, and excavated the North Carolina soil one pressure-treated post at a time.

He'd decided to go against his parents' wishes and not attend college. He was saving money for equipment to open his own fencing company. They weren't happy about the decision but accepted that it was his life, and only he could live it.

A single night changed the projection of his future. That's all it took.

Although he was not attending UNC-Wilmington, his girlfriend at the time, Kourtney Wilkins, was a student, and a member of the Kappa Sigma sorority. At a Halloween costume party, a fraternity brother got handsy with Kourtney and John laid the guy out. Other fraternity brothers jumped John and a mass brawl ensued. John and Kourtney finally snuck away from the madness and headed to John's house in Shallotte.

John had been drinking all night; Jell-O shots, whiskey shots, beer. He even took a couple hits from a joint in the bathroom. Driving home was a bad idea. Driving home in the rain was a worse idea. His Mustang GT hydroplaned and plummeted down a ditch, t-boning a tree. John awakened from agony-filled confusion to find Kourtney crushed under the passenger side door. She was awake and alert, but in an immense amount of pain. She was having trouble breathing, bones broken. She begged him to free her. John unbuckled and tried to lift the metal from her body, but it refused to give an inch. He was unaware of gas leaking. Rain was pouring through the busted windshield, Kourtney was crying, his mind a knotted mess, and in all the chaos and debilitating fear he never smelled the gas. A *whoosh* burst from around the crumpled hood. The heat was immediate and terrifying.

Kourtney lost it, screaming, and begging.

John yanked on the door and pushed and shook with all his might, all the fear, all the love for Kourtney, everything he had, and the door rose from her ever so slightly. The flames licked the dashboard until the plastic melted, moved up to the headliner which was like fat lighter. The roof of the car became a fire-breathing dragon hovering above them. John's hair caught fire; his arm hair singed. He tried to ignore the smells around him—the plastics, the metals, the rubbers, the fabrics, the human hair and flesh.

He placed his feet on the door, kicking out, arm muscles bulging. The shaking car must have caused a flaming droplet to fall from the dragon's nostril because Kourtney suddenly burst into flames. He fell back in horror as she shrieked. She twisted and clawed, her fractured feet pounding beneath the twisted metal. More pendants of fire rained down on him and he was on fire. He scurried out of the driver's side window and rolled on the wet grass. The night was suddenly a blooming ball of napalm as the car exploded. The shrieking stopped and the acrid smoke that filled the air smelled like scorched pot roast, the skin and fat of her body sizzling and popping like bacon.

John was charged with manslaughter and served five years in jail. When he returned home, he found the community less than welcoming. A few death threats were left in his mailbox. Employment was hard to find. The little money he made at odd jobs was used to buy booze. It was the only thing that muffled the screams. Harder drugs helped silence the torment further. Hooked on alcohol and drugs, John was turned down, job after job.

Kevin Teller gave him an opportunity. An opportunity to set his life right. An opportunity to make amends in the judgmental minds of the community. An opportunity to silence the screams.

In the twelve years he'd worked for Kevin, all John had done was let him down. It was as if he were cursed.

The silent HVAC unit sitting before him, snow piling up on its rusted top one thousand flakes at a time, was another sign of that curse.

John shook his head. The coffee can in the kitchen held about fifteen dollars and his wallet was probably down to nothing after last night's escapade. A repairman would want forty bucks just to look at the miserable piece of crap. *If* one was even willing to come out in this weather.

"I can't afford this right now," he said to the wind. He knuckled one bloodshot eye and sucked up a leaking wad of mucus.

Though not mechanically inclined, John's only choice was to repair the unit himself. YouTube was a treasure trove for DIYers. Of course, the cable company had cut his Wi-Fi earlier in the year for nonpayment and tax-time was still several months away. He was at the mercy of the cellular signal gods, who were always less than willing to answer his prayers.

Without much of a choice—and not liking the chances of success—John stomped across the backyard to the shop. His eyes wandered over to the dog pen in hopes that Domino was smart enough to stay inside his ramshackle doghouse. No sign of the mutt.

Good boy.

John stepped inside the ten-by-ten woodshed and rummaged around in the dark. The shed was a slight source of pride. A small tribe of Hispanics built it in the spring, and it still smelled of new lumber. The shop housed a lawnmower that would not crank no matter how many times he pulled and cussed the handle, a weed eater that leaked the petrol mixture faster than he could fill the tank, and a slew of mostly useless shit that needed to be hauled to the dump.

The one thing still worth keeping was his dad's toolbox.

John latched the lid and snatched it off the worktable. He trudged back across the yard, his head lowered. Another glance back at Domino's doghouse told him his pal was still hiding. Surprising, though, Domino hadn't stuck his head out and said hello; he always barked in excitement when John walked outside.

John dropped the toolbox in the snow beside the unit and opened the lid. He took another look back at Domino's pen. Not a peep.

Something's not right.

He made long, striding steps to Domino's pen. "Here boy," he called with a whistle. Nothing moved.

Now he knew something was wrong. He opened the door and stepped inside the pen. Hunkered down, he inspected the dog house. Empty. John inspected the fence and found a hole dug under the chain link at the back.

"Son-of-a-bitch," John hissed. "Fucking dog."

The snowfall obscured any potential tracks, so John walked in the direction Domino's digging pointed. John entered the woods, stepping over broken limbs and trees, weeds, underbrush, and the various bric-a-brac of forest floor. John whistled but got no return response.

Domino was a mixed-breed mutt. Two years earlier, Domino had mysteriously shown up on John's doorstep. It was a hot and humid Saturday morning, and John had been nursing a hangover. He heard a whimpering at the door. Lying on the porch, tongue flapping and breathing heavy, was Domino. Poor thing was in foul shape. Fur coat riddled with cuts and abrasions, fleas and ticks. The wounds were fresh, gnats and flies crawling in the blood. The dog whined again and stood on its wobbly legs. His spine and ribs were visible. John had shooed dogs away before, but with Domino he was never struck with the urge. He felt something for the animal. The dog was having a hard life. Beat down, starving to death, maimed by attackers. Still, he stood. Still, he moved forward. John related.

John brought the dog inside and spent months tending to his wounds, feeding him, showing him love, and discovered he enjoyed coming home to someone who was happy to see him. Every damn time.

The mutt had a white coat with black dots, leading to the epiphany he looked like a domino. And that became his name.

Until today, Domino had never dug out of the pen.

John's only guess was something interesting got his attention. Which was odd. The dog had been living out here for more than a year. He was used to seeing deer, rabbits, other stray animals, and all manner of wood creatures. What could have caused him to dig out?

John stopped and squinted. He leaned forward, squinted harder. A lump in the snow, could be nothing but a tree stump. Except the snow was stained red and tree stumps don't bleed. John hurried forward and pushed the crimson ice away from what lay beneath, silently praying it was a deer.

The prayer was a waste of time and energy. The bloody, torn carcass, was Domino.

CHAPTER 27

Ron and Sarah Grace stayed at the kitchen table after Jason and Skeeter had been dismissed to Jason's bedroom.

"What do we do?" Sarah Grace asked Ron.

He shook his head and sipped from his coffee cup. "I'm not sure. Seems to me we need to call everyone we know in Green Swamp."

"We only know a few people, Ron. We like it out here because we don't know a bunch of people."

"Then we call the one's we do know. Maybe they know someone else and so on and so forth. That way most of Green Swamp can be warned."

"And tell them what?"

"That's what I'm mulling over now," he sighed. "Maybe we just tell them we saw something last night out the window. Maybe a bear, maybe a wolf—*just* a wolf mind you—and I found some tracks this morning. They need to be careful and keep the doors locked and stay inside."

"That would take care of tonight, but what about moving forward? The snowstorm alone will keep everyone inside tonight but it's supposed to start moving away in the morning. What happens then?"

"If Jason's right about this werewolf, then we have a little time after this full moon cycle runs its course. Find out who it is. Hunt for it. Everyone just needs to hunker down and stay inside tonight."

Sarah Grace opened her laptop and searched for information about full moon cycles. "Full moons last for three days. But this full moon phase will be historic."

"How so?"

"Tonight's full moon will be a winter solstice Full Blood Super Moon. The first in recorded history."

"Yeah, I remember hearing that on the news yesterday. Astronomers are salivating."

"If there are any stargazers in North Carolina, they won't see anything but clouds and snow."

Ron's brow furrowed. "I wonder if this moon phase has any special effects on the werewolf."

"Like what?"

Ron shrugged. "I don't know. Does it make it stronger, hungrier, more dangerous?"

"Based on what Jason said, it's all those things already." Sarah Grace couldn't believe she was discussing werewolves. As a kid, she and her friends had sleepovers and told scary stories in the dark of her bedroom. In a circle, a single dim flashlight pointed at the storyteller's chin, face shadowed like Mr. Meaner, each recounting a tale of murder and mayhem. Always a little frightening, always a lot of fun. Screaming and giggling about it. Knowing boogeymen and monsters were make-believe. Knowing when they went to bed, a hand with sharp claws would not reach from under the bed, grab an ankle, and drag one of them into salivating jaws with rows of razor-sharp teeth.

Discovering monsters—not of the human variety—actually existed was a lot to chew on. But better than being chewed on.

Sarah Grace dialed John Munson's number on the cordless home phone. He lived half a mile down from them. Ron sometimes hired John for projects around the house; he'd installed the fence in the backyard and proved handy enough for Ron to use him to build a screened-in porch on the front of the house. John was a drinker and unstable at work, but he was overall a decent guy who just needed to get his life together. A weird tone answered her call before a woman's voice announced the number dialed was no longer in service.

"John's home phone is disconnected," Sarah Grace said, hanging up. "Again."

"You try his cell?"

"Doing it now," she answered as her fingers punched in the number. Another female voice announced the call could not be completed as dialed. "Either his cell is off or the signal is so poor it won't ring out." Sarah Grace punched in the number to Arlene Gainey.

This time the phone rang. But no one answered.

"No answer at Arlene's house."

"Why would Arlene or Cliff not answer?"

"Maybe they decided to leave before the storm. Headed west for a few days."

"Maybe."

Sarah Grace ignored the growing pit in her stomach and dialed the number to Edward's house. Edward Delaney had been a widow now for six years. His wife, Clare, had unexpectedly passed in her sleep. Edward found her when he awoke to start the morning coffee.

Sarah Grace had taken to watching over him, delivering homemade lemonade each week, making sure he was eating and taking care of himself. She worried about him, alone in that house, but he refused to move to a retirement facility.

Sarah Grace stood in the kitchen with the phone to her ear and the ringing of Edward's line tinkling around her eardrum like ice in a lemonade glass, while Ron watched her from the table. She had a moment of skin-prickling fear that Edward wouldn't answer, and they would hurry to his house and find that this monster had visited that sweet old man. She pinched her eyes closed as the disturbing image blossomed in her mind like a spring rose, the thorns dripping—

"Hello?"

Sarah Grace almost jumped. "Edward? It's Sarah Grace."

"Hey, sweetie," he said, groggy. He always called her sweetie, and, for some reason, she loved it. His gentle voice and kind nature always reminded Sarah Grace of her own grandfather, who died when she was a little girl. Maybe that was why she had been drawn to caring for Edward.

"Are you okay?"

"Yeah, just dozed off watching Clint Eastwood. When you get to my age, naps come and go as they please."

"Listen, you know me, you know I'm not a delusional person, right?"

Edward paused for a second. She heard the worn-out springs of his favorite recliner chime as he sat up from his fully-reclined position. "Of course."

"Okay, then please just hear me out and don't think I'm mad."

"I could never."

"I'm not sure how to say this other than to just say it. I believe that we, the people of Green Swamp, are in danger. It's a long story and you probably wouldn't believe me anyway, but it's important—life and death important—that you heed what I'm saying."

"And what are you saying?"

"You need to stay inside tonight. Lock your doors, your windows, and stay inside. Do not go out no matter what. Can you do that for me? Please."

"I wasn't planning on going anywhere in this weather anyway, so, yes, I can."

"Edward, it's more than just going somewhere. It's going outside at all. And it's keeping your doors locked. And—"

"Yes?"

"And have your guns locked and loaded in the room with you."

"Sarah Grace, I trust you as much as I ever trusted anyone, and for that reason I'll do as you ask. But I sure would love to know what has you so spooked? Your voice is trembling."

He was right. She wasn't aware of it while speaking but she felt the tremor in her wired-tight body. The phone in her hand clicked against her earring.

"I hope I am wrong. I have never wanted to be so wrong in my life. But if I'm not wrong, you will know tomorrow why I am so spooked."

"Are you and Ron taking your own advice? You have Jason to protect now."

"We will be unloading the gun safe shortly." She looked at Ron and nodded, who sighed with relief. "Also, Edward, could you do me another favor and call everyone you know? We don't know many people out here so I don't have numbers."

"Yeah, I can do that. Not sure what I'll tell 'em but I'll make up something."

"Thank you for hearing me. If you need anything, and I mean anything, call us immediately."

"Same. And we'll discuss this further tomorrow."

"Yes sir," she said, and hung up.

Sarah Grace leaned back on the corner and exhaled slowly. She checked the clock on the stove and saw that it was already 3:58. She hadn't made lunch, but no one seemed hungry.

I'm certainly not.

She told Edward to stay inside and keep the doors locked. But was that enough? If this animal was as strong and dangerous as Jason said, would anything beyond a bank vault keep it out?

And loaded weapons. Were bullets sufficient in stopping this creature? She remembered watching *Silver Bullet* with Ron this past Halloween on AMC and Gary Busey had a special silver bullet manufactured to kill the werewolf. Was that real or myth? If real, they were in trouble. There were no silver bullets in the gun safe and time was too short and the weather too bad to get to a gunsmith to make one. Gary used a silver necklace to make the bullet. Sarah Grace was not a jewelry hound. There was not an ounce of real silver in her jewelry box.

The questions were endless while the answers were abysmally few and far between.

But...

"We need to watch any videos we can find on werewolves. If we don't have silver bullets, can normal bullets kill it?"

"If not, we're in trouble." Ron headed for the gun safe.

CHAPTER 28

Mary pulled to a stop in the Gainey's driveway. She hopped out of the warm truck cabin and jogged up the steps. Too much was happening too fast. Lives hung in the balance, most importantly—to her, at least—Tommy's. They'd found no sign of Northern. The blanket of snow and raucous wind made it difficult to locate anything. She could be down in a ditch, covered with ten inches of snow. It would be hard for the naked eye to detect when thousands of anomalies were everywhere.

Mary opened the front door after knocking snow off her boots and stepped inside. The house was cold and dark. *Power's out.*

"Arlene? I'm back. Let's try to get him loaded in my truck and—" Mary gasped. She backpedaled until she hit the kitchen wall.

"What's wrong?" Ray long stepped through the small living room and into the kitchen. "Oh, my god."

On the linoleum floor lay Cliff, Arlene, and Misty in a spreading pool of blood. Misty's soft, white fur was dyed red, and she was cradled in one of Arlene's arms while the other arm lay draped over Cliff. Arlene was leaning against Cliff's body, her head tilted down to her shoulder, eyes closed. Both sets of wrists were sliced open and blood oozed from the cuts, the flesh white and pale. Mary knew they were dead without checking for a pulse.

Above Cliff's head on the hunter-green kitchen wall, Arlene had scrawled a message in her own blood.

All dead. Beware the beast.

Mary's fear for Tommy had already weakened her. The sight of these lovely people in a dead heap—this beautiful couple, like parents to her and Tommy and grandparents to Conner and Maribeth; Misty wrapped with care in Arlene's arm—further applied alarming pressure to a crumbling and derelict barrier.

Something in her chest cracked open. Like the sternum fractured, and everything inside spilled to the floor. Then Ray was there, carrying her to the couch, sitting next to her. Waited for her to regain her composure.

All the times Arlene had been there for her. Always willing to help. As constant as the sun. As true as the North Star. Mary had never imagined Arlene dying. She was the type of person to live forever. Life without Arlene was incomprehensible.

Mary wiped her eyes and sat up. She had lost time. Seconds? Minutes?

Ray was no longer by her side. Voices in the kitchen pulled her unwillingly toward them.

Mary felt their eyes on her. "Did someone call the police?"

"I tried, but the phone lines are down," Ray answered softly. "Probably a tree limb. None of our cell phones are getting a signal."

Mary tried to clear her raw throat. "What do we do now?"

Ray sighed and fiddled with his jacket. It was the first time Mary had ever seen doubt or question in him. "Mary, it may be a few days before someone can get out here to retrieve the bodies. Police will want to investigate. The bodies...the scene needs to be...preserved. I think we should open a few windows so it stays good and cold in here, lock the doors, and leave them until authorities can come."

Mary hated the idea of leaving them alone. It seemed inhumane. Like they were just slabs of beef hanging from a hook in a freezer. She wanted to argue against it. But Ray's point was valid and, under the circumstances, for the best. She nodded. "Okay."

"As for the message,"—Ray shook his head— "damned if I know. Buck and I were out there and didn't see anything but a mutilated—" Ray's voice trailed off.

"A mutilated what?" Mary asked.

"A deer," Buck answered.

"A deer," Ray repeated, and looked at Buck. "Looked like a bear had gotten hold of it. Could that be the beast she referred to in the message?"

"Maybe it's rabid," Buck said, his face a question mark.

"Can bears have rabies?" Garrett asked.

Ray shook his head. "It's extremely rare. But not impossible."

"What's happening in Green Swamp is unheard of," Buck said. "Maybe a crazed rabid bear fits the puzzle."

"I want to know where my husband is. If he's"—she swallowed back a fresh string of barbed wire—"dead, where's his body?"

"Well, bears—" Buck started, but a rigid glare from Ray stopped him from elaborating further. He looked at his feet and edited the wording. "Yeah, some bears are mean."

Ray closed his eyes and stood silent. Once again, Mary saw the doubt and fear in his countenance, his stance. Ray was strong but this ordeal with Northern was chopping him in half, one lethal stroke at a time.

Ray swiped a calloused thumb across his eyelids before opening them. "At this point, I have no idea what to think. But these incidents can't be coincidental. They're connected, they have to be. The how and why are the real questions. We answer those and maybe we get to the bottom of this mess."

"What's our next move?" Buck asked.

Ray stared at the floor. "If we look at this from ten thousand feet, we have five people missing and two dead truckers within fifteen miles of one another. Putting myself in Northern's shoes, hurt and concussed and on the run, I would try to find shelter, a place to hole up."

"Where would she hide?" Mary said.

Ray could only think of one place. "Pop Munerlyn's."

"Does Northern know about Pop's house?" Mary asked, thinking it would be a hard run from 211 to that tumbledown dwelling.

"She knows the swamp as well as anyone."

Buck said, "It's getting dark, so we better get to it."

"I'm going to check on my kids," Mary said. Conner and Maribeth would be devastated. Their father? Their god-grandparents? Misty? *How am I going to tell them?* "I'll meet you guys there."

The walk to her truck, the short drive from the Gainey's driveway to her own, and the entry into her home was surreal. It felt like she was floating. Maribeth appeared in the kitchen as Mary stared at the floor, trying to decide to tell them now or wait.

"Mom?" Maribeth said and stepped in front of her. "You okay?"

Her tiny voice was a jolt of electricity, shocking Mary awake.

"Yeah," she lied. *Keep it together, Mary.* "I'm okay. Um, listen, I've got to run an errand. I need you to keep an eye out for your brother. Okay? Keep the doors locked, stay in your rooms. I'll be back in a little while. Can you do that for me?"

"Yeah, sure." Maribeth was leaving the kitchen but stopped. "Mommy, the lights went out and then came back on."

"I know, sweetie. The generator is why they came back on. You'll be fine."

"Okay." She paused. "When is Daddy coming home? I'm scared of the storm."

Sometimes lies were necessary. For protection. If Tommy was dead, Conner and Maribeth would learn of it soon enough. But not yet. Despite the message written on the wall of the Gainey's kitchen, Mary held steadfast to the hope that Tommy was alive. Foolish? Perhaps. But it was all she had.

"Soon, baby. Soon."

Still, Maribeth waited, her arms around Grady, her teddy bear since birth. Mary loved Maribeth's inquisitive nature, her desire to know everything, but today she just wanted her daughter to do as she was told.

"What else, Maribeth?"

"Do you think Willow is okay?" Maribeth looked at her feet, her body twisting side to side. Her nervous tick. "It's really cold outside. She might freeze to death."

In all the confusion of the day, Mary hadn't returned to the horse stall as promised. "She's fine, baby. But I'll go check on her before I leave. Go to your room. I'll be back shortly."

Maribeth seemed to have more questions in waiting. Mary held her breath, patiently hoping she would hold them until later. Maribeth nodded and disappeared down the hallway. Hurrying out the door, Mary slipped into a heavy parka with a hoodie. She drove out to the small horse barn, parked. Willow had been a gift to Maribeth last year. Just a filly, as was Maribeth. The two would grow up together, train together, learn from one another. Maribeth loved Willow so much she asked Tommy and Mary to let the horse sleep in her room.

With that not being feasible, Maribeth spent as much time in the barn with Willow as possible. Feeding her. Watering her. Cleaning her stall. Mary was proud of her daughter. She was learning work ethic, what it meant to care for another living, breathing creature. Lessons that would reward her in life.

Mary stepped inside the barn and all thoughts of life lessons were sheared clean from her mind. Willow's stall door was closed. Beneath it, a congealed puddle of blood.

Mary's feet were cased in concrete. A single step was impossible. She closed her eyes, and, for the hundredth time that day, inhaled and exhaled to calm her over-exuberant heart.

This can't be happening.

She opened her eyes. The blood remained. It was happening.

One blocky foot rose, followed by the next. The effort was incredible. When Mary reached the stall, she cautiously leaned forward to peer inside, over the bottom half of the Dutch door. To stop the visual assault, she slapped her hands over her face, eyes, and nose.

Willow lay on her side. Her stomach was torn open, the insides emptied. Gooey organ chunks littered the stable floor, stuck to straws of hay. Her eyes were open, but all she saw was the limitless pastures of what lay beyond.

CHAPTER 29

Heavy snowfall made observing the events inside the bank difficult. Bates squinted and adjusted the lenses on his binoculars.

The masked gunman had moved the woman back behind the teller counter to hide. Another masked man held a gun on a guy in a suit and tie and pushed him to the back. Heading to the vault? A body lay face down next to a table used to fill out deposit slips.

Someone tapped Bates on his snow-crusted shoulder. "Bates, we have Heather Tice on the phone. The assistant manager."

Bates took the phone. "Heather, this is Detective Bates. I know there's a lot going on, but we need some information out here."

Heather was a panicked mess, as to be expected. "Yes, yes...uh...no problem. Wh-what do you need to know?"

"Who's inside the bank? The man and woman?"

"The man is Jarrod Howery, the bank manager. The woman should be Leigh Letson. She is the office manager. They sent everyone home when the first snowflakes started falling. They said they would close. Why are they still there?" The last question seemed more for herself than anyone else. Bates ignored it.

"There's also a male in the lobby, looks like he's wearing a uniform. Do you have a security guard?"

Heather moaned. "That's Johnson Lawrence. Is he okay?"

He needed her focused on the living. "I saw a masked individual take Jarrod to the back. Is that where the bank vault is located?"

"Yes. Ar-are th-they going to...die?" Heather almost squealed.

"No, we will get them out of there. Now listen and stay with me. The backdoor of the building—"

"The employee entrance."

"Yes, there's a badge reader. I need a badge. And the door appears to have a key override. I need a key as well, just in case. In fact, I need a grand master key if you have it. Can I send a deputy to retrieve yours?"

"Yes, I have a grand master and a badge, but I'm not supposed to give either to anyone. It's grounds for termination."

"Heather, this is life or death. You will not be terminated."

Heather paused, then said, "You're right. Okay. Yes, send someone. I would drive but the snow."

"I'm going to give the phone back to the officer who will drive over to you, okay?"

"Yes."

"Here is Officer Beckwith. Thanks for your help."

Bates handed the phone back to the officer and the uniform slid from the parking lot en-route to Heather's residence.

Bates placed the binoculars back to his eyes. Everyone was hidden from sight.

Another tap on the shoulder. "Yeah," he said, still scanning the bank.

"Gunman wants to speak to you," another officer said, holding a phone to him.

Bates snatched it and answered, keeping the binoculars on the building. "This is Detective Bates of the Shallotte Police Department. Who am I speaking with?"

"You can call me Martin."

Bates noted the vernacular intonations. Calm voice. Not hurried, frantic, or nervous. Indicative of experience in volatile situations. Military? Law enforcement? "Okay, Martin. What can I do for you?"

"You can tell everyone to go home. The storm is bad and only getting worse."

"I'm afraid I can't do that," Bates said.

"Aw. That's a shame. Maybe I should start harming the hostages. See if that loosens you up."

"You only have two hostages. If you kill them, you lose your leverage."

"I said *harm* them, detective. Not *kill* them. Listening is part of being good at your job, is it not?"

Shit! Bates changed the subject. "Can I get you guys some food? Beverages?"

"That's very kind of you to offer, but no thanks. We will not be here long."

"What's going on here, Martin? Surely you don't want to hurt anyone else. You've murdered one already. These people are innocent. At least let Leigh go." Bates used her name to gain sympathy. "She's a mother, a wife, someone's sister, daughter. Doing that shows you have a conscience and will go a long way toward helping you get what you want."

"Detective Bates, you have no idea what I want."

The line went dead.

Bates handed the phone back to the officer, and said, "Cut power to the building. And get someone from SWAT here." Then another thought. "Officer, erect a tent over my car so I don't get snowed in trying to talk to this asshole."

"Yes sir. And SWAT is en-route, sir. Coming from Wilmington. May be a few hours before they arrive."

What a mess. A bank robbery in the middle of a blizzard.

Bates checked his smartwatch: 4:05 p.m. This was shaping up to be a FUBAR situation that would stretch into the night. Dusk was already setting in, the claustrophobic cloud cover sitting low in the sky, squeezing the last remnants of light from the day.

Bates was not a hostage negotiator. He'd taken courses and received professional instruction on the subject but was far from an expert. It was a skill that required nurturing through practice. It was a talent of feel, a sixth sense, a third eye, an ambidextrous brain working both sides of the problem at once, intuition, instinct. He possessed most of those traits, but was not practiced in the art. He'd already made the mistake of elevating the gunman's threat from harm to death, planting a seed that, hopefully, would not be cultivated. If he made another error, the damage may be irreparable.

The best course of action was to end this quickly, circumvent hours of negotiating, thus eliminating himself from potential trip hazards. Doing so without harming the hostages was the real trick.

An idea teased him. It was not smart. But it would remove the hostages from harm's way.

Bates just needed an angle.

CHAPTER 30

The lights went out just as Ron sat at the kitchen table to clean the guns. Sarah Grace called Jason and Skeeter into the living room, while he set out lanterns and candles. Jason and Skeeter took a seat on the couch, watching Sarah Grace start a fire.

Ron spread a grease-stained gun cloth across the table. A battery-powered LED lantern illuminated the gun-cleaning tools: a bore brush, cleaning swab, patches, a cleaning jag, a bore snake, cleaning rods, solvent, and a luster cloth. The guns hadn't been shot in months, and though the gun safe held two dehumidifiers, cleaning and inspecting the weapons was mandatory. Especially if all this nonsense proved to be true. The last thing Ron wanted was to pull a trigger and get no response.

Ron paused to watch Sarah Grace light the logs stacked in the fireplace. As the wood ignited and the fire discovered food and oxygen, the living room livened in dancing orange, yellow, and red demons. The flames lit Jason's face. He stared intently at the fireplace, but Ron could see the boy was lost in thought.

Ron unholstered a pistol and began disassembling the weapon. Sarah Grace joined him at the kitchen table and began cleaning another handgun.

Processing everything they'd learned today was proving a monumental task. His eyes darted back and forth, to and from the silent, still form of Jason. The boy was different now—supernatural, otherworldly, and, admittedly, a bit scary.

Seeing dead people, communicating with them. The thought of Granddaddy still being here was fucking creepy. Was he there all the time? Sometimes? And when? Surely not when he and Sarah Grace were...

Ron shook his head. *Damnation.* He plunged a brush down the gun barrel throat as if to choke it.

"You okay?" Sarah Grace whispered. Her eyes read him like the words were printed on his forehead.

The shame of guilt washed over him. Ron nodded slowly but stopped mid-motion. No need to be dishonest. She was his wife. Whatever battle he was fighting internally, need not be fought alone. He moved his head side to side.

Sarah Grace checked on Jason and Skeeter over her shoulder, then came back to him. "I know," she whispered, "it's a lot. But I have always believed in ghosts. My grandmother used to call them 'haints.' She said haints were people who weren't ready to move on to their final destination. Maybe they were killed violently and wanted revenge. Maybe they died suddenly and couldn't accept their own death. Maybe they just want to hang on to life, even if it's from somewhere other than here. Whatever the case, grandma believed that the living could learn lessons from the dead. Unfortunately, most of us only catch glimpses of them. But there are a few Jason's out there. He has a *gift*. It's not a curse." Her eyes went hard. "And he is *not* a monster."

"*I know he's not a monster,*" Ron hissed back, watching an inert Jason over her shoulder. "I just don't see him like before, and I feel shitty about it. He's a terrific kid. But, he can talk to the dead. Granddaddy is still in this house. *Our* house. Where we sleep and live. That's a mind fuck if there ever was one. How do I rationalize that? How do I see him as the same sweet, traumatized little boy who needs to be loved and protected? Seems like he's protecting us."

"Jason is still the same boy he was yesterday and the day before. We just know more about him now. Ron, you've got to get a handle on this. He's our son now, and he needs us. We need him."

Ron nodded as he wiped the gun with an oiled rag. "I'm working on it." *Am I really?*

This was more about the strangeness of Jason's gift, and the unsettling idea of a dead man's ghost roaming this house, than an attempt to reconcile Ron's old feelings for Jason with the new ones.

Sarah Grace was right about one thing: he was going to have to get a handle on this. Jason was his son, no matter what. It was a responsibility he had accepted wholeheartedly, warts and all.

"Hey, Jason," Ron called.

Jason's head jerked around as if startled. "Yes?"

"Wanna learn how to clean a gun?"

Sarah Grace caught Ron's eye and smiled.

"Um, yeah, sure," Jason said, rising from the recliner. "Can Skeeter help?"

"Absolutely."

Sarah Grace instructed Skeeter on how to disassemble a rifle, while Ron showed Jason a handgun. Ron found himself settling into the normal rhythm he and Jason shared without forcing the issue. It just happened. Jason was a quick study in everything Ron showed him. It was always amazing to watch. Gun cleaning was no different. The boy seemed to have a knack for picking up things, as some people do. Ron had never been that way. He required lots of practice to master a skill. Jason was observant and his mind remembered and catalogued the lesson and movements, the deftness of fingers, the importance of light, the rules of gunsmithing.

Ron marveled at how smooth and calm Jason was at the task. How his tongue protruded from his lips as he worked the brush and rags, the whispered comments he made to the gun parts as he replaced them in their rightful spots. To the spring: "There you go." To the safety pin: "Slide right there."

Jason finished assembling the weapon, then checked the operation like a pro. He placed it on the table and said, "Done."

Ron ruffled his hair. "Great job. Are you ready for a bigger challenge?"

"Bring it on."

Ron grabbed the handle of a gun case on the floor by the table and laid it on its side. He raised the lid and pulled out an assault rifle.

"Woah," Jason said, eyes bugged out. "That is awesome. What is it?"

"AR-15. Semi-automatic assault rifle." Ron showed him the 30-round magazine sparkling with .223 Remington's.

"Bet that's fun to shoot," Jason said in awe.

"A blast. I wanted you to get experience with handguns and shotguns before we moved to this. But what the hell, let's go knock off a few rounds. Just so you know what to expect if it comes down to you needing to use this for some reason."

"Outside?"

"Yep. Outside. We can go out to the overhang on the side of the shed so we're not standing in the snow fall. You can blast away a mag. What do you say?"

Jason smiled. "I say heck yeah."

"Great. Get your hunting boots and a jacket. Skeeter, I have something for you to wear. You can fire off a mag as well."

Skeeter followed Jason.

Once they were gone, Sarah Grace said, "Thank you. I appreciate you trying."

"Like you said, we need him, and he needs us." Ron frowned. "What are we going to do with Skeeter when this is over? He and Jason act like long-lost brothers. We can't send him back to eating out of a dumpster and living in that shack."

Sarah Grace smiled warmly. "Yeah, I've already thought about that. What if we buy one of those little woodsheds and finish the inside? Put it in the backyard and run electricity to it. He could take showers inside the house but have his own space out there.

"And maybe you could help him find a job. Earn a little money."

Sarah Grace's compassion for other humans was inspiring. It was the reason they chose Jason. A newborn was available for adoption, but when she heard Jason's story, she said he was the one. She wanted to not just adopt, but to adopt a child who needed love and care. Jason had been the perfect candidate. Most people would choose the baby. The child without the emotional baggage of watching both parents die in front of him. Most people dodged that sort of challenge.

Not Sarah Grace. She wanted to love the sadness and heartbreak out of him.

Ron placed the AR-15 back in the case and latched the clasps. "Hopefully, we'll survive this nightmare to see that come true."

CHAPTER 31

Inside the gun cabinet were a lifetime of weapons, accumulated through hand-me-downs, buying, and trading. Rifles, shotguns, handguns. The prize of the collection being the Colt Army Model 1860. Handed down to his father by his grandfather. Edward once researched the gun's serial numbers online and discovered the gun had a bloody history. And was worth a bloody fortune.

Used in the battle of Little Bighorn in 1876, records were sketchy on which soldier had been issued the weapon, but it *was* distributed to the 7th Calvary, led by none other than the legendary George Custer. After killing the entire calvary, the Sioux and Cheyenne tribes confiscated all the weapons, as well as anything of value: clothing, coins, watches, food, maps.

The ownership of the gun became cloudy until Edward's grandfather, Toy Ray, bought it at an auction in North Dakota in 1927. The gun was handed down to Edward's father, Roland, by Edward's mother, after Toy Ray died of an aneurysm. Roland gifted the gun to his son, Edward, for his twenty-first birthday, and Edward had held it ever since.

Being a six-shooter, it wasn't the best choice for home defense. Here was a SIG P226 in 9x19mm Parabellum with a double-stacked fifteen round clip. Beside it lay a Glock 34 in 9x19mm with a seventeen-round magazine. Standing in the corner was a Remington pump-action twelve-gauge shotgun. Guns perfect for warding off a home invader.

However, the Colt Army Model 1860 *was* perfect for the purpose of taking one's life. He reached in the cabinet and pulled the hefty, silver-plated revolver out of its custom-made leather holster. The holster had been an anniversary gift from Clare fifteen years ago. The weight felt right and the grip fit his hand like an old catcher's mitt.

Edward returned to the living room and placed the Colt on the end table next to his recliner. He poked the glowing logs in the fireplace, stirred up some flames, then tossed two more fresh logs on top. Warmth and light. His knees popped like the wood in the hearth as he settled into his favorite chair. He used an eating tray to reload his hardwood cherry pipe with Black Tooth Tobacco. He sucked the flame into the tobacco and inhaled the warm, sweet smoke. The TV screen reflected the smoke off its black, glossy surface.

I sure wish the power was on. I could use some Clint Eastwood or John Wayne right now.

The phones were also down. No calls to Green Swampers to pass along Sarah Grace's warning.

Sarah Grace's warning.

She was sound of mind and pure of heart, but the vague, cryptic foreboding was puzzling. Why was she warning residents of this peaceful farm community of danger? What led her to believe they were in danger?

Sarah Grace suspected trouble. Edward *knew* they were in trouble.

He side-eyed the Colt and was caught by a severe pang of doubt. Was he doing the right thing? Was this the best way to handle the situation? Were there other options? And, the damning bone of contention, what would Sarah Grace think of him and his decision, sound reasoning or no?

Sarah Grace had become like a daughter, and it hurt him deeply to think what this would do to her. She had come into his life at the perfect time. The melancholy loneliness had been like a vampire, slowly sucking him dry. Once Clare passed, his desire to continue forward was dampened considerably. But he unearthed a resolve in the weeks following her death he thought impossible on the day of her funeral. Maybe it was self-preservation. Maybe it was stubbornness. Maybe it was the fear of dying. Regardless, he had continued breathing and his heart had continued beating. The sun dutifully rose in the eastern sky each morning and tired, old Edward dutifully rose with it.

Meeting Sarah Grace replenished that leaking well of hope. She was an old soul—as he had told her on several occasions—and the two of them always found interesting topics to talk about. She was fascinated by his childhood years, and the hours spent reminiscing were the highlight of Edward's days.

He always looked forward to Sarah Grace's visits and relished them after she was gone more than she would ever know.

The questions that would follow the discovery of his body were unavoidable. The answers would be shocking. That was life. Like his father used to say, "It be like that sometimes."

He checked the oval, battery-powered clock on the wall above the silent television and saw that it was now 4:15 p.m. The day was getting long in the tooth. Shadows scampered into the corners to eagerly await the imposing nightfall.

Edward puffed on the pipe, the sweet smoke curling around the cavity of his mouth before being dragged down his throat. He could feel the barrel of the pistol watching and waiting. Wondering if he had the guts to chew on lead.

An honorable question. He was wondering the same.

CHAPTER 32

John Munson sat at the kitchen table, a heavy blanket wrapped around his body. He had returned inside the trailer to find the power off. This was, of course, after he'd taken care of Domino.

He tried to dig a grave, but the ground was frozen. He wrapped the poor dog in a black plastic yard bag, duct taped the bag to ensure no smells of decay escaped and attracted the attention of hungry animals, and placed Domino back inside the kennel. He even pushed snow inside the door to keep the carcass cold and build a protective barrier. He would bury Domino after the storm passed and the ground thawed.

"Now what?" he asked the cold, darkening trailer with its brown paneled walls, and dreary thrift mart furniture. *Go down to the Elliot's. They have a fireplace. And food.*

He frowned at imposing. Ron and Sarah Grace were fantastic people who had helped him in the past and would do so now, but—

But what?

He wasn't exactly sure, except he wasn't one to impose. Which was bull; he had imposed on people plenty.

John wrestled with these conflicting thoughts for a few minutes before deciding to drive down and visit for a while. Warm up in front of the fire. Maybe talk to Ron about coming to work for him. Explain his desire to straighten up and get his life in order.

Decision made, John pulled the heavy, still damp, coat off the counter where he had spread it out to dry—*Good luck without heat*—and slipped his arms inside. Zipped it to his neck. The house key dropped in his pocket as he pulled the door shut.

John concentrated on the plan moving forward. Ask Ron for a job. Make it his life's mission to show up every day, on time. No more drinking, no more drugs. He was going back to his early school days of *Just Say No.*

And if Ron says no? This was the negative voice. The side of him still traumatized from the wreck. The narrator of his damnation, the author of his nightmares. Since that hellish, life-changing night, the negative voice had commanded his life and all decisions made. It was his weakness to reject that destructive force.

No more.

"I'll go back to work for Kenny," he said to the howling wind. "I'll save my money and buy some equipment, then go into business for myself. Just watch and see."

The negative voice laughed.

It was just the wind, he thought, without conviction.

The storm increased in power and pitch, buffeting him almost off his feet, oblivious to his threats.

He climbed inside the truck, pushed the clutch to the floor, and turned the key. The engine clicked but wouldn't turn over. Then he noticed the headlight switch was on. Which meant the battery was dead. He placed his forehead on the cold steering wheel and waited for the rage to pass. The anger was quickly replaced by a melancholy defeat that made his feet lethargic during his walk.

The Swamp carried an eeriness he had never seen before. No traffic on the road, none of the residents out and about. The noise of the world dampened to mute. No sounds but the uncanny call of the wind. Like the moans of the dying, and the whispers of the dead.

John picked up the pace.

The Elliot's home was a modest Craftsman, but it was quite beautiful. The tapered columns, the peaked eaves, the Craftsman touches around the windows and doors, all lent the house a slight fairy tale quality. John stepped onto the screened-in front porch just as a burst of gunshots sounded from behind the house.

He ducked low and waddled around toward the back to see who was shooting.

"It's Ron, Jason, and Skeeter shooting an AR-15," Sarah Grace called from the kitchen window.

"Skeeter? Dumpster diver Skeeter?" John found Sarah Grace's pretty face framed between the curtains.

"Yes, that Skeeter." The look on John's face must have been comical because Sarah Grace smiled. "It's a long story," she said. "I'm actually glad you're here. We need to talk. But first, why don't you check on the boys? I'm sure Ron'll let you pop off a few, too."

John was not interested in remaining in this brutal cold, but he went anyway. Beneath the huge oak tree beside the Elliot's house, little snow covered the bare dirt. A swing hung on one branch—a massive thing that splintered into sharp, wooden fingers—and the wind pushed it back and forth as he passed.

The backyard was expansive and open. At the rear of the yard, near the wood line, sat a metal building, fairly new and styled to resemble the house. Beside Ron's new shop was an old weather-worn shed that Vernon built in the sixties. The rusted tin roof was almost black from oxidation. Ron mentioned replacing the roof last year and had asked John if he was interested in doing it. The answer had been yes, but

Ron never got in touch with him about it. Maybe in the spring next year.

On the side of the shed was a lean-to, which housed Ron's tractor, and next to the tractor stood Ron, Jason, and Skeeter. Ron was showing Jason a large, intimidating gun.

Skeeter saw John appear through the fog of snow and pointed. "John's here."

Ron turned. "John," he said in surprise. "You walk down here?"

John quickened his step to get under the cover of the lean-to. "Yeah. My power is out and I have no heat. And my truck wouldn't start. Was freezing already. Now I'm really freezing."

"We'll go inside in a minute and you can thaw out in front of the fire. I'm letting Jason shoot this AR."

"In this weather?"

Ron looked at him with an unreadable expression. He said, "We all have to be ready. Including Jason. So yeah, in this weather."

John wasn't about to ask what Ron meant, so he shivered while Ron instructed Jason on how to hold the gun, release the safety, sight it, and pull the trigger. The blast was brilliant and clipped. Jason took his time and followed Ron's direction. The kid was young, but he took to shooting naturally. Once the magazine was empty, Ron showed him how to remove the empty and replace it with a fresh, fully loaded clip. Ron then repeated the lesson to Skeeter, who was a little clumsy to start but got the gist after a few tries. John was still wondering how Skeeter came to be here.

"You wanna try?" Ron asked him once Skeeter finished.

"Nah, I'm good," John answered. He just wanted to go inside.

"Okay. Let's head in. I pulled out my Coleman stove for Sarah Grace, so there should be a hot pot of coffee ready."

John moaned at the thought.

He followed the others to the screened-in porch, shrugged out of his jacket. Hung it next to the other wet jackets on a hook screwed to an old piece of driftwood that had been upcycled to make a coat rack. His wet boots were dropped next to a cluster of other boots. The central heat was off but inside the house was toasty. John sighed as the warmth sent tingling sensations through his fingers, face, and feet. The aromatic scent of coffee was so heavenly that he shuddered.

The daylight was winding down quickly now. Though some shadows remained, the house was well lit with candles, oil lanterns, and battery-powered lamps.

John moved through the living room and into the kitchen and settled at the table across from Ron. Jason and Skeeter grabbed a battery-powered lantern and headed down a hallway.

"Here you go," Sarah Grace placed a steaming cup of coffee on the table. On the side of the white cup, in a cheery font, **SMILE**. A yellow smiley face with red hearts for eyes grinned back at him.

"Thank you," he said, and took a sip. The heat arrived in his belly and blossomed like an atomic bomb. "Sarah Grace, this is the best coffee I've ever had." And it was the truth.

"Thanks. Just Golden Son Dark Roast with some hazelnut creamer. Killer combo."

John noticed Ron staring at him and dropped his eyes to the mocha-colored liquid steaming in his cup.

"You look like shit, John." Ron's voice was deep and cutting.

The words stung like a slap, even if he knew they were true. He hadn't looked in the mirror this morning but his burning, itchy eyes were the tell-tale signs of bloodshot. This afternoon's beer had done nothing to wash away the residue of last night's coke or the film of George Dickel from his tongue. He hadn't shaved in…what?…six or seven days? He took a shower yesterday morning, but none since. His clothes were dirty because the washing machine belt broke three weeks earlier and rather than buy a new belt, he spent the money on booze and blow. The smell of musty sweat hung around him like an aura.

"Yeah, I know," John mustered. He continued to stare at the coffee, unable to face Ron's disappointment.

"I thought you were quitting that shit."

This was not how this little excursion was supposed to go, John thought. He said, "I did for about a month. But the nightmares came back."

Sarah Grace sat beside him. "John, there are therapists who can help with that."

"Therapy costs money. And I don't have any."

"But you have money to buy beer and coke. I'll never understand how addicts and alcoholics are too broke to buy food and other necessities but are not too broke to buy drugs and alcohol."

John's face flushed, anger rushed up his neck. He rose to leave but Sarah Grace placed her hand on his arm and firmly pulled him back down.

"We're trying to help you, John. Because we care. That's all. But we won't say anything else about it, okay? We're glad you're here because there are things happening that we need to talk about." Sarah Grace looked to Ron, silently pleading with him to drop the third degree.

Ron seemed unwilling, his face flat and expressionless. But he sighed, "Whatever. Kill yourself if you want. Sarah Grace's right. We have bigger problems."

John again felt the sting of humiliation. Disappointing these two people hurt him somewhere deep inside. He took a sip of coffee to help swallow the jagged shard of broken pride lodged at the back of his throat, and asked, "What bigger problems?"

CHAPTER 33

Beckwith handed Bates the keys to the bank and a badge to the reader on the back door. Bates stared at the objects as if they were live grenades. In truth, he knew them to be exactly that. If anyone breached the building, the robbers would kill the hostages, and this whole situation would blow up in his face. As a last resort that might be necessary, but he had to exhaust all possibilities before making that call.

He was still chewing on an idea. Not a smart one. But it accomplished several goals at once: the release of the hostages and the displacement of this stand-off from the bank. Bates wanted these guys in the open, where he could see them.

Problem? He was putting himself in harm's way.

Better me than them, he thought. *Look at the bright side. If this goes south, as it probably will, I'll get to see Susan sooner rather than later.*

A knuckle tapped on the driver-side glass. Bate's rolled down the window and a mobile phone was placed in his hand.

"Bates."

"Ready to listen, detective?"

"All ears."

"Good. I want your men off the property. Once that is done, I want a four-wheel drive truck—with snow chains—parked at the back door. When we are a safe distance away and I see no tail, I will release the hostages.”

“That's a no go.”

“Oh really? Okay.” The phone shuffled and Bates heard the bank robber's muffled voice tell his partner, “Shoot him in the leg.”

“No, wait, wait,” Bates shouted in the phone.

“Yes, detective?”

“Take me. Take me and let the hostages go. I can bring my radio so we can hear what the police are doing. I can help you get where you want to go. Then you can let me go. Or not. My wife died from brain cancer a month ago. I honestly don't care if I live or die. So take me and I will have everyone clear the property and have a truck here in thirty minutes.”

“Hmmm. That's an interesting proposition.”

“It's a win-win. I want the hostages safe and you want to get away. We both get what we want.”

Bates held his breath and silently prayed for the guy to take the deal.

A plan was forming. Probably wouldn't work, but it was worth a try.

“Suppose I'm interested. How do we do it?”

“Release the woman now. Once she's free, I remove everyone from the site but me and my patrol car. Once the truck arrives, I will get behind the wheel, pull it behind the bank. One of you come out and get in the front seat with me. Gun pointed at me, of course. Then you let the man go and climb in the back seat. I take you where you wanna go. Once there, we go our separate ways. However you want that to mean.”

“That's a nice plan. How do I know the truck's not bugged?”

"You don't. But it doesn't matter. As long as I'm in the truck, no one will do anything. You keep your directions to me limited and simple. No one will know where we're going."

A long pause. "Alright, detective. I will let the woman go. But hear me and hear me well. If I feel the slightest sliver of doubt or deceit about this plan, I will begin removing vital parts of this man's anatomy, piece by bloody piece. Got it?"

"Got it. Send her out."

Bates jumped out of his car and silently rejoiced when a woman in her mid-thirties, light brown, shoulder-length hair, wearing a beige trench coat, black slacks, and beige leather boots, unlocked the front storefront doors and step out. She stopped and stood still, and Bates almost fainted with panic at the thought this was a trick. But the shadow of a figure moving behind her told him she was being used as a human shield while one of them relocked the door.

Leigh Letson took a quick peek behind her, then carefully walked toward a deputy who made his way to her. As soon as Leigh touched the deputy, she broke down.

The officer led her to Bates's car and sat her in the backseat. "Wait here for a few minutes. Detective Bates wants to speak with you. I'll get you a hot chocolate."

Bates finished relaying his plans to Officer Beckwith. The policeman nodded, affirmed his understanding of the orders, climbed in his own car, and barked orders for everyone to move back.

Deputies put their guns away, climbed in their patrol car, and left the bank parking lot. Bates eased inside the warmth of his cruiser and twisted in the seat to face Leigh. Mascara streaked down her cheeks like war paint. Her eyes held the I-Can't-Believe-That-Just-Happened emptiness of shock. Her hands trembled in her lap.

"Leigh? I'm Detective Bates. Can you hear me?"

After a silent moment, Leigh's wet eyes slowly lifted from her lap to meet his. She nodded. "Yes." The words rode a tremor like a pot-holed street.

"Are you hurt?"

She swallowed. "No. I'm fine," she said silently. Then added: "Physically, anyway."

"Can you answer a few questions for me? Then you can ride to the station. We need to get an official statement before you go home. Unless you need to go to the hospital."

"Okay. And, no, I don't need to go to the hospital."

"Can you tell me anything about these guys? And I don't mean physical descriptions. I'll get that soon enough. I mean what they talked about. Did they say anything about their plans? Where do they want to go? Names? Details like that."

"The one holding me was called Martin and the guy holding Jarrod was Roger. I don't think that's their real names. They joked about it."

"Joked how?"

"Um, Roger called Martin 'lethal weapon' and Martin laughed. My husband loves action movies and I've sat through those *Lethal Weapon* movies a hundred times. The main characters are Martin Riggs and Roger Murtaugh. Martin and Roger."

Ah. Made sense from an ass backwards point of view. "Anything else?"

"They whispered a lot, but I heard them mumbling about Wilmington. I may be wrong, but I think I heard 'boat.'"

The pieces of the plan are falling into place, Bates thought with encouragement. "Okay, Leigh. You have been great. Thanks for answering these questions. Officer Kincade will take you to the station now."

Officer Kincade opened her door and Leigh followed him to his car. Promptly, they left the parking lot and disappeared in the fog of snow. The parking lot was now empty except for him.

The phone on his console rang. "Yes?"

"Nice work. So far so good. Keep doing what you're doing and this will be over soon enough."

"The truck will be here shortly."

"Good." The line went dead.

Bates called Beckwith. "Yes, sir?"

"They may have a boat in Wilmington. Call Wilmington P.D. and put them to checking all boat landings. Maybe put a man at each one. Just in case my plan fails. Otherwise, move forward with what we talked about. 17 toward Wilmington. Ten-four?"

"Ten-four, sir. Good luck."

Bates disconnected and exhaled a lung-full of nervousness and doubt.

No turning back now.

The cell in his hand chimed again. Chief Lowell. Rare and troublesome. This was not good news.

CHAPTER 34

The world had dimmed to a wretched gray. As night blended with the pallid snow, the Swamp illuminated to an eerie, muted tinge. The brilliance of the snow cast a glow that allowed them to muddle through the powder without flashlights, though each of them were equipped with one.

Buck had been to Pop's house before, long after Pop died. He had sat on the front porch and eaten Vienna sausages while listening to the echoing bray of Redbones and Blueticks from miles away as the hound dogs tracked a deer. As long as the hounds were not headed in his direction, he could relax and munch on snacks. If suddenly the trumpeting turned toward him, the action would pump up a considerable notch.

The house suffered significant deterioration. It had been dilapidated then. Now it was positively leaning onto itself. The roof sagged, the walls tilted, the porch canted, as though a chasm was opening beneath it, the ground ready to swallow it whole. Decayed boards, crumbling shingles, rusty nails, broken memories, lost souls, and all.

Green Swamp had decided to reclaim as much of the place as possible while it waited for complete ruination. Vegetation and bushes pushed from the outside while vines blanketed the walls. The house was a condemnable death trap. Buck couldn't imagine anyone taking refuge inside.

His memories of Pop were spotty, having mostly known him during childhood. What Buck remembered most was how feisty Pop had been for such a small man. Pop ran about five-foot-five and pegged out at 130 pounds. Once you met him, you learned his attitude far exceeded his height and weight. He had been all piss and vinegar, hellbent to appear ten feet tall and bulletproof. He was not intimidated by anyone. One had to be scared to feel intimidated and Pop feared nothing, which was the reason his death was unexpected and shocking.

Pop had wrapped his lips around the greasy barrel of a twelve-gauge and choked on what it fed him. The gruesome nature of the death had been enhanced by the fact it had occurred during the summer months and Pop was not discovered for over a week. Cliff Gainey had been the unfortunate soul to find the body. He admitted the scene visited him frequently in his sleep. He told his breakfast buddies that in those nightmares, Pop's body leaned forward in the rocking chair, raised his left hand, and pointed into the woods. A coagulated moan blew bloody bubbles from his exposed esophagus as his bony finger—chewed to the nub—prodded at the air, insisting Cliff seek out the object of the dead man's attention.

"What's he pointing at?" Linwood Williams had asked one rainy Saturday morning down at Bob's Grill, while gumming a piece of bacon.

"Don't know." Cliff shrugged. "I wake up before I see it. Every damn time."

Buck tried to imagine finding something like that, then dreaming about it every night, a constant reminder of the ugliness of life. He stood in the yard while a flashlight strobed around inside that old house and shivered. Not from the cold—though it was cold enough to freeze the tits off a warthog—but from the thought of such a possibility.

Speculation about Pop's decision to end his own life had run rampant through the swamp for years following the discovery of his body. Pop was too mean to go gentle into the great beyond. If you called eating a buckshot burrito gentle. Pop was a Vietnam vet, and a surviving P.O.W. from that war. He was a fighter, an arguer, a flip-off-the-world scrapper who, like a mongrel, refused to break even as life bent him in half. The notion that one random day this wiry man said, "Fuck it" was flimsy. No one else truly bought it, either. They sifted through the excuses for years and grew tired of the endless speculation. A logical reason was settled upon and little by little the incident was pushed to the back of the community's memory until it was mostly forgotten.

Inside the battered house, Ray's flashlight beam danced like a spotlight. A sudden crash was all it took to get everyone out of the weather and on the porch.

Buck stabbed the beam of his flashlight inside the doorway. "Ray? Are you okay? Ray?"

"Damn it to hell," Ray answered, his voice muffled and dusty. "I fell through the floor. I'm in the basement. I think I broke my goddamn ankle."

"Hang on," Buck called. He paused as headlights pulled to a stop in front of the house. Mary.

Buck knew something was wrong immediately. Her body language said so. "What happened?"

"Willow's dead," Mary said. She looked tired. "Something tore her open."

This bear sure is making the rounds. "Sorry, Mary. I know how much Maribeth loved that horse."

Mary nodded, looked around. "Where's Ray?"

"He fell through the floor. I'm going to help him out. Be right back."

He searched around for a set of stairs, mindful of each step he took. He noticed a seam in the faded brown wall paneling in the hallway. Buck slipped his fingers in the gap and tugged. The door screeched open. Mossy blankets of spiderwebs stretched and broke apart as the door revealed a tight set of stairs leading down. He chopped through the webs with the flashlight as he descended. The treads creaked but held until he reached the earthen floor.

The space was cramped and busting with piles of crap everywhere. A wooden worktable was loaded with the bric-a-brac of a backwoods mechanic. Buck's flashlight skimmed across file cabinets, a wooden chest with a hasp and lock on it, engine parts, a set of bald tires with the wire exposed, a broken mirror, and finally landed on Ray. He sat on the dirty, oil-stained floor. His pants leg was up as he self-examined his ankle.

"Wanna take the boot off?" Buck asked.

"No. The boot will help hold the break in place. It's swollen so bad I'll have to cut the boot off anyway."

"Any sign of Northern or Tommy?" Buck asked, knowing the answer.

"Not a thing." Ray grimaced. "They weren't here. At least not in the house."

"What now?"

"Now you help me to my truck. Then I'm running home to get the walking boot my farmhand Oscar used a few years ago after he stepped in an old post-hole and busted his ankle. After that, I'm coming back out."

"Ray, Tommy is my best friend. He's like a brother to me. I want to find him, but being out here in a snowstorm in the dark is liable to get someone killed. Maybe we should wait until daybreak. The storm will be moving away by then and we'll be able to see what we're looking for."

Ray emphatically shook his head. "That's ten hours of waiting I'm incapable of doing. The rest of you are certainly welcome to go home and wait till daybreak and there'll be no hard feelings, but I will not stop until I find my daughter. If I have to go all night. If I have to fight a fucking bear with my hands, I'm not calling it. My baby is out here somewhere, and I'm gonna find her or die trying."

"Yeah, I've heard you Easons got guts for miles and the determination of a platoon of blood-thirsty soldiers," Buck sighed. "If you're not stopping, I'm not stopping."

"This is going to be a long, painful night, son. I feel it."

Buck nodded grimly. He felt it, too.

CHAPTER 35

The bedroom was darkening, the battery-powered lantern growing brighter. The room was also substantially chillier than the kitchen and living room. Not freezing cold. Yet. He would return to the living room in a minute; he just needed some alone time.

Jason plopped down on his bed. Skeeter sat in his gaming chair in the corner. The chair had been his first birthday present with his new family, and he loved it. It had built-in speakers in the headrest and a subwoofer in the seat. Games were a lot more fun to play when sitting in that home theater.

Addie, lying at the foot of the bed, barked and scrambled to the floor, the hair on her back rising. She stared at the corner, and barked again.

A buzz scratched his bones. Like hair clippers on a chalkboard. The sensation always preceded a visit. Mr. Vernon wanted to talk.

"Skeeter?" Jason said, his eyes on a shadowed corner of his room. Mr. Vernon hid there, his chalk-white eyes barely visible in the gloom. "This is going to be weird. Don't wig on me okay? Everything is all right."

Skeeter leaned forward in his chair but said nothing.

"Down," Jason said to Addie, pointing at the floor. She hesitated but finally settled on her stomach, a low growl creeping from her throat.

Mr. Vernon stepped from the shadows and the eager wash from the lantern illuminated the ghostly figure. Jason noticed the light seemed to shine through Vernon, caressing the darkness behind him.

Mr. Vernon was a haggard man, rail-thin and pasty. The old brown suit he wore was disheveled and soggy with body-fluid excretion. His head was bald, save a few wispy white strands of pillow-bent hair. His arms hung limp at each side and Jason couldn't help but notice his hands were huge, his fingers long and slender. A nose-wrinkling odor drifted from the man, like cheap cologne, sweat, and vinegar.

Jason had spoken to Mr. Vernon twice before. The first had been a short conversation. Mr. Vernon had expressed his displeasure with them living in his house, and his disdain for the upgrades and renovations. The second visit had been a little more cordial. The dead man offered some insight about Ron. Some comical treats. Some embarrassing truths—like the Alfalfa joke.

This visit carried the air of foreboding. Menace wafted from the ghost.

"Mr. Vernon?" Jason said. The apparition stared at him with blank, milky eyes. "Are you here for a reason?"

Mr. Vernon appeared as if he had nothing to say. But then: "The night approaches." His voice was slow and brittle, the words like rotten wood which crumbled from his lips. "Hiding within, lurking in wait, is the end."

"We know about the monster. We know it may come tonight."

Mr. Vernon's leathery eyebrows furrowed—crackling like a paper bag—and his face darkened. "It *will* come. Brings the slaughter. Buckets of blood. Vengeance will have its way."

Vengeance? Jason wondered. But said, "What do I need to do to be prepared?" He glanced over at Skeeter to see how he was handling this. Found him engaged. He could only hear one side of the conversation, but he was getting the gist.

Mr. Vernon sighed, his lifeless eyes moving to the ceiling. "No preparation exists. It harbors the stink of death on its breath. It cannot be stopped. You must flee."

"The storm is too bad for us to leave. We have to stay and fight."

"Then you will die. Your restless, tormented soul will roam the cold black with me. Forever." Mr. Vernon returned to the corner and disappeared as the shadows devoured him.

Jason looked at Skeeter. "We're in trouble," he said, and hurried to the kitchen.

Ron, Sarah Grace, and John were deep in conversation but hushed when he burst in the room.

"What's wrong, honey?" Sarah Grace asked.

"I just spoke to Mr. Vernon. He says we can't win this fight. He says we will all die."

John's expression twisted into bafflement and confusion.

"How does he know we can't win?" Ron asked, ignoring John. "Without a doubt?"

Jason fumbled with an answer to the question, because if there was one thing he had learned about ghosts, it was this: "They are never wrong."

Ron mulled this over. "What was his advice?"

"We should leave. Before nightfall."

"That's impossible. It's five after five. Sunset has started. And, oh yeah, by the way, we have a storm dumping more snow on top of the two feet already on the ground. I have one four-wheeler and a truck with no snow chains. We'd be lucky if we made it five miles. We have no choice but to hunker down, wait it out. If it comes, we'll be ready."

Jason nodded. But they were doomed.

It would be nice if his father made another appearance. Maybe provided more guidance and clarity.

Jason wondered again for the hundredth time what his dad meant when he said the dumpster diver was their only hope.

Surely, it's not what I think.

CHAPTER 36

The wind picked up as the temperature dropped another degree. Weather forecasts called for lows to drop in the low single digits by morning. One of the coldest winter storms in North Carolina history, and Bates was stuck in the middle of a bank robbery and hostage situation.

Susan had loved winter. She had asked Santa for snow on Christmas Day every year. Her mother, Diane, said Susan had made the same request every year since she was old enough to make such requests.

Each year, the two of them vacationed in Colorado to ski. After the doctors discovered the brain tumor, Susan asked for one final trip before her strength waned and the cancer sunk its vampiric tendrils deeper in her body. Crested Butte, Colorado was her requested destination, and it was the best trip they had ever taken. The mood on the flight out had been melancholy, but once they stepped off the shuttle from the airport, the heavy-heartedness evaporated. The majestic humps of snow-capped mountains rising into the fluffy clouds and the crisp fresh air had done for them what no medicine ever could.

A week of skiing, eating, live bands, and adult beverages had been good for their souls. And, as it turned out, a much-needed rest to prepare them for what was to come. The sleepless nights, the sickness, the incontinence, the weight loss, the hair loss, the tireless battle to win the fight at all costs, the remorse of a losing war, the shattering news of defeat, and, finally, the overwhelming grief when her final breath was drawn.

When Bates saw snow, he saw Susan, and his heart wept.

A tap on his window yanked him from those traumatic memories. He thumbed a wet spot from the corner of his eye, and pressed the power window button, pushing snow and ice from the glass. The wind whistled through the two-inch crack as an officer looked in at him. "Yeah?"

"Truck's here and ready, sir," the officer yelled over the wind. The collar of his thick jacket was turned up and his head tucked down in the protective cover like a turtle. "Full tank of gas and some snow chains. Had to really hunt for those damn things."

"Thanks. Give me a sec then take this cruiser back to the station."

"Yes, sir." The officer added. "Chief Lowell is on the way, sir. He is steaming mad you declined his call. Told me to not let you leave."

"Is that what you're going to do?" Bates asked. He declined the chief's call knowing the man would order him to stand down.

The officer smiled. "I turned my back and you hopped in the truck. Nothing I could do about it. Better make it quick though. Chief's ETA is less than ten."

As the window slid back into place, the phone on his lap rang. "Yeah?"

"I see the truck in the parking lot. Why are you not in it yet?"

"The truck just got here."

"Clocks-a-ticking. You have five minutes to be waiting on us at the back door." The line went dead.

Works for me, Bates thought. *In ten, I'll be fired.* He climbed out of the car and handed his Glock, badge, and cell phone to the officer.

Bates eased the vehicle behind the bank, leaned across the console, and opened the passenger-side front door. After a moment, the back door cracked open. A masked head poked out and searched the area. Satisfied everything was as promised, the robber ducked into the front seat of the truck, dropped a cloth bag between his feet. Behind him was Jarrod, the bank manager, his face white as a sheet, eyes wide and traumatized.

"Open the door," the second masked man said from behind Jarrod.

Jarrod, a cloth bag in one hand, opened the door, and was roughly shoved in, the second robber climbing in after him and slamming the door.

"Hey, what the—" Bates began to protest but the masked man in the front seat poked him in the chest with a Smith & Wesson.

"If I were you, detective, I would drive."

"This wasn't the deal. You have to let him go."

"I don't have to do jack shit. But you do. Now drive."

Bates looked back at the pale face of Jarrod, his lips trembling in fear, and said, "No. Not until you let him go."

The masked man laughed. "Okay, have it your way. Roger?"

Roger removed a six-inch knife from inside his jacket and deftly sliced it across the leg of Jarrod's blue dress pants. Jarrod screamed, jerked back in the seat, and clinched his leg as blood seeped from the wound.

Bates growled at the masked man. "You son-of-a-bitch."

"I told you to drive. Now, do you want to resist further? Roger is really good with a knife. He can carve his name in Jarrod's chest if you want."

The world flashed white. This was not how Bates imagined this going. Now an innocent man was in the line of fire. "Okay," he said in resignation, hands slapping the steering wheel. "I'll do it."

"That's a good boy," Martin said.

Bates slid the gear into drive and exited the bank parking lot, turning right. No signs of police activity existed but Bates knew they were back there, following at a distance. The heavy snowfall was beneficial in masking their movements. A plan—like the one he had in place—depended on many moving parts all working together. Bates liked the odds better when he was the only hostage. Now, with Jarrod in the equation, the plan would need a lot of luck sprinkled in to have a chance of success.

Main Street merged onto Highway 17. The road remained clear of accumulation, the salt brine doing its job. In the backseat, Jarrod whimpered.

"Can you put something on his leg?" Bates hissed.

Roger glared at Bates in the rear view. Bates held the gaze.

"Do it." Martin instructed.

Roger huffed but did as he was told. He cut the sleeve off Jarrod's suit coat and split it. He wrapped the wound on Jarrod's leg and tied a knot to hold it in place. Jarrod whistled a cuss word when the knot was cinched.

"So, what's the plan here?" Bates asked Martin.

Martin stared out the windshield as if he hadn't heard the question. Bates's eyes skirted across the rearview mirror and found Roger watching him intently.

Martin may be the mouthpiece of the two, but Roger will bear keeping an eye on, Bates thought. What did Bates see in Roger's eyes? Madness? He seemed volatile. Maybe he was someone always ready for action, the coil forever tense and ready to spring. *Or maybe he was not a fan of the hierarchy.*

Time was short and exploiting that potential weakness in the partnership may not come to fruition but it was worth noting. If—

"The plan," Martin finally answered, "is for you to drive to Wilmington. The roads should be good most of the way. You do that and do not try anything funny, you and Mr. Banker will be released unharmed."

"I'm supposed to believe that?"

"Doesn't matter what you believe."

Bates changed the subject. "Since it's nobody but just us girls, when did you come up with this plan? This snowstorm came out of nowhere. You're obviously using it to your advantage. This kind of operation would take time to scheme."

Martin laughed. "A detective until the end. Got to know all the answers to all the questions."

Bates waited. He was not actually expecting an answer and was rewarded with silence.

Several miles ahead lay the first phase of his plan. He could only hope all the items he requested were in place and ready. If not, he was going to have to see where this went in Wilmington. They would have the advantage then.

And the chances of getting out alive would be drastically reduced.

CHAPTER 37

The pipe glowed bright as Edward pulled on the tobacco, dimmed as he blew smoke from the corner of his mouth. The house was almost fully dark now. The only hint of light from the glowing coals in the fireplace and the bowl of his hardwood cherry.

In the silence, in the darkness, he waited.

This day was bound to come. He had known it his whole life. The sin deserved its penance. Wasn't that the reason Jesus was sacrificed? Atonement for sins?

Revenge always collected that which was owed, one way or the other.

Edward was young. Doing as he was told, following the guidance of his elders. But he knew it was wrong. Then, just as now. And that was enough.

In spite of the damnable act, he had lived a good life. Shouldn't be possible to commit such an atrocity and go on to find love and happiness, wallow at night in the arms of serenity. His serenity being the love of his life.

He met Clare in Holden Beach at the flea market. Edward was always attracted to antiques, even as a young man. A curiosity passed to him by his father. Also, a lover and collector of items most people called junk.

One antique store he liked to frequent back then was The Rusted Bucket, housed in said flea market. Items of every shape and size packed the shelves and lined the walls. Old magazines, mirrors, furniture, lamps, trinkets, toys. You name it, The Rusted Bucket probably had it jammed in some dusty corner.

In one such dusty corner, Edward came upon a prim girl attempting to remove a piece of art high on the wall above a junked-out shelf. He first noticed her legs. She was stretched so thin her dress rose to show a frowned-upon amount of thigh. Impossible to miss, for a boy in the prime of puberty.

Edward stepped in to give her a hand when her foot slipped, her elbows slammed into the shelving, and the whole damn contraption leaned over the girl like a coming landslide with intentions to bury her for all antiquing eternity. Edward saved the girl that day but paid the price for his chivalry. The shelf and all its contents landed on him instead. It took ten minutes to dig him out from the rubble.

During his claustrophobic burial beneath the mound of junk, the girl somehow convinced the owner of the shop that the display had just tipped over—so dangerously overloaded with clutter were those shelves—and the brave young man underneath all the clutter was a hero. Saved her from certain death. By the time Edward was freed, the owner was handing out free gifts to Edward's father and the girl's mother in hopes to avoid a lawsuit. The poor, distraught fellow even submitted handwritten IOUs to the families for a free gift on a return visit.

The girl introduced herself to Edward outside the shop. Clare. It was love at first sight. At least, for Edward. Took some time for Clare. She liked him a lot, and told him such. But she was a practical girl with dreams and aspirations of being an actress. She was moving to Hollywood in a few years. Gonna be famous. Light up the silver screen.

No sense tangling with a local farm boy who was going nowhere in a hurry. Hero or no.

The yearly fair did her in. He invited her, she said yes. They met in the parking lot and walked in holding hands. He was shocked she allowed him such a brazen act. She smiled like she enjoyed it. Cotton candy, kiddie rides, and, finally, the Ferris wheel. A jalopy, if he'd ever seen one. The operator was missing as many fingers as teeth. They boarded the death trap and hung on for dear life. The wheel stopped spinning halfway through the first rotation, which left them at the top. Clare gripped his arm, her pink, polished fingernails latched onto his tanned bicep, and trembled with fear. It took a little coaxing to prize her eyelids open. Once Clare allowed herself a peak, she gasped in surprise. The view was spectacular. The sky was tinted a deep purple and glazed in burnt orange as the sun sank to its knees in the west. A light breeze carried the Atlantic Ocean on its salty breath. Lights from the fair below sparkled and flared, the sounds of laughter carried to the stars.

As Edward—Eddie, she called him—took it all in, his eyes met hers. A thrill like he had never experienced tap-danced across his arms and back. When Clare looked at him, she looked *into* him. Past the charming smile and easy demeanor. Past the wiry farm boy with the land caked under his fingernails. Her eyes dove into him like an experienced swimmer. She saw his fears, the endless love he already felt for her, his mediocre dreams of a house with a picket fence and a dog and children and a good job. She saw it all. It frightened him but made his head spin all the same.

Clare leaned forward, ignoring the clicking and clacking down below as the ride operator tried to repair some broken part, and kissed him. Her mouth opened and he tasted the sweet chocolate she'd eaten earlier. The thrill turned electric, and his nerve-endings sizzled. The

Ferris wheel finally resumed its rotation, but it wasn't until the operator cleared his throat that the two realized the ride was over.

Edward drove Clare down to the beach and the two walked along the sandy shores, the waves crashing at their feet before slinking back out, just to crash again. Clare talked and Eddie listened. Eddie talked and Clare listened. Just two young kids figuring it out, life spread before them to the horizon.

Eddie asked Clare to be his wife less than six months after that first date. She said yes, and the rest was history.

"Best damn day of my life," Edward said. A bang at the back door placed an exclamation at the end of the statement.

He leaned forward in his chair, peering around the living room wall into the dining room. The back door was beside the dining room table. He caught a flash of red through the window, just before the old residential door was slashed in half. The pieces clattered to the floor in splinters, the glass shattering. Two red coals floated through the never. A smell of rotted meat and brimstone wafted toward him.

Finally, after all these years. Vengeance.

Eddie took another hard pull on his pipe and sat back in his chair. While his left hand held the pipe in place, his right hand lifted the Colt Army Model 1860.

The air shifted and the stink blew over him like pipe smoke. The two eyes, boiling with misery, crept toward him. A growl rattled at the back of its throat.

"I knew you'd come one day," Edward said around his pipe. "But you're too late. I've had my fun, lived a beautiful life. I get to see my Clare now." He placed the gun to his head. "So fuck you and your revenge."

Eddie never heard the hammer click.

CHAPTER 38

"What is this?"

Bates smiled. On the inside. No way was he allowing it to reach his lips. Instead, he looked at Martin with disbelief. "I don't know. Looks like a wreck."

Up ahead, as planned, fire trucks, wreckers, and ambulances blocked Highway 17 to Wilmington. Police cars were scattered about. A coroner's truck—not his idea, but a nice touch—was parked within sight. The vague silhouette of Officer Beckwith motioned them to follow an orange DETOUR sign. Bates turned left onto Highway 211.

"Where are you taking us?" Martin spat. He had lost a modicum of control and was not happy about it.

"Calm down." Bates soothed him. "Highway 211 runs through Green Swamp to Bolton. In Bolton, Highway 74 will take us to Wilmington. We're still on track."

"If you are playing me—" Martin said. He shook his head without finishing to indicate how bad it would be.

"Yeah, I caused a pile-up to play you." Bates snarked. Of course, he was responsible for the pile-up. Except there wasn't a pile-up. He had the van from the accident earlier today moved down to that intersection, parked an eighteen-wheeler crooked, staged all available emergency service vehicles with lights flashing and bulbs spinning to block the view of the ruse, called on any willing firefighters and EMS personnel to run around like chickens with their heads cut off, and an officer to wave them along the detour route.

Now the situation was headed into unknown territory. 211 was also blocked by wreckage, which would reveal this was indeed by design. Bates had to make his play before they reached the wreckage. Thankfully, 211 was an unsalted mess. The road wasn't even visible. There were no tire tracks to show him where to drive. The truck's high beams were having trouble pushing past the curtain of snow cascading from the black sky. Not ideal travel conditions but perfect for what he had planned.

Now I just have to not wreck before I get to a certain point on the road, Bates thought, straightening taller and leaning forward to place full concentration on the task at hand.

"I can't believe they sent us this way," Martin said. He, too, was leaning forward, his body wound tight. "They know our situation. Why send us this way?"

A sliver of concern needled at Bates. Martin was getting to the root of the ruse quicker than anticipated. Bates needed to spread the story on, nice and thick. "They know there's an innocent civilian and a police officer in this truck. They know this is life-or-death. They know your demands. Shitty as it is, this is the best way to get you to where you want to go. The other option would have been for us to sit at that intersection for hours while they clean up the mess. Hours spent sitting in this truck with fire trucks and police officers moving all around us. I'm sure they deduced that was a recipe for disaster."

Judging Martin's body language and eyes, Bates knew he hit the mark. Martin said, "How far is Bolton?"

"Almost fifty miles."

"Shit." Martin looked around at the wall of trees on either side of the road. "Is there not a shortcut somewhere that will take us around the wreck and put us back on 17?"

Now we're talking. Bates said, "I think there's a dirt road about ten miles up that cuts through the woods and brings us out about five miles past the wreck. But it's backroads, running through the woods. It'll be shorter but we'll have to be careful. I don't know what shape those dirt roads are in."

"Can't be worse than the crap we're plowing through right now. When you get there, take it."

Bates nodded. *So far so good.*

"What happened to your wife?" Martin asked, taking Bates by surprise.

Her death always stung and, he imagined, always would. "She, uh, died of brain cancer."

"Sorry to hear that," Martin said.

Bates could read people, their voices, eyes, body language, twitches. Martin was sincere. "Thank you."

Bates slowed when he was close to the back road. He saw it almost too late. He resisted the urge to stomp the brake. He pressed the pad gently, slowly turning right. The rear tires wiggled but straightened once the tread dug into the dirt that made up Middle River Road. The headlights ran up the claustrophobic, tight trees on either side of them. The snowfall was lighter here. The tree canopy overhead acted like an umbrella with holes, repelling most of the precipitation, but still allowed enough through to keep things interesting.

"This is a spooky place at night," Martin said, his voice low as if talking to himself.

"The local folklore says Green Swamp is haunted," Bates replied, and acted as if he didn't catch Martin's head snap toward him. He continued. "I've never seen anything. I've hunted out here a few times, been in the tree stand by four a.m., everything so dark you think Earth has floated through a black hole. When it's that dark and quiet, you hear all sorts of things. It's the mind playing tricks. But, still, the noises will creep you out."

"What kind of noises?" Roger asked from the back seat. Sitting forward, suddenly intrigued.

"Well, mostly breaking tree limbs, rustling leaves. Things you could easily disqualify as dangerous or weird. Then there's the moaning. Like someone whose sorrow is so excruciating the body has to relieve the pressure. Like the vent hole in a tea kettle. The most god-awful thing you ever heard. I get goosebumps thinking about it."

"But you never saw anything?" Roger again.

"Nope, not a thing. Well, except a deer, which I chose not to shoot."

"Why go hunting and not shoot the deer when you have it in your sights?" This was Martin.

"Because I wasn't shooting it to feed my family. I had meat in the freezer, I had food in the cupboards. I was shooting it for sport, for the fun of it. To show my buddies. Smile over that dead innocent animal and take photos to post on Facebook and Instagram. Didn't seem right." Bates was quiet for a beat. "I see enough death on this job. I haven't been hunting since."

"That's admirable, detective," Martin said. "You're a better man than me. I would have pulled the trigger and mounted the head."

Bates said nothing. Martin *had* pulled the trigger and a man was dead.

The point of the conversation was to distract and relax them. They were strung tight, but he felt the intensity ease down a few notches. They weren't on high alert for a trick play. Though one was coming.

Skeeter's run-down shack passed by on the left. Odd that the house was pitch black inside and no smoke poured from the chimney. Surely, Skeeter wasn't inside without heat.

"Someone live there?" Martin asked.

"Yeah. Name's Skeeter. Local dumpster diver. A harmless hobo. The community watches out for him. Some of the restaurants donate food, the county dump sites allow him to scrounge for anything he finds useful or sellable. I give him money every now and then. He's a good guy. Was dealt a bad hand at birth and has been fighting against it all his life. Just trying to survive."

"Looks empty."

"Yeah, I noticed. If I get out of this alive, I'll swing by for a wellness check."

Martin was noncommittal on that subject.

Bates came to an intersection and took a right onto what he knew to be Little Red Road, named such by some long-ago dweller of these parts for its slick, clay surface. The treetops opened and the accumulation became significant.

Bates braced himself mentally. The shit was about to hit the fan.

As he rounded a soft bend, the right front tire blew, and the truck slewed back and forth. Bates slammed on the brakes, and the rear of the truck slipped into the shallow ditch framing each side of the road.

"Goddammit!" Bates exclaimed, dramatically slamming his hands against the steering wheel. He hoped his acting was on point.

Martin jumped out, cussing. Bates climbed out and stood in the high beams, staring at the flat tire in disgust.

"We can't change the tire with the truck leaning in the ditch like this," Martin complained. "Try to pull out onto the road."

Bates hopped behind the wheel and made a show of trying to maneuver the truck from being stuck. Martin even pushed against the bumper. The chains acted like shovels, digging through the snow and into the slippery clay dirt.

In the pitch-black woods surrounding them, Bates caught movement.

Time to get this party started.

Roger joined Martin to brainstorm. Bates reached into a door compartment and deftly removed a hidden, black SIG P365 XL. He pushed it under his left leg. Jarrod's eyes met his in the mirror. "Stay calm, but get ready," Bates murmured under his breath.

Bates barely finished the sentence when all hell broke loose.

CHAPTER 39

Jason's exchange with his parents was baffling. Ron and Sarah Grace were two of the most stable people he knew. They were as solid as the ground. But the idea some monster was waiting for nightfall so it could hunt and slaughter everyone in Green Swamp was hard to grasp. And now Jason was bringing Vernon into the fracas. Saying he *spoke* to the former owner of the house. And Vernon spoke back! A man who had been dead for how many years?

"Time out," John said, using his hands to form the universal sign language for stop everything. "Just time out. You guys are pulling my leg, right? This is a prank, yeah? Crazy monsters and speaking to the dead, this is just you guys fooling around?"

Sarah Grace smiled, but it failed to travel from her lips to her eyes. "Every part of me wishes I could say yes. I'd love to say April Fool's. But this is no joke."

"This is as real as it gets." Ron added. "It sounds crazy, we all know. I'm still processing it myself."

"What conv—" John was cut short when Jason shouted in surprise.

"What's wrong?" Sarah Grace asked, leaping from her chair.

Jason looked at John, his eyes wide and pained. "What happened to Domino?"

It took a moment for John to speak out loud. No way in hell Jason knew to ask such a thing. He hadn't even told Ron and Sarah Grace, yet.

John cleared his throat, and said, "Um, yes, he's dead."

"I know. I see him. He's a mess."

"What happened, John?" Ron asked.

John was still staring at Jason when he answered. "He got out of his pen. I found him in the woods. He was split open." He whispered the next part for Jason's sake, though he had a burning feeling the kid knew all the details, anyway, "Insides hanging out. Must have happened fairly early in the night because he was frozen." John followed Jason's eyes, trying to see what he was seeing. There was nothing but tile flooring. To Jason: "You see him now? Here?"

"Yes. He must've followed you."

"Is he..."

"All torn up?"

John nodded dryly.

"Kinda. His coat is bloody, but mostly stuff is hanging from underneath him...out of his belly."

John closed his eyes, unable to believe what he was hearing and yet unable to *not* believe. He had always considered the possibility of ghosts as plausible. The essence of a person remaining after the physical body had moved on. Especially if the person was, say, murdered brutally, life stolen when so much life was left to live. What was impossible about that? Had mankind not been created from nothing? Whether you believed in the scientific or the biblical, it amounted to the same. From nothing came humans, whose ideas created cars, words, mathematics, astronomy, houses, machines, paved roads, factories, schools, churches, AI, and all the amenities (good and bad) enjoyed by humanity that weren't in existence at one point in time.

If something can come from nothing, wasn't it probable the residue of a person—their soul, if you like that better—could remain under the right circumstances? John thought it not only probable, but damn near fact.

Catching glimpses of Kourtney Wilkins, usually nothing more than a flicker in the dark, gave credence to this hypothesis. If there was anyone who died in a manner so brutal eternal peace was unattainable, it was her.

The part John was having trouble getting a firm grip on was Jason talking to them. As if they were as present as himself. The boy was communicating with the dead.

"You can speak to ghosts?" John asked slowly.

"I don't know how I do it. I just can."

"John," Sarah Grace butted in, "Jason saw his real father last night. His deceased father. He gave Jason a sort of bird's-eye view of this monster. He showed him Skeeter. Said Skeeter is our only hope."

"Only hope how?"

"We don't know," Ron said.

"Is it possible you could be wrong about this?" John asked Jason.

Jason shook his head. "I wish I was."

"Okay." John twiddled his thumbs. "Some sort of beast will be coming for us tonight. And you think it might be a werewolf, but you don't have confirming evidence to support that theory." John paused. "So, this could be a rabid dog, right?"

"It could be," Jason answered. "It may be a coincidence this is happening during a Full Blood Super Moon. It lasts for about two hours. That may be when the creature strikes. It may be when it is at its strongest. Lots of maybes. But there's one truth I do know. It is coming, whether we like it or not. Whether we *believe* or not. Whether we're ready or not."

"We'll be ready," Ron said.

"If it is—and that's a big if—the kind of wolf we're facing is important," John said to Ron. "If it's just a wolf, then bullets will kill it. But if it's a werewolf, we'll need silver bullets. If the legends are true, that is."

"I don't have silver bullets," Ron said. "I have guns, ammo, a bow with arrows, a few knives. If we shoot it enough, surely, it'll die."

John wasn't an expert on werewolves. His knowledge existed from movies and a few jailhouse books. The lethality of standard brass casings was nothing but speculation at this point. "Sounds like we have no choice but to roll with what we have."

"What's the plan?" Sarah Grace asked Ron.

Ron sighed, his eyebrows scrunched. "We need to fortify the house. The shutters need to be closed and locked. Hopefully, that protects the windows. Lock the doors and place a chair underneath the door handle to jamb it from opening. We load all the weapons and move to the middle guest bedroom. No exterior windows or doors leading to the room."

"Like a tornado," John said quietly, more a thought than statement.

"Exactly." Ron nodded. "We'll take turns for watch duty. Resting is important. It's going to be a long night, and everyone needs to be sharp when and if things go sideways."

The kitchen was tense and heavy with fear and uncertainty, but no one said a word.

"John, you and I will go outside and close and lock the shutters. Sarah Grace, you, Jason and Skeeter move the guns to the bedroom."

Sarah Grace parted the kitchen curtains. "What if it's outside right now and you're walking straight to it?"

"That's why John's going with me." Ron hefted the AR and slapped home a magazine. "I'll lock the shutters while he watches my back."

CHAPTER 40

Ray strapped the walking boot tight. The pressure caused the ankle to pulse like a heart. He popped four ibuprofen, filled a thermos with coffee, and rejoined the group in the living room. They stood quietly by the fireplace, warming their bodies in preparation for spending the night outside.

"We should switch to ATVs," Ray said. "Should get through the snow better."

"Okay," Mary said. "But I need to ask a favor before we get started."

"Shoot."

"My kids are home alone. Conner has been running fever all day. I don't want them to spend the night alone. I would generally send them to Arlene's"—Mary trailed off, lowered her head, swallowed hard—"I would like to bring them here, if that's okay with Maggie."

"Absolutely," Maggie answered from the doorway. She was in her pajamas and wrapped in a house coat. Furry slippers donned her feet. Her hair, which had been ponytailed earlier, was now down. Gray streaks accented the brown. "It would be our pleasure."

"Let's go get them," Ray said, slipping into a dry coat.

Mary hugged Maggie. "Thank you."

"No thanks required."

Ray led the group to a band of ATVs. "Mary, you ride with me," Ray said, passing out keys. "Buck—you, Garrett, and Brent follow. We're gonna get the kids, bring them back here to Maggie, then head over to Tin Shed."

"Why Tin Shed?" Buck asked. "We already looked there."

"Because we know for a fact that's where they were. We'll try to predict where they could've gone based on what we know. Only play I can think of right now."

"Should we split up?" Brent asked. "Cover more ground that way."

"Under different circumstances, I would say yes. But there are too many unknowns for that. Safer if we all stay together."

Ray hit the garage door clicker to open the roll-up door and hit it again once they were outside to close it. He drove slow down the driveway, the snow now completely hiding the road.

"You know what I'm confused about?" Mary asked.

"Don't leave me guessing," Ray said.

"Behavior."

"Behavior? What behavior?"

"The bear." Mary twisted slightly in her seat to talk directly to Ray, as if imploring him to take this seriously.

Maybe she wasn't aware that nothing in his lifetime had ever been more serious. "I'm listening."

"Let's say it is a bear, since that's most likely. In a single night, this bear attacked Northern and *four* hunters in *two* different locations separated by several *miles*. It also slaughtered a horse housed in a stall some fifteen miles from those attacks. How likely is that? I'm no bear expert, but the behavioral pattern seems off."

Ray had to admit it was a long shot. Bears were not known to be aggressive toward humans unless humans were aggressive toward them or their cubs. Tommy, Cliff, Jerry, and Steve were seasoned hunters with years of experience in these woods. They would never make a move toward a bear. And certainly not in the middle of the night.

There was something else that had been nibbling away on his thoughts all evening as well. "Do you remember when the kid was killed at the haunted hayride back in October?"

"How could I forget? Conner was planning to go the next night."

"Pete Dawson is an officer with Shallotte P.D. and stops by the store once a week. A few days after the murder, we were talking about it. Hell, everybody was talking about it. I asked him if they knew what killed that poor boy. He looked around the store to be sure no one was within earshot and told me that *officially* it was a bear. But then he said, *unofficially*, the autopsy was inconclusive."

"How can that be?"

"That's what I asked. He shrugged, paid for the goods, and left."

"Could the coroner be inexperienced in animal attacks and not know how to classify what he saw? It's not like we have lions, tigers, and bears snatching people in the middle of the night around here."

"Maybe. Seems like if he was unsure, he would call in an expert, though."

"Not if the public, the media, the mayor, and every-damn-body else is screaming for answers. He may have been forced to make a judgment call and move on."

Ray nodded. Made sense. "So, these may not be bear attacks. Is that what you're getting at?"

"I don't know what I'm getting at. Not even sure if it matters at this point. I just want to find your daughter and my husband."

No disagreement from me, Ray thought as the ATV plowed through the snow on 211. Northern had been a slight child at birth. She weighed five pounds two ounces, even though Maggie went full term. Once she got older, started school, it was easy to see she was smaller than the other five year olds. Ray had assumed she would remain that way the rest of her life; skinnier than most, shorter than average, ridiculed about her size against societies impossible measuring stick.

But farm life will grind you up or shine you up, and Northern began to shine around the time she slipped into her teenage years. She gained weight, grew four inches seemingly overnight, and by the time she was sixteen, she was stunningly average. She was the same height as most other girls. She was no longer the scrawny kid she had been in elementary school. Her blonde hair grew thick and wavy—*Where did that come from?*—her features filled out, and the woman she would become began to form. It had been a high school fashion show as a junior that opened Ray's reluctant eyes to the effect she had on boys. The whistles every time she graced the stage had been the first sign. The gathering of males around her after the show was over had been the second.

While growing up and maturing, Northern had an effect on her father as well. Ray had never been good at small talk. He lacked the gift of gab, that innate ability to converse with any *one* at any *time* about any *thing*. Years on a farm, toiling away in solitude—with nothing but the land and the animals as company—had not developed him socially. He had always been a contemplative person, happy to linger in his own thoughts. Or sit by the fire and read a historical novel of some war where men went away to fight for some damned thing called duty and returned home in a box. He had lived in his thoughts all his life and had been most content there.

Northern changed all that. As she got older, her desire to help on the farm grew with her. At six, she was cleaning horse stalls, feeding and watering them, feeding the chickens, milking the cows. By eight, she was working in the fields with the hands. At ten, she was driving tractors on her own. By fifteen, she was operating the combine with the confidence of a veteran.

She loved being outside and always wanted to help Ray with whatever he was doing. He discovered something about children: they were inquisitive as hell and wanted to know *everything*. Her bubbling chattiness never failed to brighten his day, and, over the years, he came to depend on it. He learned to open up. He learned that she was his daughter and open and eager to know his thoughts on a vast assortment of topics, no matter the flavor. He used those talks to teach life lessons—the ways of the world, the meaning of discipline and respect and character and hard work and responsibility. He wanted to instill as much good as possible inside her.

What he was never aware of, not until today, was that she, all along the way, every second of every day, was teaching him. How to be a better man, a better father, a better husband (once admonishing him for being unnecessarily short to Maggie one ill-tempered morning, which he acknowledged with an apology that evening at the dinner table), a better boss to the year-round and seasonal workers, and a better communicator. The world was a better place with her in it. Ray refused to believe she was no longer here. Maybe it was foolish hope. Maybe.

"You okay?" Mary asked as he approached her driveway.

"Yeah. Why?"

"You went somewhere inside for a minute."

"I do that a lot. Northern broke me from the worst of it. But I'm an old dog and old habits die hard."

"How did she break you from it?"

Ray was not a sensitive man and had been accused of being emotionally vacant, but in front of this stranger, the knot loosened in his chest and his vision blurred. Tears gushed as he pressed the brake and placed his forehead on the steering wheel. The ATV crunched to a stop in the middle of 211. A dizzying flash of Northern's life skipped behind his weeping eyes.

The doctor handing the screaming bundle to him in the delivery room.

Her fussing red face as her first tooth cut through inflamed gums.

Her first shaky steps as he beckoned her forward.

Christmas morning when her face lit up as bright as the Christmas tree from all the presents.

A squealing five-year-old Northern steering the tractor for the first time.

Her first day in kindergarten as she clung to his leg and hid her face from all the scary strangers, and her excited return home when she realized there was nothing to be afraid of.

Her first bike ride.

The birthday parties, the celebrations, the school events, the high school graduation.

And—the kick in the gut—her kissing him on the cheek the previous night before walking out the door to go on a date.

Someone tapped on the door, but he ignored it. Mary's body quaked against his own. He found a measure of comfort in the shared grief, weird as it sounded; someone understood what he was going through, empathized with him, and directed no judgment at the hard old man whose calluses were finally bleeding.

After what felt like an hour, he eased upright to dab his burning eyes. Headlights shone in the mirror from the ATV behind him, the reflection causing him to wince. He moved his head to the side so he could look at Mary. Her eyes were bloodshot, cheeks puffy. "You okay?"

"We're never going to see them again, are we?" Mary asked, her voice cracking.

Ray placed his shaking hands on the steering wheel to steady them. "I want to believe with everything inside me that we will. I know my daughter. She's a fighter to rival a marine. She's alive goddammit."

Ray pressed the pedal, and the ATV resumed its steady crawl through the torrential weather. He turned into Mary's driveway, thankful the entrance was boxed with dormant azalea bushes on either side, the driveway itself invisible. Ray stopped by the front door where porch lights bragged. "We have a generator."

Mary ran inside. Shadows bound by the curtained windows as she hustled the kids outside and into the back seat of the Polaris. She jumped in beside Ray with a huff.

"Okay," she said, knocking snow off her shoulders. "I think we're ready."

Ray nodded and pulled back out on 211. The boy and girl sat quietly in the back seat. The older one, Conner, wore a toboggan with a deer emblem on the front, curly tussles of light brown hair rolling from around the edges. His dark blue eyes were watery with fever and his pinched cheeks were flush. The younger one, Maribeth, was wrapped in a flannel blanket. She was smallish, meek, and obviously not sure what to make of the situation. No doubt Mary had informed them of staying with Maggie. Conner seemed outwardly okay with the circumstances. Maribeth looked scared of being left with a stranger, and her body language verbalized the sentiment.

"Hey," Ray said, inflecting a jovial tone to his voice.

"Hey," Conner answered, meeting Ray's eyes in the mirror.

"Hi," Maribeth answered quietly after Mary shot her a look.

"What's Santa bringing you two for Christmas?"

Maribeth visibly straightened at the mention of Santa. She was young enough to consider Christmas the best time of year. "I asked for a new saddle for Willow. That's my horse. She's more beautiful than a unicorn."

Ray checked on Mary. She was looking out the window, discreetly wiping her face.

"A saddle, huh? That's a nice present." Ray found Conner in the mirror. "What about you, Conner?"

"A drone."

"A drone? What do you want to use a drone for?"

"So I can fly over the woods and look at the animals. If dad's not home soon, maybe we can use it to look for him." Conner's head slumped.

Walked right into that one, Ray thought grimly.

"Are you helping my mommy look for my daddy?" Maribeth asked.

Ray nodded. "Yes. My daughter is also missing. We are working together to find them."

"Thank you," Maribeth said. "I hope your daughter is okay."

Ray pulled up beside his front porch steps. Mary hustled Conner and Maribeth through the miserly wind across the porch to where Maggie waited in the doorway. Ray watched Maggie wave Mary off as she ushered the timid pair inside. Before the door closed, Maggie had Maribeth talking.

It was her gift. The ability to put everyone at ease, especially children. Maggie's voice was as comforting as hot chocolate. Her mannerisms soothing and inviting. She looked at strangers like best friends, her eyes imploring them to open up and vocalize whatever was on their mind. She listened to the dullest of stories like they were riveting tales of hair-raising adventures. Never failed to impress Ray.

Mary fell in and slammed the door, watching her children disappear into the house. Safe. She half expected Maribeth to burst into tears, calling for her mother.

"Maggie will take care of them," Ray said.

Mary wiped her eyes. "I know. Your wife is incredible. It's not that. I'm worried about tomorrow and the days after. If Tommy never comes home. What then? How do I explain this to them? How do I raise them with this hanging over their head?"

"You can't think like that."

"I try not to, Ray, but all I see is Cliff. He was the toughest man I had ever met. And something attacked and killed him. What chance does my husband have to survive something that killed Cliff?"

"I don't know. But Tommy has you and those beautiful children waiting at home. If that's not a reason to fight, I don't know what is. You have to hold on to that with both hands and feet."

"I'm trying."

The drive to Tin Shed was slow going. Now that the sun had completely abandoned the east coast, the conditions worsened. Ray had traveled these roads his whole life; it was only his familiarity with Green Swamp that allowed him to maneuver through the backroads and shortcuts without winding up stuck in a ditch or flipped over in a ravine.

He stopped in front of the campsite with his headlights washing the area. Buck pulled beside him, lending more light to the site.

Mary checked Tommy's tent. She crawled inside. The movement sent cake-sized slices of snow cascading off the fabric.

Ray lifted a flap and peered inside. "Find anything?"

Mary sat by a duffel bag with a shirt balled in her hands as she held it to her face and wept silently. A paperback stuck out from under the edge of the sleeping bag.

"We have to find him."

"We will. Let's keep looking."

Ray ducked out. Buck was searching behind the tarps of the Tin Shed. Garret was in one tent and Brent was inside the other. They both crawled out and shook their heads.

"Nothing," Garrett said.

Brent conceded. "Same."

Ray examined the surroundings, thinking. *Why had they left the campsite at the same time with their weapons?*

First possibility: they went hunting.

Second possibility: they were awakened by the explosion on 211, went to check, and were attacked.

Seemed logical to start with the tree stands. If that rendered nothing, then they could explore the truck explosion possibility.

None of the stands in this area were designed for more than two people, and that was pushing it. They went to four separate stands.

"I think we should check the four closest deer stands," Ray said. "One is about six hundred yards to the west. Another is about the same distance to the north, and another is about eight hundred yards due east. I think a fourth is behind us a few hundred yards. Mary and I will take the stand to the east. You three check the others."

"How did Cliff get from here, all the way to his house?" Mary asked. "That's over five miles as the crow flies. And he would have had to crawl across 211 and up the side of the road to his house. I have been up and down that road multiple times today, just like you guys, and I never noticed a body or a blood trail." She paused to let it sink in. "So how did he get there?"

She had a point. Ray rode the four-wheeler down 211, searching for signs of Northern, and he hadn't noticed signs of a body dragging along in the snow. *This damn mystery keeps giving more questions than answers.* "I have questions of my own, but I think we need to eliminate the knowns."

Mary said, "But none of this makes sense."

"That's an understatement."

Ray took Tin Shed Road to Knotty Stump. He went off-road once he was parallel to the stand. He parked next to the ladder. He would have preferred to climb it himself but the walking boot made that impossible. Mary climbed carefully but quickly. Her foot slipped once on the ice-coated rungs but she never wavered. She disappeared inside the blind for two minutes, then climbed back down.

"Nothing. An empty can of Vienna sausage and a half-empty water bottle. The grease from the Vienna's is still slimy."

"Who eats Vienna's?"

"Cliff. Loves the things. He was in this stand recently."

A horn blasted in the distance. Three quick bursts followed by three more.

"They found something," Ray said, and gunned the engine.

CHAPTER 41

"GET DOWN! GET DOWN NOW!"

The commands were shouted as six men in white camouflage emerged from the woods. Big, white, SWAT patches donned their chests. Each held an assault rifle, and the barrels were pointed at the bank robbers. Martin flinched but recovered quickly. He pulled his pistol and popped off two shots as he scurried low around the bed of the truck. Roger added his own barrage and ducked beside Martin behind the quarter panel.

Bates hopped out from behind the steering wheel and pointed his pistol at Martin. "You're under—" Arrest was what he was going to say, but his shoulder went numb, and he was thrown to his back, halfway under the truck.

Feet shuffled as shots rang out. Bullets pounded the truck metal with hollow thunks. A tire whistled flat, something under the hood *whooshed* as a bullet punctured a hose. Bates checked his shoulder—it was beginning to burn. Blood leaked from a hole just above his armpit. A quick assessment told him it was superficial. A bone may have been nicked but nothing was broken.

"I'll kill him!" Martin threatened. He held Jarrod at gunpoint and used him as shield as he backed into the woods. Roger hid behind the two of them. "I'll kill him if you come closer."

"There's no way out of this," a SWAT officer said. Michael McKnight, former green beret, current Wilmington P.D. SWAT commander. "You can surrender now before this goes any further. No one has to get hurt here tonight."

It happened in slow motion, like a movie skipping frame by frame.

Bates was sliding out from under the truck, rolling to his side to aim his pistol, when a creature—no animal he'd seen was that large—exploded through a stand of brush. One second Roger ducked low behind Martin, the next he was gone, leaving nothing but a trail of intestines.

Martin turned, just in time to see the thing disappear into the darkness. He forgot about Jarrod. He forgot about the commandos pointing fully automatic assault rifles at him. He pointed the gun at the trees and whipped it back and forth, hunting for the creature. Jarrod ran into the arms of the stunned assault team. McKnight blinked, looked at Bates for direction.

Before Bates could make a decision, the beast galloped out of the cover of darkness again and leaped onto Martin. One paw swiped at the bank robber and his head spun off his shoulders like a top. It paused as it took in the crowd of shocked onlookers. This gave Bates time to log what he was seeing.

Some sort of abnormally large wolf. But worse.

Its eyes burned like chunks of roasting coal. Its head was long and sleek, its snout dripping with clotted flesh and blood. Its body furry and muscular. Talons as long as butcher knives protruded from its paws. The claws glinted in the flashlight beams stabbing out from the assault team's guns, as if made of polished steel.

The animal roared, batted Martin's head at the officers like a baseball, then disappeared while the commandos dodged the blood-spurting body part.

McKnight helped Bates to his feet. "What the hell was that?" His face was white and pallid, eyes searching everywhere, on high alert.

"I have no idea." Bates said. Then it hit him, the pieces clicking into place. The way it happened always satisfied the detective in him. This...creature...was responsible for the tractor trailer accident twenty miles from where he now stood. The tufts of hair he found caught in the trailer door hinges came from the animal he just saw. He was sure of it. A normal-sized wolf was not capable of reaching the height of the door hinge. But the wolf that decapitated Martin certainly met the criteria.

"What do we do, sir?" McKnight was sweeping his flashlight across the snow-coated tree trunks.

"We need to get out of here. Now."

"We can push the truck out of the ditch and drive out of here." McKnight offered.

"It has a flat tire and bullets hit the engine. It's useless now. Where are your vehicles parked?"

"We drove ATVs in off 17. We have four of them. They are three miles back. The highway is about ten miles past that. I didn't want to chance you missing the mark and driving further. We could've been spotted."

"Do you have radio comms?"

"No sir. We didn't want to chance someone speaking, or the thing squawking, as we snuck in. We needed total shock and awe on this one."

"Understood." Bates surveyed the surroundings and detected no movement. "Okay, we fall back to the ATVs. Wedge formation, civilian in the middle. He is the innocent and must be protected at all costs. Flankers move in reverse. Eyes and ears open. Quick and quiet. Let's go."

The team backed into the woods and moved to formation without a word of discussion. Practiced and well-rehearsed. Each step caused a sledgehammer of pain to pound Bates in the chest and down his arm. He had no choice but to grin and bear it.

This was his first time being shot. Part of his training had been learning to mentally prepare for the inevitability of such a wound. Most people who were shot automatically assumed it was a death sentence and panicked. Bates had been taught not to panic. It was a mentality. Years of instruction to callous the brain.

I wish my pain receptors were callous. This fucking thing hurts.

During Susan's final days, the pain had been intense. She'd wailed at times, talking crazy, seeing dead relatives, objects that didn't exist, cussing aloud. A steady drip of morphine had been the only thing to keep the worst of it away. Bates had prayed for the pain to stop. He told her he wished he could take it from her, and she told him to stop being silly. "I wouldn't wish this on my worst enemy, much less my husband."

Eventually, the pain had stopped. About the same time as her heart. She fought the pain all the way to grave, and while it had the final say, it went silent, bloody, and bruised.

If she can do it, so can I.

McKnight threw a fist up—*Halt*—then flattened his hand—*Down*—while each soldier searched the quadrant for which he was responsible. The wind whispered around frozen tree limbs as it pushed more snow through the cracks. A thin *Pop!* sounded from an eastward position. Outside of that, Green Swamp was blanketed by a haunting silence.

McKnight rose, the potential threat having not materialized. He turned to motion forward when the beast sailed out of the murk and flashed past McKnight before anyone could react. In a blink, the thing was gone. McKnight stood ramrod still, frozen in place until the top half of his body tilted away from the bottom half and landed face-first in the snow. All the slick, gleaming organs packed inside his abdomen slid out and unfolded on the snow, the bastard colors austere against the saintly white. Steam wafted from the entrails. The pair of legs swayed side to side as if moved by silent music. After a moment, a hushed moment where terror overtook every man in this small squad, the legs took one shaky step forward before buckling at the knees.

Fear broke one soldier, and he unleashed a volley of gunfire in the direction the beast had disappeared. It was blind fire without worry of target. It was reaction, red-hot and scare-hazed. The team babbled in panic, jabbering nonsense, unsure what to do without their team leader to issue orders.

"Get your shit together, soldiers," Bates hissed. "We have to keep moving. Nothing we can do now but get the fuck out of here."

The soldiers stiffened. The voice of a superior, untarnished by bull-shit or politics. The words cut through and reminded them of their duty. The soldiers formed a circle around Jarrod, and they moved with methodical determination.

Not a minute passed before Bates heard the attack coming, a wink before it burst from the darkness. Bates twisted toward the screams. Two men were eviscerated, the steamy contents of their abdomens piled at their feet. In unison, teammates until the end, the bodies crumpled into the snow.

"It's picking us off," Bates said to the remaining four men. "We'll never make it to the ATVs." The only chance for survival was shelter. He knew of only one place out here. "Follow me. Jarrod, you're going to have to run, you hear me? Knees to chest. Stay on my ass. Let's go."

Bates was not a regular at the gym—had not been since Susan died—but his legs remembered the concept and the adrenalized electricity of current affairs gave him an extra boost. He bound through the trees, dodging low-hanging limbs, zigzagging around obstacles, jumping over fallen logs, his breath hot in his face, his skin sweaty under his clothes. He heard feet stabbing into the snow behind him, the grunt of exertion, the clink of equipment hanging from utility belts. He crossed Little Red Road and reemerged into the cover of the forest. Skeeter's house was only a few hundred yards further.

Almost there.

Another scream from behind proved this a premature celebration. Still, Bates dared not look back. The grunting had transformed to panting and whimpering.

"Ah, fuck," someone shouted. Then they were gone.

A clearing appeared and Skeeter's snow-coated shack came into view. Bates glanced back and found Jarrod loping right on his heels without effort, not even winded. One officer remained, and he was damn near pinwheeling trying to run as fast as possible without falling face first.

Bates slid to a stop behind a longleaf pine. Jarrod and the officer slid beside him. Bates waved them forward. "Get to the house. Kick the door down if you have to. Get inside. I'll be right behind you. GO!"

The thudding of feet faded away. Bates squatted down, his knees popping. Movement in the distance, off to his right, black on black, barely discernible. Low-slung and slow, a prowlers stance.

Maybe it lost sight of us. Wishful thinking. More likely, it was creeping around to flank the cabin, attack at an angle without line-of-sight. The thing was smart, almost military in its advancements, attacks, maneuvers. Military-trained animal? Loose in the woods? Somehow escaped from where?

Bates was unaware of any sort of government-owned/operated facility in Green Swamp. If there was a lab where bioengineered super monsters were being created, it would be classified and hidden underground. He wasn't privy to such high-ranking information, his pay grade lightyears below "need to know".

No matter. Now to decide on the next move. The thing was too far away to take a shot. If he made a run at the cabin, he would be attacked. Bates liked his head attached at the shoulders, thank you very much.

Stealth. Lethargic and scary, but the best option. He slipped down onto his stomach like he was easing into a swimming pool. The snow spilled over the collar of his coat, the ice melting against his heated skin. The least of his worries.

Bates belly crawled, and thought, *At least it's soft.* His shoulder hurt so bad it was numb, which was fine by him. He watched for any indication his movements were attracting attention as he pushed forward. The animal was no longer visible. Being this close to the ground, he should feel or hear the thudding of feet if there was an attack imminent.

His focus was so narrow, radar on high alert, that he arrived at the house without realizing he was close. He crawled up the weather-worn steps and tapped on the door. It opened and he was hauled inside.

"Oh, thank God," Jarrod said, giving him a quick hug. "We thought, you know, you weren't coming back."

"Thanks for the confidence," Bates said quietly as he beat the snow off. "And keep your voice down."

"Where is it?" The officer was at the lone window, peering out through the murky glass.

"Not sure. It was creeping through the woods to the north ten minutes ago. Then I lost sight of it."

"Whose cabin is this?" Jarrod whispered.

"Skeeter's. The dumpster diver."

Jarrod's face lit up in recognition. "Oh, yeah."

"What now, detective?" The officer tiptoed over to him, waiting for a reply, an order, a directive.

"What's your name?"

"Watts, sir. Dakota Watts."

Watts was practically a child. Short, black stubble on top of his head, a few acne spots on his otherwise smooth cheeks, frame in the beginning stages of bulking up. "Nice to meet you, son. Bad circumstances, though."

"Yessir. Same here."

"This thing is sneaking around out there like it's flanking us. Maybe it knows where we are, maybe not."

"*What* is it, sir? Do you know?"

Bates shook his head, his lips a tight straight dash.

"Suggestions?"

"We can't go running around the woods. It'll pick us off one by one. We have to hunker down, stay quiet. If it comes for us, we give it all we got."

"We don't have much, sir. We thought this op would be a wham, bam, thank you, ma'am. No shots fired. Come in low and fast, wearing our meanest unhappy faces, waving around bad ass artillery, and those boys would drop to their knees faster than a hungry hooker. We had no operational knowledge such a hostile existed. It's the goddammedest thing I've ever seen." Watts' wide eyes stared at the wall, saw nothing but the slow-motion replay of his friends and co-workers being slaughtered.

Bates squeezed his shoulder. "I know how you feel. Been there. And I'm truly sorry for what you've seen and been through. But now is not the time to get sentimental. That's for later. Stay in the here and now, and we'll get out of this. Copy?"

Watts swallowed the sadness, pity, the need to mourn. He nodded as his eyes glazed over with the soldiers' scrum. "Yes, sir. Copy."

"Let's search the cabin. Maybe Skeeter has a gun, a knife, anything that can be used for a weapon." Bates added: "Also cleaning supplies."

"We housekeepers?" Jarrod asked, confused.

"Bomb makers," Bates replied.

CHAPTER 42

It was all confusing, hard to follow. Dead people talking, a monster coming, Ron and John about to go outside to board up the windows, standing guard like the Army.

But the house was warm, the food was good, the coffee full of energy, and no one called him names.

The name-calling was the worst. He pretended not to hear it, wasn't important enough to acknowledge. But sometimes the words were like wasps. The stings sharp and fiery, leaving him feeling swollen all over. Later, at home, when it was just him alone, he would hear the echoes of those nasty names as they bounced around in his head, spiked rubber balls that drew blood with every ricochet.

What made people so hateful?

This was a question he asked himself a lot. He wasn't bothering them. He wasn't calling them names. So, why? To make themselves feel better? That was probably the answer, as mysterious as it was. Who felt better by being mean to another person? He could only shake his head and wonder.

Thankfully, this family was unlike any he had ever been around. They cared for one another, displayed affection in every mannerism. He wasn't even part of the family and Sarah Grace patted him on the hand and shoulder, her kindness soft and warm.

As a child, Skeeter had wondered what it was like in homes like this one. When he watched movies and the Christmas tree was decorated—presents stacked beneath the branches, the dining room table adorned with holiday decorum—he had wondered what it would be like to wake up on Christmas morning and walk in the room to see all those gifts. Skeeter had always found nothing. Not a single present. Not even a Christmas tree. In his life, he could only remember receiving one present for Christmas. Two years before Joe died, his dad gave Skeeter and Joseph a special edition of Big Bank, a popular board game of his youth.

A few game pieces had been missing but it was otherwise in great shape. He and Joe had played it a lot. After his brother went away, the game sat under the bed collecting dust. Skeeter found it one day and played it alone. Still had the game, occasionally played it. The white die was dirty, and the silver game pieces were tarnished with finger grime. That was okay. It was only dirt. He tried to keep the Tall Female Bank Manager piece clean because he liked her. She looked like a manager.

He kept expecting the silver to flake off, or turn green, but, no, it shined when polished. The ragged cardboard game box said on the front the game pieces were exclusive to that edition, special in that they were made of real silver.

Silver?

Yes, that was right.

"Holy moly," Skeeter said in excitement. His stomach fluttered when everyone looked at him. He was not comfortable with attention.

"What is it, Skeeter?" Ron asked. He and John were standing at the front door. About to go outside to close the shutters.

Skeeter liked Ron but was a little intimidated by him. He looked at Sarah Grace.

"It's okay, Skeeter." She soothed. "You're with friends."

Skeeter took a deep breath to steady his nerves. *Friends, yeah.* He liked the sound of that. "I know where we can get some silver."

"You do?" Jason asked, his eyes full of spark.

"Yeah. At my house."

CHAPTER 43

"What you got?" Ray asked, run-hobbling toward Buck. Garrett came running, and Brent arrived a moment later.

"First, I noticed these," Buck said, pointing at gashes in the bark. From four feet off the ground and up as high as twelve feet, the skin of the tree was slashed ragged, fissures several inches deep in some places. The sap of the tree oozed like blood. "Then I noticed this." Buck bent over and pointed at what appeared to be blood spatter dried on the bark near the base of the tree. "Then that." Buck pointed up at the tree stand. Frozen blood-drops draped from the cracks in the boards like tinsel.

Ray dropped to his knees and dug away the snow. Scraggly spires of weeds sprung up as the ground was exposed. The dirt was red.

"My god." Mary breathed.

Ray climbed awkwardly to his feet and looked up. The two bottom rungs of the ladder were broken. Hoisting someone up was the only way to reach the next available rung.

Or...

Ray hobbled back to his ATV and pulled it under the rungs. Mary started to climb up, but Ray stopped her. "We don't know what's up there. One of the boys should go up."

"Fuck that," she said flatly, and hurried up the ladder. There was a cry of surprise as Mary disappeared into the stand. Muffled calls. "Steve? Steve? Can you hear me?" Mary poked her head out the doorway, shouted, "Steve is up here. He's...he's dead. We need to get him down."

There was a heavy silence as reality kicked in. Steven and Cliff were dead. The others—

"Come down." To Brent, Ray said, "You and Garrett get the rope out of my ATV, climb up, and throw it over that branch right there. It's strong enough. Tie one end around Steve and you two lower him down. Mary can help balance the weight and be the guide."

It took ten minutes to ease Steve's lifeless body out the door. The rope creaked from the weight. Mary held his hand and guided him into the back of Ray's ATV.

They gathered around and stared at the dead man, his white face, purple lips. His puffer was ripped and crisp with frozen blood.

"What are we going to do with him?" Buck asked. "Isn't it a crime to mess with a deceased person's body?"

"Probably, but we need to know what's going on. I'll happily go to jail if this helps me find my girl."

"How does this help?"

"I should've looked closer at Cliff, but I had no idea these incidents were connected. Now that I think they are, I want a look at the wounds."

"You've got to be kidding."

Ray shook his head. "I'm taking him over to Pop's house. I want to lay him on the porch and open up all this torn clothing, look at the skin."

"I don't understand why that's necessary." Buck protested.

"Because if this is a bear attack, it's the strangest damned thing ever. Mary mentioned earlier that the behavior of this bear is weird—unusual—and the more I think about it, the more I see she's right. This bear hunted these people down and attacked them. That's very rare. Maybe even impossible. Something's not right, and I'm going to find out what."

Buck relented with a sighing shrug. "Okay."

The trip to Pop's took five minutes. Ray's insides were a knot. Each body found was another strike against Northern surviving. As humans, we are drawn to the negative, the bad. Like flies on shit. That's why the news reported death. Why shows like *Dateline* were so popular.

Ray believed Northern was alive, but the pointed roots of negativity continued to jab at his flesh like a blunt needle, looking for a vein to slip inside, worm its way throughout, embed in his heart, bleed him dry of resolve, empty an Eason of iron will. Ray shook his head as he pulled close to Pop's front porch. *Damn if I give up on her. Ever.* It was body or bust.

Buck and Garrett carried Steve to the porch and laid him down. Ray unsheathed a machete he kept in the ATV for snakes and began cutting away the torn clothing. He tried to ignore the way the lifeless body shook as he pulled and tugged at the cloth, which was stiff from frozen blood. The final layer of thermal undergarments was cut open. Ray pulled back the flaps and gasped. Steve's skin was a milky purple and riddled with gashes. His sternum was exposed, shattered rib bones poked through the flesh, his abdomen leaked out of an eight-inch slice. It was a miracle he was able to climb into the deer stand. Pure adrenaline and white fear drove him up that ladder, two powerful natural stimulants unrivaled by man-made drugs.

Ray closed his eyes and inhaled a crisp ration of lung-burning air to allow his overwrought emotions to calm. A human being lay before him, his body mangled beyond belief, but right now he needed a clinical perspective.

As the lids raised, he forced himself to look at the wounds. Not as tears in the flesh but as indicators of the crime, details imperative to solving the case.

Patterns emerged. One set of gashes across the chest stood out, five side by side, spaced at almost even intervals, the three in the middle long and deep, the outside two slightly shorter and shallower.

"Bears have five claws," Ray stated.

"Right," Buck answered. "But only four register."

Ray nodded. "This animal has five distinct claws. What leaves five distinct claw marks?"

"Dogs have four," Garrett answered. "That's the only one I know."

"Wolves?" Ray asked.

"You think a wolf did this?" Mary asked. She was on her knees beside him, trying to see what he saw.

"It's possible. We have wolves in Green Swamp. I've seen a few in my life. This would have to be a big wolf, though, abnormally large. The wounds are long and deep. So deep the claws shattered bone."

"Wolves only have four," Buck said. "I think."

"The cuts are clean," Mary said, shining her handheld flashlight on a cut that was not marred by other damage. "See how this one is flayed open? Looks like a scalpel was used."

"Bears rip and mangle," Ray said.

"Is it me, or does everything about this indicate it was not a bear?" Mary asked.

"I don't see how it could be." Ray conceded. "But I don't see how it's not."

"Because..." The question hung in the air.

Ray was too distracted to answer. A nibble, a peck, some memory was trying to gnaw through his consciousness and make an important announcement. He could almost see it, hear it, feel it. Was there information hidden away in the dark that could provide answers to this puzzling situation?

"Ray? You okay?" Ray heard Mary ask, but her voice was faint, a whisper in the stiff wind.

An image popped into his head: the legendary lean-to on Tin Shed Road. Crippled with time. Worn by weather. But still standing, happy to show off the tattoos and scars from a life spent in Green Swamp.

"Scars," Ray said.

"What scars?"

Ray hobbled to his ATV and slung himself inside the warm cabin. Mary climbed in next to him without a word.

Ray saw it with his mind's eye. He knew what was there. Just wanted to see it one more time. Let the others see it as well.

He slid to a halt close to the tin shed, the blue tarp rustling in the wind, again using the headlights to illuminate the area. He couldn't remember which post it was, but he knew it was there. Over time, many hunters had carved their names in the skin of the posts. Here was Pop Munerlyn's scratchy knifemen-ship. Here was Tommy's mark (a heart with Tommy & Mary in the center). Here was Mack Little (a descendant of Green Swamp founder and war hero Christopher Little). Here was Solomon Larsen. And, finally, the scratch marks from the infamous Tin Shed bear attack.

What Ray remembered most about the scratches was how clear and perfect they were. Canted slightly to one o'clock. Someone a long time ago had felt the need to preserve and protect the marks by coating them with clear polyurethane. This was the only spot on any of the four posts that was not black with weather and cracked with rot.

Ray had not looked at these marks in years, but they were as remembered. Four scrapes, with not a trace of a fifth. The claw marks were not extremely deep—less than half an inch—and the edges of the marks were crumbled, the hairy fibers of the pretreated wood torn not sliced.

"My father told me the bear that attacked Levi Stuart was big," Ray said, his voice elevated to work through the wind. "The largest bear ever seen in Green Swamp. These are the claw marks from that day. As you can see, these are nothing like the marks on Steve Gainey. Whatever killed the Gainey's is a lot bigger than the bear that attacked Tommy's granddaddy. And that's a big fucking problem."

CHAPTER 44

"Woah," Ron said, pumping his hand up and down. "We are not wandering out in the dark, through Green Swamp where this thing is hiding, to find some silver game pieces that probably are not real silver anyway."

"Ron," Jason pleaded. "My dad said Skeeter is our only hope. This *has* to be what he was talking about. It has to be. And that makes it the most important thing we can do."

"It *may* be what he was talking about. But it may not be. I am not putting our lives in jeopardy going on some fool's errand we don't even know is necessary."

"But—"

"There is no 'but', Jason. The answer is no. That's final. We are staying here, hunkering down, fortifying our position, and waiting for sunrise."

Jason, deflated, stormed down the hallway with a battery-powered light in his hand, Skeeter on his heels.

John and Sarah Grace stared at him as if he were the bad guy. "Got something to say?"

Sarah Grace shrugged. "I think we need to consider this."

"Consider what?" Ron huffed. "Going out in a storm, at night, through a forest, with some unknown murderous creature rampaging around, to retrieve toys that are probably plastic? That's what we should consider, huh?"

"We wouldn't know anything about any of this if it wasn't for Jason and Skeeter. So far, they haven't been wrong."

"They haven't been right, either. I hear all this mumbo jumbo, but I don't see any real proof. So he can talk to ghosts, wonderful. But we're running on faith here. Nothing more. I will not risk any of our lives on faith."

"You may be risking our lives anyway," Sarah Grace said, and walked away.

Ron looked at John. "You wanna argue, too."

"Nope. I agree with you."

"Good. Let's close these shutters."

The wind had picked up, the temperature had dropped another ten degrees since they came in from shooting guns, and the world was cast in a weird dusky glow. Every horror movie he'd ever seen held some—or all—of the elements he was dealing with today: monster, boy who speaks to the dead, disbelieving adults, stormy weather. A battle to the death usually preceded the end credits.

This would make a good story, Ron thought.

Ron latched the first set of shutters closed.

What were the odds a monster was on the way to slaughter them? A million to one? A trillion to one? At least that. Probably more.

What's the odds a boy can converse with the dead? Grandaddy's voice chimed. *Quadrillion to one?*

"Yeah, yeah, whatever," he mumbled as he twisted the latch.

"What?" John called back. He was on guard like a Secret Service agent: gun at the ready, searching everywhere for anything that remotely resembled an animal, innocent or not.

"Nothing."

Ron turned the corner of the house and the wind sliced through his clothes like razorblades. His gloved fingers were already numb. He quickly banged the shutters closed, flipped the latch, and hurried to the next one.

Five minutes later, he and John were beating the snow off their boots on the front porch and practically dove inside the warmth of the house.

John said, "I hope my water pipes don't bust. Be just my luck."

Ron went to the sink and smiled. Sarah Grace already had the faucet set to drip. "Good job, honey. You are trained well."

"You're a good teacher. I've got pillows and blankets, some candles, and a few snacks in the middle bedroom. You guys ready?"

"Almost," Ron said. "Where are Jason and Skeeter?"

"I knocked on Jason's door a few minutes ago and told them to gather their stuff. They should be out soon."

"John, help me with the guns and ammo."

The weaponry and ammo were moved into the bedroom. Long guns stood in the corner, muzzles up. Handguns were lined side by side on a dresser, a smoke wagon platter waiting for the barbecue to begin. Each locked and loaded. The ammo was stacked against the mirror of the dresser, the top boxes open, the brass twinkly, even in the meager candlelight.

"Let's barricade the door," Ron said. "Go get Jason and Skeeter."

Ron assessed the room, impressed with the setup.

"Oh no." Sarah Grace appeared in the doorway, her face bleached of color. "They're gone."

CHAPTER 45

I am a dead man, Jason thought grimly, as the ATV hammered through the snow on Lilypad Road. He was shocked they got away without being chased down. After he and Skeeter were out the window, Jason noticed they were leaving tracks in the snow. He worried Ron or John would see the footprints as they shuttered the house, the adventure over before it started. But Ron was distracted, a lot on his mind, and John was focused solely on the woods surrounding the property, waiting for the slightest movement to go commando.

Pushing the ATV from under the lean-to, Skeeter hid it behind the shed until Ron and John went inside. Jason cranked it up and eased through the woods, feathering the throttle so the engine noise would remain at nothing more than a purr. He knew of some paths that cut over to Lilypad.

Skeeter's cabin was six or seven miles away through Green Swamp, via backroads. If his luck held, Jason hoped to get there and back within an hour. He doubted his deception would hold for a whole hour but, then again, maybe it would. His new parents were busy preparing the middle bedroom. It would take a while.

Jason was still a little miffed. He tried to focus on the ribbon of road curling out through the dark, stormy night before him, but his mind continued to stomp backward.

After all the proof he had given them, that this was a life and death situation, they still doubted him. Sarah Grace believed most of it, but she held her reservations close to her chest. Ron believed at times, but other times was blatant in his skepticism. This told Jason he was not truly convinced of anything Jason said and therefore, by virtue, thought Jason was lying. Ron was going through the motions, nothing more. It was dangerous and likely to get them all killed.

Running blind through Green Swamp in the middle of the night, during a snowstorm—and with a monster lurking—was dangerous and foolish, and likely to get the two of them killed. But foolishness was needed if they hoped to survive the night.

The monster *was* a werewolf. He had no ironclad proof, just a hunch. A feeling. Based solely on the dream-trip last night from his deceased father.

As they floated across the sky, his father had made a puzzling statement, almost as if talking to himself. Jason had forgotten it. But now, he understood the relevance. "When the full moon rises, so does the beast."

Jason initially took it to mean when the night falls, the monster will rise. Now, he was certain it was a clear indicator of the attacker. "When the full moon rises" was the important part of the clue. His father didn't say, "When the moon rises." As in *any* moon. He said, "When the *full* moon rises." What beast was known to rise during a full moon? A werewolf.

Who was the werewolf? Where did it live? Those were great questions. Jason knew only a half-dozen people living in Green Swamp. With a population of about one hundred along Highway 211, pointing to the exact person responsible in a sensible amount of time would be impossible.

Jason wrote a research paper for school on Green Swamp, and while studying the National Natural Landmark, he found Green Swamp actually covered over 13,000 acres of North Carolina. The area of Green Swamp where 211 trickled through was only a small portion of the conservancy. Logic said this person could live somewhere other than on either side of 211. Probably someone like Skeeter who lived alone in the woods with no family and no one to care.

A terrible idea dawned on Jason.

What if Skeeter is the werewolf?

Ridiculous. It was nighttime; the moon was hidden from sight by the cloud cover, but the potent pull would have caused Skeeter to transform by now. Right? Plus, he'd been with Skeeter when Domino was attacked. Right?

Jason glanced at his friend. Skeeter's eyes were squinted against the frosty wind, his cheeks red, but he showed no signs of distress. No extra tufts of hair slid out of the pores in his cheeks. No yellowed fangs protruded from around his lips. No hooked claws inched out of his fingertips. He was normal Skeeter.

He couldn't believe he was having such thoughts. Skeeter had been with him all day. It was Skeeter who remembered he had silver pieces. Skeeter even tried to discourage Jason from sneaking out to run this crazy errand.

"Turn here," Skeeter said, pointing to a road veering to the right.

Jason slowed as he turned to help maintain control and not skid into a ditch. A truck with a flat tire zoomed past.

"Almost there," Skeeter advised.

When Skeeter's shack came into view, Jason gasped. A monster—huge, menacing—was tearing at the front door, flinging shards of metal through the air. It was covered in wiry fur. Sinewy muscles rippled under the dense coat. Dagger ears pointed from the top of its head. The snout was long and mean, housing rows of yellow, snarling teeth.

It relentlessly assaulted the door. The thin metal was shredded, its foam contents breaking off in chunks. With every manic swipe, the thing growled and grunted, foamy saliva blowing from its mouth.

"Holy shit," Skeeter said, barely audible.

Jason's foot had involuntarily lifted from the accelerator when he saw the creature, but now he slammed the pedal.

Skeeter turned to him with wide-eyed bewilderment. "What—"

The ATV hopped the decrepit stairs and slammed into the side of the distracted werewolf. It screeched and flew across the yard, slammed into the side of a tree, its body contorting as it bent around the pine, and dropped into the snow. It rose to its feet and stumbled sideways, momentarily dazed.

The ragged door Jason opened, and he yelped at the three men standing in the doorway.

"Get inside!" A voice ordered. The owner of the voice towered at six-foot-three and was framed like a linebacker. He brandished a gun and motioned for them to come on.

The werewolf was still staggering around. Jason didn't want to be out here when it regained its bearings.

"Come on," Jason grabbed Skeeter by his arm, pulling him out of the ATV and into the house. The tattered door was closed behind them. A chair was stuck under the lock as a makeshift door stop.

Skeeter looked at the three men. "What are you doing in my house?"

"I'll explain later," the big man said. "I'm Detective Bates of Shallotte P.D. I've seen you around town, Skeeter."

Skeeter nodded, his face dawning with recognition. "You bought me lunch one time."

"Two actually, but who's counting?" Bates took in Skeeter, then Jason. "Who's this?"

"My friend, Jason. He lives on 211. He sees ghosts."

Bates nodded. Took the news on the chin, never flinched. "Where do you live, Jason?"

"2521 Green Swamp Road."

"Do either of you know what's going on? For the life of me, I can't see any normal reality where the two of you are out riding an ATV in the middle of the night during a god-awful snowstorm. I've got two tractor trailers wrecked and burned on 211, I've got a wolf the size of a fucking pick-up truck beheading people in the woods, and now you two show up from nowhere." Bates's laugh was full of crazy. "I believe in coincidences, but not like this."

Jason bit his lip, contemplating his options. The guy was police and, therefore, governed by logic. Nothing about this situation was logical. Bates was bound to reject the explanation, right?

"You won't believe me."

"After what I've seen kid, I now believe in Santa Claus, the Tooth Fairy, and the fucking Easter Bunny."

Jason huffed in hopes oxygen would organize his thoughts. "The monster outside is a werewolf. I saw it in a dream. The dead man who once owned our house confirmed it. Skeeter was at my house when he remembered he has silver game pieces with his board game. You need silver to kill werewolves. We snuck out and came here to get the game pieces to make bullets. That's it."

Jason was relieved Bates was not overcome with laughter. "Okay, that's a bit much to take in, but I'll bite." Bates looked at Skeeter. "Where're the silver pieces?"

Before Skeeter answered, a sound like a car wreck erupted from outside. It was followed by another attack on the weakening front door.

"We may not live long enough to use the silver," Bates said as he hurried to the kitchen, where half a dozen glass bottles with rags sticking out the throat lined the counter.

"What's that?" Jason asked, though he watched action movies with Ron all the time and had a fairly good idea.

"Homemade Molotov cocktails."

CHAPTER 46

"The only animals I know to have five claws are weasels, badgers, creatures like that," Buck said.

Those marks were not made by a weasel. Mary mused. A thought occurred to her, though she had no idea why. "Could we go back to the tree stand where we found Steve?"

"Got something?" Ray asked.

"Not sure." Mary frowned. *Maybe.*

It was like a word that you know but can't quite think of, right of the tip of your tongue. Something about the four and five claw marks.

Mary appreciated Ray's silence on the return trip to the tree. It allowed her time to mull over what she was thinking.

Back at the tree, Mary examined the slashes in the bark. On the side, separated from the other wild, overlapping gashes, was a clear set of marks. There was something familiar about the pattern. She removed her glove and placed her right hand over the impression. She gasped.

"You have got to be kidding me," Buck argued.

The imprint was grotesquely larger than Mary's hand, but the similarities were irrefutable. The thumb mark was shorter than the other four fingers and the middle finger was longer, the pinky the shortest of the main four.

"These are human."

CHAPTER 47

Pitter-patter heartbeat, short of breath, skin crawling with fire ants, can't think, pacing the room. Words piled up on her tongue. Every sentence tumbled out as if spoken by a pickled drunk. "Can't believe he'd gone and went there. Ron, if anything...something happens. It's so dark and cold. That thing could be out there. Just waiting. I don't know what I'll do if anything—"

Ron placed his cool hands on Sarah Grace's warm cheeks. Her eyes settled on his. Her thrumming body tuned down a notch. Ron was like that. A calming balm to her cracked worries.

"Easy," Ron said, his voice smooth as almond milk. "You can't help if you get wound up."

As a child, Sarah Grace had been prone to panic attacks. Abnormal circumstances, stressful situations, unusual occurrences had brought them on. When she was fourteen, during a basketball game, a girl from the opposing team had badgered her relentlessly—calling Sarah Grace names, drawing multiple fouls with her dirty game tactics—until finally, Sarah Grace went into panic mode. She sat in the middle of the court and cried until her mother rescued her.

Sarah Grace had entered treatment and over time learned tactics to stop the fits when she felt the oncoming rush of turmoil. After a while, she'd learned to squash the tightness in her chest before it started. Eventually the attacks stopped and were forgotten.

"I'm okay," she whispered to her husband. Surely this wasn't a sign the attacks were returning. "It's under control."

He released her face and held her tight. "What do we do?" she asked, nuzzled against his chest. "Our boy is out there."

"I'm not sure," Ron whispered, his voice unsteady.

"I'll go find him," John said from the kitchen. "I know where Skeeter lives. You two stay here."

"I can't ask you to do that," Ron said.

"You didn't. I volunteered." John shrugged. "Besides, I'm still not completely convinced of all this anyway."

Sarah Grace hugged John. "Thank you."

"I'll have to borrow your truck," John said.

Ron tossed him the keys. John hurried outside. Sarah Grace watched him out the kitchen window. John pushed the snow off the windshield and thawed the glass. After what seemed an eternity, the truck eased out of the driveway and disappeared into the night like a wraith.

Ron placed his hands on her shoulders, kissed the back of her head. "He'll be okay."

"You don't know that."

"I don't know that he won't, either."

Ron was great at making comments like that. Common sense sayings that sounded easy to follow and incorporate into daily habits. Not so easy to put into practice.

Guilt laid on Sarah Grace's heart.

Jason was a strong boy. What he had endured in his short time on this planet was nothing short of horrific. Yet, he laughed, smiled, told jokes, pranked both his parents all the time, made silly TikToks with

Sarah Grace (garnering him over 4,000 followers!). He was a typical pre-teen boy in all the ways that counted. The strength it must take to crawl through a thousand miles of barbed wire and come out with nothing more than a few cuts was extraordinary.

All he had been through, and now this. She was his mother, Ron his father. They were supposed to protect him from the sharp objects that left scar tissue. They were to remove anything that caused him fear or pain. Here, in this house, he was to know nothing but unconditional love. The warmth of security. Peace of mind.

Instead, he was fighting evil. This demon was different than those in his past, but evil, nonetheless.

He deserved better from them. He deserved better from life.

"Ron?" Sarah Grace turned.

"Yes?"

"I believe our son," she said. "Completely." His brow furrowed in confusion. Before he could say anything, she continued. "I choose to stand by him no matter what. I choose to back his play from this moment forward. Because I want him to know that no matter what, he's got me. He's been ridiculed and doubted his entire life. He needs someone to break that cycle." She tapped herself on the chest. "I'm breaking that cycle." She paused a beat to let that sink in, and watched Ron's eyes soften. "It's time for you to choose. No more riding the fence, waiting for some sign to tell you what to believe. You can believe in our son and me, or you can go to the bedroom, go to sleep, and we'll take it from here. The flip-flopping is over."

Ron blinked. "What if he's wrong about all of this?"

"What if he's right?"

"If he's right, God help us," Ron said, throwing up his hands. "If he's right, everything we know is open for discussion."

"Is that why you're still fighting this? Because of what you think you know?"

"Werewolves aren't real, Sarah Grace. Ghosts aren't real. It's fiction, make-believe. If we discover they're real, then the possibilities become endless."

"If ghosts aren't real, how does our son talk to them?"

Ron was silent, his eyes blinking rapidly as he shuffled to find a logical excuse to explain the mystery. He sighed. "I don't know. I can't explain it. Maybe Scully and Mulder can help."

"Then why are you trying? Stop with the what-we-learned-in-school bullshit and accept that there are questions with crazy, impossible answers. If you can't wrap your head around the concept of ghosts and werewolves, fine. Just try being a father that tells his son, 'No matter what, I've got your back.' Why is that so difficult?"

Ron stared at his feet, dejected. "He's out there right now because I refused to hear him."

Cupping his chin with her hand, Sarah Grace drew his eyes to hers. "That's why this must change. Halfway isn't good enough. It's all in or all out. If it's all in, you stand by his side and back his every move. Doesn't matter if you agree or thinks it's crazy. You back him. All the way."

Sarah Grace waited in silence.

Ron nodded with measured assurance. "Yeah, maybe I'm having trouble with the supernatural shit. But I don't have a problem standing behind Jason." A faint smile. "I'm with you guys no matter what."

"Thank you."

After a moment: "I've got to get out to the shop."

"Why?"

"I need to heat up the hearth and prep the loading press. I've got a silver bullet to make."

CHAPTER 48

"Hold on, boy!" John shouted to the truck as the tail whipped around. He twisted the steering wheel to the right to fight the pull of inertia. For one breathless moment, he was sure the truck was sliding into the ditch. But the tires caught a pebble, a grit of sand, a blade of wiry weed. Grinding against the straggly sides of a prayer John sent out to whoever—*whatever*—was listening, the tires lurched the truck forward.

John exhaled a shaky breath. He leaned forward, resting his forearms on the steering wheel, the heat from the defrosting vents rolling over his face in waves.

What a day.

If he'd known how the last five hours were going to unravel, he would've snorted the remaining crumbs of cocaine off the nightstand and gone back to bed. Unconscious bliss was preferable.

What to think of all this. A boy that can see and speak to the dead. A werewolf out to satiate its bloodlust. Silver bullets. Snowstorms.

Like a damned horror movie.

I wonder who'd play me? Johnny Depp? He wondered. *Nah, Ryan Phillippe, for sure.*

Maybe the best thing for him was to take Jason and Skeeter home and head back to the trailer. The hall closet held a few musty blankets.

A camouflage fleece blanket was folded on the couch for Domino. He could crawl under all of them and wait for sunrise. Tomorrow the storm would be over, and he could work on the HVAC to get the heat back on. Worse came to worse, he would borrow the old kerosene heater Ron used in his shop.

Thought you were turning over a new leaf, the negative voice nagged.

"Tomorrow." He huffed. "I'll do better tomorrow, for fuck's sake."

Right now, he needed a snort to settle his nerves. He hadn't had anything since late last night—early this morning—and his skin itched beneath the surface, the backside of the flesh. His teeth felt like they might fall out, and he licked at them with a furry tongue, knowing he was in the initial stage of withdrawal. The shakes would start soon if he didn't feed the demon raging inside. He'd known men who did anything—*anything*—for a hit, even self-harm. Maybe a razor down the forearm would let him scratch that fucking itch.

Hell, even a beer would help. Maybe Skeeter had a brew or a shot of bourbon.

John rounded the last turn on approach to Skeeter's shack and the first thing he noticed was an upside-down ATV in the middle of the road. In the dark, snow falling, he wasn't one hundred percent sure, but it looked like Ron's.

The next thing that caught his attention was the giant wolf clawing at the door and the wood walls around the door frame. The thing stopped its attack, now aware of his presence, and turned its burning eyes on him.

It took two steps on its hindquarters—*Walking like a man*—before dropping to all fours. Its teeth flared from its snout and, while John couldn't hear the growl, he felt it in the deepest chambers of his heart.

What do I do?

Hit it?

Get the fuck outta here? He couldn't do that; Skeeter and Jason were in the shack.

John's mind went blank, taking in the beast as he clawed at his forearm. He was frozen with fear, withdrawal, and the shock that everything Jason said…was true.

Someone—a head—appeared in the shredded doorway, just a silhouette at first. A body followed and the person was recognizable. John had seen him before. His size was his calling card; a tall glass of water, built like a pro football player.

Dwayne Johnson would play him in the movie.

The wolf crept toward him, the hair on its back spiked straight up, spine bowed like a spring ready to uncoil. It was focused on John, unaware of the guy stepping out on the small porch. With a lighter in his hand. And what? A bottle?

"The fuck?" As soon as John asked, the question was answered.

The big guy lit a dangling rag from the mouth of the bottle. The flame licked up the rag in a greedy gulp. The linebacker said something—a muffled sound, drenched in panic—and the wolf halted, its head flipped around. He threw the bottle, and it exploded like a grenade against the monster's pelt.

Flames clung to the wolf, lighting its raging body in an orange-yellow glow, the burning, melting hair billowing black smoke as the beast howled in pain. Flecks of singed hair and skin dropped to the snow with a *hiss.*

Howling again, it darted into the woods, a fiery torpedo. John watched it dance through the trees.

He heard a muffled shout. On the porch Jason, Skeeter, the linebacker, a man dressed in all black tactical gear, and a scared-to-death guy in a suit jumped up and down, shouting for him to pick them up.

John accelerated, careful not to overdo it, eased around the ATV, and pulled to a stop by the cabin. Jason hugged John from the back seat. It was the hug that reminded him he was alive and safe—for now—and as his brain sank back into his body, he realized the itch had gone. Only for a moment. Small victories, right?

"What—" John began.

"Go! Go! Go!" The linebacker shouted in the seat next to him.

John went, driving as fast as he dared down Little Red Road, when he detected a strong scent. Not gasoline. Chemical. "What's that smell?"

The linebacker held up another bottle. "Just in case it comes back."

"How do I know you?" John asked the linebacker.

"I'm Detective Bates with Shallote P.D. You gave me information back in the spring when some fencing equipment was stolen from your boss's warehouse."

Ah, yes. "Thank you for finding that stuff. I thought I would have to dig each post by hand."

"Did your boss apologize? I remember him blaming you rather publicly."

"He did in his own way. Which is to say...no, he did not." John caught Jason's eyes in the mirror. "Jason, I'm sorry I didn't believe you. You were right all along. I don't know how that's possible, but you were right."

"I understand," Jason said, holding John's gaze. "Now you know."

"Your parents are worried sick. You shouldn't have run out like that."

"I know, but I had to. Ron doesn't believe me. Not really. I knew this was a werewolf and our only chance of killing it were those pieces of silver. I did what I had to do."

"Speaking of silver," John said, tense with anticipation, "did you find them?"

Skeeter held out his hand. In the palm were four figurines cast in silver.

"You're sure they're *real* silver?" John asked.

"So the game box says," Bates answered with a deep gulp. "We'll see."

If those aren't real silver, we are in real trouble. He didn't dare say it aloud, fearful it might jinx the whole damn thing. Whether or not that thing was a werewolf was to be determined, but it was definitely a wolf. The largest wolf known to man, if John had to guess.

"Jason," John said from over his shoulder, "does Ron still have the bullet cast and press machine? Please say he does."

"He does."

"Phew. Good news." A question suddenly occurred to him. "How are you in the middle of this, Detective Bates?"

"Long story," Bates answered, continuing to scan the dark woods surrounding them. "We'll get to it later."

"Do you know what's going on?" John asked hesitantly.

Bates recounted everything he'd been told. Turned out they were on the same page. Tangled in a weird fucking mess.

"And you believe all that?"

"Did you see that thing? Hell yeah, I believe it." Bates eyed him with scrutiny. "Why? You don't?"

"I didn't at first. Then I wasn't sure. Jason said things that made me want to believe, but..."

"The story was too crazy." Bates finished.

John nodded.

"It was easy for me because I watched an entire SWAT team get eviscerated by that thing. I saw it up close and personal. That's no run-of-the-mill animal indigenous to Green Swamp. Hell, I don't think it's indigenous anywhere." Bates paused before adding: "I also have a little insight that assists my belief in what Jason says."

"Such as?"

"Let's get to Jason's house and I'll tell everyone."

CHAPTER 49

A roaring engine. V-8 by the sound of it. Ray heard it before he saw it.

"What's that?" Mary asked, stepping away from the gashed-up tree.

"A truck."

"Who else would be out in this mess?"

"Someone desperate," Ray said, opening the door to the ATV. "Let's get out to the road. See who it is and what's wrong."

Ray found a flat, open area beside the dirt road, and waited. Headlights appeared through the foggy mist of snow and then a black truck with a shiny grill. Ray climbed out of the warm cabin and waved his flashlight as the truck slowed to a halt. Dark silhouettes jumped from the cab.

"Ray?" a faintly recognizable voice called. "What are you doing out here?"

The man stepped into the headlights and Ray almost cried with relief. "Hot damn, Bates, that you?"

The giant man approached Ray, patted him on the shoulder. "You guys shouldn't be out here, Ray. It's dangerous. And not just because of the storm."

Ray squinted at Bates. Curious thing to say. Like he knew something. "We're beginning to realize just how dangerous. People have been killed."

"Killed?"

"Two that we know of. Cliff and Steve Gainey. Mary Stuart's"—he nodded at her—"husband, Tommy, and another friend, Jerry Landon, never returned from a hunting trip, and...Northern...never returned home after a date last night."

Bates stumbled back in shock. "Northern is missing? Have you reported this?"

"Maggie called this morning. They said she needed to be missing for twenty-four hours before they could do anything."

"Jesus Christ," Bates growled. "You should've called me, Ray. I was out here already."

"The wreck?"

"Yeah. I was called out because it was unusual."

"Unusual how?"

"Let's just say it wasn't an accident."

"Where you guys headed?"

"Jason's house," Bates said, pointing at a boy of about twelve. "His parents are Ron and Sarah Grace Elliot."

Ray wondered why this child was out in all of this but held his tongue. More clues. "I know of the Elliots." Ray had an idea. "Sounds like we all have information to trade. Can you go get Ron and Sarah Grace and meet us at my house. There's a lot going on and it sounds like you know something that may help explain some of it."

"Anything to get away from what we've seen tonight," Bates said.

"Which is?" Ray asked as Bates trudged back to the truck.

"At your house." Bates added: "And be on the lookout. For anything."

Ray twirled his finger—*Let's go*—at his crew and hobbled through the ever-thickening snow back to his ATV. He followed the truck until it turned left on Camp Branch Road. Ray continued straight. The tents at Tin Shed were barely visible when he flew by. Ray had the pedal to the floor.

The conversation with Bates worried him. Without saying anything, the detective had said a lot. He wanted to get away from what he'd seen tonight. He referenced something dangerous. Told Ray to be on the lookout. References, Ray believed, to the owner of the marks in the tree bark, and, inevitably, the killer roaming Green Swamp.

What could make those marks?

Mary was right; the impressions matched a human hand, but humans didn't have razor-sharp claws that left two-inch deep incisions. A keen-bladed ax at full swing couldn't do that.

"A human can't be responsible for those marks," Mary opined, and Ray jumped.

She reading my mind? "I think we're close to finding out what's going on," Ray said. He turned down Two Mile Road and stomped on the gas. He wanted to be home. He wanted the detective to arrive. He wanted answers.

"Maybe," Mary said, "but Northern, Tommy, and Jerry are still missing."

"We've looked everywhere we can think to look. I don't know where else to go. If the detective knows something that can help guide us to our next step, I'm all ears."

"You think he does?"

Ray nodded. "Absolutely."

CHAPTER 50

Sarah Grace was too relieved to see Jason and Skeeter get out of the truck to be perplexed by the three new guys. She hurried to the front door as it opened, grabbing Jason in her arms and swirling him around while smothering him with kisses. "I'm sorry," she whispered in his ear. "So sorry."

"It's okay," Jason said, pulling away. He reached into his pocket and produced four silver figurines. "We got the pieces."

"Great. Ron's in the shop, heating up the cast."

"He is?" Jason asked.

Sarah Grace understood at the skeptical tone. It was warranted. "Yes." She hugged John, thanking him. Embraced Skeeter. "I'm so glad you guys are okay, but who are these gentlemen?"

"Detective Bates, ma'am," the oversized guy said. His hair was buzzcut and his pale skin was red from the cold. He carried sadness in his eyes, the weight of it tugging the corners down toward his cheeks. "Sorry for the intrusion. This is Dakota Watts. He works with me. And this is Jarrod Howery, bank manager at Duffer Brothers." Her expression must have required a follow-up, because Bates said, "Long story."

Sarah Grace's eyes were taking him in when she noticed red droplets on the front of the detective's jacket, then a seeping bullet hole just above the armpit. "Are you shot, detective?"

Detective Bates looked down, inspected the bullet hole, and nodded. "Yes, ma'am. A lot has happened tonight."

"Sarah Grace," Jason said, stepping between them, "we have to go to someone named Ray's house."

"Eason? Ray Eason?" She was confused. Three strange men—one shot—with blood spattered on their clothes, were standing in her living room, and now Ray Eason was being thrown into the mix. "What's going on?"

Detective Bates held up a hand. "Mrs. Elliot, there are things that need to be discussed. Ray wants us to meet at his house to share what we know."

"Why?"

"Because his daughter is missing, some hunters are dead, and two more could still be out there."

"And," Jason added, "we just saw the thing I've been warning you guys about."

This is crazier than imagined, as if that was possible. Sarah Grace paced the floor, trying to fit the pieces together, round pegs for square holes.

"Ron's preparing the hearth and press machine to make the silver bullets," Sarah Grace explained. "If you saw it, and it is what Jason says it is, he needs to finish."

"Let's do this," John suggested. "Why don't all of you go to the Eason's? Dakota and I will stay with Ron in the shop. We can be on watch while Ron makes the bullets. Then we'll join all of you in a little while."

Sarah Grace wanted to say no. She agreed only because she could see Jason thought it the right thing to do. She had made a pact to follow his lead. "Alright. Not happy about it, but...alright."

"Grab the Molotov off the front porch and take it with you." Bates advised Dakota. "Damn thing hates to be set on fire."

"Follow me," Sarah Grace led them to the middle bedroom where the small arsenal was assembled.

"Nice," Bates exclaimed. He snatched up a shotgun from the corner, racked the pump. "You guys were prepared."

"Not prepared enough, apparently." Sarah Grace stuffed a Taurus 9mm in her back jeans pocket.

All of the weapons were confiscated. Sarah Grace, Bates, Jarrod, and Skeeter loaded into a Ford Explorer. Jason came running out after locking Addie in her kennel. He hopped in, carrying his backpack. Sarah Grace wasn't sure why he needed it but was too worried about leaving Ron behind to ask.

John and Dakota hurried across the yard and disappeared inside the shop. The Explorer wasn't four-wheel-drive, but Sarah Grace was confident she could grapple her way to the Eason's without putting them in a ditch. She backed the SUV from under the single garage shed but stopped when Ron rushed out.

"Give me a sec," she said.

Ron met her under the cover of the garage. "John filled me in. You okay?"

"I don't like leaving you here," she shouted over the wind.

"I'll be okay. You get to the Eason's and be careful. I'll be there shortly. Love you."

"I love you." Sarah Grace hugged him. She wanted to never let go. An unpleasant feeling stirred deep inside. The day's events had left her shaken, her nerves frayed. She knew better than to give credence to gut premonitions, but she couldn't shake the sense that she would never see Ron again.

She watched him jog back to the shed and felt helpless to stop the coming nightmare.

"Everything alright?" Bates asked, as she climbed behind the wheel.

"Not really."

The drive to the Eason's was slow, taking close to forty-five minutes, with Sarah Grace easing around turns to avoid losing control. Bates informed her she would have to go the back way. When Sarah Grace asked why, Bates was silent.

The detective was twitchy on their trek through the woods. Jason had said they saw the monster, but no one was saying where said monster was currently located. Was it stalking them right now? Creeping in the shadows? Waiting to pounce?

The Explorer exited the woods of Green Swamp without interference. She turned between the gaslit flames and pulled up to the front porch steps. The door opened. A pretty, melancholy woman stood in the doorway, the glow of a warm home radiating around her. She was no more than forty, brown wavy hair, five-foot-six, wearing khaki utility pants and a puffer vest.

"Come on in." She waved.

Sarah Grace held Jason's hand as they climbed the stairs. She could feel the gritty crunch of salt under her boots, but snow and ice continued to try to accumulate on the brick.

The woman shook hands with Bates, who was first to the door. "Hi, I'm Mary. They're waiting for you in the dining room. Coffee's in the kitchen."

Sarah Grace shook hands with the woman and introduced herself, Jason, and Skeeter.

"Glad you're here," Mary said and closed the door. "Hang your jackets by the door and head to the kitchen."

The house was warm and smelled of percolating coffee. The living room housed an enormous fireplace where a log the size of a washing machine burned. By the window, a Christmas tree alluded to a holiday season that lacked the spirit of holidays past. Sarah Grace again felt a tug of regret. Jason was dealing with more trauma rather than being excited about his first Christmas with them.

The kitchen was built to cook for a hundred people. No doubt such meals were prepared on a regular basis.

Sarah Grace carried a steaming mug into the dining room, and seated herself next to Bates, whose wound was being treated by Maggie Eason. The detective hissed every time Maggie dabbed the bloody flesh.

Jason and Skeeter slipped past Sarah Grace with mugs of hot chocolate warming their hands and sat at the table. Seemed everyone was here. Except for Ron, John, and Dakota.

"Good evening," Ray greeted, his eyes moving to each person in attendance. "Thanks for being here. Over the last twenty-four hours there have been some crazy things happening in Green Swamp. I thought it best if we all gather and tell what we know. Collectively, we may be able to figure out what is going on."

Ray started at the beginning. He told them everything he knew. Everyone in the room listened and responded with shock, awe, curiosity, and fear. Sarah Grace bit back a sob when he recounted finding Cliff, Arlene, and Misty. They hadn't left town, after all; they had left life.

Sarah Grace shook her head in surreal disbelief.

"We found Steve about two hours ago in a tree-stand off Camp Branch Road. He, like his father, suffered a terrible mangling. Animalistic, rabid. He bled out in the tree stand. On the side of the tree, in the bark, we found cuts and gashes like nothing we've ever seen. Whatever attacked Steve tried to get to him when he got into that tree stand. And whatever attacked him was big with claws at least six inches long. My guess, this is the beast Cliff referred to in his message.

"As far as Northern, Tommy, and Jerry go, we don't know where they are. Detective, can you offer any details about the wreck that may be helpful?"

Bates recounted the details and what the investigation had uncovered thus far. He added that no evidence of Northern was present at the scene. "I found hair fibers stuck in the hinge of a trailer door. Not human hair. It was odd, I thought, so I retrieved samples. I did a little checking and found the hair fibers to be inconclusive." He paused and gauged the reaction of the room. Leaning forward, elbows on the table, he gripped the coffee mug, and continued. "You all may remember the little boy who was killed at the Creepy Swamp Haunted Hayride. DNA from that incident was inconclusive. I now believe this is the same animal responsible for that."

"I thought you guys said a bear killed that little boy," Mary said.

"Chief Lowell made a judgment call based on the findings. The only animal that could come close to such savagery was a bear. A big one. The thinking was the DNA samples were compromised at the scene. Public pressure, Governor Mason leaning hard for answers, the media frenzy, somebody had to be blamed, yada yada."

"So, the bear killed by hunters a week after the accident wasn't the animal responsible?" Sarah Grace asked.

Bates shook his head. "Apparently not. Looked right at the time though."

"Does anyone know what this beast is?" Mary asked, looking around the room.

Jason raised his hand slowly. "I do. Some of you already know, as well. The ones who don't, will think I'm crazy. But I'm not the only one who saw it."

Bates nodded grimly. "He's not lying."

"It's a werewolf," Jason announced. No one breathed, just watched him. "And for some reason, it wants to kill us all."

CHAPTER 51

Did he say werewolf?

TF? Craziest thing Ray ever heard.

Except it fit. Somehow, it slid into place like it belonged. He worked it over and found no holes in the theory. A full moon last night. A full moon tonight, with a Full Blood Super Moon happening in the wee hours of the morning. Should look wicked as the Gates of Hell, with the snow and cardinal tints of lunar shading blending together. The injuries to both Cliff and Steve were the same as the gashes in the tree. The marks suggestive of human anatomy. A werewolf was a human who transformed into a beast during a full moon.

It all fit.

Except for, of course, the obvious. "Werewolves aren't real," Ray heard himself say aloud.

The way Jason looked at him—like a child still learning the facts of life—made Ray avert his eyes to his calloused hands.

"I know," Jason said carefully, "it's hard to get around. If I didn't have a special knowledge of the supernatural, I wouldn't believe it either. Things exist that are...unexplainable. That's a fact." His voice was confident now. Sarah Grace nodded for him to continue. Telling him his words were worth hearing. He stood. "This *is* a werewolf. It *has* killed people, and it *will* kill more if we don't find a way to stop it."

"The only chance we have," Sarah Grace added, taking Jason's hand, "is to put aside our disbelief, and hear what my son is saying. He hasn't been wrong yet."

"As I said,"—Bates locked eyes with Ray—"he's telling the truth. I saw the thing, big as day and twice as scary. It took out five members of the Wilmington SWAT team right in front of me. The most terrifying shit you could imagine in a dozen lifetimes."

Ray decided to set aside the werewolf idea. He'd come back to it later. He needed to find his daughter and chasing the validity of folklore was no help. "Okay, I'll bite. It fits, I get it. But *my daughter* is still out there somewhere. *Tommy* is still out there somewhere, along with Jerry. How do we find them? How does this information about a werewolf help us?"

"Maybe we're looking at this all wrong," Garrett said.

"Meaning?" Ray asked.

"A werewolf is a werewolf only at night. When the moon rises, right?"

"Yes."

"Well...that means it's a human during the day, and the days *between* the full moon cycle. With me?"

Everyone nodded, waiting for the punchline.

"Humans live in houses. And this human must live in Green Swamp, or somewhere nearby. As soon as the moon rises, it comes out."

"And," Bates wagged a finger, his detective antennae ramrod straight, "the first killing in Green Swamp was a month ago. The Ramirez boy. We could potentially narrow it down to new residents. At least start there."

"We find the murderer, maybe we find the missing," Garrett said.

"How do we find out who recently moved to Green Swamp?" Ray asked. He wasn't sure if this was the correct path to venture down but hunting the woods had given them nothing but one dead body and endless questions. With no clues to the location of his daughter, maybe it was the best option.

"Generally, I would call it in," Bates said. "But with no radio, cell service, or landlines, we're forced to go old school."

"Old school?" Sarah Grace asked.

"We brainstorm. You guys live here. What do you know? Who's new to the neighborhood? Ray, have you noticed anyone new in your store?"

Ray saw new faces every day. Lots of tourists traveled 211. Heading to Southport, a place made famous by those *I Know What You Did Last Summer* movies. Heading to Holden Beach. Heading to Myrtle Beach. So many faces they blended together. Only the regulars stood out. Still, he felt a tickle of recognition. Not a face, but a conversation. He tried to home in on it while the others threw in bits and pieces of what they knew.

It was Maggie who helped him whittle a shape from the fog of memory. "Didn't we have a lady come in a few weeks ago and introduce herself?" Maggie whispered to him. "Said she bought the Houghton House."

That's right. Ray had heard gossip and small talk about a massive renovation underway on the property. The old, dilapidated house—rumored to be haunted— had been finally bought and placed under construction. The woman who bought the property stopped in to buy some fresh fruit. She introduced herself. "Victoria Naughton," Ray said over a lot of murmuring.

Everyone quieted, conjuring a face to go with the name.

"The realtor plastered on every billboard in Brunswick County?" Bates asked.

Ray shrugged as his thoughts scrambled down the rabbit hole of belief. He felt his heart hammering at the idea they were making progress. Somehow, without leaving the dining table, they were making progress. "She's new to the Swamp. Maggie and I met her a few weeks ago. She renovated the Houghton House."

"Said she moved in *that* week," Maggie added.

"She came to my house yesterday," Mary interjected. "Was super friendly. And beautiful. No way it's her."

"Why did she come to your house?" Bates inquired. Always asking questions.

"Her SUV's battery was dead. Needed a jump. I drove her home and jumped off her car."

"See anything unusual?"

"No. Everything seemed normal."

"The first case I ever worked as a detective was a missing sixteen-year-old girl." Bates reminisced. "Interviewed the girl's distraught parents. She was hanging out with a bad crowd, cutting school, smoking pot, not studying, you know the cliche. She was dating this guy, twenty-five. Her parents forbid her from seeing this guy. She ran away, was never seen or heard from again. Obviously, the boyfriend was our prime suspect. I go talk to him. He was very upset. Showed me his phone where he had tried calling her over a hundred times in the last twenty-four hours.

"While talking with him, his parents were present. For some reason, the dad was giving off weird vibes. A real clean-cut guy, always wearing golf attire. He said all the right things, was emotional, invested in the investigation, helpful in all the ways we needed, but something just kept poking the detective in me.

"You see, what I realized after multiple talks with him was though he appeared distraught, those emotions never reached his eyes. Hard and dark all the time, always astutely attentive to what I was saying, to the activities of others around him. Then I caught him staring at my partner. She was an attractive young detective, stares come with the territory. But, again, those eyes. He hid everything with displays of sadness, but he couldn't hide the lack of depth in his eyes.

"I took a closer look at him and discovered he had contact with several currently missing women over his lifetime, cases that'd gone cold. He became suspect number one, and I finally nailed him when I put his cell phone and the girl's cell phone in the same spot on the night she went missing. He met her to give her a ride to his house, but raped and murdered her instead. We found the body, confirmed the crime and criminal with DNA, and closed the case. He's now sitting on death row."

"Moral of the story?" Ray asked.

"Just because all seems normal, doesn't mean it is. We should vet this Victoria," Bates suggested. "Maybe we pay a visit disguised as a wellness check. Good neighbors and all."

CHAPTER 52

The chances the game pieces were actual silver was monumentally low. Ron threw out a small "Thank you" when they melted rather than catching fire.

He carefully poured the melted silver from the crucible into the buckshot mold. He held his breath in hopes the mold retained its shape under the intense heat. He waited a moment before dumping the shot in cold water. The water bubbled and fizzed with steam.

The preferred ammo for this situation was shell casings for a handgun, but he lacked molds that would withstand the 1,763 degrees necessary to melt silver. The buckshot mold was now warped but being steel allowed it to hold up long enough for the shot to harden. The game pieces contained enough silver to make one shotgun shell. A nerve-racking concept. No spares for misses. No extras for mistakes.

No point worrying about something he couldn't control. If one shell was all he had, then one shell was all he'd need.

As a child, Ron had watched his grandfather move deftly around this reloading table. The dies, charts, primers, chamfering casings, deburring tools, load densities, and an encyclopedia's worth of other arcane hand-loading terminology and practices. His grandfather's fingers were always smooth and economical in motion, his hands continuations of the machines placed on the table before him. He had consulted charts full of precise numbers that meant nothing to Ron at the time, but which Granddaddy had sworn by. The hours spent listening to the old man regale Ron with stories of hunting and fishing and life in Green Swamp had been the highlights of his day. He cherished those memories with a fondness that caused his chest to tighten when he thought of them. He missed Vernon, and hoped the lessons learned in this shed over twenty years earlier would serve him well tonight.

The irony that his grandfather was now helping from the grave was not lost on Ron.

Ron prepped the shell-loading machine, but stopped when John said, "Uh oh."

Ron's heart skipped. "What?"

John's face clouded with fear, and he mumbled a hushed, "It's here." Dakota moved from the opposite side of the shed to observe. John pointed out the window at a sharp angle to the left. "There."

"I don't—" Dakota began, then paused. "Looks like a shadow."

"Shadows don't move like that," John whispered. "And they don't have eyes that glow red."

Ron squeezed in, squinted through the fog of snow. He pressed his forehead to the frosty glass and cupped the sides with his hand. For an instant, nothing. Movement from his left wrenched his eyes in that direction.

The monster stopped in front of the shed and locked its fiery eyes on his. Ron stumbled back, lost his footing, and smacked the concrete floor with his ass. "Get back," he hissed and spider-crawled backward.

The window exploded inward. The cheap, metal blinds clattered to the floor amid a spray of insulated glass. One charred arm burst through the opening, and in a blink, the top half of Dakota's skull slid off the lower half. The bowl of hairy bone cracked against the floor, the contents plopping out like congealed oatmeal. Dakota's finger squeezed two shots into the floor, his nervous system spasming in shock.

John yelped and dashed to the back of the shed. Ron scrambled to his feet beside John. Jason had warned him of this monster. It was really real. A fucking werewolf. A creature of the night, tethered to the moon like a dog on a leash. It tore at the window, its knife-bladed claws slashing and mangling the vinyl frame and wood-casing holding it in place. Jaws snapped, ripped, tore at the material. Its eyes flared like hot coals. Like its skull was a flaming furnace.

Flames.

"The Molotov!" Ron shouted at John.

John leaped across the room where the bottle sat on a workbench by the second window. Dakota had placed it there to be close at hand, while he looked out that window.

Most of the monster's burned upper body had managed to squirm through the hole. It continued to claw at the opening to widen it. The growling was maddening. The promise of mayhem more a guarantee than a threat.

The fur coat and flesh beneath was charred black, blistered raw in places. Damage from the first Molotov. But through the quivering mass of rage, Ron was amazed to see what appeared to be gray patches of repaired flesh and hair dotting its scorched hide. Rejuvenating.

Dear god. Ron ducked as the Molotov flew from John's hand. It burst into a napalm thundercloud, washing the animal in its molten hail.

An inhuman screech bellowed from its blistering throat as it disengaged itself from the window. Disappeared. Silent. The men were thrust into the unknown—couldn't see it, couldn't hear it—for a few seconds, before a howl pierced the belly of the night like a switchblade, emptying its bowels on the land below.

"Fuck me." Ron spat. His knees were so weak he used the workbench counter as a crutch. Deep breaths. Closed his eyes to concentrate on slowing the blast-beating heart that threatened to punch a hole through his ribs.

"You okay?" John asked. He popped the ring on the dusty fire extinguisher Ron had never used and sprayed the fluffy mist on the flames. The shed smelled of rank chemicals and meat, a nauseating combination. Ron checked on John to see how he was reacting to that reek; John had smelled it before. If haunting memories were rising from the dead, John wasn't showing it.

"I think so." But then: "You need to watch for that thing in case it comes back. I have to finish this shell."

John tossed the extinguisher aside and grabbed the assault rifle from Dakota's clinched fist. He retrieved a sheet Ron used to protect the ammo-reloading equipment from dust. Covered the dead soldier and his still-twitching right foot.

Only the sheet made it worse. With every jerk, the entire sheet moved as if being dragged off the body by an unseen hand. Like one of Jason's not-so-imaginary friends. John uncovered the foot. Let it shake.

Ron finished prepping the shell-loading machine. He deprimed a shell, dropped a primer, pushed in the powder, plugged a wad, added the silver double-ought, and crimped the casing.

He grabbed the shotgun he'd taken with him when he went out to the shed, ejected the unused shell, and popped home the supercharged, werewolf slaying, silver-balled casing.

"Let's go."

CHAPTER 53

The doorbell chimed. The chatter stopped. Sarah Grace jumped from her chair. When she returned, she was accompanied by—Bates presumed—her husband Ron, and John.

"It just attacked them," Sarah Grace announced breathlessly. She looked at Bates, her watery eyes sad and tired. "I'm sorry."

An entire squadron of men. Good men with families. Wives and children who would never see their loved ones again. Lives stolen while they weren't looking.

Bates nodded. What else was there to do?

"What happened?" Ray asked, standing now, back stiff.

"I was making the shotgun shell with silver shot," Ron began. He replayed the attack, John thwarting the creature with a Molotov, and their arrival to the Eason's. "There is one thing that may be pertinent."

"Yeah?" Ray asked.

"It looked like it was already healing from the burns of the first Molotov. Some of the fur and skin was charred, but I made out significant patches of skin and hair that looked...new." Ron paused for impact. "This thing can rejuvenate itself."

"That's why we need the silver bullets," Jason said. "It can't come back from that."

"I'm sorry, Jason," Ron said, moving to his son. "I was wrong. So wrong."

Jason nodded. Accepted the somber man's embrace.

Bates was glad to see the unity happening before him. With everyone present. It was needed. This beast was a killing machine. If they stood any chance, it was as a group. Strength in the pack. No coincidence, a wolf motto.

"This is real?" Ray asked the room. "A werewolf?"

"Yes." Jason nodded.

To the extent of his knowledge, Bates knew one could become a werewolf by being bitten by a werewolf. Except, now he remembered that movie with Michael J. Fox where the character—*What was his name?*—found the condition hereditary. It was a comedy, and the transformations were not driven by the moon, so probably not a lot of significance. Unless the condition *was* hereditary.

No time to chase that lead. Didn't matter now, anyway. Three questions were all they needed to answer: *Who* was the werewolf? *Where* was the werewolf? *How* do we kill it?

Ron was here with the silver. Which left two questions. Which circled back to possible suspects.

"Ron, do you know the realtor, Victoria Naughton?" Bates asked.

"I know *of* her." Ron shrugged. "She renovated the Houghton House. Why?"

"Her name came up in conversation. She's new to Green Swamp. Coincidentally, she moved into her new house around the same time the Ramirez kid was killed."

"The beautiful blonde-headed lady,"—Ron deadpanned—"who sells million-dollar North Carolina properties is a werewolf. That what you're saying?"

"Nope. I'm saying she moved to the area at the same time this started. That makes her someone we should visit."

Ron thought about it for a moment. "Let's go."

Bates only wanted a few men going. Leaving the Eason house unprotected was dangerous. Who possessed the shell with the silver buckshot, that was the conundrum. In the end, he decided the buckshot should go with them. They were walking into an unknown situation completely blind. Chances were, this lady was not a werewolf, but better safe than sorry.

"Okay," Bates announced, "Ron, Brent, and Buck will join me at the Houghton House. The rest of you stay here and keep brainstorming."

"I'm going, Bates," Ray said. "My daughter is still out there."

"Me, too." Mary stood in defiance.

Bates shook his head. "I need someone to stay here. Ray, you're hobbled. Mary, you're a—"

"A woman? Yeah, I noticed. But I'm still going."

"I was going to say...you're a *mother*. With two small kids." Bates raised his hands in defense.

"If my legs were missing,"—Ray gritted—"I'd walk with my arms."

Hard-headed country folk! "Fine. Brent, Garrett, and John, you three stay here and watch over the wives and children. Those coming with me, we're mobile in two minutes. Weapons up." Ron captained the vehicle. Ron, Mary, Buck, and Ray tried to squeeze into the back seat. Too tight. Buck elected to sit in the bed.

"I've been out in the cold all night," he quipped, when Mary offered to sit on someone's knee. "Few more minutes won't kill me."

The truck bobbed and weaved down the driveway. Ron took the trek slow. Traveling was a rigorous test of concentration. At least the snowfall was not torrential like it had been, even if the wind was still screaming like a locomotive whistle.

No one spoke, all lost in their own trains of thought, contemplating the chances that Victoria was the culprit. No doubt writing her off because of her stunning good looks.

It was a common event in American culture. Prejudice, based on looks. Beautiful people—in designer clothes, driving imported vehicles—were overlooked, assumed innocent. While the less fortunate—and those of color—were pulled over, harassed, targeted on bias. Hell, Bates was guilty of it himself.

Objectivity would not allow her looks to be the deciding factor of guilt or innocence. If she was home, she would be innocent. If so, cast the net wider and see who was next to consider.

If not...

Ron eased to a creeping crawl as he turned the wheel. The entrance to the Houghton House sloped down ten feet, and they all held their breath as the truck slid to the bottom. Ron removed his foot from the brake and resumed his travels.

The wooded entryway spread-eagled after fifty yards. Open fields on either side of the driveway stretched a hundred acres to the furthest snow-crusted treelines. The land was bare of crops, the season of harvest passed, now a white, unblemished blanket. To Bates's right, a swatch of empty ground announced a house once occupied the space. It was the set of the trees, the natural gas tank rusting to metal-flaked dust, the warped electrical pole, the collapsed swing-set like the bones of a prehistoric animal. This was where the Houghton House had been built and stood until Victoria came along and moved it.

Bates had heard the history of the Houghton House. The deaths inside its walls, the suicide. Was the house haunted, the timbers cursed? Or were the occupants cursed, coincidentally drawn to the house by some unknown entity? Could it be a little of both? Two afflicted souls drawn to one another by an unseen force in the universe.

Either way, this land—and the history of the Houghton House—would eventually fade. Victoria, removing the house from eyesight would speed the process.

These killings, however, would live in infamy. The tales would be endless, the recounting bloated with half-truths and embellished drama. The number of deaths greatly inflated. Wounds that would never heal.

Timeless, Bates thought. *The stuff of legend and lore. Like werewolves.*

The truck trudged through another canopy of trees, the opening a dark tunnel transporting them to another dimension in time and space.

"Her new house," Mary said, causing Bates to flinch from the sudden end of silence, "is just around the next bend."

"Tell me about her," Bates said to Mary. He wanted a sense of the real estate Viking before the formal introduction.

"Very pretty," Mary answered. "Stunning, actually. Perfect teeth, hair, skin. It all looked effortless. Like she woke up looking like that."

"Not her physicality. Her behavior. The devil is in the details. What did she say? How were her eyes when she spoke?"

"Eyes?"

"When she said something amusing and smiled or laughed, did her eyes react?"

"I don't—"

"It's easy to miss. But once you see it, you'll always see it." Bates let the lesson go as the house slid into view. "What did she talk about? Not you, her?"

Mary told him about the meeting as best as she could recollect.

"After a few minutes, she got around to her car not starting. I drove her over and gave her a jump. That's it."

The truck stopped in front of the garage, leaving Bates no time to further dissect the conversation. The house was gigantic. Modern farmhouse. White vertical HardiPlank with black trim and accents. Straight out of a magazine.

Which added another question to the pile he was sorting: why use the skeleton of the old house, add new limbs, wrap it in new flesh, and call it home? Why not just build everything new? The Houghton House had strong bones, withstanding decades of hurricanes, the gnawing persistence of termites, the cracking weight of time. But today's technology lent itself to producing lumber impervious to nature and its furious digestive track. It would be cheaper to build a new home than disassemble an existing house, move it here, and add on. Made no sense.

"All of you wait here," Bates said, as the truck engine ticked like a metronome, and the wind whistled a death song in the tree hollows. "Let me check things out."

Silence greeted him.

Simultaneously, three doors opened, and everyone exited the cab. The truck bobbed as Buck hauled himself out of the bed. Left alone in the passenger seat, Bates said, "Glad we had this conversation," and stepped into the cold.

Bates climbed the wraparound porch on his tiptoes. Silent as a mouse. Long, black-framed windows lined the front wall. Inside, the soft glow of lamps suggested occupancy but confirmed nothing. Bates squinted through the sheer fabric of the dreamy curtains blocking the view inside but was only able to ascertain blurry images.

Nodding at the group, Bates instructed everyone to step closer. He whispered, "Buck, you mosey around the house. Stay quiet. Come back and tell me what you see." Buck nodded, surprisingly light-foot-ed on his departure. "I'm going to ring the doorbell, you three find a crack in the curtains and see if anything moves."

"Something wrong?" Mary asked.

Bates frowned. "Detective radar is beeping."

Bates eased to the door and pressed the doorbell, a fancy thing with a built-in camera. A chime tolled from inside, long and adequate at waking the dead. He listened close for thudding feet. Neither heard nor felt a vibration. He raised his eyebrows to the window gawkers. Each shook a head.

An empty house was not a confession of guilt, but—

"Hey, guys!" Buck whispered hard from off the porch. "There's basement doors back here. Someone's beating on them."

CHAPTER 54

Antsy was the best word for it. His feet wanted to move, go some-where. Jason pushed his chair back, let his legs carry him to the living room. He stood in front of the fire for only a moment before retreating a few steps, the heat so intense he thought his pants would combust. A glowing chunk of wood broke off and plopped in the ashes. Lay there smoldering, the glow pulsing like a heartbeat.

Not unlike the eyes of the beast. Hot with hatred. Fed by a savage, primal instinct. Driven by its need to kill.

Why?

That was like asking why ghosts exist? Why his real parents loved drugs more than him? Why this gift/curse? Search as he might for answers, the universe remained silent. Stubborn in its dereliction of duty.

He had hoped for another visit from his father. For some reason, the dead man only chose to appear in his dreams. Unlike Vernon, who walked through walls, and pointed his Nosferatu fingers at Jason like accusations.

Jason only needed a little more information from his dad. A hint as to who was responsible for this.

And why.

Back in Strongsville, Jason was bullied by a guy named Terry—a big, dumb jerk who wore designer clothes and laughed at Jason's thrift store outfits. One day, Terry was hounding him relentlessly, in class, down the hall, at lunch, at recess. So much so, Jason cried. Terry really poured on the name-calling then. The onlookers laughed and joined in the fun.

Jason asked Terry, between sniffles, "Why are you doing this?"

Terry smiled his goofy, awkward smile, and said, "Because I can."

Maybe that was the reason this creature was hunting them, but Jason wasn't convinced. No basis to feel that way. Just a sense there was more to it. A purpose. Random as the killings looked at first glance, a pattern existed. He was sure of it.

"You oka—" Sarah Grace began as she entered the living room, but stopped when the lights went out.

Jason held his breath and listened. No sound, save the crack and pop of the fireplace. With the thrum of the generator now stilled, the silence was loud.

"Jason, come here," Sarah Grace said firmly. Jason moved to her without argument.

From the dining room, Brent spoke words that froze Jason's bone marrow. "It's here."

"Get upstairs, now," John said through gritted teeth to Sarah Grace. "Take Jason, Maggie, Jarrod, and Skeeter with you."

"I'm staying," Jarrod said. "Give me a gun."

Maggie grabbed a candle and led them upstairs. The clicks and clacks of weapons being checked for clips and capability followed them to the second floor. Maggie ushered them into a bedroom and closed the door. "Stay here and be quiet. Watch Mary's kids." The door latch sprung into the strike hole with a click.

"But—" Sarah Grace began to protest but stopped speaking to the departing thud of footsteps.

Two dark shapes rose in the bed. "What's going on?" A boy's voice. Scared but trying to cover it up.

"It's okay," Sarah Grace said softly. "My name is Sarah Grace. I'm a friend of your mom's."

"I want mommy," a little girl cried.

Sarah Grace moved through the gloom and sat on the edge of the bed next to the whimpering silhouette of the girl. "What's your name, sweetheart?"

"Maribeth." Small and frightened.

"Maribeth, your mommy will be back soon. Until then, I will stay with you."

"Where is she?" the boy asked. Older than Maribeth, but not by much. Maybe Jason's age.

"I know you two are scared and confused. But right now, I need you to listen carefully." Silence greeted her. "We need to be very quiet. No talking. Okay? It's very important."

A shotgun blast from the first floor reinforced Sarah Grace's warning. Maribeth screamed and jumped into Sarah Grace's arms. "Skeeter, get over here."

Skeeter came to her obediently. Sarah Grace patted the bed beside her, but Skeeter shook his head. He pulled a handgun from his pocket and turned to the door, his stance shifting wide and ready.

"Skeeter, what are doing?" Sarah Grace's voice shuddered like her body.

"I'll protect you."

From the first floor came a barrage of gun shots, the sonic register of each indicative of the type of gun being fired: a boom signaled a shotgun, a pop signaled a handgun, a tap-dancing stream signaled a semi-automatic. A full bullet buffet being fed to the beast.

A roar followed by a shattering scream. Glass broke. The house quavered like a small child after a frightening nightmare. Another tortured screech.

Jason's body involuntarily flinched with every heart-piercing sound. These people were dying right below him. Slaughtered like sheep. The bullets no match for its savagery.

All went quiet. An old clock on the nightstand patiently ticked off time-defying seconds.

Jason sat on one knee in Sarah Grace's lap, Maribeth the other. Skeeter held his shooter's stance, gun pointed at the door, daring to even breathe. A thud on the steps caused him to jump. A small, squeaky cry popped from Sarah Grace's lips like a cork. She cinched her arms around Jason and Maribeth and pulled them tighter.

Jason rolled to the side, wrenched from her grip. "Jason, no," Sarah Grace whimpered, her fingers clawing against his back.

He crawled to the front of the bed and opened his backpack. He had grabbed it on the way out the door, not even knowing why, just instinct. Inside was the dinosaur tooth-shaped rock his father had given him during a trip to the mountains, before all the bad stuff happened. One end was rounded, the other pointed like a fang. It wasn't much, but it was a weapon. And something was better than nothing.

He crawled back to a frantic Sarah Grace—*My mother*—and sat next to her.

Another thud on the steps rippled through the floor joists, sub-flooring, and hardwood, to Jason's body. The beast was in the house, mounting the stairs. Slowly, deliberately. Stalking its prey. Relishing the hunt. The smell of fear permeated the air like buttered popcorn.

An additional percussive resonance accompanied each thump. Claws striking the lacquered wood with every step.

Jason adjusted his grip on the dino tooth, his fingers shifting the rock in his palm for the best fit.

Skeeter turned to Jason and nodded. "Be good. Stay in school." Then, before Jason could process what was happening, Skeeter belted through the door with a menacing shout. The gun—an old school six-shooter—boomed once, twice, three times, before it clattered to the floor and an awkward, off-balance tumbling thump repeated until it reached the first floor.

Jason was blinded by tears. His chest constricted, squeezed by his bursting heart. Sarah Grace smacked her hand over her mouth.

Jason wiped his gummy eyes. The darkness in the corners of the room shifted. Jason's bones buzzed. Vernon's ghostly face pushed forth as he surfaced from the hellish depths of what he called the Cold Black. His body followed. Beside him, Megan stepped from the darkness. She was just as he remembered: black hair, eyes, and teeth, pink frilly dress, greasy black streaks of fluid dripping down her thighs. Domino barked, leaping into the room. Two more figures followed, a surprise: the hanged twins, the ropes still dangling from around their necks, WE LOVE MYRTLE BEACH glowing in the dark.

The room was full of the dead. Jason was at a loss. *Why are they here? What's going on?*

The twins turned to him, their heads moving as one, and spoke in unison, the voices oddly melodic, a capella. *"You helped us. We are here to return the favor."*

Before Jason could think anything else, a thump from outside the door announced the arrival of the monster. Two fiery eyes danced through the doorway and stopped to browse the cowering food supply. Thick rivulets of red liquid dribbled from its homicidal maw. Glinting, protruding claws scraping at the floor.

It stepped through the doorway and just enough nightglow existed to preview the bringer of death.

It stood five feet high on all fours, back arched, the burned fur jutting out like porcupine spikes. Ron had been right. Patches of new fur were present as it rejuvenated the damage. Blazing eyes sat on each side of its skull, tilted forward slightly to give a more menacing countenance. Its legs were thick with muscle, the gray rippling with every step. The claws gauged chunks of wood from the pre-finished floor.

"*Jason,*" Vernon grumbled, "*when I say, throw the rock.*"

He knew enough to trust the dead.

Out of his peripheral, another figure emerged from the blackness. His father. Tongue lolling, half his face missing. When he spoke, the words were a jumbled soup, but Jason heard them clearly in his head. Just like the dream. "Because that rock has silver in it. Not enough to kill it. But enough to maim. No healing that damage."

Holy shit!

A smallish boy appeared from Jason's right, stepped out of the hutch against the wall. He carried his head in his hands like a basketball, his chest open and empty. His eyes sought, and found, Jason. "*Get ready.*"

Two more men joined the room. One older, one younger. Father and son, Jason believed. Same shaped head, same eyes, similar lips. Both bodies ripped to shreds. They said nothing. Just watched the beast, their faces scowling masks of fury. Pissed, and rightfully so.

Vernon pulled his eyes from the monster to each of the apparitions in the room. Together, they all nodded as if some unknown accord had been reached. Megan's sad eyes rested upon Jason. *"This is our last trip from the Cold Black, Jason. We will move to the next phase of our celestial journey. You have helped us all. We return the favor in hopes this gives you peace."*

A blonde woman stepped into the room. Must be Northern. But there wasn't time to contemplate.

Vernon shouted, *"Now!"*

Jason never wavered or wondered. He simply chucked the rock at the creature creeping toward the bed. The rock left his fingers in a lazy tumble, but after having only traveled three inches, the ghosts of past and present stomped forward and pumped their arms out as if striking an assailant in the chest. The dino-tooth rocketed forward like a bullet from a high-powered rifle, striking the werewolf in the flank.

The beast was thrown, screeching like a banshee across the upstairs landing, where it barreled through the banisters of the stairs and plummeted over the edge. A spectacular crash announced its arrival to the ground floor. The smashing of tables and chairs, windows and walls followed. A pained howl penetrated the house as the thing bashed through a window. Silence greeted its departure.

The ghosts departed as well. Vaporized like smoke up a chimney. Not even a goodbye. Jason felt a pang of regret. He hadn't let his dad know that he need not worry about Jason anymore. Sarah Grace and Ron were good people. He would be okay.

His dad probably knew that already. If his father could manifest himself at a time like this, then he knew Jason was receiving the kind of care needed to raise a good human. One bred to be a good father and husband himself. A productive member of society.

If he knew all those things, maybe he could be at peace. Like Megan said.

Sarah Grace shuffled beside him. She was dazed, her eyes almost vacant. "You okay?" she asked.

"Yeah. You?"

"What just happened?"

Jason explained.

"Is it dead?"

"I don't think so." Jason climbed to his feet. "But my dad said it wouldn't be able to heal the damage. So, there's that."

Jason helped Sarah Grace to her feet. Now they had to navigate the house of carnage. Seeing Skeeter was not on his bucket list. The stranger had become a friend, then a brother, in a span of less than twenty-four hours. Impossible to explain, but true nonetheless. Jason owed it to Skeeter to see that he was properly cared for. And if they made it out of this alive, to see that he was properly buried.

"You two stay here," Sarah Grace instructed Maribeth and Conner. Maribeth clung to her brother, her face white. "We'll be right back."

Skeeter's body was gone, but his head lay on the floor by the gun. Jason snapped back into Sarah Grace's arms, pinching his eyelids closed to halt the perverted images. Sarah Grace moaned and held him tight.

Jason had seen so much pain and death. When he first moved in with Ron and Sarah Grace, he wondered when the dream would end. When would he wake up and find himself still in that dirty trailer, the smell of cigarette smoke and sweat and helplessness baked into the brown wall paneling? He feared it every night he went to bed. That reality would reinsert itself, return him where he rightfully belonged.

But each morning he woke in his new bed and found his new mom in the kitchen making him breakfast. His new dad would ruffle his hair as he rushed out the door for work.

Little by little, he began to trust the bad things were behind him. The fear dissipated. He opened up and even made friends with Jesse Griffin at school. Life settled into an easy flow and Jason was truly happy for the first time in his life.

Now this. This immense pain in his chest, but deeper. Like on the backside of his chest. A hurt so profound he thought he would break in half. He wanted to scream but what good would that do? Relieve the pressure? Perhaps. But the pain was never going away. Not for Skeeter. The brother he never had.

Sarah Grace allowed him to step away when he was ready. Jason nodded at her. He crept to the bedroom in which they had hidden, borrowed a pillowcase from a pillow next to Maribeth, and returned to Skeeter's head. Sarah Grace moved to protest but stopped. Jason rolled the head gingerly into the pillowcase and cinched it closed.

"I just want to put it with the body," Jason said sadly, rising to stand. "Then I want to kill that thing. Once and for all."

CHAPTER 55

Each impact shook the doors and rattled the padlock. Bates dropped to his knees in the snow and knocked. The cellar doors were not like the old wooden ones from back in the day, rotted and weak. These were new and made in America. Hollow metal doors and frame, steel-stiffened and heavy gauged. No doubt galvanized and insulated to resist the climate. Breaking the hasp was not impossible, but not easy either.

A shout answered Bates's knock. A voice, muffled but unmistakably male.

Mary squealed and draped herself across the doors, yelled into the crack between the pair. "Tommy! Tommy! Is that you?"

"Mary?" came the muffled reply. "Yes! Holy shit, yes. It's me."

Mary melted into a frenzy. She kicked and pounded on the doors like a child throwing a tantrum at the supermarket. Ray stepped forward, placed his hand on her back, and shushed her. "Stop that!" he whispered harshly. "We don't know where *she* is. You need to quiet down."

Mary jerked but stopped yelling. She placed her face to the crack again and said, "Hang on. We're getting you out."

Ray looked at Ron. "Do you have a crowbar or tire iron in your truck?"

"I have both," Ron said, and disappeared.

Ray waited for Ron to return. He watched the woods and house for any signs of movement. Dark and creepy was all he found.

But one positive: Tommy was alive. What that meant for Northern, he was unsure, but it was a win, and a much needed one.

Ray was one giant step closer to the truth. *I just hope my baby girl is still with us.*

Ron burst around the corner with a tire iron in one hand and a crowbar in the other. He handed the tire iron to Bates and jammed the crowbar under the padlock. Bates hooked the flat end of the tire iron under the other side of the padlock and together they prized with all their might. The hasp was welded to the doors and fought their advances. Over and over they repeated their attack. Buck joined in. The craftsmanship was solid.

"We live in a disposable society." Ray huffed. "Nothing is made to last. The one damned thing we need to be disposable is built like a tank."

When everyone stopped to rest, a muffled call came from inside. Bates put his ear to the door. "Say again."

"There's another way in," Tommy replied. "A tunnel. Maybe you can get it open from out there."

Ray took inventory of their surroundings. If it had been summer, with the thickness and camouflage of foliage growth, he wouldn't have seen it. Winter had stripped the trees and bushes of their leafy coats, and the snow illuminated the forest floor. Two hundred yards away, the land rose like a mound on one side, but went flat on the other. Like the entrance of a cave.

Ray pointed. "There."

Mary was already running. Her short legs worked hard to pound through the snow, knees tapping her chest.

Ray was handicapped by the cumbersome boot, which dragged in the snow like a boat anchor. He stopped halfway, unstrapped the Velcro, and left the relic where it fell. To his surprise, the pain was minimal. Running was out of the question, but a brisk walk was only mildly uncomfortable.

He arrived to find the others shining a flashlight in the hole. It looked more like a bear cave than a cellar entrance.

"You sure?" Bates asked Ray.

"Hell no. But those aren't bear tracks." He pointed at the trampled snow under foot. Clear prints moved around the side of the mound. The tracks, to no one's surprise, matched the marks in the tree.

Bates followed the trail, stopped mid-stride. "Check this out."

Ray discovered yellow snow. "She marked her territory. It's a warning to any creature who dares enter her lair."

"Probably marked every tree surrounding this place." Buck added.

"Consider us warned," Bates said. "Now can we get Tommy and get the hell out of here? This place gives me the heebie-jeebies."

Nodding, Ray shuffled back to the cave entrance. Hesitation bred cowards, so he entered the tunnel without pause.

Ray had never been in the military, but he had watched documentaries on Vietnam. The tunnel rats had burrowed passageways underground for hidden travel and sneak attacks. Some passages required the tunnel rat to belly crawl for miles through a hole the size of a coffin. Dirt crumbling around their body every inch of the way. The most claustrophobic shit imaginable.

This tunnel was marginally better but terrifying just the same. Old wooden beams formed bracing. In spots, newer trusses had been installed. The tunnel made a soft descent, and as they moved lower below ground level, the air became damp and colder. The dirt walls dripped with moisture, the floor goopy with slick mud. The darkness coagulated here, thick with rot and mildew.

"This tunnel looks old," Bates whispered behind Rays ear.

"I've heard," Ray whispered back, "there were underground railroads in Green Swamp that served as a safe haven and transportation route for fleeing slaves during the Civil War. Never seen one until now."

"That's why she moved the house further back," Bates said. "To be closer to the tunnel."

Ray nodded.

Someone yelped behind Ray, and he spun to find Mary climbing to her feet. She wiped mud from the seat of her pants, then nodded to continue.

The going was slow. His foot throbbed, but he hardly noticed. His full concentration lay ahead while his ears listened to what was behind. When the door came into view, his tense muscles relaxed the slightest.

Mary pushed past him and rushed forward. She frowned in disbelief when she found nothing but a rotating latch across the door. No padlock.

"She uses this tunnel as an animal," Ray explained. "She wouldn't be able to pull out a key and unlock a padlock or deadbolt." Ray shone his light on the metal door. The paint was marred by long knife-blade scratches. Rust bled through the exposed metal. "See."

"Makes sense," Bates said.

Mary was lifting the latch when a mewling growl echoed down the tunnel walls.

"Uh oh," Buck whimpered.

Ron stepped away from the group, raising the shotgun loaded with the one and only silver cartridge.

"Get inside," Ray demanded. "We only have one shot. We have to make it count."

Ron said, "I can hit her."

"This is her territory. She knows it up, down, and sideways. If you miss, we all die right here, right now, and they'll never find the bodies. We have to be smart."

Ron paused for a second. He lowered the gun and joined them.

Mary threw the latch and pulled the door. The hinges moaned as the door opened just enough to slide a body through. A warning snarl rumbled from the darkness. A wet thud chased toward them, the beast now sure strangers were in its midst.

Ray shoved everyone inside, squeezed through the crack and slammed the door just as the werewolf assailed the door, the blows and slashes like a demolition derby.

Inside the cellar, several hasps with open padlocks dangling from them were welded to the face of the door. Ray slapped the hasps closed and dropped the padlocks through the holes. The metal door rattled violently against the frame.

Mary and Tommy were locked in each other's arms, frantically grasping and groping, clinging to the impossibility. Tommy was battered and bloody, but he wasn't missing any limbs.

"How are you here?" Mary asked breathlessly. "Why did she kidnap you?"

"I—"

"Let's save the reunion for later," Ray said, inspecting the dank space. The room was bare, save a mattress in one corner. A five-gallon bucket and a roll of toilet paper sat in the opposite corner. A small room the size of a walk-in closet was empty, except for a nightgown lying in a heap on the cold concrete floor. "What is this?" Ray asked Tommy, nudging the nightgown with his foot.

"That's...uh, her nightgown. She changed in there. Commanded me to stay seated on the mattress, out of sight." Tommy swallowed, his eyes gone back to the memory. "She went in as a pretty blonde and came out"—he pointed at the door still being battered by the monster—"like that."

"The stairs lead to the first floor, I assume?"

"Yes," Tommy answered. "The door is locked. I can't figure out the code on the push-button pad. I've tried all night."

Ray looked the door over. Steel construction, tight in the jamb, push-button lockset. No kicking that thing in.

Turning to Tommy, he asked, "Have you seen my daughter, Northern?"

Tommy's eyes dropped to the concrete floor, like rocks falling from a cliff. His lids slid shut and he inhaled deeply.

It was all the answer Ray needed. He blinked, found himself falling to the floor, unable to breathe. He was so tired. His body drained of all strength. His brain went straight to rejection. No way was his baby no longer alive. She was an Eason, goddammit. Guts five miles long and tough as Kevlar. And *young!* So much living left. A man to marry, a child to bear for Ray and Maggie to spoil rotten. No way this was true. No way.

But a glance back at Tommy and his hard, sad eyes, Ray knew it to be true.

For the first time in Ray's life, clutching at his chest from the concrete floor, he considered giving up. What was the point? He could lie here on this cold floor and let the werewolf rip him to pieces. It would be over in seconds. He had no doubt he could handle that kind of pain for a few measly seconds. Especially to never know anything anymore.

Maybe, if there was such a thing as heaven, he would see his baby girl again. Maybe she was waiting for him right now, just beyond the threshold between the dark and the light. A shadowed silhouette, hands outstretched, blinding white background of such majestic sights his simple mind was unable to fathom. She would be laughing, happy to see him. Together, hand in hand, they would walk through golden pillars, down a path of bleached stone, and trumpets would sound their arrival. All the pain in the world would be worth it if Ray could be with his little girl.

"Take my hand," someone said.

Northern?

No. Mary. She stood over him, her hand open and ready to haul Ray to his feet. For a fleeting second, he thought he wasn't interested. The idea passed quickly. He was an Eason, after all, and "quit" was not in his vocabulary. He slapped his palm into Mary's, and she yanked him to his feet.

Through the pulsing fog, Ray's breath coming back to him, he noticed a silence. "Where did she go?" he whispered.

The cellar was silent. The house above was silent. *Is this a trick? To lure them out in the open? Probably. Be smart to stay in the cellar. It was safe. She can't get in. At the moment.*

A crash at the top of the stairs made the decision for him. The metal door leading from the house into the basement shook as blow after blow battered its metal skin.

"We have to make a run for it," Ray said. He threw the padlocks on the floor, bolted through the door. The tunnel curled up and spat him into the swirling snow. Every instinct in Ray screamed "Run" but he ducked low and moved to the house. He led the group around the opposite side where no outside lights revealed their movements. In the silence of the night, the sounds of Victoria attacking her basement door were brash.

A thirty-yard dash and they were diving in the truck. Ron twisted the ignition, gunned the throttle, and snatched the gear shift into drive.

"Go!" Buck screamed from the truck bed. "Go Go Go!"

Ray spun in the front seat to see a werewolf leap from the front porch and bound toward them. The truck fishtailed in the snow as it fought for traction. The wolf closed the distance quickly and Ray knew they were dead.

But the tires snagged on something—a rock, a chunk of grass—and the truck leaped forward and picked up speed. The beast, however, kept pace, the glow of the taillights washing the nightmarish thing in a red haze. The trees parted, on the right was a field, on the left the spot where Robert Houghton first built his beloved home.

As Ron pushed the truck up the dirt road, the werewolf slowed, then stopped. "What's it doing?"

It raised its head and the last thing Ray saw before they careened onto 211 was the world washed in crimson.

The howl of the beast announced the arrival of the Full Blood Super Moon.

CHAPTER 56

Blood dripped from the walls. Even the twelve-foot ceilings were dotted with arterial spray. Sarah Grace's feet slipped on a puddle, barely saved herself from going ass over tea kettle. She tried to shield Jason from the carnage, but that was impossible. Body parts lay scattered on the smashed dining room table, the floor, the doorway. The smell of copper and shit poked at her gag reflex, running its putrid fingers down her throat to provoke a gut purging reaction. Sour, chunky bile surged into her mouth, and she dashed over Skeeter's headless corpse into the kitchen, straight to the sink. The faucet ran on high while the yellowed contents of her stomach splattered against the stainless steel.

When Sarah Grace's stomach stopped seizing, she cut off the water, leaned against the counter, and waited for the nausea to pass. Jason wrapped his arms around her, his embrace warm and comforting. Something that made sense amidst all the crazy.

After a moment, her stomach calmed enough for her to move. She wet a dish rag with cold water, wiped her face. Rinsed away the sour gravy marinating on her tongue.

Something moved in the corridor leading into the kitchen and Sarah Grace protectively jumped in front of Jason. She cried out when she saw it was Maggie. She ran to the woman.

Maggie embraced her. "You okay?"

"I don't think I'll ever be okay." And it was the truth. Those stark images continued to flash behind her eyes like her brain was taking snapshots, saving the photos for a later nightmare.

"It seems that way." Maggie acquiesced sadly. "Until it doesn't. Which may be weeks, years, or even decades. Time is funny like that." Maggie closed her eyes. "I saw that thing right outside. Jesus, I was so scared. Did I really see a werewolf?"

"You saw it," Sarah Grace said. "It was real. Jason and I saw it, too. The bodies in the dining room say it was real."

Maggie's eyes went wide. "I was so scared, I ran. Lord, help me, when I saw that vile thing, I dropped my gun and ran." She started past Sarah Grace. "Are they all dead?"

Sarah Grace firmly held her back. "Yes. You don't want to go in there."

"I should've fought with them."

"Then you'd be dead, too. There's nothing you could have done."

A commotion from the front of the house. The entry door crashed open, and feet pounded through the living room. A bellow of anguish erupted through the house as Ray now saw the slaughter. She pulled Maggie and Jason toward the foyer, into the living room where Ray sat crumpled on his knees. Everyone else stood in shocked disbelief.

"Ron?" Sarah Grace called. They all jumped in surprise. Ron bolted to her and Jason, pulled them tight.

Ron blubbered. "Where's Skeeter?"

Sarah Grace and Jason's white faces provided the answer.

"Dad!" Conner called from the top of the stairs.

Tommy took the stairs two at a time until he reached his children.

The living room became a funeral home as weeping held sway over the night, while stiffening bodies lay nearby. Sarah Grace held steadfast to the two boys in her life, greedy in her need to be sure they were here and not a mirage. Ray and Maggie sat on the couch, holding hands. Buck stared blankly into the fire, lost in his own briar-thicket of thoughts. Mary continued to hug her family on the stairs. Sarah Grace realized one missing person was found, but the others weren't present.

She whispered in Ron's ear. "Where's Northern? And Jerry?"

Ron's eyes snapped to Ray and Maggie, and he shook his head slowly.

Northern dead. Steve and Cliff Gainey dead. Jerry Landon dead. Two truck drivers dead. The Ramirez kid now a known victim. John, Garrett, Brent, Jarrod, and Skeeter dead. How many others?

What now?

Bates, who had put on his detective glasses to assess the crime scene, rejoined them. "We have to kill this fucking thing."

"Why not hunker down? Wait for daybreak." Buck's voice was monotone. "Kill her after she changes back."

"You can kill a human?" Bates asked.

Buck was noncommittal.

"Why don't you arrest her after she changes back? Put her in jail. Let the government take it from there." This was Mary. Obviously not sold on the idea. Just running through the options for the sake of posterity.

"That's not a bad idea," Bates said, brow furrowed in thought. "Except the government will do what the government does. Take the beast alive, run a million tests, look for a way to weaponize her DNA, then kill her when they have what they want. I trust the government to handle this like I trust Covid came from a wet market in Wuhan."

"Look," Ray said through gritted teeth, "this monster has killed without mercy. A child was slaughtered during a hayride. A *fucking* hayride." Ray's voice escalated. "We're not waiting for daybreak. We're not waiting for her to change. We're not arresting her. This ends tonight."

Ray checked each and every one, locked eyes, and waited for a confirming nod. Sarah Grace gave her affirmation, as did Ron and Jason. No one protested. Not even the detective.

"Okay," Bates said. "What's the plan?"

Ray threw the curtains open wide. The Full Blood Super Moon illuminated Earth like Hell had conquered the angels, taken control of the kingdom.

From an unknown distance, a piercing howl eviscerated the infernal sky.

"I wounded her bad, but she's at her strongest now," Jason said. "She will come for us."

"Then we need to be ready," Ray warned.

CHAPTER 57

A rat bit her bloody cheek.

She jumped awake with a screech, knocking the hideous rodent across the cave. Tiny legs squirmed across her arms, up her pants legs. She kicked and beat, hearing insectile bodies crunch and spew their vile innards. Water bugs. A constant irritation in this abandoned cave. She brushed away the disgusting carcasses, killing any strays before they could escape to torment her later.

Time was an illusion now. She pondered how long it had been since she was brought here. The darkness was constant, so deep was she hidden. Light failed to make the journey. Lost interest just past the cave mouth.

A day was her guess. Maybe two at most. Bound to a chain, shackled to the stone cave wall. For what purpose? The questions rattled on, over and over. A broken record.

When she first awoke to rats knotted in her hair, licking the blood from her head wound, she had lost her mental stability. The panic and fear had been overwhelming. Strange, pitch-black place, chained like an animal, rodents tangled in her hair, bugs creeping inside her filthy clothing to feast on the grimy sweat and blood leaking from dozens of abrasions. It had been too much.

After cracking the backs of several rats and ridding the immediate threats from her clothes, she'd settled into a state of helplessness. Whatever the reason for being here, she had resigned herself to the idea that the end was near. She would die, and no one would know where she was located. Her body would never be found.

Then a surprise. Shocking, actually. It shook her to her core.

A visit. From a human. Not the frightening creature that ran her off the road. Not the same beast that chased her across a field in the dim glow of moonlight.

An older woman. Very pretty. Her perfume so remarkable, so heavenly in that ungodly place, Northern had almost fainted. The woman carried a bright, battery-powered lantern, washing the stony cave walls in white. She was being saved. Somehow this woman knew she was being held captive and came to the rescue. Her eyes swam in an ocean of tears as her head went light with relief.

"Well, hello," the woman had said. "You're awake."

Strange thing to say. "Ye...yes." Northern had rasped. "Can you help me? I'm chained."

"Sorry," the woman had said with a pleasant smile taped to her lips. "I'm afraid I can't do that."

"Why not?" Northern had needed to know but *wanted* nothing but silence. The answer might be worse than being chained to a cave wall.

"Because, I need you right here. I have plans for you."

"I don't understand," Northern gasped. Her lungs had suddenly stopped working.

"I know," the woman had said. "Maybe I can at least explain. I think you are owed that much. After all, you had nothing to do with why I'm here now. Doing what I'm doing."

Northern had continued to suck on the musty cave air, trying to throttle her lungs awake. Concentrating on not losing consciousness, she remained silent.

"It's a long story, but I'll give you the short version," the woman had stated as she lowered herself to the cave floor, crossed her legs, and placed the lantern beside her. "My name now is Victoria Naughton. It wasn't always. I changed it. Before I moved back here to Brunswick County. I wanted to keep my identity a secret. You'll understand. But before I can tell you about why I'm here now, I need to tell you about then."

CHAPTER 58

"My birth name was Winnie Kittle," Victoria started. "I lived in the Houghton House as a child. I was three when my father hung himself in that house. For reasons no one ever figured out. At least, that was the story told to the public." Victoria went away, back in time, and told the story.

The truth of her father, George Kittle, was much more sinister than a suicide. George, owner of Kittle Furniture, was lynched by Green Swamp residents. Earl Eason led the lynching after he caught a wolf eating a baby calf. For months, local farmers were hit, night after night, by a creature slaughtering and eating their livestock. Horses, chickens, goats, cows. The cost to replace these animals was too much to suffer, so a 24/7 watch was set. The night—or early morning, as it were—Eason Farm was hit, it happened that Earl Eason was the watchman. Earl decided to try a snare after Levi Stuart said he had shot the wolf the month before, to no avail. Said that double-ought did nothing but make the wolf mad. Said it ran off like it had been stung by nothing more than a BB.

Earl decided to catch the wolf and make damn sure it didn't escape. The capture occurred just before dawn. Nearby farmers came running as the news spread through Green Swamp. The wolf was caged inside a dog pen while Eason waited for all to arrive. The plan was simple. A firing squad would unleash a fusillade of steel at the beast and end its reign of terror once and for all.

As the sun crept toward the orange sky, most of the Green Swamp farmers in attendance loading their weapons with the gleam of payback in their eyes, the wolf fell to its side, started trembling. To the horror of all those watching, it transformed from beast to man.

The naked man, recognized as George Kittle, begged for his life. The farmers saw a heathenism likened to witchcraft. George was evil. He brought that evil to their land, slaughtered their cattle, and now, with the taste of warm blood on his tongue, would naturally succumb to cannibalism next.

"Earl Eason,"—Victoria ticked off through gritted teeth—"Pop Munerlyn, Edward Delaney, Vernon Elliot, Cliff Gainey, Lionel Gainey, Samuel Kindred, Levi Stuart, Jerry Landon, Martin Landon and then Chief-of-Police Horace Adams participated in the lynching. My father was dragged from that cage, buck naked, kicking and screaming, begging for his life. They hog-tied him, tossed him in the bed of Earl Eason's truck like a piece of trash, and drove him out to the big oak tree at the corner of the farm."

Northern knew the tree. She had laid under it many a day and napped in the shade while a summer breeze cooled her sweaty skin. It was a giant. Thick limbs, sturdy.

"They threw a rope over a branch, tied a noose. Stood my father in the bed of the truck, draped that death necklace around his throat, and pulled the truck from underneath him. The fall wasn't far enough to break his neck. No mercy extended in this killing. Oh no. He strangled to death. Kicking. No longer screaming. Just croaking for air, Adam's apple not even bobbing because the rope was crushing it. It didn't take long—a few minutes maybe—but to my father, it took a lifetime.

"I have imagined a million times over what he must have been thinking. What he must have been feeling as he gasped for the tiniest breath. I like to envision that he thought of me, my sister, and my mom. It's how I stay somewhat sane.

"But research shows that more than likely, his mind was in survival mode, his body reacting to the lack of oxygen. No time to think of us. Maybe as he died, his central nervous system fired off its final signals, and in there somewhere, he saw us. Memories of birthdays, bedtime book readings, first bike rides.

"Regardless, he died. Murdered by men you have grown up respecting because you never knew them to be bigger monsters than my father."

Northern had remained silent for the duration. She had trouble believing it, though. "So, your father was a werewolf? Is that what you expect me to believe?"

Victoria had smiled without humor. "I don't really care what you believe. I simply wanted to explain why you're here."

"You haven't explained anything. I'm more confused now than before. What does my grandfather lynching your father have to do with me?"

"Because," Victoria said, climbing to her feet, "I am going to turn you into a werewolf. They'll have no choice but to kill you like they killed my father. And that, my dear child, will be my vengeance."

"Your revenge, you mean," Northern spat.

Victoria smiled, and in the dim glow it looked like her lips spread impossibly wide. "I will have my pound of flesh. And eat it, too."

CHAPTER 59

The 100x100 metal building where Ray stored his ATVs, four-wheelers, lawn mowers, and an old K-5 Blazer once belonging to his daddy, was chosen for the last stand. Metal panels sheeted both the outside and the inside, making the walls formidable. A few windows were installed high on the walls to provide daylight in the building. Too high for a werewolf to climb through. Only a pair of double doors, two single doors, and four automatic garage doors led into the space. A raised loft hunkered in one corner, a spot for the field hands to unwind after a long day in the heat.

Victoria had slashed through the generator, leaving it incapacitated. But Ray owned half a dozen more. A 10,000-watt Steel Power Plant generator was quickly connected into the buildings circuit panel, and, voilà, let there be light.

Being a farmer, Ray owned a wide assortment of chemicals. Bates quickly read through ingredient lists, found what he needed, and set to making the explosives. The Molotov cocktails had not stopped the beast, but they had hurt it. They needed any advantage they could get.

Ron, Tommy, Ray, Buck, and Mary moved the all-terrain vehicles in front of the roll-up doors as extra protection. One roll-up door was left unfortified on purpose. Further preparations were made, plans unfolding one idea at a time.

Maggie, armed with a semi-automatic, remained on the second floor of the main house, protecting Maribeth and Conner.

Jason and Sarah Grace barricaded the man doors of the metal building. As he and Sarah Grace screwed sheets of plywood over the double doors, he decided to confide a mystery that bugged him. He leaned in close, kept his voice low, not ready to disclose this information to Ray. "When we were in the room, beside the bed, remember how I said ghosts were there? They saved us?"

"Yeah?"

"Something's been nagging at me but I couldn't get a grip on it until now."

"And that is?"

"Vernon was there. Domino was there. Megan was there. So was my dad. And who had to be Cliff and Steve Gainey; they were all torn up so I can only assume it was them. An older woman who I think was Mrs. Gainey. A Hispanic boy was there, the Ramirez kid I presume." He winced at the memory. "There was the faintest outline of a blonde lady. Her hair was dingy-blonde. But..."

"But?"

Jason found Ray on the other side of the building, to be sure he wasn't within earshot. "Northern was not there," he whispered. "If she was killed by this thing, she should've been there."

Sarah Grace brushed a stray hair from her frowning face. "The blonde wasn't her?"

"No," Jason said. "I've looked at the pictures in the house. Northern was bright blonde and tall. This was an older woman, shorter than Northern. Maybe five-nine."

"You think Northern's alive?"

"Yes," Jason stated. "I think it's a good possibility."

"We don't need to tell Ray until this is over," she said. "He'll go running into the storm hellbent on finding her. Probably get himself killed."

Jason nodded his agreement. He had already reached the same conclusion. Northern had managed to stay alive this long. She needed to hang on a little longer. She was strong. Obviously, an Eason.

"Let's go!" Ray shouted and waved his arms for everyone to meet in the middle. Several long, plastic folding tables were pushed together. Guns stacked on top. "Grab your weapon, get in position. Jason, I want you and Sarah Grace upstairs in the loft."

Jason wanted to protest, but Ray was in no mood. He was only a kid, but he knew controlled rage when he saw it. Ray Eason was positively bursting with it.

Ray handed Jason a rifle and Sarah Grace a shotgun. "Locked and loaded."

Jason followed Sarah Grace up the stairs to the loft. Several leather couches were positioned around a coffee table. A kitchen table and chairs sat near a small kitchenette. A big screen TV was mounted on a wall, perfect viewing from the couches.

Each of them dragged a chair from the kitchen to the loft balcony and propped the gun barrels on the railing for support.

Down below, movement stopped, except for Ray. He manually raised one of the garage doors to five feet, locked it in place. Reaching into a five-gallon bucket, he retrieved a ragged scrap of shirt, dripping with blood. The shirt Garrett had been wearing.

Ray eased outside just beyond the threshold of the door and shook the cloth to dribble blood in the snow. The trail led from the yard to a noose of steel cabling positioned on the epoxied concrete floor, fifteen-feet inside the building. The noose was the end of a length of cabling that snaked over a motor hoist beam and attached to a towing winch on the front of the K5. Lying under the Blazer with the controller in hand was Ron.

Ray dropped the blood-soaked shirt in the middle of the noose, made a final check that everything was as planned. He jog-limped to the light switch by one of the man doors. "Lights out!" Banged off the metal paneling, and the building went almost pitch black. Three can lights with dimmer switches remained on low. Just enough to see. The red wash of the Full Blood Super Moon peaked through the high windows and tiptoed inside the raised roll-up door but made it no further.

Jason sat in silence and listened. The building creaked, its metallic bones and galvanized skin flexing beneath the bullying push of the wind. Something clanged.

Sarah Grace nudged his arm. Her first finger unfolded from her palm and pointed at the roll-up door. A shadow was creeping through the red glare cast by the Full Blood Super Moon. The shadow became a figure, and Hell followed.

CHAPTER 60

A stab in her chest was the first sign something was wrong. Northern pounded a fist against her sternum to dislodge the discomfort. Instead, the pain spread through her lungs to her ribs. Her hand lying on her stomach detected a swelling. Her gut distended, a rib cracked. She snatched her blouse open in time to see her torso extending. Her bra strap popped and dropped in the dirt, her breasts shrinking while her chest expanded.

Her eyesight had acclimated to the pitch-black cave, which allowed her to witness the shifting of her body as she experienced a brain-numbing flood of sensory overload.

The seams on her already tight jeans burst and the denim cloth unfolded like flayed skin. Thigh muscles rippled as they thickened. Her quads grew longer, moving her knee lower on her leg. Her feet lengthened as long, razored claws slid from the tips of her hairy toes.

Her ears burned as if a blowtorch lit their tips. The bones of her face fractured as her jaw, chin, and nose elongated. Thick spears of hair sprouted from pores all over her body. The fur rippled as it grew.

Northern crawled to all fours. The pain, so intense in the beginning, subsided, replaced by pleasure. Every bone break and restructure felt like a professional massage. Bone growth sent shivers down her morphing spine. Hair proliferation tickled the flesh like a lover's caress.

Smells exploded like fireworks in her nasal cavities. The musty dank earth. The faint but ever-present trace of human perfume. The rank, filthy coat of scurrying rats, their foul breath. The pungent odor of blood, sweat, and urine soaked in the ripped clothing beneath her paws.

A tittering rodent attempted to slip by, and she used the opportunity to test her newfound utensils. A pointed claw spiked the creature like melted butter. It emitted a dying screech before she slipped it in her mouth. A gush of warm innards soaked the insides of her mouth. Not the best. But not bad.

She crept across the cave and through the tunnel. The world was new and fresh. Sensations galore. An infinity of scents. Pounding heartbeats of critters, both mighty and meek. The call of blood, the promise. So loud—deafening.

She jogged the rest of the way and hurtled from the mouth of the tunnel into the snow. She danced around in the cushy stuff, cold against her paws. But a new scent hooked her nose and pulled her through the night. She moved like she knew where she was going. Until, at last, she climbed a small hill. Standing at the top, her muzzle to the moon, was another. Kindred spirits, like creatures. United, the bond instant. Mother and child.

Mother was injured. The cutting smell of burned flesh. The gape of a menacing wound. But she was strong, fight still left in her. The leader of this meager pack. The mother howled and the child understood, the words as old as existence.

Let's hunt.

CHAPTER 61

Motherfucker!

The first black shadow was accompanied by a second.

Ray blinked in disbelief. How was this possible? All the attacks had been perpetrated by a single creature. No signs of a second assailant existed.

The feeling of defeat was overwhelming. They were not prepared for two. The second was slight compared to the first, but fierce, nonetheless. The glint of razor-blade claws pranced around the room like a nightclub disco ball, advertising the bloodletting to come.

Ray hid behind a massive tool chest loaded with socket wrenches, screwdrivers, and hammers. He watched the two creatures advance into the building, stances wide and ready to attack, and debated what to do. The smaller werewolf helped make the decision when it advanced on the bloody scrap inside the steel cable loop.

It stepped inside the loop and licked at Garrett's shirt. A whining zip snatched the cable, taut around the upper half of its torso, yanking the kicking and mewling creature airborne. The larger wolf roared and attacked the steel cable. Sparks flew as claws and tightly-wound steel threads met with a twang. Bates darted out from behind the Blazer with a Molotov in hand. He lit the fuse but was stunned when the creature covered the distance in one leap. The flaming bottle slipped from his grasp and shattered on the concrete. A puddle of fire spread, licking the tires of the Blazer. Ron rolled from beneath the Blazer in the opposite direction to escape the flames.

Bates, in blind panic, dashed up the stairs to the loft. Ray cursed. He jumped up and down, waving his arms, shouting to halt its advances up the stairs to where Sarah Grace and Jason hid.

The diversion worked. It leaped from the loft and dove at Ray. In mid-air the beast burst into flames. Ray rolled sideways as it slammed into the tool chest. Tools clattered across the concrete. For the third time tonight, the beast was on fire, its sickening screech like drill bits to the ears.

It bashed against an ATV, and the napalm lit the Polaris on fire, sending orange flames climbing toward the ceiling. The tires of the Blazer had caught fire as well, thick black acrid smoke filling the building, choking the oxygen from the air.

Ray wasn't about to let the hazard of smoke inhalation stop him from shutting it inside. He took a wide berth around the wolf swinging in the noose, still fighting for its freedom. He dropped the roll-up door closed with a bang. Ron hurried to his side with the shotgun, silver bullet ready.

The creature tried desperately to extinguish the fire that engulfed it from perverse head to meat-cleaving toes. It flipped, rolled, contorted, rubbed against the floor, the metal paneling. The flames continued to burn its bubbling flesh. Even consumed with murderous rage, the creature slowed from fatigue and debilitating agony. Ray stepped closer, pressed the shotgun against his shoulder, and, without hesitation or remorse, pulled the trigger.

The blast was brilliant against the deflective properties of the concrete floors and metal paneling. Quarter-sized holes scattered across the animal's charred hide, blowing chunks of black flesh away.

It bellowed, body trembling and stretching. Without any further drama, it rolled to its side and moved no more. The fire continued to be fueled by oily flesh, even as the transformation occurred. Arms shortened, legs retracted as the scorched hair receded, claws retreated. Inside a minute, the creature that had slaughtered innocent citizens was nothing but the badly burned, nude body of Victoria Naughton. Her blonde hair was burned to her scalp, except for one blonde patch.

"RAY!" Mary screamed.

Ray spun on his heels and blinked. His brain was slow to fully comprehend what his eyes were seeing. Northern was dangling from the steel noose which, only a moment earlier, had held a rabid werewolf.

"Ron!" Ray yelled as he ran to her. "Lower the winch!"

His naked daughter was lowered into his arms. A coat was tossed over her unconscious body as Mary gently disentangled her from the noose. Ray carried her through the snow into the charnel house and up to her room where he laid her in her bed.

Ray remained by her side until she awoke six hours later.

CHAPTER 62

Only silence existed. And darkness. And peace. Turmoil had consumed her, animal instinct rife with survival and bloodlust. Luckily, she had escaped its awful grasp. The tranquility was nice, soft. A soothing touch, inviting her ever so gently. She floated with it, on a magic carpet, cool breeze brushing her hair like her mother used to do when she was little, so tender.

Northern became aware of sounds and a bright light against her eyelids as she slipped even-keel from sleep to wakefulness. She was tired but she wanted to see, having sat in darkness so long.

Her eyelids fluttered open and the first thing she saw was her rugged but handsome father. He stared at her with tears dripping down his cheeks.

"Hey, sweetheart," he whispered. The toughest guy she had ever known broke down and wept like a baby. So profound was his display of emotion, she, too, joined. Her mother rushed in and the family cleansed themselves.

Cheeks moist with salty tears, Maggie and Ray pulled back, mere inches, to allow her some space.

"What happened?" Northern asked. She was terrified to know.

"We can discuss all that later," Ray said. Her parents shared a look of agreement.

But Northern needed to know. It's why she opened her eyes rather than sleep longer. "Please."

Ray and Maggie shared another look, this one unreadable. Ray nodded. "Okay."

"The last thing I remember was being held in a cave. Rats were biting me, bugs crawling over me. A woman visited. Older, but very pretty. She told me an incredible story." Northern met her father's stare. "About Granddaddy. About a lynching."

Her father's eyes told her it was true. "She's not lying about that. It was a long time ago."

"For just killing a cow and some chickens?" Northern asked. She was so ashamed.

Ray's eyes turned stony. "Is that what she told you?"

Northern was confused. The phrase "two sides to every story" popped into her head. "Yes. She said all he was doing was killing cattle, and you farmers decided to put a stop to it."

"Northern, I was not born an only child. I had a twin brother, Larry. It's a family secret. Or, rather, family history we prefer to keep secret."

"What—" Northern began.

"Daddy woke in the middle of the night to a child crying. He ran to our room to find the window open, and my brother gone from our bed. I was still asleep, didn't know any of this was happening. He went out hunting for Larry and found his body parts scattered like breadcrumbs. At daybreak, with a group of farmers by his side, Daddy followed the body part trail. It went straight to the Houghton House. Two of Larry's toes were in the grass by the goddamn front door. George Kittle was in bed sleeping, naked. Still had blood around his mouth. Thank God his wife and daughters were visiting family and not home." Ray wiped his face, his breathing rapid. "They hung

George in the living room, Northern. No arrest. No day in court. Judge, jury, and executioner."

Northern wasn't sure what to say. Undisclosed family history. All the reunions over the years and no one ever mentioned anything about the bloody history of the Eason clan. Her father had a brother, she an uncle. Lynching and hanging the man responsible like the Wild Wild West. It was a lot to take in.

I need a nap. Let this information marinate. "Can I rest for a while?"

"Of course," her mom said with a pat. Maggie pulled Ray out of the room and the door clicked shut.

Northern nestled her head in her pillow and slipped back to the silent darkness.

CHAPTER 63

The next few weeks were filled with revelations.

Victoria Naughton was, in fact, Winnie Kittle. Her mother and sister had died, leaving Winnie to sharpen her desire for revenge.

Dozens of journals found in her home disclosed the angry ravings of a suicidal maniac, hellbent on vengeance.

Details were sketchy with gray areas and missing time periods, but Victoria was not born cursed with werewolf. The affliction was not passed to her father's offspring. After the death of her mother and later her sister to suicide, she had sought someone to grant her the wish of anathema. For fifteen years, she hunted. Victoria finally found what she wanted in a remote village, hundreds of miles south of Entre-Rios, Brazil, deep in the uncharted forests. A shaman spent days chanting over her while she lay staked to the ground. She was fed disgusting broths. Weird hieroglyphics were painted on her body with foul-smelling stains. She claimed to have seen the wolves of her ancestors, another generation in a long lineage. They greeted her with open arms.

Her first full moon was spent in a cage. She felt the change and embraced it. The pain, the ecstasy, the bouquet of blood, the mouth-watering musical thump of heartbeats. She broke out of the cage and slaughtered the entire village, including the shaman. *"I feasted upon his guts like spaghetti."* She bragged in her journal.

Victoria returned to the states, bought a house in Wyoming, and tested her abilities. She spent years learning to harness the power through meditation and yoga. She devoured books about the mind and how to manipulate it. She had yet to master the talent of halting the shift once the full moon rose into the black sky, but she was consumed by the desire to have complete control. *"It's only a matter of time,"* she wrote.

She moved back to Brunswick County with a new name, started a real estate business and renovated the house she was born in. Blinded by revenge, she set a plan in motion. And almost saw it become reality.

Her killing spree had been going on longer than the month period she lived in Green Swamp. An uptick in reports of missing homeless people and prostitutes along the Grand Strand had been coming in for months. The body in the field helped solve some of those cases. Carrie Puckett, 29, a sex worker from Myrtle Beach, South Carolina, was picked up by Victoria and never seen again. Until Cliff, Tommy, Steve, and Jerry happened upon her corpse while investigating gunshots and car crashes.

Jerry Landon was found eventually, deceased and mutilated.

Victoria's final journal entry shed light on the mystery of how Cliff managed to crawl home from the attack site miles away. Victoria wrote:

My car won't start. I think the battery is dead. Maybe a neighbor has jumper cables. I must go find the old man. I had to drop him in the woods before I made it home. I lost track of time, and the sun was rising. I felt the shift. He shouldn't be too far away, but I can't carry him as Victoria. I'll need my vehicle.

Yeah, I'm walking to the neighbor's house across the street.

CHAPTER 64

As the investigation continued, everyone involved nervously waited. Northern had been bitten by a werewolf, transforming into one. Research suggested, albeit fictional, the tie was severed once Victoria was dead. Without evidence to support the theory, the parties could only wait.

One month after the incident, several days after the New Year, a full moon marched into the night sky. Northern, out of an abundance of caution, locked herself inside the dog kennel and chained her leg to a post. Ray and Maggie held watch along with Sarah Grace, Ron, Jason, Mary, Tommy, Buck, and Bates—armed with a tranquilizer gun—just in case.

She never even growled.

CHAPTER 65

The story fed to the public was Victoria Naughton was a serial killer responsible for the deaths of eleven Green Swamp residents and six people from Myrtle Beach. The deaths of the two bank robbers, Charlie Dunning (Martin) and Pete Labriola (Roger) and the SWAT members were blamed on a mission gone wrong while attempting to arrest the robbers. This was simply too crazy a story to even hint at the truth.

The department decided not to amend its findings on Benji Ramirez. Nothing would change the outcome now, and the information would only tarnish the department's credibility.

The murders ran hot in the news for weeks, but another mass shooting displaced it, and the media hustled away to feast on the fresh blood.

CHAPTER 66

The following Thanksgiving, the survivors, now bound by something greater than blood, gathered in the Eason's dining room to celebrate the holiday. At first, the history of the room held the parties silent. Less than a year earlier, amputated parts were placed in body bags and liters of blood were mopped from the floor. Ray had paid a local contractor to gut and renovate the room, but new paint and flooring couldn't cover the trauma left behind. Ray, sensing the strained mood, took control.

He rose with a wine glass in hand and tapped the side. The ring influenced all eyes and ears to rest on him. "I want to thank all of you for being here. I can see this room leaves you uneasy, and understandably so. Some—or all—of you may be wondering why we're celebrating here. I debated moving the table in the living room, maybe out to the building. This was considered out of respect to those who died, as well as for you.

"I decided to keep it here for several reasons. First, those who died in this room did so defending all of us. They sacrificed their lives to give us the *opportunity* to be here tonight. I think it would be disrespectful to have it anywhere else. We celebrate together in honor of them. With them. If there is such a thing as the Hereafter—and Jason has proven that to be the case—then they are with us now. That's worth rejoicing, don't you think?" Every head nodded. "The second reason is a little personal. For me and for you. You see, this house was built on land owned by the Easons for a hundred years. Blood, sweat, and tears shed in the soil we harvest for crops, for food. What kind of man, what kind of Eason, would I be if I packed up and ran for the hills? I'd be an embarrassment to my father, my grandfather, my great-grandfather. Everything they worked for would be for nothing.

"I raise this glass and send a toast to Garrett, Brent, Skeeter, Jarrod, John, Cliff, Steve, Jerry, Arlene, Millie, Benji, Dakota, Domino, Winnie, the SWAT members, and those from Myrtle Beach. I raise this glass and send a toast to each of you. I raise this glass and say Happy Thanksgiving."

Glasses rose, nods of approval with multiple "hear hears" ringing across the table. The speech worked as hoped; chatter bubbled from mumbled utterances to the lofty sounds of small talk, and finally, to laughter.

Family. A word of strength. Sometimes made stronger through tragedy. As was the case with these neighbors. Forged by fire. Now the sum of their parts.